# RITES OF INHERITANCE

'I've come to claim my dowry,' Margaret Parr announced to her brother when she walked into his drawing room.

'Then I presume that you are getting married,' he said tightly. 'And who is the unfortunate gentleman?'

'Robert Dillon,' she said, looking him straight in the eye.

'He's a Catholic! No Parr ever married a Catholic. No dowry for a Parr who marries a Catholic!' he cried at her in anger.

He looked at her. Silently she loosened her dress and let it fall to the floor. Then she undid her bodice and exposed her breasts.

'I am going to strip naked. Then I am going to walk naked out of this house and ride into Williamstown crying out that my brother stripped me and deprived me of my dowry.'

'Stop, stop,' he told her wearily, 'I will get the money.'

He returned with  was aware of the hal beside him and coul body. Her breasts alr she bent forward to

'We are now enem attend your wedding your children bastard

Michael Mullen lives in Castlebar, County Mayo with his wife and family. He is the author of four previous novels, and his most recent, *The Hungry Land*, was published by Corgi in 1988.

# Rites of Inheritance

## Michael Mullen

**CORGI BOOKS**

*For Kate*

## RITES OF INHERITANCE

### A CORGI BOOK  0  552  13488  0

First publication in Great Britain

PRINTING HISTORY

Corgi edition published 1990

Copyright © Michael Mullen 1990

This book is set in 10/11 pt Perpetua
by Colset Private Limited, Singapore.

Corgi Books are published by Transworld Publishers Ltd, 61–63
Uxbridge Road, Ealing, London W5 5SA, in Australia by Transworld
Publishers (Australia) Pty. Ltd, 15–23 Helles Avenue, Moorebank,
NSW 2170, and in New Zealand by Transworld Publishers (N.Z.) Ltd,
Cnr. Moselle and Waipareira Avenues, Henderson, Auckland.

Made and printed in Great Britain by
BPCC Hazell Books
Aylesbury, Bucks, England
Member BPCC Ltd.

# Chapter 1

It was autumn in the woods. Leaves choked the pathways and lay scrolled and brittle under foot. No wind stirred the branches and the silence was filled only with the bell from the stable yard which rang at wide intervals, muted by the great bowls of the trees. A little younger than the great house itself, they had matured through a hundred years, carrying the high canopy of the woods on their vaulting branches.

Two figures moved sluggishly through the masses of leaves along the main pathway. They had come from Ballinrobe and seemed exhausted after their journey.

'I'm tired and I wish to rest,' the hunchback Toby Drew complained to the blind Piper whose hand was placed on his bent shoulder. 'I have got lost many times in these woods. I know how these paths are tangled.'

'Well, we must be on the main pathway,' said the blind man patiently. 'We should be nearing the burial place soon. I hear the men knocking on stone.'

'You have a sharp ear.' The hunchback looked up at the blank face which stared ahead with a fixed gaze.

'Listen. Can you not hear the sharp sound of the chisels and the hammers?' the other asked, firming his grip on the thin shoulder.

The two men listened for a moment and picked up the ringing sound of iron on stone.

'Follow the direction of the sound; it will take us where we are going. But please hurry, I must be in place before the funeral arrives so I can sit and order my thoughts. They have been in turmoil all day.

'It's four hours since I put food in my mouth. I must eat,' whined Toby Drew. 'You said you would feed me well and have me well bedded when you took me on.'

'Have I not fulfilled the promise? I have shared my last crust with you.' It was an argument they had had before.

'It's the cold that makes you hungry,' the hunchback said sulkily.

'I'll find you food later at some pub. Keep silent and leave me to my thoughts. Just lead me towards the sound.'

'Sounds, sounds! Had you ever eyes?'

'Eyes that once looked on the most beautiful woman born, and nostrils filled with the scent of her body,' the blind man said, his voice elegiac. 'And I watched her ride on the sea meadows, her hair flowing.'

Toby Drew moved forward. 'I have only smelt the sweaty women in back kitchens of the pubs and the eating houses,' he said over his bent shoulder. 'Lumpy women who stirred me up.'

'Lead me towards the burying place,' the piper commanded, angry now.

'If I had food in my stomach I'd be silent,' snarled Drew, and wiping his wet nose on his coat sleeve, he trudged forward through the woods.

Toby Drew was a half-finished figure. His warped spine hooped his body downwards so that he had to stretch up his neck to look directly forwards. In a lazy mood he looked at the pathway before him. He disliked the Piper who was fastidious in his habits and his conversation and lived in some inner world of his own to which there seemed no access.

'How could he have scented the most beautiful woman ever born and who was she?' the hunchback asked. He had been with the Piper five years, during which they had kept only the company of rough men and unfinished women. He mulled over the images in his confused mind as they shuffled along.

'It must have been before I met you,' he said later out of sequence.

'What?'

'The woman you were talking about. The one that smelt well.'

'It was many years before I met you.'

'So I was thinking. So I was thinking,' Drew said sniffing and fell once more into silence.

After another half hour or so they arrived at the path leading towards the family graveyard and the hunchback led him up a small incline beside it. The Piper sat down on the stump of a tree and placed the pipes beside him, drawing his great coat about him as he waited. The hunchback sat by his side. Through the silver-birch wood he could see the lake shimmering and gazed at the splinters of light, sharp like the glint of silver coins.

The piper also stared ahead, but his eyes were white and unfocused, a greyish mass sealing off all light. He was a tall, blond man with white skin. Even the large coat which was of a shapeless character could not conceal that he had wide shoulders and slender hips. His forehead, tight and sensitive, bore the tensions of blindness. As he listened to the bell toll through the woods, he remembered the woman of the great house who had come to him many years ago. Her body had been as soft on his fingers as the touch of silk.

Sergeant Grinling, with two constables riding beside him, felt satisfied as he rode from Ballinrobe. He had broken the Fenian circles in Mayo and Galway and soon he would be recalled to Dublin to take up a new position at Dublin Castle. Possessed of a sharp, incisive mind, he was firm in pursuit of his ideals and he rode through the narrow, limestone-walled roads without fear. His colt revolver was loaded, ready to be drawn at an instant. Twice he had shot men in close combat when they tried to ambush him and even the Fenians feared his calculated ferocity.

Before he left the barracks he had closed the file on John Dillon. With neat copperplate handwriting he had described the final journey of the coffin from Galway, listing the Fenian sympathizers who had accompanied it to Dillon Hall. He had long suspected that Elinor Dillon knew of her husband's activities and made a note to order a party to search the house for evidence against her.

The two policemen, heavy and undistinguished men, had been reluctant to accompany the sergeant. They preferred the security of the town and the high barrack walls and looked suspiciously from side to side as they rode behind him. They feared the presence of the Fenian menace; some of their own colleagues had been sympathetic to the cause.

'It's ill-advised. Ill-advised, I tell you,' Constable Goff had muttered to his companion as they saddled their horses that morning in the stables at Ballinrobe Barracks. 'Many of the Fenians have not been rounded up. The American is still at large and there are others gone to ground. The death of John Dillon could be the spark to blow up the keg and we could go with it. I'm telling you, it's ill-advised.'

The other man agreed. He preferred the easy duty of the town with its military presence, its official order. They had mounted their horses reluctantly and waited apprehensively in the cobbled yard for Sergeant Grinling.

Now the horses were moving forward in a single line, the sound of the hooves muffled by the crisp leaves.

The shot rang out, splitting the silence, and the two constables reined in sudden shock. Sergeant Grinling, with his stiff upright back, continued to ride ahead. Then he fell backwards on his horse, carrying the stirrups upwards towards the horse's head. The two constables urged their mounts forward to look down at the face where a neat splotch of red on the forehead showed the bullet mark. Grinling lay on the horse's back for a moment, his head on the tail, then he tumbled sideways on to the ground. The horse dragged him forward a few feet so that the side of the sergeant's face furrowed the leaves and then stopped. The two constables looked at each other and turned their horses rapidly but awkwardly in the confined place, desperate to get out of the wood in case they too were cut down by the hidden snipers.

'It was coming to you, you bastard. Now everything is square,' said Desmond Hogan as he took the spent case from his gun and put it in his pocket. He stood upright and brushed his body print from the leaves, acknowledging his luck. There were two entrances into the wood from Ballinrobe and Sergeant Grinling had been unfortunate in choosing the wrong one.

He did not bother to see if the sergeant was dead. At fifty yards his aim was accurate and he had been thirty yards distance when the sergeant had come into range. The smell of cordite still held the air for a moment, then it dissolved. Hogan moved away quickly for he had further business to attend to and a horse was waiting for him at the edge of the woods.

Bartley Gaynor heard the single shot among the trees but continued to carve the dog from the wood he held, nicking carefully at the roughed-out head until he was satisfied that he had secured a good image. His cabin was filled with half-finished dogs. He was never satisfied with his work but it kept his hands occupied as he sat indoors and listened to the sounds about him. A squat man with vast shoulders, he possessed immense strength even in old age. His face was dark with grime, the cuticles of his nails rimmed in dirt and there was a greasy shine from his clothes.

'Time to go, Feather,' he told his dog who had been following his carving with appreciation. He looked at his model once more, turned it about in his hand and left it aside, then rubbed his face and squeezed his nose between thumb and finger. 'If that shot signifies what I think it does, then an enemy lies dead in the woods and we have some business to attend to and no barking. Do you hear me, Feather?'

The dog understood.

Gaynor left the cabin and made his way through the thickets where the wild laurels and rhododendrons grew until he came to a small hill from which he had a good view of the pathway. Below him he saw a solitary horse standing alone, secured by the body of Sergeant Grinling. He stood there listening for some time, but there was no sound in the wood and he went down to where the body lay.

'A neat shot if ever I saw one,' he remarked, looking at the face with its gaping mouth. 'He measured rightly between the two eyes.' He stood up and kicked the inert body.

'Who's God Almighty now?' he asked. He contemplated the figure for a moment and then kicked it again. 'And that's for giving me the gun butt on the back of the head. May you roast in hell with Martin Luther and his wife the nun.'

He moved in closer to the body and heaved it another kick into the ribs. 'And that's for kicking Feather, the day you searched the wood.'

Going through the sergeant's pockets, he found two items of interest: a black notebook, with writing he did not understand and a bright knife with two blades. He put them both in his pocket. He showed no interest in the gold sovereigns which had jingled at

9

each kick. He stood up, leaving the horse and body in the pathway and went to the marksman's position. Taking a bunch of twigs, he swished away the traces of the assassin, found the gun hidden in a cleft of a tree and wrapped it under his coat. Later he would secure it with the others in a safe place. All the while he was engaged in these activities, the funeral bell continued to toll through the woods.

Dillon Hall was in mourning. All day a steady stream of visitors had made their way up the wide, pebbled avenue to the open space in front of the house. Those who had never come before were impressed by its setting and its fine proportions. The limestone fronting carried a balcony which overlooked the great lake and its small islands. The portico and pilasters were finely chiselled with the family coat of arms carved on each pillar and the proportions of each of the three storeys above were balanced and perfect. Beneath the house lay the kitchens and store rooms, with their low-vaulted rooms, heavy-ribbed and solid. To the back of the house lay the tunnel, through which the coaches came on wet days. Above the tunnel stood a parapeted walk leading to the orchard and the stables.

On this day of sorrow it was not necessary to use the great tunnel, for the sky carried only tufts of cloud and the sun was warm and drew scents from the autumn wood. The Partry Mountains, to the west, were deep purple, the valley lines sculpted out by the light.

The tenants had formed a gapped crescent before the front door. They were men and women who had put on their best clothes for the occasion; the men in rough woollens, the women in coloured dresses, looking out from behind their shawls at the small stream of visitors arriving at the house in open carriages. Many of them wept openly. They could recall the days when the famine had blighted the land, when the cattle and sheep had been slaughtered in the cobbled yard for food. They could also recall the moment of exultation when Pegasus won the Grand National in 1846 and Eddie Cooney had run to the villages bearing the news soon after it reached the house. People had rushed from their small cabins and flocked to the racecourse where Elinor Dillon stood in triumph.

Very few of the landed gentry came to pay their respects; John Dillon had threatened their very existence. He belonged with those

10

who had plotted against established authority and had paid for the consequences of his crime. In their eyes he was guilty of treason.

In the hall, directly inside the double doors, the huge coffin lay on oak trestles. It was made from a shell of lead and a shell of deal. At each corner of the coffin, on brass candlesticks, four thick candles burned steadily, filling the hall with a heavy odour. Within the coffin, hands piously knit, John Dillon lay finally at rest. His face, despite the care taken by the servant women who had washed and dressed the body, was marked by the ravages of prison: the lips sagged over the white teeth, the ears were the colour of grey clay. The days of solitary confinement had left their mark on all his features.

Elinor Dillon sat in a great chair in the middle of the hall. Beside her stood her son Peter and her daughter Catherine. He was dark and tall like his mother, his sister, though not as tall as her mother, had the same sensual lips and, it was said, the same determined mind. Her hair was blond and neatly set about her head. Like her mother she spoke French fluently and possessed an uncanny knowledge of horses. All night Catherine had wept before the dining-room fire, reflecting on the pleasant days she had just spent in France at the château of her uncle and of the voyage home with her father. He had promised that he would ride with her across the mountains when he had finished his business in Galway. And then everything was thrown into confusion. The man lying in the coffin, grey-haired and worn, was not the man who had waved to her on the quay a month earlier.

At forty, Elinor Dillon was still a woman of outstanding beauty. Her firm, tall body carried a proud head with fine features and her hair was lustrous and black and fell freely on her shoulders. She possessed an air of authority which had impressed both her enemies and friends. Dillon Hall had been brought through difficult times through her stewardship and she had made hard decisions to ensure its survival.

At twelve o'clock Elinor Dillon signalled to the servant that the doors should be closed and the family retired to the drawing-room. In the great hall the blacksmith, with the aid of the two farm hands, soldered the edges of the lead coffin. When he was satisfied that the seams were fused, he took the great deal lid and

11

secured it with ornate brass screws. Then he removed the stove and soldering pot from the main hall and knocked on the drawing-room door to indicate that he had finished. As the family emerged, the great doors were drawn open and eight men from the estate came forward to take the heavy coffin on their shoulders. They moved slowly through the doors and down the steps.

The monks from Partry monastery formed a double line before the coffin. They moved forward in their brown habits, chanting in Latin. Directly behind the coffin Elinor Dillon followed with her daughter and son. Behind them walked Tadhg Mor, the mute giant who was Elinor's protector, and, at some distance, the tenants of the estate.

The cortège moved down the avenue and then along the edge of the lake, where the sedges, sere and stiff, brushed drily against one another. Birds, disturbed by the presence of so many people, took flight from among the reeds and settled further out on the lake.

As the procession approached the walled cemetery the Piper took his chanter, placed it on his knee and began to play. It was a slow air, full of haunting echoes. He had composed it a long time ago by the sea and it had the rhythm of the tides about it. Elinor Dillon turned towards the sound and saw the blind man, his eyes fixed and staring, sitting on the stump of the tree. A small vein quivered in her neck as she looked at him, and Toby Drew the hunchback, partly hidden by the undergrowth. He had locked his knees into his body with tight arms.

The cortège had reached a walled plot in which, surrounded by sombre yews, stood the mausoleum. It carried the remains of the generations who had lived at Dillon Hall, including the mad daughter Maud Dillon, who had been dredged from the lake.

The heavy coffin was set on a stone shelf within the vault and almost immediately the stone masons began to set the stones in place. The crowd remained quiet while the work was in progress, but just as they were about to disperse a man emerged from the trees carrying a rifle. A bugle was slung across his shoulders. He stood alone before the silent gaze of the mourners and then, lifting the rifle to his shoulder, he fired a single shot over the mausoleum. While the echo was still ringing round the trees, he

12

placed the bugle to his lips and sounded the last post. Many wondered why Sergeant Grinling had not been present at the funeral to ensure that there would be no firing party.

With her daughter and son, Elinor Dillon made her way along the lake path. She looked up briefly at the place where the piper had sat and played his lament, but there was no sign that he had ever been there.

Lord Daniel Parr was surprised that no one had brought him news of the funeral; he had expected a visit from Sergeant Grinling for there were certain details to be attended to before the large file on John Dillon was closed and dispatched to the Castle in Dublin. He shrugged and looked at the fire glowing in the grate. There was a chill in the autumn evenings which left his fingers numb. He wrapped an ornate blanket about his thin shoulders and sat back in his chair, feeling the satisfaction of vengeance.

With a deafening crash, the plate glass shattered in the great study. Fragments flew in all directions. Parr threw himself to the floor, his heart pounding, waiting for the shots that must follow. When he was certain he could hear nothing but the moan of the wind through the broken glass, he got gingerly to his feet and brushed off some of the shards sticking to his breeches, cutting the palms of his hands and making them bleed. Shaking and white with fear and rage, he looked at the object which had been thrown through the window. It was a lead coffin lid. He stretched out his hand and with a bleeding finger traced the outline of his own name which had been scored into the surface by a sharp instrument. Then he turned and tugged at the bell rope.

'Why did you not come immediately? Are you going deaf, man?' Lord Daniel Parr said as the servant ran into the room. 'Have the soldiers returned from Galway?'

'Oh, they have other business bothering them, my Lord. News has just arrived in the kitchen that Sergeant Grinling has been shot through the head on the way to Dillon's funeral. They are scouring the countryside. And worse still, my Lord, some of your horses in the stables have been blinded. Their eyes were slit and they are gone mad! We gave them the free run of the yard but sure they don't know where they are.'

13

Parr made a hasty assessment of his position, his sharp features pinched with thought and fear. He was isolated on his great estate and knew that he must act quickly and hope that he could survive the night.

'Bolt all the doors and draw the shutters on the windows. Have candles lit in all the rooms so that I can see the enemy if he enters. And bring me my guns. Load and line them on the hunting table in the great hall.'

Lord Daniel Parr drew up an armchair and ordered the servant to bring him a bottle of brandy and a brandy glass which he placed on the table beside him.

'If the vermin come I'll meet them like a lord and I'll take ten of them before they touch me. They tried before and failed. See that the fire is kept fully fuelled and check the guns at the stroke of each hour. Tomorrow order will be restored.'

He filled his glass with brandy and settled down to wait.

Elinor Dillon opened the great windows and stepped on to the balcony, wrapping her cloak about her against the autumn cold. A full moon to the east threw a path of silver across the lake and she could make out the silhouette of the islands with their mass of willows and sally. The great burden of the estate and the house now rested upon her shoulders alone and the lands belonged to her and her blood. She alone, and perhaps Tadhg Mor and the Piper, knew her secret and the strange tides of fortune that had brought her to Dillon Hall.

She went indoors and drew the doors behind her just as Tadhg Mor entered and asked her if she needed any attention.

She shook her head. 'You have been with me a long time, Tadhg. You know the secrets of my heart more than anyone else,' she told him as he moved to the door.

'This house is now yours, Lady Elinor,' he remarked, and then, he added, 'We have come a long way from the sea.'

'Do you miss it?' she asked, looking into his face.

'Sometimes I hear the waves in my ears. But I would not return to the island or to the Captain's house if it were still standing.'

'Good night, Tadhg. You have always been by my side during the good times and the bad times.'

'Good night, Lady Elinor. We never knew what the future held

14

when we left the ruined house many years ago.'

He opened the door quietly and closed it without a sound. For a large and seemingly awkward man he possessed a great gentleness.

Elinor poured herself a glass of wine and sat down in the deep leather chair, looking at the portraits of the Dillon family which hung about the walls of the library. No Dillon blood flowed in her children's veins.

# Chapter 2

Robert Dillon chose to be alone in the library. He was a tall man. His face and hands were fine-boned and his skin had the bright patina of porcelain. His eyes were remote and thoughtful, characteristics he had inherited from the Le Febres of Château la Prade. Their portraits stood about him and here more than anywhere else he felt that he belonged to a long line of aristocrats with their roots in medieval Europe. The Dillon family was represented by the dour portrait of his father and the ebullient one of his brother George who lived in Paris and who had taken charge of the vineyards in the Loire Valley and the warehouses at Quai de Bercy in the east of Paris. He was a man of the world with no great interest in books; his knowledge came from contact with men.

From the room Dillon could gaze reflectively on the lake with its islands and watch the sun rise out of the east; on mornings when a mist covered the lake the scenery could be as delicate as that in a Chinese print. But there were also black days when his mind was so filled with the fragility of human existence that he wondered if he should pursue the biography of Marie Antoinette on which he had been long engaged. Two miniatures stood on his desk to remind him that he must continue with the task. One depicted the young Queen at the court of Versailles, elegant and dressed in blue satin, lace edging the material. There was a suggestion of strong breasts, a fullness and certainty of being. The

15

other showed a gaunt woman, 'the Window Capet', without her false teeth, her cheeks sunken, a peasant bonnet on her head as she went on her way to the guillotine. What had begun as a romantic notion of a tragic life had changed during the years as Dillon began to perceive that the reasons which had destroyed the French monarchy could also destroy the great estates of Ireland and that its destruction would be caused by more than a rabble. The philosophers of reason were dangerous men; the French disease would spread to Ireland. The book was expanding his ideas of history.

Now, sitting before the log fire which the young groom Paddy Begley set most mornings, he recalled the long months he spent with his brother after coming down from Cambridge. He had been eager to experience the fine pleasure and culture of France and had stayed with George in the château close to the Forests of Saint Cloud.

The brief event which was to change his life occurred one morning when he decided to ride through the king's forest. It was a vast place and he knew that he would not be discovered if he rode at the very edge of the estate. A mist lay about the bowls of trees and reached to the chest of his horse: it was an ethereal and rare moment for the mist would soon be burnt by the sun and the forest would reappear to view. Robert Dillon rode quietly, enjoying a deep solitude, his mind filled with pleasant, unconnected thoughts.

His reverie was disrupted by the sound of horse's hooves somewhere in the distance. Leaning forward he peered into the mist to see a figure emerge, a vague and ghostlike appearance which for a moment made him think he was dreaming. It began to take solid form as it approached and he saw it was a solitary horsewoman. She was startled when she saw him and for a moment seemed about to turn away, but instead she reined her horse with an expert hand and moved in his direction. Even at a distance he was impressed by her appearance: she held her head proudly with a serene expression although he could detect a youthful vivacity on her lips. She could not have been more than twenty-three, he thought and he wondered what she was doing alone in the forest at such an early hour.

16

'Good morning, my lady. You startled me,' he said to her as she patted the neck of her horse.

'And indeed you startled me! I did not expect to meet a stranger here. How did you find your way into the forest?' she asked, laughing.

'Why, through one of the side gates. The place has always been a mystery to me – I have ridden about the walls and wondered what secrets it held. This morning under the cover of a morning fog I decided to enter – and here I am, although I must slip out again soon. But, why do you ride alone? It is dangerous for a lady to ride without an escort. Are you one of the ladies of the court?'

'I am, but I like to escape whenever I can. The air is so fresh here and the forests are so immense and simple like the woods about Vienna.'

'Vienna!' exclaimed Robert. 'Are you not far from your home? Do you not wish to return to the simple way of life in that country? I have heard that the court at Saint Cloud is a corrupt place full of intrigue.'

'I must stay. I married a French gentleman,' she said in explanation. A curious smile played about her face which he did not understand.

'And how did all that come about?' he asked.

'It is a long story, full of political diplomacy which is tedious to relate. But where do you come from? I'm sure the details of your life are much more interesting than mine.'

'Ireland,' he told her softly.

'I have only seen Ireland on a great map. It seems so remote and on the very edge of the world. Tell me about Ireland as we ride along this path. It is better to turn left here, you know. We are too close to the palace. The king's soldiers would be quite angry if they discovered you here.'

He was aware of her firm back and the good control she had over the horse as she rode beside him. He looked across at the saddle and reins; they were made from the finest leather. He told her how his father had made his fortune in France and then returned to Ireland with a French wife to establish a house there, and described Dillon Hall and its surroundings.

17

'And do you dance at this great house and have servants?' she asked seriously.

'Yes, we have dances, but not in such a formal fashion as you have in the great palaces.'

'And are the people poor?'

'Yes. But not as servile as the poor of France.'

'How do you mean, servile?'

'I have seen them in the fields,' he gesticulated around. 'They are like beasts of burden. They seem to do their master's bidding without question and I can detect little spirit.'

'And should it not be so? Has it not been ordained to be like this?' she asked in genuine puzzlement.

'I do not think so. You may feel that you are safe within these forest walls, but I believe that the times are changing.' He turned to look at her.

'You think too much. Thought is a bad thing. You should be happy,' she told him, turning from the drift of their conversation and looking ahead, shading her eyes with one hand. By now the mist had partially vanished and the vista between the great trees had been opened up.

'I shall race you to the gate,' she announced and would have urged her horse forward had not a group of mounted soldiers suddenly appeared from the thickets on the right. Beside them ferocious dogs barked, their teeth wet with vicious saliva and the forest was suddenly alive with noise. The soldiers drew their swords and formed a circle around Robert Dillon. His companion directed them to stay their anger and, turning to him, said, 'You have discovered the mystery within the walls; I will never discover the mystery without.' With an enigmatic smile she rode away, leaving him staring after her.

A soldier took the reins of his horse and drew him roughly aside. 'You trespass in these forests! Do you know I could have you thrown in the Bastille for your arrogance? Who are you?'

'I am an Irish gentlemen,' Dillon replied with some dignity. 'Take your hands from me. Have you some law which prevents me speaking to a lady?'

'Yes,' said the other shortly. 'When you speak with the Queen of France you are beyond the law. I will escort you out of this forest.'

18

Robert Dillon did not speak while he was led through the pathways to an obscure gate. He was filled with a sense of awe. He recalled the face of the lady, the colour of her hair, her simplicity and their conversation. He was aware that she was in her own prison, wide and spacious though it was, and that she had little knowledge of what was going on outside the great walls. He knew that she must be stifled by court life; he had read of its frustrating manners and etiquette and from that moment on he would follow her fortunes with great interest. Long before the fatal days of the Revolution and the guillotine he began to gather material on her life.

Next day he told his brother enthusiastically about his encounter with the young Queen as they rode through Paris.

'You are impressed by their elegant ways, the great châteaux, the vast acres and their stables,' George told him. 'Look at the poverty of the people here, crowded into narrow streets which breed hatred. In the countryside the peasant is weighed down with taxes – he is an ox of burden, a chattel without privilege who can be put down and buried in an unmarked grave. And look at the revolutionary yeast, at the writings of Voltaire so popular with the bourgeois intellectuals. His message is easily understood. And look at the success of the American War of Independence! I tell you, there is revolution in the air. . .'

'And where shall you be if the Revolution comes?' Robert asked as they passed across Pont Neuf on their way to the Latin Quarter.

'In my vineyard or at the warehouse. The French cannot do without their wine. I keep detached from politics and I always have a means of escape – I know every ship which sails out of Paris.' George was suddenly serious.

'And will the Revolution succeed?' Robert pressed.

'How should I know?' George shrugged. 'But it seems to me that already the long fuse to the powder keg has been set alight. The aristocracy and the Church have been given fair warning but they will not heed and they are fat and full and too lazy to change their ways. I think it is inevitable. Kings have lost their heads before.'

In the September of that year they had gone to the vineyards.

George examined the grape harvest on the chalky hills of Vouvray and decided that they should ride several days further south to the small estate in the Auvergne on the lower slopes of the Massif Central.

They rested for a day after their journey in the main house, occupied by the foreman. The next day he ordered out an old man, Jacques, to saddle two horses and pack provisions of food and wine for two days. The peasant, who moved slowly about the warm courtyard with its red weathered-tiled outhouses and rough masonry, picked out two sturdy horses. It was he who had introduced George to the wild, primitive countryside as a young man of eighteen and there was a strong bond of friendship between them.

'I clear my mind and my heart in the mountains,' said George as they waited in the yard for Jacques to saddle their mounts. 'Here man is tested by the landscape; in the city he is pitted against man. Some day I may come and live the life of a peasant like old Jacques here. He is not bothered by history or the latest fashion in Paris. He has his own answers and they come out of the soil and are part of it. Rousseau should have known him.' He laughed. 'He might have corrected some of his wilder notions.'

'Have you read Rousseau?' Robert asked in surprise.

'Oh, I have given him a cursory glance. I knew all that before I read Rousseau. Of course my favourite is that old agnostic Voltaire, but beyond that I learn from man. Why clutter the mind with learning?'

George enjoyed the open spaces where the earth was fertile and the sun beat down on the ripened grape. As they moved further into the mountains Robert, too, felt his mind gradually set at liberty. He enjoyed the delight of living for the moment, eating with the peasants around their rough tables and sharing their humour. He loved the rough utensils they used at table and the manner in which they ate their food.

They stopped off at remote villages and watched women trampling the grapes in large barrels, singing medieval songs as they did so. They watched them sickle rye and oats on pockets of warm land and on one occasion they spent a whole day flailing wheat on a barn floor until their bodies ached and their clothes were drenched in sweat. That night George had danced to a tambour and fife with the women of the village.

'Do you ever think of Dillon Hall?' Robert asked the next morning as they journeyed on into the mountains along a dusty track.

'Look at the clear sky,' George said, pointing to the high arc of blue. 'Smell the resin from the pines. Feel the warm wind on your body. I have no wish to return to Ireland and I rarely think of Dillon Hall,' he answered in a definite voice.

As they rode further into the mountains the brothers talked less, the silence in the valleys and the pines filling them with a sense of tranquillity. Their journey forged a bond between them which was to strengthen as they grew to manhood and took on the burdens of the family.

More than a quarter of a century later Robert Dillon could still recall the night they slept in the small valley close to a mountain stream. The air was dry and warm and they had built a small fire and roasted a chicken they had bought from a peasant woman. As it braised above the fire they opened two bottles of wine and began to drink. It was while drinking the wine and looking into the heart of the pine fire that George told Robert all that he knew of their ancestry. It was a strange story which would haunt Robert all his life. Although their ancestry could be traced into royal houses, somewhere on the way the blood had become tainted. George had searched out every corner of the family history and had proved that the fatal defect turned up in each generation.

'It is fixed in the blood, I tell you,' he said as he poked the fire. 'No breeding will dilute it. And that is the reason why I shall never marry.'

'And you believe that this strangeness will show itself again?' Robert asked.

'Of course it will. I have traced our mother's family here in France and I tell you, the female line carries madness. It may not be the madness which confines people to lunatic asylums but it generates oddness and a strange behaviour. You know that they say in Vouvray: Ah, the Le Febre women, they are all mad.'

'And you believe that our mother was mad?'

21

'I'm certain. You may not remember her, but I do. I can recall clearly the way her face would distort and she would become strange. After your birth she was taken from the house and brought to Galway – I can still hear the whispering in the library – and when she returned she was never the same. She took to walking by the lake edge and singing French songs remembered from her childhood. One of the servants was set to watch her and I recall the day that he rushed through the house, screaming for my father while I followed on his heels. We found her hanging from a rafter in one of the outhouses. I can still recall the men undoing the knot and easing her head out of the noose. She was still alive, so they had time to call the priest and that is the reason she is buried in sanctified ground.'

Robert looked at his brother, caught in the light of the fire. With his open shirt, wild hair and sunburnt skin he looked like a Romany. When he had finished speaking, he put the lip of the clay jar of wine to his mouth and drank deeply. Some of the wine poured down his chest and stained his shirt.

'And you believe that it runs in the female line?' Robert persisted.

'Uncle Michel, the curé, told me all these things. He was a wise old owl and had a very sharp French mind. He was what you might call ungodly. He had a bastard child by a servant woman who still lives with him at le Petit Mont. The child is married now and has two sons and a daughter and she is strange. You ask me how I am certain of these things. I have seen them for myself. I tell you that we carry a congenital defect in us. There are whores enough in Paris to take the edge off my lusts. Perhaps I should not have told you these things, but in the heart of the mountains and away from civilization and feeling insignificant under the stars it is as well that you should know them. You, I know, will marry and the estates will pass on to your children. You may keep the secret to yourself or you may tell it to your wife, but it is a heavy responsibility.'

'And what would you advise?' Robert asked, taking a branch and marking out abstract images on the dust before the fire.

'You will know yourself when the time comes,' said George, passing him the jug of wine. 'Drink to the pagan gods, brother.

Drink to the gods of wine. You must follow your destiny and I mine.' And for some reason he began to laugh. 'Existence is folly. Enjoy the day for what it is worth. Be like the old peasant Jacques. He accepts life with its tragedy and with its joy. He knows how to live!'

They both fell silent. They looked into the heart of the pine-wood fire, and listened to the spit of the resin drops as they shot from the flames. The burning branches collapsed and sent out a shower of bright sparks which danced for a moment in the darkness and died. The sound of the stream was soft in their ears. Close by, the horses, tethered to a fallen tree, stirred in the darkness.

'Why do you choose to tell me these things upon such a beautiful night?' Robert asked, looking up towards the bright crust of stars. 'It seems such a cruel disclosure.'

'One is honest in the mountains.'

'Then why did our father marry a woman who was clearly strange? He must have been aware of these things.'

George took a handful of dust and let it fall evenly in light trickles through his fingers.

'Soil. The possession of the earth, property. Remember that Father was the third son of an impoverished squireen sent to work in the wine warehouses of Galway. He was intelligent and learned to speak French so he came to France to work in the warehouses here. The marriage alliance brought him property and even a coat of arms. The Le Febres can trace their line back to the court of Henri II and he was married to one of the Medicis. Father saw an opportunity and took it and when he returned to Ireland he could build Dillon Hall and set a coat of arms above the door and on the pillars. He made a very good bargain. . .'

George spoke with the voice of one who knew the ways of the world. He could take a large view of events and was shrewd in his dealings with men. He admired wealth and, though still a young man, had taken over the family business and extended the property and export trade.

'Let us sleep, now. We have a way to go before we reach the mountain pass. Then the flat plains drenched by sun will show us that we are back again in vine-growing country.' He took a large,

23

coloured blanket and handed it to Robert. Then he wrapped his own blanket about him, placed his head on the hard saddle and fell asleep.

They rode through the mountains for two further days. The valleys became more fertile, the villages more numerous, lying in the blue haze of summer, sleepy and tranquil. The small mountain pass soon ran into a rough road, which led to a village where they rested for the night before making their way back towards the estate vineyards. As they entered the cobbled yard, they could see Jacques sitting on a stone bench scattering oats to cheeky hens. He strung the oat bag tight with a rope and came slowly towards them, his steps ponderous and old. In some way he reminded Robert of the crags and mountains through which they had just passed and he knew that he would never again make such a journey.

Robert Dillon recalled all these things as he sat before the log fire. Moving to the library window he watched as Paddy Begley came into view. He was driving a horse and cart and sitting on top of a precious box of books he had just collected from the mail coach at Ballinrobe. He took his clay pipe periodically from his mouth when he wished to spit a jet of saliva to the ground as he had seen his elders do.

Looking down as the cart approached, Robert Dillon realized that his great work would occupy many years of his life and felt yet again the familiar surge of desperation as he contemplated the enormity of his task.

Suddenly his attention was drawn to his daughter who, with hair sweeping behind her, came out of the wood path and forced her horse forward across the great lawn in the direction of the fences. The beast pulled up and refused to take the fence. Maud jumped from the saddle and brought her whip down upon him again and again until he whinnied in pain. Her elder brother, Matthew, who had been riding behind her at some distance, quickly dismounted and rushed towards her. He grasped her hand to stop her beating the horse and the two of them fell forward. Matthew pinned her hand to the ground and Robert Dillon could see her body shaking with anger, her teeth snapping at his arms.

As the surge of anger left her, and Matthew got to his feet

24

brushing his knees, Robert turned from the window, disturbed at what he had seen. Maud was now fourteen years of age and this strangeness was already a frequent characteristic of her behaviour. Physically she was an attractive young woman but during the last two years an odd look had begun to appear in her eyes. In fury she had thrown plates at the servants and several times she had brought her whip down on the back of the stable boy who had not groomed a horse to her satisfaction. Robert recalled the night he had sat with his brother at the blazing pine fire close to the stream and the history of the family had been revealed to him.

# Chapter 3

The Parrs in blood and bone held a firm allegiance to the British Crown and the Protestant faith which had been proved in each generation. Parrs had fought in all the great battles which had convulsed Europe and America, and in the village chapel of Williamstown marble medallions and brass plaques testified to their bravery and loyalty. They had provided colonels and captains for the armies of the Empire and they felt they were as British as families living in the shires.

To their tenants they were known as 'the spore of Cromwell'. The soubriquet had been passed down, generation after generation. Tradition had it that in the seventeenth century Madcap Parr had chained rebels together on the Corrib Bridge in Galway and thrown them into the rushing waters. It was believed that he had tossed babies on to the bayonets and swords of his soldiers and that he had sent Catholic women as slaves to Barbados. There was very little definite evidence that these atrocities had ever occurred, but they remained ingrained, like dirt, in folk memory. Parents frightened their children into obedience by threatening that they would send for Madcap Parr to deal with them, although he had been dead for over two centuries. The more prosaic facts spoke of a Cromwellian captain who had been given five hundred acres of land to farm in Mayo, ill-natured land, more suitable to rearing sheep than fattening cattle. He married into a neighbouring family and extended his holding down into the fat flatlands and the generations which followed extended their lands, their influence and the rough house he had built. By the end of the eighteenth century the old house had been pulled down, the present great house set out among trees and the Parrs were the owners of six thousand acres of good land.

John Parr took possession of the title and house on the death of his father in 1772. His marriage to Elizabeth Hoxten of Surrey brought much needed money into the family. The great house was reroofed, a new strain of horse introduced to the stables and the estates in Surrey added to the family inheritance. Elizabeth was a tall, gaunt women with an ungainly walk; even the artist commissioned to paint her portrait for the great gallery could not flatter her: among the portraits of the woman gracing the walls, that of Elizabeth Hoxten stood out for its flat, featureless quality. She faithfully produced six children and then she conveniently died. John Parr, now secure in his fortune, chose a young beauty for his bed and his middle age and spent nine months of the year on his English estates, leaving the running of his affairs in Mayo to his eldest son, David.

David Parr had been educated in England. He had the dour character of his ancestors and he took a keen interest in the estates, treating tenants like chattels. He had a keen eye for young, unmarried women and at a whim would send a servant to fetch one when his lusts burned. Once he had got a woman with child, he settled her and her husband on the estate, feeling that he had built up a blood bond about him as his father had done. He was attended by a small army of rough men whom he had drawn from his father's bastards, united in blood and spirits and loyal to his bidding. They rode with him through the countryside at night time when his spirits were restless and were feared for their angers and their savagery. Many of them also followed Valentine Parr, David's younger brother. He was heavy and dissolute and his eyes had a sad, lecherous look. At night, he played cards with the men in the stables, gambling cautiously, his wet eyes looking at the fan of cards, his awkward fingers bending the corners. While he waited for a wager to be placed, he would pull his raw nose with his fingers. He had lost and won fortunes at the card table.

The four Parr sisters lived on at the house in one of the wings, called by the servants 'the convent', isolated from their brothers. The sisters, it was commonly predicted, would follow trivial pursuits, observe time and events pass with due reserve, die without issue or dowry and leave both themselves and the great house intact. To this end their elder brother had introduced Parson Nugent into their service. A former army officer who had taken the cloth, he had rigorous beliefs in the purpose of the Protestant faith. His hold over his timid flock came from physical strength, his thunderous voice, his powerful fists pounding his conviction into the pine pulpit.

'The Catholic Church is not a bride. It is a whore. The Pope, the very Antichrist in garish investments, leads ignorant people to damnation with his bulls and his anathemas! Have you heard about the bad popes and the women popes? Well, let me tell you and let me tell you at length for it is a subject with which I am well familiar. Let me tell you of the successor of Peter cavorting with the loose women of Rome. Let me tell you about the Jesuits with whom I am also well familiar. Trained military men – don't be taken in by their black habits – their founder was an officer in the field, and a Spanish one at that. But let me return to immoral popes and the loose women of Rome. . .'

His sermons were filled with wild excitements and the rich music of the Bible and, although his knowledge was shallow and pictorial, he could rapidly stitch together quotations from various books to prove his point. He had a few favourite themes, one of which was a description of the brothels of Rome and the manner in which whores were introduced into the papal bed. He described the interior of the brothels with great exactness and some enthusiasm, quickly moving from the papal bed to the Irish peasant cottage, with its idolatrous images. As his sermons came to an end, his voice would become soft and pious:

'You are the salt of the earth, the wise virgins, yours will be the nuptials of heaven. About us the vileness of corruption, votaries of venery. Here lilies grow in the oasis, the air is laden with perfume. I stand amongst the blessed, unabused bodies of intact women,

27

flesh of virgins fit for gods. Here there is the peace and the pearls of great price.'

His sentences and his logic were not always coherent but they had a strong influence upon the isolated minds of the Parr sisters and for five years they were subjected to his wild images. Three of the sisters were drawn into Nugent's strange world of erotic hates and fears, but Margaret Parr did not share the plain appearance or frail body of her sisters nor did she possess the mincing tones of their voices, or their rigid attitude towards Catholics. She enjoyed physical work in the great garden where she grew vegetables and flowers and would spend long hours digging the earth and preparing it for seed. She took pride in her work and was abusive towards gardeners when their ridges and flower beds were ragged and careless. While her sisters were caught up in the religious fervours of Parson Nugent she preferred to walk in the hills or ride her horse across the wide lawns and fields.

She refused to attend service in the Protestant church built by her ancestors at Williamstown. Her brother had called her to task the first Sunday she had absented herself, standing with his back to the blazing fire, dressed in an elegant frock coat and ruffles.

'You realize of course that you were missed from church today? You realize also that this will be the subject of conversation and gossip at every table in the county? The fact that you rode past the carriages as they made their way home from church was more than an insult to the congregation: we built the church; I expect my family to attend services there. You may not be aware of it, sister, but it behoves us to give an example to others. You belong to a class which sets the fashion and the fashion you have set this morning has in no way added to our reputation. I expect you to attend church each Sunday morning from now on.' He spoke in a dominating voice, his elbow placed on the marble slab of the mantlepiece, dangling his gold chain in a manner to impress upon her the importance of his opinion.

'I refuse to obey your orders. I do not believe in religion and I see no reason why I should waste my time in a stuffy church starched and clean when I would prefer to be riding. You speak of example, but what of my father's bastards who inhabit the estate?

28

Is that not flying in the face of your established church? And what of your own indulgence? The tenants are your slaves; the women your concubines. And you introduce a mad parson to our family table, one who sees the Bible as a battlefield and good and evil the struggle between England and Spain. I have watched his male part harden in front of me as he speaks of the Love Songs of Solomon or describes the brothels of Rome. He's not a pastor! He has done untold damage to the minds of my sisters – if they have minds,' she added enraged.

He looked at his sister carefully. She was now twenty-two years of age with a full body and heavy breasts. He realized that if he did not immediately stamp his authority upon her she would spread dissension throughout the house.

'I will not have such vile slanders spoken against one who comes with the finest recommendations!' he shouted. 'Your suggestions come from a corrupt mind. Nugent is a man of the cloth—' he would have carried on concerning the dignity of the cloth, but Margaret interrupted.

'The man is a charlatan! He is clearly mad and I will not listen to him or attend church.'

David Parr was taken aback. He fought to regain control of his cold voice. Looking keenly at the face of his sister, he said 'I should have you horse-whipped. You are a Parr, remember.'

'And I have the Parr angers!' she retorted. 'I have seen young women brought into the stable yard at dusk. I have watched them walk across the quadrangle and up the back stair. I know what goes on. I have seen your bastards in their arms.'

He suddenly felt vulnerable, ashamed. 'It is not true.'

'It is true,' she insisted.

He moved forward quickly and with an open palm slapped her across the face with a sharp smack 'Silence! You have pried too much on my privacy.'

'I am a Parr,' Margaret said, her face reddened where he had hit her. 'Had I been a man I would own land and play a dominant role. I refuse to obey your orders any more or be subjected to your will. You will not master me as you master my sisters and the peasant women. I am tired of your repression and I am tired of this house.'

He hit her again and again on the cheek. She held her face firm and took each angry blow, her eyes glaring stubbornly at him. Blood trickled down her chin and dropped on to her white dress where it stained the material. Finally he relented.

'Leave if you wish. Make your own life. You do not belong here. I do not wish to speak with you again.'

'Nor I any wish to speak with you. Give me the Dower House and I will live there. If I stay here both of us will lead lives of misery – I can give you full guarantee of that.'

'And how will you sustain yourself at the Dower House? You have no money,' he said with a sneer on his lips.

'Then I will marry a peasant and come for my dowry. I mean it: I will not be bullied by you.'

He looked at her angry face and knew that she would not hesitate to follow her threat.

'Knowing how stubborn you are I will settle one hundred pounds a year on you,' he said, his mind working rapidly.

'I do not trust you.' She stood her ground.

'Very well,' he said. 'I will have a solicitor draw up the papers.'

She did not thank him or say goodbye. She swept out of the room, banging the door behind her, and walked directly to her room to pack her trunks. Her sisters, aware that something of great import was happening, came to her room and gathered about her, twittering with anxiety.

'I am saying goodbye to this house and its stifling atmosphere,' she told them. 'I cannot tolerate David any more.'

'And how will you survive on your own?' one of them asked, surprised at her angry gestures.

'Living alone presents no problem to me and some day I intend to get married and have children and have a man in my bed and rule my own house.'

The sisters grouped together as they listened to her words, a little frightened at what was happening.

'Do we know the gentleman who will ask for your hand?' another asked, wishing to nibble on some information.

'I do not know myself. He could be a black man as far as I know, or a yellow man, or an Indian,' Margaret laughed.

30

'As long as he is not a Catholic. As long as he is not a Catholic,' they warned her timidly.

She looked at the three frail figures, almost indistinguishable in appearance, and went towards them, wrapping her arms about them as if to protect them.

'I will miss you very much,' she told them. 'You are dear to me and so frail. Won't you come with me? There is room for all of us in the Dower House.'

'Oh, we could not do that! We are not brave like you. We had better stay here. But you will come and see us for Sunday high tea and tell us everything that is happening? It is important for us to know what is happening.'

'I shall not be returning to the house,' Margaret said finally. 'I will say goodbye here and now and if we should see one another again it will only be at a distance.'

The three sisters began to shake with tears, patting their eyes and noses with linen handkerchiefs as they had been trained to do. They did not sniff as this was considered impolite. Margaret hugged each one of them once more before she left her room for the last time.

She did not look at the great house as the carriage emerged from the yard and into the main avenue. Its splendid roof, with huge slates brought all the way from France, its high and twisted chimneys, its parapet and bow windows held no attraction to her. She was free of all its social demands and, above all, free of the heavy presence of her brother. She had broken loose at last.

At the turn of the century it seemed strange that a young woman should set up at a Dower House on her own and it was the main subject of conversation for some time. The rumours were various: some believed that she was carrying her brother's child and that she had been ordered to remain within the estate walls; others said that her sensual appetites were so strong that she had employed two young men from the estate to attend to her passionate needs; others believed that she was mad and had been confined within walls and protected by servants.

She was familiar with the Dower estate and had watched it falling into decay over the years. It was remote from her brother's

31

mansion and had been used to finish cattle for the market. On her arrival she ordered her servant to make ready a bed and to prepare a simple meal for her.

'I shall return in four hours' time and I expect that the house will be in order, the furniture dusted, fires burning in the grate to banish the unused smell of the place. This house has fallen into complete decay: the drains are clogged; the avenue needs scuffling; the apple trees have not been pruned in years. You have become lazy and lost all pride in yourselves.'

Margaret rode the bounds of the Dower estate, noting which walls needed repair and where trees needed to be felled. She returned four hours later to a warm house. Next day she journeyed to Galway and engaged a solicitor to draw up an agreement between herself and her brother. She wished to have a lease of ten years on the estate and in the event of marriage she expected a dowry of one thousand pounds. She also insisted he grant her a stipend of one hundred pounds a year. She listened carefully while the solicitor explained her statutory rights and the conditions of covenants.

David Parr signed the documents. He was happy to be rid of her and two hundred acres of land were of no great account to him. Eventually they would revert to his possession anyway, and knowing his sister they would be improved during the tenure.

The next five years passed quickly and pleasantly for Margaret Parr. Under her direction the estate was transformed: unnecessary walls were flattened, scrubland was cut back, trees felled and cut into long timber beams which were sold in Galway. The walled garden was brought into production and she employed a gardener from the local village to maintain it.

She had an obsession with order. Each morning at eight o'clock the bell in the tower above the farmyard sounded to begin the measured day at the estate. Men and women made their way into the great kitchen where they were served a large breakfast. At half past eight Margaret appeared with a plan of the day's work: the men were assigned to the stables and the land; the women were given their duties about the house and the dairy. At one o'clock the bell sounded again for dinner. The meal consisted of meat and vegetables, a strong diet unusual in the locality.

'It is not charity,' she told a local squire, 'and I am not giving them expectations of plenty. You cannot expect people to work unless they are fed and you cannot expect to run an estate unless people know what to do. If they are not pleased then there are other tenants I can invite in to replace them. They are worked hard and if they have cause to complain they can come to me and I will listen to them.'

'The Irish peasant will not submit to such order. It is foreign to his nature. They are shiftless liars,' the squire insisted.

'No, but their landlords are shiftless and they imitate them. It is a scandal the way the land is abused. It is not worked to its full worth,' she protested.

'And you educate them!' he told her with amusement. 'Teach them to read and write and you set the seeds of rebellion in their minds.'

'If they read and write they will set some value upon themselves. It makes them less than beasts. They know I am rigorous and fair. And don't tell me that I give them a bonus for extra work – of course I do and I make more money in that way. It should be obvious to any farmer that this is the way to run an estate.'

One of the outhouses had been changed into a small school. It contained rough desks, some books she had purchased in Galway and some writing material. Each week she visited the classroom to mark the progress of the children.

At the beginning some of the tenants had been resentful. Their resentment was focused on a man called Hughs. In protest he maimed one of her cattle. When she saw how cruelly the beast had been treated she was furious and called soldiers from Galway into the estate to protect her animals. The tenants were questioned in her office in the presence of a constable. They quickly confessed that Hughs was the culprit.

Immediately she dispatched the soldiers to his cottage and they dragged Hughs to the yard where he was trussed to the back of a cart, while the tenants gathered about him in a circle. Margaret took her riding whip and moved forward into the centre of the circle. In the presence of the soldiers she tore off his shirt, raised the whip and brought it down five times on the man's back. The strokes raised blue weals on his unwashed skin.

33

'Now take him and throw him out of the estate. If he returns I will shoot him. I will not have a savage maim my cattle.'

Hughs was mute with humiliation. A woman had whipped him and that scar would remain in his memory when the weals on his back had healed. He was marched between the soldiers down the main path to the gate. The tenants looked in awe at Margaret Parr. She was twenty-four years of age and she had now complete control over the estate.

'If Hughs returns and anyone present has any connection with him then they too will be thrown off the estate. Now return to your work. The hay is ready for scything, the weather is good and I have wasted a whole morning on a villain.'

All that day she rode through the fields while the men cut the hay, moving evenly forward towards the ditches. They worked at some distance from each other. There was the wet scent of root and flower in the air, which filled her body with pleasure.

Within three years she had improved the estate beyond recognition and, through the sale of cattle and sheep, it showed a profit of three hundred pounds. She set out her costs and profits in a large ledger and each evening she had the servant light a candle in her small office where she sat planning the next day's work and entering her costs for the day.

For two years she had her eye on the estate of John Sherlock which bordered her own land. The pasture had been coarsened with rushes and ragwort and in wintertime part of it lay under water, the tracks through it muddy and without foundation. The tenants were lazy and ate at the table of their master who was more interested in his hounds than his land. She knew that he was in debt to the merchants of Galway who refused to give him more credit.

One day she decided to approach Sherlock and make him an offer. She rode along the bank of the river which cut through the two estates and looked at the dark, sullen waters stained with iron and turbary. Finding a place where the river was level with the land, she forced her horse into the water. Near midstream it had to swim forward and took fright for a moment but then gained confidence. She emerged from the river and rode up to the ramshackle house with its broken windows. She knocked on the

34

door with the knob of her riding whip and when the servant opened it she brushed past him and strode into the large kitchen. It was low and dank and filled with the stench of dogs and unwashed bodies. John Sherlock with some of his men was playing cards at the table.

'I would have private words with you, Sherlock,' she announced. The men, knowing her reputation, slipped out of the kitchen.

'What could we say to one another?' John Sherlock asked. 'A river divides us and you hold rank on me. Did you come to whip me? I own this land and could have you driven from the estate for trespassing.' His voice was slurred. It was evident from the half-empty bottle beside him that he had been drinking whisky.

'That will be unnecessary,' Margaret said coolly. 'I come to you with an offer: I will buy the river meadows from you. At present they are worthless, but I will offer you two pounds an acre – unless you would like to sell the whole estate?'

'No Parr will buy me out,' said Sherlock grimly. 'But I'll sell you the river acres for three pounds an acre. There are two hundred acres of water, so that, Margaret Parr, comes to six hundred pounds.'

'Very well. I'll have my lawyer draw up the deeds and we will meet in Galway next Saturday.' She turned and left the house. The stench of the kitchen was overpowering and she felt that she should wash her body when she returned to her house.

The following Saturday the deeds were signed. On Sunday sappers from the military barracks in Galway placed two barrels of gunpowder under Ashley falls and lit the fuses. From a distance on a small hillock Margaret Parr watched the explosion lift a heavy mass of granite into the air. Even before the rocks had fallen back into the stream, dark water rushed through the new cut. She looked upstream at the sluggish river which had kept part of her land and the land of John Sherlock sodden and useless. It was beginning to find a lower level.

John Sherlock, playing cards with his tenants, heard the explosion. He rushed from the kitchen and saddled his horse. He could see a puff of black smoke moving across the trees as he pushed his horse forward through the woods towards the river.

When he looked at the breached waterfall and Margaret Parr seated on her horse on the hillock he knew that he had been deceived. Within five days large trees had been felled in the wood and thrown across the river to form a bridge: Margaret Parr rode across it and took possession of her own land.

She rarely appeared at public functions at Galway. Instead she preferred to visit farms and watch horses mating or study the nature of the earth. She took delight in the presence of sleek cattle and thoroughbred horses and had formed a keen eye for judging the quality of a horse.

One Monday in May 1806 she dressed in her riding clothes and saddled her best horse to set out for the estate of Robert Dillon on the lake shore of Lough Mask. It was a bright day and as she descended the hills of Partry she could see the estate beneath her. The Georgian house built on the wine money from France by Patrick Dillon stood on a gentle incline above the wide expanse of lake with its many islands. Behind it were the beech and oak woods and circling the woods the wide limestone fields with rich grass. She could make out the large paddock where the Dillon thoroughbreds were exercised each day. Patrick Dillon had purchased only the best stock and his son Robert had taken a keen interest in improving the breed. She reined her horse and gathered in the view. She remained on the brow of the hill for half an hour. Then she stirred herself and made her way towards the estate.

She recalled that Robert Dillon was a Catholic. It had been bred in her since she was a child that Catholics were verminous, unwashed peasants who worshipped chalk statues. She tried to banish these thoughts from her mind as she came closer to the house and dismissed them finally at the gates. She had come to buy a stallion and that crossed the barriers of religion.

As she approached the house itself she observed the coat of arms with its hooded falcon on each limestone pillar. She knocked at the door and a servant invited her to enter the hall, where she looked about her at the magnificent marble staircase, and the family portraits obviously painted in France. She felt clumsy and out of place.

A door opened on the first landing and she looked up to see a tall figure emerge, elegantly dressed. He carried gold-rimmed spectacles in his hand and she was certain that he had been just interrupted in his reading.

'Forgive me, Miss Parr, for keeping you waiting,' he called out as he came down the staircase. 'I received your letter a week ago. Welcome to Dillon Hall! I'm sure you are exhausted after your journey. You must join me in some refreshments. Let us go to the drawing room where we can talk.'

She was impressed by his friendly manner and his sharp, intelligent face. He opened the drawing-room door for her and she entered a room with blue wallpaper and light furniture embroidered with blue brocade.

She sat on one of the armchairs and, as he sat down opposite her, she had a better chance to assess him. He was a man of about thirty-five years of age with fine skin and hair greying at the temples.

'You must have some of our port. It is a good quality and quite firm.' He poured two glasses of port and passed her one.

Margaret felt a certain awe in his presence. He had some remote quality about him that she had not observed before and she felt uncomfortable in her rough riding clothes which seemed out of place in the room. She stiffly sipped the port: she rarely drank wine.

She realized that she had not spoken a word since she entered the house. 'I hope I have not intruded on your work,' she began awkwardly, sitting rigidly in the chair.

'I welcome such intrusions,' he said kindly. 'Writing is a slow process. One is never certain where one's thoughts will lead. This morning they have led me into a maze.' He observed her closely as he spoke. She was a young, heavy-fleshed woman and seemed to find the drawing-room uncomfortable. Her face was ruddy from exposure to the sun and her hands, too, indicated that she did not shirk physical work. She bore little resemblance to the women of her station, who normally fretted about trivial matters and petty gossip and this attracted him.

'I'm told that it is run on model lines. You have earned a name for yourself in the county. Tell me how a woman can have such an interest in farming.'

He listened patiently to her while she told him of her involvement with the land she had purchased and how she had reclaimed the water meadows by blasting a waterfall to release the water and change the level of the stream. He was totally attentive to all she said.

'Of course I should not forget that you came to see our stallions. I will have James bring them from the stables. We can stand on the balcony and you can have a clear view of their quality.'

He led her upstairs and into a huge room lined with books. In the centre of the room stood an oak table with several reference books opened on its surface. Before the chair lay a half-finished page in neat writing. They went forward to the windows which he drew open.

'My mother often stood here on summer days,' Robert said as they walked on to the balcony. 'She loved this view. I'm sure she longed for France. I doubt if she were ever happy here.'

Margaret Parr looked towards the lake with its many islands and the feathery hazel and silver birches. There was a bright, luminous quality on the waters and quiet parcels of cloud moved eastwards from the mountains. At that moment she was captivated by the lake. She had looked only on heavy farmland and a sullen river which curved sluggishly about her estate.

Then her attention was drawn towards the three stallions. They were black with shiny coats and their tendons and muscles were powerful as they moved about the great lawn. Their confirmation and breeding were perfect: the rich limestone land had given their legs great strength and she knew that their bones were dense and firm. The good structural formation gave them both confidence and strength.

As she observed the quality of the horses she realized that she had made a mistake. She could not purchase such fine animals.

'I'm afraid I could not buy one of these animals. I thought perhaps I could have started my own strain with a Dillon stallion but I never realized that they were of such an outstanding quality.'

'So they live up to their reputation?' he asked, sensing her keen pleasure in the animals.

'They have been well-bred. They know it themselves as they pass before us. They carry proud heads and they have long, sloping

38

shoulders and deep chests,' she remarked, never taking her eyes off the horses.

He looked at the rapt expression on her face. It had a heavy, earthy beauty. She was a remarkable woman, confident of the earth and animals. 'Have you a thoroughbred mare?' he asked.

'Not clearly thoroughbred, but I have a good mare. She has sturdy qualities and she comes from the same breed as Queen of Hearts. Sorrento was her dame.'

'Then bring her to the stables and have her covered by one of my stallions. They are perhaps too fine for rough racing in the west of Ireland. They need to blend with strong sinew and muscle. They have been brought to perfection. Their offspring needs a dash of common stock.'

'And what are your cover charges?' she asked in a forthright voice.

'Nothing. I would dearly wish to see a strong foal produced by the mating of two such horses. As I said, we breed thoroughbreds but they need to be mixed with other qualities.'

'Very well. I, too, would be interested. I think a mixture of the strains could produce an interesting animal and perhaps one with less pride. It could produce a horse with both speed and strength.'

They left the open balcony and returned to the main hall. Robert Dillon walked with her to her horse and held her arm as she mounted. It was an unnecessary gesture but the touch of his hand on her arm stirred pleasure within her. She smiled and thanked him. Then she turned her horse and rode away.

As she returned home across the hills she reflected on her encounter with Robert Dillon. She was attracted to him because they were opposite in many ways. She was drawn to him because there was fine breeding in his face and in the lines of his body, but like the lines on the thoroughbreds he perfected, he needed a strong woman to sustain his estates.

That was the first of many visits to Dillon Hall. On her return she brought two of her mares and watched with Robert from the balcony while they were covered.

Robert Dillon and Margaret Parr were drawn towards each other. For the first time in her life Margaret Parr was feeling the pleasure of love and Robert Dillon began to haunt her mind. Even when she was going about her day's work his image came before her and she would find many reasons to visit his estate. One day he invited her to ride with him across his lands and watched with amusement as she looked at the fields. They were clearly in need of attention and she could see where neglect had set in.

'There is so much that could be done with the scrubland,' she told him as they sat on their horses on Dromashionnaig and looked at the acres covered with unproductive rough bush. When she looked at him she was surprised by the expression on his face. There was a tenderness there which she had not witnessed before.

'Then why not supervise its clearing? Set it out in parkland. And if necessary drain the marshland,' he suggested teasingly.

'But I would have to come and live here!' she said, surprised.

'Marry me, then, and you can renew this land. I think you could improve the estate and that you truly belong here.'

'The thoroughbred mating with the strong mare,' she said with an earthy laugh. The image was firm and struck a deep chord in his mind. He looked at the strong body, the thick hips and breasts. The estate needed such a mistress.

He bent towards her and kissed her on the lips. She threw her arms about him and drew him down towards her. He felt the strong, firm flesh of the woman on his body.

'You will have to become a Catholic,' he told her as they rode home through the woods. 'It is very important to the family tradition. And you realize this will cut you off from your own? I hope you have considered all the consequences of this step.'

'Send me one of your priests,' she said humorously.

'It is a serious matter,' he told her.

'I know it is a serious matter, but marriage existed ever before there was Catholic and Protestant. I am not a religious person and my conscience is not troubled by such matters.'

It was obvious to Robert Dillon that she did not care about their religious differences or the finer points of theology: she would not tire her mind with such tiresome details. Her allegiance was now to Dillon Hall with its horses and cattle; its maturing woods and the acres which needed reclamation and her mind sang with ideas as she rode home to the Dower Estate.

*　　*　　*

40

'I've come to claim my dowry,' she announced to her brother when she walked into his drawing room unannounced, whip in hand. Her entry and her direct statement took him by surprise.

'Then I presume that you are getting married,' he said tightly. This was their first conversation in five years.

'That is obviously correct. I never intended to remain a virgin,' she said.

'And who is the unfortunate gentleman to whom you are going to get married?' he asked with sarcasm.

'Robert Dillon,' she said, looking him straight in the eye.

'He's a Catholic! No Parr ever married a Catholic! You are clearly mad. Have you lost whatever wit you ever possessed? Dillon is the spore of small squireens from Cong. You are marrying beneath you. You know if you walk through that door you will never return again,' he roared at her.

'I do not expect to. I came for my dowry and I presume that I can have it. It is part of the contract drawn up between us.'

'No dowry for a Parr who marries a Catholic!' he cried at her in anger and pounding his fist on the mantelpiece.

'Don't speak viciously about Catholics. What do you know of their doctrine?' she snapped at him.

'And, pray, what do you know about it? Have you been corresponding with the Pope?'

'I'm a Catholic,' she said, a certain vicious delight in her eyes.

'Explain yourself,' he cried in a shrill voice.

'I've been baptized by a priest. I have been accepted into the Church of Rome. I worship statues.'

'Get out! How dare you enter this house! You have disgraced the family and I will not have you here. You will have no Parr money – it is out of the questions, unthinkable!' He had lost control of himself and his voice and logic were garbled.

'I will and I shall have it now,' she said, stamping the ground with her foot, 'It is mine. It belongs to me.'

'There is no way you will extract a thousand pounds from me,' David shouted, sweeping a vase off the mantelpiece, and crashing it to the floor.

He looked at her. Silently she unloosed her dress and let it fall to the floor. Then she undid her bodice and exposed her breast.

41

'What are you doing?' he asked in a confused voice.

'I am going to strip naked. Then I am going to walk naked out of this house and ride into Williamstown crying out that my brother stripped me and deprived me of my dowry.'

He looked at her eyes. She was telling the truth. 'Stop, stop,' he told her wearily. 'I will not have my family disgraced. You have brought enough disgrace on us by turning to Rome. Wait and I will get the money. Get dressed while I am away.'

'No. I'll remain the way I am until I have my money,' she said firmly.

He returned with a bag of sovereigns and counted them out on the table. He was aware of the half-naked woman standing beside him and could smell the scent of her body. Her breasts almost touched the table as she bent forward to count the coins. Satisfied that she had the correct sum of money she poured it back into the purse, put the purse about her neck and dressed.

'We are now enemies,' he said as she opened the drawing-room door. 'I will not attend your wedding and I shall consider all your children bastards.'

'Consider what you will,' Margaret said carelessly. 'This is a joyless place. We shall meet at the race tracks and the hunting fields. The Catholic horse will beat the Protestant horse. I will breed them to be winners. Soon I will have an estate of my own. You would have immured me in the left wing like my other sisters, but I would have none of it. . .' She spat at his feet and walked out of the room.

David Parr did not move from his position by the mantelpiece as he watched her ride down across the parklands on her horse and take the stone wall with ease, disappearing at last into the avenue. He reflected on her final departure. She had brought infamy to the house; she had turned her back on her heritage; she had become a hated Catholic.

Robert Dillon and Margaret Parr were married in the small Catholic church in Cong with only two witnesses. That evening they set off for Dublin from where they made their way to London and then to Paris.

Robert Dillon never revealed to his wife that there was a doubtful strain in the Dillon family.

42

# Chapter 4

Robert Dillon sat in the library ashen-faced. He took a stud book and began to leaf through it. The names of the sires caught his eye and his interest: Abbot's Trade, Buckler, Minden, Pecker – they were like some long chant. But his mind returned to his wife who was now in labour.

They had been married for two years. During that time he had taken delight in her strong, sensual body. Soil, sinew and seed were in her blood. Her mind was uncluttered and her sexuality was direct and powerful. There was a total naturalness about the woman which both frightened and attracted him.

He had given the care of the estate over to her on their return from Paris, impressed by her singular determination and the way she had set out to restore order. She immediately began clearing the forty acres of scrubland edging the lake. She went to Galway and secured the services of the prisoners at the jail, bringing them in great carts to the stables where rough bedding had been set out on the floors. Each night soldiers stood in the great yard guarding the doors and each morning, after a breakfast of gruel and bread, the prisoners were marched to the scrub. They laboured all day for three months, tearing the stubborn roots from the soil until it was ready for seeding.

Robert Dillon had argued with his wife concerning the use of prison labour. It offended him that men should be used as slaves and he refused to visit the yards while they were imprisoned there and to examine the great clearance they made close to the lake.

'They must be returned to Galway. Or at least have the manacles removed,' he told his wife in a distressed voice when they argued about the matter.

When she spoke her voice was hard and her logic clear. 'You ask them if they wish to return to Galway. I have heard them talk. They prefer the open land to the enclosed walls of the prison. The stable bedding is comfortable and fresh, the food is wholesome. You talk of the evil of the prison sentence, of men receiving harsh sentences for small crimes, but I did not create the prison sentence or the penalties the judges hand down and this is the lesser of two evils.'

'It it dreadful to think that these men spend their lives like caged animals. There is an innate goodness in man; it is only circumstances which make him evil. Any system or civilization which endorses such harsh treatment and treats men as chattels is evil.' He would have quoted texts to her but she brushed his words aside.

'I know nothing of these matters. I know that these prisoners are well treated. And if the manacles are removed then they will escape. They were brought here on condition that they remained chained to each other. I am sorry if it offends you but it is my decision and I will abide by it.'

Each evening he listened to the jangle of chains as the prisoners plodded home from work. Once he had gone to the window and watched them, with bent backs and expressionless faces, make their way up in a sad line along the pathway. They were flanked by soldiers with whips and guns.

When the work was finally done, they were loaded on to four huge carts and drawn by heavy horses to Galway. They seemed to show no interest in the beauty of their surroundings as they were driven away and Robert felt that the reclaimed land would always be tainted. One prisoner had died as he drew a root from the ground, a quiet, silent death. He had a frail appearance and had been put in prison for larceny. The manacles were taken from his feet and he was brought to an outhouse. Later he was buried in the local cemetery in his prisoner's clothes. Nobody was certain of his name and with the passing of time the incident became part of folk memory.

Margaret Dillon worked tirelessly on the estate: she thinned the woods and sold the timber; the drains were cleared and the bog partially drained; new strains of cattle and sheep were introduced from England. Her mind eagerly absorbed all the new changes which were taking place in farming and she read periodicals and books avidly, rigorously planning the work of the farm. Fields that had lain fallow for years were drawn into production and clover was set in order to make them fertile again. The water mill crushed the corn not only for the Dillon estate but for other landowners as well and during the winter, cattle were taken from the fields into an enclosed paddock and fed with crushed oats and

44

turnips. Many of the tenants objected to the change in the old ways but Margaret Dillon was obstinate and pursued her own beliefs.

Robert Dillon no longer had to run the estate. The burden of making small decisions or dealing with the tenants was taken from his hands and gave him ample time to pursue his studies in the library. He had a small book published in London which met with only modest success. It was a study of the peasantry in England and in France on the eve of the Revolution, but the critical attention it received from a number of historians encouraged him to begin the biography of Marie Antoinette which would engage his mind for the rest of his life.

As he sat in the library, alert for sounds from the rooms above, he heard hurrying steps in the hallway. He rushed forward and opened the door.

'Has the child been delivered?' he asked Mrs Conway who was running down the great stairs.

'Not yet, sir. The final pains have started and I must fetch hot water and some towels. I will come to the room immediately and tell you when the child has arrived.'

He returned anxiously to his seat, but discovered that he could rest no longer. He began to pace the room. Then he opened the great windows and stood on the balcony. It was a warm night, no wind stirred the trees and the moon was soft on the lake.

Behind him the doors were pushed open. He turned to see Mrs Conway standing there.

'Congratulations, sir, on the birth of your child,' she said, smiling.

'Is it a boy or girl?' he asked impatiently.

'A boy, sir. A fine baby boy with plenty of air in his lungs. Listen!'

He could hear the voice of the male child crying. The tautness left his face and he began to smile. 'When all is in order I shall go and see the mother and child. But something for your service, Mrs Conway.' He drew five sovereigns from his pocket and passed them to her. She looked in amazement at the gold coins in the palm of her hand.

'God bless you, sir. And may the boy grow healthy and strong and may he have a long and happy life.'

She drew the doors closed and left him to his thoughts. He sat down and buried his hands in his face. His body trembled. Gradually he took control of himself and reflected on his good fortune. His boy would grow to be a healthy man. He would have a male heir to his estate and the flaw had been avoided.

Much later he entered his wife's room. Margaret was resting on deep, white pillows, with a smile of pleasure on her face and the baby in her arms. She decided to call him Matthew.

During the course of the next eight years three other children were to be born at Dillon House, two boys, John and Edward, and a girl, Maud. The girl showed no odd traits during her first years of life but by the age of ten a strange stare had developed in her eyes and by fourteen she had an uncontrollable temper. Her beauty was apparent very early in life. Her fine features she had inherited from her father and her red passionate hair from her Le Febre grandmother. Her body was agile and even as a child she could handle horses expertly.

Robert Dillon took a distant interest in the education of all his children. A room was set aside and he employed a French and a general teacher. Margaret realized that the French estates would fall to one of her children, most probably Edward, and she was insistent that the children learn to speak French colloquially, rather than by rote. Her husband questioned her decision. He could not understand why they should not have abundant grammar.

'One must understand the logic of language. It is a rational thing,' he complained when he observed what was happening.

'They will be fit to learn the grammar when they are older if they so wish. I have visited other houses where children have learned French grammar. They can neither speak nor pronounce the language. It is an absurd practice and I will not abide by it. Language like everything else must be practical and of some use. The children will learn to speak French with a proper accent and from a proper teacher.'

She recalled her own embarrassment in France during their honeymoon. She would not have her children laughed at by her brother-in-law.

Robert Dillon pursued his studies in the library and became

46

remote both from his wife and his children. Margaret had given him heirs to the estate and she was now active in its affairs. When she surveyed it from Drom a Shionnaigh she felt that it belonged more to her than to her husband. It yielded more now per acre than any other property in the vicinity, the financial accounts were accurate and detailed and she had fulfilled most of her ambitions. But there was one ambition that she had not fulfilled: she had once vowed that a Dillon horse would beat a Parr horse on every racecourse in Connaught, but her brother possessed two horses which, he boasted, could not be beaten. Margaret Dillon now set out to breed a winner. She attended the birth of each foal in the stables, hoping that some day the perfect colt would be born out of one of her stallions. She had had several victories over him, but she had yet to win the coveted Galway Plate. She knew she would not be satisfied until the strain at the stables was so perfect that she would beat her brother into second place so she studied the dames and sires of each foal watching their traits with a keen eye as they developed. She stood at the centre of the paddock and watched them pass before her, but always there seemed to be something missing: the strains were not mingling as she wished.

Since her departure her brother had married. She was surprised at his choice of wife. She came from a neighbouring estate and was neither beautiful nor intelligent. As their children grew up, the two families saw each other at a distance at the race meetings and an instinctive rivalry developed between them.

'They regard us as Catholic upstarts, but remember that when the Parrs were yeomen our ancestors were riding to Paris in carriages and we still possess estates in France. So take pride in your lineage,' Margaret Dillon told her children.

When Matthew and John Dillon raced across the country on their horses they remembered that they must outwit and outride the Parrs on every occasion. Every victory meant honour to their family. Their father stood hopelessly by while this rivalry was nurtured within them.

'You are sowing the seeds of division,' he told his wife. 'This rivalry can be turned to hate. Catholics and Protestants live tolerantly together on the continent, even in England,' he argued with his quiet logic.

47

'This is not England or the continent. My brother despises Catholics and I will not be despised. He gave me a thousand pounds for my dowry, but should have given me ten thousand for the improvements I made to his estate during my time there. I will never forgive him.'

The three Dillon boys had a high degree of intelligence. The mornings spent in the study gave them a knowledge of general affairs, a grounding in Latin and a ready knowledge of French. Early in their lives they became aware of the world of politics and read the Hansard reports from the House of Commons so that they became familiar with the great political dramas which took place there. At breakfast time they argued with each other over political events in England and France. Robert hoped that one day one of them might take his place as a Liberal Member for the Constituency of County Galway.

'As a leading Catholic family we must have a representative in the House of Commons,' he insisted. 'It will confer dignity on us and on our family. Remember that you come from a long line of men who have been in the service of the French state and they are the consummate politicians.'

Matthew and John Dillon joined in the political heave in 1830, the year after Catholic Emancipation. John Fahey the first Catholic candidate was to challenge the Right Honourable Denis Blake. They spent eight days campaigning in the towns of Galway, standing beside the candidate on his carriage and felt the pulse of power about them. They noted the eager faces of men caught in the excitement of the time and canvassed the names of the freeholders who would vote in favour of their candidate. Everywhere they went they were followed by their tenants brought together by the enthusiasm.

On the day of the polling the Protestant landlords mustered their voters and, accompanied by dragoons, marched them to Galway. It took three days to cast the votes, each voter coming forward to declare his candidate and it became obvious that the Parr candidate would win. When his victory was declared a faction fight broke out in the town. Matthew and John Dillon led their tenants forward calling out, 'Death to the Cromwellian Bastards! To hell with the Parrs!' For two hours the faction fight

48

continued. Time and again both factions assembled and charged at each other down the main street, calling out abuse and brandishing cudgels. As men fell bleeding on the street they were trampled on or dragged away to some tavern by their friends. Only once did the fighting cease and that was when John Dillon and his first cousin Daniel Parr faced each other with bare fists. They fought viciously for a quarter of an hour until Daniel Parr was knocked out by an upper cut to his chin and was carried away to an hotel.

Two hours later when the fury of the crowds had been wasted and the dusty street was wet with blood, the dragoons arrived from the barracks. They drew up a line at the end of the town, discharged a volley of fire over the combatants heads and charged with drawn swords. John Dillon grasped one of the dragoons as he bore down upon him and dragged him from his horse. He wrenched the sword from his hand and carried it away as a prize.

Robert, standing at the window of an hotel, looked down at the fury which burned in his sons. The rivalry with the Parrs had now turned to a hatred which would never be quenched and he felt ashamed and humiliated at their behaviour. He left the window and sat before the fire regretting his own remoteness. His wife had too strong an influence upon them; he feared for the consequence of their hate.


That night Matthew and John did not return home. They spent the night drinking in the taverns with their tenants and friends, discussing the day's events and their chances in the Galway Plate.

'And there we'll have another chance to show the Parrs from what metal we are made. Whitelock will thunder home to victory. Place your money on Whitelock for since the day he was foaled he was agile and well-formed,' John Dillon shouted, waving his tankard in the air.

The election changed the two young men and they became aggressive and wild, abandoning interest in the estates so that even their mother could not control them. They became strong-willed and hot-headed and their reckless riding was talked about in Galway and Ballinrobe.

During this time their brother Edward, who had a less excitable temperament, went to a boarding school in England. He was studious and determined and each summer he made his way to Paris where he stayed with his Uncle George. He fitted easily into the fashionable society of the period and spoke fluent French. After reading law at Cambridge, he spent a long summer at Dillon House, but seemed ill at ease and had frequent arguments with both his brothers on political questions. He was an abstemious drinker, exact in his habits and did not associate with the rough company his brothers kept. Finally, in the summer of 1834, at the invitation of his uncle he set off for France; he was to return to Ireland only on three further occasions. Meanwhile Matthew and John Dillon followed the wild course of their lives. Matthew had a more stable temperament and even in drink never fell into excess, but John, on the other hand, was extremely volatile. On some occasions after a week's hunting and drinking he would return to the house unshaven, lock himself into a room and brood. Then after two days of solitude he would shave himself, put on clean clothes and set out again on his horse for some race meeting or other.

During these years Maud Dillon too was a cause of concern to her father. She would fall into deep depression and wander through the woods, forgetful of time and place and some nights she would not return at all. Invariably she was discovered on Monk's Island which was only a short distance by boat from the house. She told her parents that she heard strange voices speaking to her and that she had seen a monk passing across the water and entering the woods and she would enter a deep depression that might last for a week. It would be followed by a strange energy and she would take her horse and gallop furiously across the countryside, taking high ditches and wide streams.

When Robert Dillon sat by his great fire and considered his life on New Year's night, 1837, he recognized that it was flawed. His great task remained half-finished. Already he had assembled three thousand handwritten sheets of manuscript but the work was untidy and several issues remained unclear and there were large gaps in his research.

He was satisfied with his eldest son Matthew. At twenty-six he was finally taking an interest in the estates. He had borrowed books from his father's library and he would come to discuss politics with him. They had spent pleasant evenings by the great fire in serious talk. His son Edward wrote at regular intervals from Paris where he obviously found French society suitable to his temperament and had invited several acquaintances from his Cambridge days to visit him at his uncle's château. He had a wide interest in European politics and his English friends had invited him to visit their homes in England. He believed that through their influence he could extend the family interests in England.

His son John was his main disappointment. Handsome and well-formed, he lived a loose life, frequenting the whorehouses of Galway, and challenging men to drinking bouts which lasted all day. There were rumours that he had wounded a man in a duel in the woods of Lough Corrib. He returned to Dillon Hall infrequently, choosing to live in a cottage on a small estate with his dogs and his horses.

Robert left his armchair by the fire and, opening the windows, went on to the balcony. It was a frosty night and the huge expanse of park below shimmered with frost. The moon hung low to the east and formed a cold path on the water. Man under the constellations was an insignificant and troubled thing.

# Chapter 5

The limestone island, standing like a great black mass on the sea, had dominated their lives. They had never been away from its presence; they were born on its high surface and they fished at its base. They had never heard the soft song of an inland bird; the raucous cry of the gulls hungry for fish gut was in their ears from birth. The sound of the sea beating in anger against the cliffs set them to sleep and in winter, secure in their low stone cabins, they watched the spume rise into spray and carry across the fields. They led a hard, primitive life, the sad advent and withdrawal of waves marked the coming and going of time, of men and the wearing down of the island.

'Take warning from the Wind, Tadhg, and for God's sake don't move the curragh from the slipway today,' the old man told Tadhg Mor as he watched him loosen the rope about the granite bollard. 'I've seen the sea in all its moods over seventy years and today of all days it's in an awkward mood. No sign is right – even the cry of the birds is strange as if they expected a storm.'

Tadhg Mor was a young man of enormous strength. His massive figure, with its wide shoulders, dominated all the other islanders. His head was solid, his face roughened by salt spray.

'The mackerel are running to the east of the island. I saw the waves flecked with their bodies from the cliff. I'll take my chances with my brothers. The silver and gold is out on the sea and not in the scrapings of the field,' he said, taking the boat and lifting it down the slipway to the sea. No other man could lift a boat single-handed. The old man, smoking his pipe, looked in wonder at his great strength, thinking to himself that Tadhg Mor was a hot-headed young man with no care for his safety or that of his brothers.

Later, he watched their easy rhythm and light stroke take the black canvas boat out of the narrow harbour and to the sea, heavy grey waves unsettled and awkward. The old man watched them until they wrung round the cliff. It was the last time he was to see them.

They moved far to the west, riding across the crests of the waves. Their skin boat was as light as a feather and answered easily to the pull of the oars as the wind freshened and a low mist moved in from the south, coming between them and the island. They suddenly felt scared: with the island no longer visible, they were alone and unprotected.

'Let us return, Tadhg,' the brothers pleaded. 'There is a strange humming in the wind and it freshens steadily.'

'I'll not let the mackerel pass the island. It's our last week on the sea. Soon the storms will be about us and there is naught we can do but watch from the cliffs.'

His body moved in rhythm to the oars. The sea began to mount

52

into ever-larger waves, sweeping the foam across the ridges.

'Turn back, Tadhg! Turn back. There is black evil in the heart of the sea. It is angry and we should respect it. In the name of God and Mary turn back!' one of his brothers called as Tadhg heaved the frail boat across the mountainous waves. His voice was thinned by the sea noise.

'Turn back! Turn back!' they both shouted.

By now the wind was hard and steady. It whipped up the waves and threw them out of sequence. Looking into the vague distance they saw the huge wall of water rise in front of them before it caught the boat sideways and turned it over, casting all three men into the sea.

Tadhg Mor grabbed at one of his brother's bainin coat and with all his strength drew him towards the curragh, clawing into the tar surface to grasp the frail ribs beneath. He pushed the terrified man on to the boat's black back.

His youngest brother was lost; there was no sign of him in the boiling waters. *I'll have this death on my soul*, he thought. *Oh, God save us. Bring us to a safe harbour.*

He looked at his brother whose face was grey with fear. His eyes bulged and Tadhg Mor thought they might burst. 'Hold on, hold on,' he cried. 'Don't leave the boat. It will carry us to safety.'

Time and again the seas pounded down upon them but they held on grimly to the ribbing of the boat. Then it happened. The boat was heeled over and by the time Tadhg Mor had struggled to the surface, his brother had disappeared. Looking about swiftly, he thought he caught sight of him on the crest of the wave, his mouth drawn open with fear. Then he himself was carried down into the confusion of water.

All day the storm raged, but Tadhg Mor held on to the boat, his body growing colder. While he was still able to move his fingers, he took off his leather belt and, forcing a hole in the canvas, pushed it round the main rib of the boat and buckled his hand to the rib.

Night came. The sullen mist darkened. The storm continued. All night Tadhg Mor was tossed on the water, secured to the frail craft buffeted by the tides and currents. He had begun to lose all hope, but fought with his fears. He would not give himself easily to the sea; it was a hostile and cruel element but all his life he had lived in its presence. To keep awake he began to recite Irish poetry in his mind, reciting the same poems again and again, concentrating on each line, each syllable.

Day came slowly on to the sea and with it the wind eased and the mist cleared. As the sun began to shine over even water Tadhg Mor drew his head up wearily and looked to the west. He could see islands and hills but the cold was in his body now, his limbs were numb, his fingers purple and he knew he was slipping away. He had survived a night but now he was going to die. Before he lost control of his mind he tried to recall the words of the old songs but found he could not. Hope was failing within him. The sea had beaten him; it wished to take him into its dark waters, down to the long, tawny seaweed, down to the craws of marauding sharks. He fell into a coma, knowing that the sea would quietly draw away the final life heat.

Elinor O'Donnell had listened to the storm in her attic room. The noise of the wind tearing itself on the trees and the sound of branches brushing dryly against each other satisfied her. She had tried to remain awake, but the thunder of the storm and the pounding of the waves on the beach close to the house set her into a deep sleep.

When she awoke in the morning, the storm had passed over and the sea was calm again. Putting on her rough clothes, she rushed down the rickety stairs, through the kitchen and out into the yard, where she mounted her horse and set off towards the sea. Galloping barebacked along the long white strand, her black hair caught by the morning breeze, she felt a rich sense of excitement.

Her father, an adventurous man, had smuggled contraband from the continent into the small ports of Galway. Those who remembered him as a young man said that he had been handsome once when he had brought home his French wife from Saint Malo and settled her in a large, rambling house close to the sea. He had known the coast so well they said that he could bring his small brig blindfold through gaps in rock shoals, but one night he had missed his bearings and the keel of the brig was torn on a reef. With his

54

two companions he made the shore on a small boat, but as he watched his ship pounded apart next day by the waves, his interest in the sea snapped and he became a heavy drinker and began to gamble the small fortune he had acquired. Elinor could not remember him as a sea captain; she remembered him only as a heavy, sullen man, rough in drink and quick in anger. As a young girl she had come between him and her mother when he tried to hit her.

'Forgive him for his angers,' her mother had said in her strange voice. 'You do not know the torment in his mind. He is a sailor and the better part of him died with his ship.'

As Elinor O'Donnell rode across the strand these memories were banished from her mind. At twelve she was almost a fully mature woman and her beauty was apparent even to the dull eye. She would be tall and dark-haired and her shoulders would be wide. From an early age she had taken care of the stables and the cattle, clearing out the dung when John Kelleher was drinking with her father. Her mother had taught her to read and write and chattered with her in French. She acquired the language without difficulty and she sang French songs of her mother's home village with simple charm.

Drawing her horse to a halt, Elinor's eye was arrested by a black object floating on the sea. For a moment she thought it might be a dolphin or a dead shark, but when she looked more closely she could see that it was the back of an upturned curragh with a human hand strapped to it. She urged her horse into the water and forced him to swim towards the boat. As she approached she saw the body of a man, his mouth half-open, apparently dead. She bent down and tied the reins to the leather strap and with her foot urged the horse to swim towards the shore. As soon as they reached the shallow water, she dismounted, reached forward and unbuckled the hand from the boat rib. She looked at the grey face and the dull patches of sunburn. She had been to the wake houses and this man had all the appearance of death upon his face.

Drawing him up the beach to the sand dunes, she laid him flat on his back and looked again at the face. She was certain that he was dead. She opened his rough shirt and felt for a heart pulse with her thumb, but there was no suggestion of life in the body.

Turning to look at the staring face again, she was astonished to see the right eye flicker and close.

'He is alive! He is alive,' she cried and, jumping on to the horse, she rode to the house to tell her father and John Kelleher what she had discovered floating on the sea. Reluctantly they came with her to the beach.

'You must be mistaken,' said John Kelleher when they stood looking down at the motionless body. 'No one could survive the cold sea. He is dead. You imagined you saw a flicker in the eye.'

'No, I am certain,' she cried.

The two men placed the heavy body on the back of the horse and brought it up to the house where they stretched him out on the floor beside the fire and removed his clothes. Elinor had never seen a naked man before. His huge body was muscular and hard. There was rough hair on his chest and crotch. John and her father wrapped a blanket about him and set logs on the fire, then they returned to their game of cards on the deal table. Periodically they came and looked at the figure.

'I tell you he is dead. I've seen shipwrecked corpses before. He has the colour of death on his face,' her father told her.

'But I saw a flicker of life in his eye,' Elinor insisted. 'I'm certain he's alive.'

All day she sat by the inert figure lying in the grey blanket. It was not until evening came that the eyes opened and blinked.

'He's alive! He's alive! Look!' cried Elinor dancing with excitement.

The men rose from the table and came to stand over the man. They looked at the open eyes.

'He has returned from the half dead,' her father said. 'He has been given the second gift of life. He owes his life to you.'

After a long vigil through the night, the man's limbs began to move and the head stir. Elinor bent down, lifted the head and induced some warm soup into his mouth. He drank it slowly, never taking his gaze from the young woman. After he had eaten, she rested his head on a pillow and he fell into a deep sleep. All the next day he slept before the fire, his breathing regular and deep and on the second night she left him alone in the kitchen and went to bed. When the family woke in the morning he was sitting

56

in the great armchair by the fire.

He never spoke. The men tried to talk to him both in English and Irish but he remained mute and distant. He stared fixedly ahead of him. His mind seemed unhinged.

'I hope we haven't a mad man on our hands,' John Kelleher said nervously.

'Leave him by the fire. Perhaps he will talk in a day or two,' her father suggested. 'Remember he has suffered greatly. Only his strength has carried him through.'

They left the kitchen and went in the direction of the sea-shore. Elinor was left alone with the immense man she had rescued from death. He turned towards her and began to talk.

'You have saved my life. Even on the sea-shore I could hear your voice. It was like a bell.'

'How long were you at sea?' she asked.

'I do not know. I do not care to talk about it. It was black and it was terrible. I will speak only with you. I have no wish to speak with others any more.'

'Very well,' she said. 'Speak with me if you wish.'

From that day he would speak only to Elinor and then when they were alone. From the beginning he followed her everywhere and when she rode along the strand he sat on a small hillock and watched. When she returned to the stables he brushed down her horse with care and affection.

Elinor discovered that his name was Tadhg Mor, that he had been the cause of his brothers' deaths and that he had no wish to return to his island. He told her also of the hours he had spent in a deep coma and of the strange and fragmented images which had poured into his mind.

The bond of affection which grew up during the following three years was intense. Tadhg Mor went with Elinor to the fairs and stood close by, observing her, watching her grow in beauty. At fourteen men turned their heads when she rode by on her white horse. At an early age she had a presence which commanded respect; a maturity of mind suited to a grown woman.

Tadhg Mor slept in a small room in the attic with a window towards the sea. He slept in a huge bed which he had made for himself. On the bed lay a large loose bag of feathers upon which he lay in great comfort. He kept the window open so that the sound of the sea was always in his ears. Elinor taught him to read in English and to write simple messages on paper. It was a slow and arduous task. He began to till the fields close to the house so that the family never lacked for vegetables. He did not approve of the drinking and the gambling which went on in the kitchen. Some days Valentine Parr and his men rode into the yard with bottles of whisky and a sheep carcass which was set to roast on the great spit. They drank and gambled in the kitchen for days, sleeping on rushes which Tadhg Mor cut on the hillside. They gambled fiercely on the toss of a dice or face on a card. Gambling was a passion with Valentine Parr. One evening Tadhg Mor was working in the loft above the stables. Two men entered. He recognized Parr's voice.

'I've set my eye on the young woman and I declare I'll have her when she's ready for plucking. We'll let her ripen in the breasts and haunches for a little longer.'

Tadhg Mor remained rigid until they left, when he descended and entered the house. He remained mute by the fire, taking orders from the men. He fetched them meat and poured them whisky. His mind boiled with instinctive anger.

*The drunken Protestant cur*, he thought to himself. *But he'll not touch the girl. There is no way he will defile her while I stand close by her and watch her every day of my life.* He carried logs in for the fire where the sheep carcass was roasting slowly. The kitchen was filled with pipe smoke, the floor slimy with spit. He watched the heavy, sowlike face of Parr as he looked at his cards. With greasy fingers he moved them about into a strategic position. There were ten sovereigns on the table. Men watched carefully for the final cards as Henry O'Donnell lost his wager to Valentine Parr.

'There is no beating Parr with the cards or the dice,' his men called out. 'He was born lucky.'

'Deal again,' Valentine told them, 'and I'll give you a chance to win back your losses. We'll double the bets.'

Henry O'Donnell was frightened and said cautiously, 'No, we'll keep the bets to five sovereigns a hand.'

'He's no man, lads,' Valentine laughed. 'He's no man at all. Afraid of losing a few sovereigns. A mean man.'

Henry O'Donnell saw Parr's henchmen grinning at him. 'Deal the cards and I'll go and fetch more sovereigns,' he told them drunkenly. 'The devil deals you cards, Parr.'

'It's no devil. It's lady luck,' he called after him, then leered at his men and whispered. 'Some day I'll force him to lay his daughter's maidenhead on the table. That will be the game that will be talked about until time runs.' Tadhg Mor looked on with a blank face.

'Did the fool hear me?' he asked, worried that his intentions might be made known.

'It doesn't matter,' one of his men told him. 'He can't talk and he is soft in the head. He doesn't even know his own name.'

'Well, have him cut me meat – I'm hungry,' he directed. Tadhg Mor cut a braised strip from the back of the carcass and brought it to him on a fork.

'Put it on a plate, you fool. Parrs were reared with silver.' He snapped back with his hand and hit him on the mouth. Tadhg Mor felt a shock of pain as his cheek was torn by a ring. The meat fell on the floor and the dogs tore at it, snapping and snarling. The other men laughed at Tadhg Mor's bovine eyes as he took a plate from the sideboard, cut more meat on to it and placed it before Parr.

That night Tadhg Mor had a nightmare. He was chained to a wall in a cellar. On a bed in the room Valentine Parr took his pleasure of Elinor O'Donnell. He roared out and woke, covered in sweat.

'What disturbs you, Tadhg? Was it the sea? Were you in the storm again?' Elinor asked, kneeling beside him in her rough nightdress.

'You are safe,' he breathed, touching her dark hair.

'Of course I'm safe. I'm always safe with you beside me.'

'Yes. I will let no harm come to you, ever.'

'What harm could come to me,' she asked laughing. 'Go back to sleep. You are safe in this house from the storms and the sea.' She left the room and he fell into a deep sleep. Frequently the nightmares returned. During the day as he tilled the fields he often recalled the drunken leer on Valentine Parr's face. He was a dangerous man. He must be vigilant.

Tadhg Mor watched as the estate by the sea was gambled away. Each year some field or wood was lost, or the cattle which grazed on the sea pastures. One day some of Parr's men came to take Elinor's white horse. One of them mounted it while Elinor wept at the stable door but just as he was about to leave the yard Tadhg Mor moved forward, caught him by the waist and wrenched him from the saddle. Holding him above his head he threw him on to a heap of dung. When the second man protested Tadhg Mor hit him on the jaw, the loud crack indicating that it was broken. As the men staggered to their feet and rushed from the yard, Tadhg took the reins of the horse and led it back to Elinor. Then he walked quietly back to the field and began to mould the potato ridges.

Elinor's mother died quietly in her bed. Elinor, her brother Kevin and Tadhg Mor were beside her during the final hours. Her father had gone to a race meeting in Galway and they had no idea when he would return.

'Take care of my daughter and son, Tadhg Mor. I place them in your care. I know you understand what I say and I trust you to be a wall about them.' He pressed her hand in understanding. She turned to her daughter, talking in French for half an hour. When they were finished she lapsed into unconsciousness, and died. They wept together beside the bed. Tadhg Mor placed his great arms about them and gathered them close to him. Kevin only eight years of age, called for his mother. These children's lives had been placed in the great giant's care.

# Chapter 6

Robert Dillon watched the madness grow in his daughter. She was subject to wild fits of rage which blew up in her mind like a tempest. Her obsession with horses was extreme. She had studied veterinary books and more than once she had dissected a horse to study its organs and discover what caused its death. There was something frightening in such behaviour. She often left the house to return a month later, when she kept to her room, having food brought there. The predictions made by his brother George had come true. Robert Dillon kept the secret in his mind but as he grew old it troubled him. Should he have remained single like his brother in France? Through his marriage the family estates had been maintained . . . the name had survived. He worked slowly and pleasantly in his library. There remained such an immense amount of research to be done on his work that he lost interest in the estate. He did take an interest in the political changes in Ireland and in Europe and it was obvious to him that the effects of the French Revolution were spreading beyond the borders of France.

Maud Dillon first saw Captain Bagnall steeplechasing at Tuam. He was a quarter-master who bought horses for the regiments, his keen eye discerning defects at a distance of ten yards.

He had an arrogant bearing as he entered the field, his blue uniform tightly fitting his lithe figure. His black beard was cut close to his skin which gave him a hard ascetic appearance. He rode a mare called Hildegarde.

Her eyes were clear and she had a confident gait as he took her through her paces close to the crowd who had gathered at the starting line. Maud saw that he was a vain man, certain of his skill. He was running against Sir Harry Christian's horse and his peas-antry were at hand to encourage him. They threw their caps in the air when he appeared in his top hat, black tails and riding breeches. Captain Bagnall continued to exercise his horse, bringing her from a walk to a canter, then taking her easily over a practice jump.

The five-mile course was over rough terrain, hard soil, a river and a final hedge. Dressed in crimson riding clothes she followed the movements of the captain. He suddenly turned towards her, a cold glint in his eye as he appraised her body. He studied women as he did horses, looking for fire and breeding. Having stared for some seconds, his interest returned to the field of horses.

The starter called the riders to order. She watched every move-ment of the horses carefully. Captain Bagnall had positioned himself to the left of the line. The starter read out the wagers and conditions of the race before bringing his whip down on his saddle.

Captain Bagnall moved quickly into the lead, holding himself firmly on the horse. He took the first wall with elegance. She watched a rider thrown over the fence on to the hard ground, the horses behind jumping over him. Later it was discovered that he had broken his leg. Sir Harry Christian urged his horse forward, lashing at its thigh with his whip. He moved with great speed on the flat, leaving Captain Bagnall five lengths behind. At the stream, Sir Harry Christian made the fatal mistake of jumping too early. His horse failed to land securely on the bank, its back legs slithering into the water. He beat it furiously as it struggled awkwardly from the river. Captain Bagnall landed close to him, his horse moving in perfect rhythm across the spongy ground. He rose easily to the fence and romped home twelve lengths clear of Sir Harry. The crowd cheered Captain Bagnall as he moved through them, patting the horse on the rump for her performance. He seemed unmoved by his victory but gazed at the lady in crimson riding the thoroughbred horse.

The riders retired to Uptons Hotel in the Square, followed by a milling crowd who discussed the great race. They admired good horsemanship and Captain Bagnall had proved that he could handle a horse on a difficult course.

She followed at a distance, her eyes never leaving Captain Bagnall. She signalled the groom to stable her horse and went inside the familiar hotel. The squires of Galway and Mayo held their wild parties in the great panelled hall at the back. She had played cards here during long nights and she knew most of the people present. She was the only woman who joined the company of the men in the large hall. The table bore decanters and a candelabra with three tiers of candles which brightened the room. The walls were hung with the four prints of *The Phantom Riders of Nacton*. It celebrated a steeplechase by midnight and suited the wild mentality of the squires and military officers. Sir Harry Christian had once led a group of riders across country on a moonlit night and had returned to the hotel with a broken arm for his efforts.

They sat about the table and the servant carried the dinner on silver plates to the great table. Sir Harry Christian looked with contentment at braised backs of fowl and well-cooked meat presented to the guests. He was pleasurable man who loved horses, wine, food and women. No great thought had ever disturbed his mind. He signalled to his guests to take their chairs about the table. Without turning to left or right, Sir Harry Christian plumped a partridge on to his plate, tore off a leg and sank his teeth into its substance. While he ate he dashed out some wine into a large glass and drank it quickly. He felt enormously happy, surrounded by friends and well regarded. He had challenged the best horseman in the British army and had acquitted himself well.

'Had I been ten years younger and not carrying weight and Raby Hunt beneath me then by God it would have been a different story. It was the soft ground that got me. Curse the soggy ground. Damn hard for a light horse to carry a heavy man over that. And then the fence was badly placed for me.'

'It could have gone either way, Sir Harry,' a companion remarked.

'Damn it man, I know. Been thinking that all the time riding through the town. Went at the fences too hard.' He belched with satisfaction and looked at the table. He pushed his plate aside and called for another. A clean plate always suggested to him that he had eaten nothing and was still hungry. He carved some beef and heaped the strips on to his plate. Now he could eat in comfort, lean back in his armchair and enjoy the good company.

'How is Squire Quiller's lad?' he asked.

'Broke a leg at the first jump, sir.'

'And the horse?'

'Had to be put down, I'm afraid.'

'Young fool. Didn't go with the mouth of the horse as it descended. Destroyed a fine horse; should be whipped. Don't see why his father lets him ride at all.'

Gradually he got pleasantly drunk, his face glowing with importance. He proposed a toast to the King which was brief and one to the Tuam Blazers which was much longer. Catching sight of Maud Dillon he proposed a toast to her great beauty and horsemanship. She had slipped in when the guests had taken their seats and sat at the end of the table.

63

'To the gallant company, and gallant it is, and no finer found in these realms or any other realm, a toast.'

'To the gallant company,' they all toasted, including Captain Bagnall who had relaxed into an easy mood. He had unbuttoned the neck of his uniform and, like the others, talked only of horses. She listened intently to his conversation which dwelt on all the defects he had encountered in horses.

'Never knew you could tell so much from the pulse of a horse. Why I listen to them break wind and can tell if a horse has a bad appetite. And if they quid, well, damn it, I know that it's plain disordered. I pride myself on having good horse sense. But I never gave much care to pulse. You tell me now that you can tell what is wrong with a horse by feeling its pulse.'

'Not always, but I can be accurate. Did you know that the heart rate is faster in a young horse than an older one? Tell me the normal pulse of a horse.'

'I'm damned if I know, sir,' the squire answered, leaning across the table in interest.

'A guinea if you guess correctly.'

'Seventy beats to the minute,' he hazarded.

Before Captain Bagnall could reply Maud Dillon answered, 'Thirty-eight beats in a normal animal.'

'Very good. The lady has earned a guinea,' he said, a cynical expression on his face. 'And for five guineas, can the lady tell me what age were Eclipse and Pocahontas when they died?'

The table fell silent for a moment, all looking at Maud Dillon. She thought for a moment, before replying firmly, 'Eclipse was twenty-six years of age and Pocahontas thirty-two.'

'Well, captain? Is she correct?'

'No. Pocahontas was thirty-three years of age,' he answered never taking his eyes from her.

'A year don't make no difference. The lady has won the wager.' Most of the company agreed, but Sir Harry Christian could see the anger growing in Captain Bagnall's eyes and quickly intervened.

'Could the learned gentlemen tell me what a hickey is?' he asked, getting their attention immediately and smiling pleasantly at their confusion.

'I'll wager a hundred guineas that none present can tell me. In fact I will raise the wager to three hundred guineas.'

He let them guess for five minutes, by which time the unpleasantness which had threatened his meal has been averted.

'We give up, Sir Harry,' they finally told him.

'It is quite obvious that I am dealing with uninformed horse traders. The best veterinary books will tell you that a hickey is a white spot on a black mare's backside.'

They looked at him for a moment then exploded laughing. Captain Bagnall returned to his conversation, seeming to have lost interest in Maud Dillon.

She took only a desultory interest in the people about her and continued to stare at the fine arrogant face. Men had always wanted her company at racecourses and balls and she had dismissed their attentions irritably, but this man behaved as if she were a kitchen maid. Waves of violent hatred and violent love passed through her mind.

Gradually conversation became impossible. Bottles of drink were carried into the room and set on the table. One squire fell off his chair and then crawled under the table to sleep. A group began to sing a hunting song about Sir Harry Christian. By early morning most of the squires and military men were snoring by the fire or across the table.

Captain Bagnall never lost his composure, drinking until the morning. He buttoned his uniform, looked at the prone figures with disdain and made his way up the stairs to bed.

Maud Dillon followed him without invitation as he had expected. He made love many times with precision but did not utter her name once. She cried out with pleasure as his massive strength broke in her.

Next morning he dressed, ate a huge breakfast and left the hotel. The stable boy had his horse saddled and he rode out of Tuam towards Galway.

She watched him depart from the window which overlooked the stable yard, following his movements across the yard and through the gate. She hated his detachment and beat on the window in anger. No man had ever treated her like Captain Bagnall. She wished to be humiliated by him. Reflecting for a

65

moment, she rushed down the stairs and out into the yard. When her horse was ready she rode furiously out of the yard. She caught up with him five miles outside the town and rode beside him for some time but he took no notice of her. When they reached Galway she followed him into the barracks' stables where he dismounted and indicated the she should take his horse. She lived with him until he was recalled to London, becoming known in the county as the captain's whore.

# Chapter 7

Tadhg Mor was fearful that the threat made by Valentine Parr would be realized. He watched Elinor's father lose all interest in life. The land became fallow, the fences overgrown and the walls broken. The cattle were never sold as they served to pay gambling debts. The outer fields were lost at cards and the house had fallen into decay. Weeds grew on the gravelled square before the house and the shrubs which her mother had brought from Galway and planted along the avenue were left unattended. On wet nights the rain poured through the gaps in the roof left by fallen slates. Elinor had once loved the storms, but now she feared that it might carry off the roof.

Elinor O'Donnell had matured into a woman of sixteen, her breasts firm, her carriage certain, and she had an air of authority about her.

Her twelve-year-old brother Kevin depended on Tadhg Mor to protect him. His father neglected him and in aimless anger had beaten him savagely, later asking his forgiveness. Tadhg Mor tucked him in at night and he knew that he was close by if anything happened, but never spoke to him as he did to his sister. He had wide, firm shoulders and his strength was growing. There was a lonely quality in his mind, his blue eyes intense with dreams.

Their father rarely shaved and his clothes smelt of sweat and urine. He slept when he was stupid with drink, sometimes for twenty-four hours.

Always he asked about Valentine Parr, the ugly leer on his face often in his mind. Valentine Parr was plotting against him. He had already won his fields and his cattle. Henry O'Donnell did not possess the courage to drive him from his house. Some day he would win back all he had lost to Valentine Parr. He would mend the broken fences, perhaps buy a ship and sail for France. Parr could not always be lucky.

All night Elinor and her brother were excited, barely able to sleep. They had polished their saddles, set out their best clothes and Tadhg Mor had given them each a sovereign which he had saved for them during the year. They would be away from the house and their father for some days, seeing all the wonders of the world at the Ballinrobe Fair. Elinor looked forward to meeting her aunt, who owned Upton's hotel. She had beds prepared for them there. She had worked in a hotel in Galway and later, with money inherited from her father, she had purchased Upton's. She had built up a prosperous business and had little sympathy with her brother-in-law's drinking and gambling. The Piper would be coming with them. He always came to the house in spring, when the daffodils were in full show on the high field. They kept watch for the Piper on the mountain road. He would sit under the bent hawthorn bush and play 'Piping Tim of Galway'.

'The Piper has come, the Piper has come,' they called to each other. He brought sweets for Kevin and a ribbon for Elinor.

A tall man with blond hair, his skin was as white as milk, his fingers long and nimble. He had once been a landowner in Clare but for some reason he decided to hand over his property to a cousin and take up the life of itinerant Piper, visiting the great houses, playing his pipes and telling stories.

His eyes were covered with a grey mist which blurred objects and Tadhg Mor told Elinor that some day the Piper would be completely blind.

When the household had gone to bed Kevin crept down to the Piper and asked him to tell him the history of Ireland. He recited the great legends which fired his young imagination, sad tragic tales of the Celtic past. When he pressed the Piper further he told him of the more recent history and Kevin O'Donnell began to

67

understand how the old Gaelic order was destroyed and a new English order came into being.

It was a golden morning when they set out for Ballinrobe, the sea behind them even and without tension.

They passed into a gloomy valley, the stone of the steep hills breaking through the gorse and moss like mange on the back of an old animal. A river, fed by wild thin streams, rushed down across the bare expanses of granite.

High in the mountains on a flat ledge of earth and surrounded by stunted trees lay an eighteenth-century hunting lodge belonging to the Parrs approached by a winding walled road, partially concealed by trees. It caught their interest as they moved up through the valley.

By midday the two horses were tired. The Piper had walked beside the young boy grasping the saddle edge so that he would not lose his direction. He tried to draw the scenery into his memory so that when vision failed he would have it stored away.

Tadhg Mor walked beside Elinor, marvelling at the manner in which she had developed during the years. And then he thought of Valentine Parr. He must be careful when they arrived at Ballinrobe.

They sat on the bank of a river and Tadhg Mor brought out the satchel of food which Elinor had prepared the night before. The bank was dry and she set out a linen cloth on the grass. Tadhg Mor peeled off his rough stockings and set his feet in the cold water. He sat motionless and took delight in the summer day, excited at the thought of the great fair. He looked forward to the horse races and the sideshows, to the continual excitement of three days when the world was filled with noise and bustle.

They ate their meal and while Elinor gathered up the plates and cutlery the Piper played a quiet summer air for them. His face was transfixed, his eyelids closed over his failing sight, yet he possessed a physical beauty which attracted her. She felt the strange wish to touch his face and the white skin under the linen shirt. She woke from her reverie and gathered the plates.

They continued their journey, the land becoming more fertile, the trees plentiful and luxuriant. She was aware of order and the settled appearance of the land, in comparison to the rough and grudging terrain by the sea. She saw a great house, with spacious lawns and well-proportioned façade. Sleek cattle grazed under the shades of the tall trees. She wondered who lived in the wide rooms and how they passed their days.

At Ballinrobe the traders had set up their coloured booths and the square was filled with activity. Elinor was fascinated by the stalls as they passed through the confusion of people. In one there was an array of ornaments which caught her eye; rings and bracelets secured by coloured ribbons caught the sun and were changed into mysterious objects.

'Rings and bangles for the pretty lady,' the woman at the stall called up to her. 'Rings and bangles for her fingers and wrists to delight the man she will marry.'

She passed on from the sound of the woman calling. In another stall a vendor had set out delph plates ringed in blue and patterned in the centre. A street balladeer sang songs from a torn book, rubbing a wet drop from his nose between his lines. A group of children gathered about him, miming his actions. Beyond the canvas booths stood the great warehouses. Grain was carried from the Ports of Galway and Westport and stored on the wide floors. In other buildings were sweating piles of cattle hides, filling the building with offensive smells which found their way out to the street. And everywhere on the square were shebeens, set up for the three days. Men were reeling through the confusion, carrying great ashplants, ready to settle old scores through faction fights. Tadhg Mor looked anxiously about him as they moved through the fair. He had no wish to be caught up in a brawl and feared the presence of Parr's men. They might set upon Elinor and carry her off as they had done with young girls from the estate.

A wide straight space had been left open on the square, leading directly on to the Kilmaine road. During the day the horses were raced along this road. Napoleon's quarter-masters had once visited this town to buy horses for the French cavalry. The Ballinrobe steeplechase which officially ended the fair finished at a limed line in the centre of the square.

Elinor and her brother were excited, their eyes were filled with the wonders of the fair. Each year they came to Ballinrobe and each year they returned home with gifts which they had received

69

from their aunt. They spoke of nothing but the great fair for weeks afterwards.

When they reached the stable yard Elinor left her horse with Tadhg Mor and rushed into the kitchen. Her aunt gathered her into her arms and then inspected her, surprised at how she had matured. She noted the firm breasts, the well-formed hips, the dark, lustrous hair and the black pupils on her eyes which would set men's hearts beating.

She was curious to see the huge man who accompanied Elinor and noticed that his eyes followed the young girl wherever she went. It seemed strange and a little disturbing. She had heard something of the man who had been washed up by the sea, and how his mind seemed to have been partly unhinged by the experience. She would have to question Elinor about him later. Tadhg Mor and Kevin went back to the great square while aunt and niece sat down to talk. The conversation was light and dealt as much with fashion as it did with the fair. Then it became more serious.

'It seems strange to me that a young lady should be companied by a mute man,' she began.

'But he is a friend,' she told her aunt.

'And you trust him?'

'Of course I trust him, I feel protected in his presence. He is obliged to me because I saved his life. And he is needed about our house more than ever. You often said that I needed somebody to take care of me.'

'But I was not thinking of somebody whose mind is touched.'

'It is not touched,' Elinor said firmly. 'He knows what he is about. He takes care of the farm and ensures that our life runs smoothly.'

'Then why does he not return to his home?'

'He told me he would never return to the island. He caused the death of his brothers and it has brought him great shame. He wishes to stay at our house.'

'I have not heard him talk. To me he is a mute,' her aunt told her.

'He only talks to me. He cannot or will not talk to others. He wishes to be left alone. And I feel safe when Parr and his men come to gamble.'

'How far has the gambling gone? Will your father never learn from his mistakes?'

'I do not know. I have seen Parr enter his winnings in a book he carries. My father has also to sign it. And Parr sells him drink. Sometimes I fear that something terrible is going to happen.'

'Valentine Parr is dangerous. Some day your father will have to honour these debts. That house is no place for a maturing girl or for that matter your brother Kevin. You should come and stay with me and I shall train you in the ways of the hotel and the town. There is much you have to learn concerning the ways of the world.'

'But I must take care of my father. Some day I will come, Aunt, but it would mean that I would have to give up the sea and the strand and the hills which lead up to the mountain. I would pine in a town.'

'You cannot stay forever in that bleak windswept house. Your mother would wish you to come here, and soon you will be a woman and will have to give serious consideration as to how you are going to spend the rest of your life. In four years' time you might marry, and where will you find a decent man of quality unless you find one here or in Galway?'

'But I am too young to marry. And four years is a long way away and I have father to take care of.'

'He must take care of himself. You owe it to yourself to leave that house and come and live with me. But we will talk of these matters later. We are becoming too serious. Tomorrow we will visit the milliners and I will buy you the very latest in fashion.'

The conversation led easily into clothes and small-town gossip. They did not feel the time pass and when Tadhg Mor and her brother returned from the fair it was almost time to retire. There was still some daylight in the western sky when they made their way to the comfortable beds at the top of the hotel. From the windows they could gaze out over the square and to the country beyond. The luxury of clean, scented linen sharpened her sense of excitement. Elinor lay awake thinking of the wonderful days which lay ahead.

The Ballinrobe steeplechase took place from Kilmaine Crossing to the central square. It was held every year and marked the highest point of the great gathering. At dawn the bookies had set up their blackboards on the square giving odds for the day. They

71

were dressed in bowler hats, coloured waistcoats, tailcoats and corded breeches. It was evident that Captain Bagnall, the quartermaster from Galway Barracks was a clear favourite on Clasher. He had been stabled at the military Barracks and it was rumoured that the horse had been purchased for King George. It was evident from those who saw him that he was a quality animal. It was said that he had an alert eye and even temperament and well-set neck.

That morning when Clasher emerged from the stables, the crowd gathered about the great gates to get a close view of the animal. The rumours had not been exaggerated. It looked healthy and sharp and tossed its neck with disdain as it passed through the crowd on the way to Kilmaine Cross, five miles distance from the square. Later Captain Bagnall emerged, followed by Maud Dillon. She rode past with a haughty air, her eyes set on the far distance.

By now the odds had fallen to one to six and continued to fall steadily during the day. The bookies were worried over the odds: all the money in the fair had been placed on Clasher. Only John Dillon stood a slight chance of keeping close to him. He was reckoned eight to one but very few bets were taken on him. He had come to Ballinrobe with his friends, and spent the night carousing at Upton's hotel. But after three hours of sleep he emerged fresh-shaven and dressed for the race.

As he ate breakfast his sister entered the room and threw a bag of sovereigns in front of him.

'Well, John Dillon, will you take my wager? I have heard you boasted last night that you could beat Captain Bagnall. Now let us see if you are so certain this morning.'

His sister seemed a stranger to him and not the young girl who had ridden with him across the Dillon estate many years ago. She had changed into a strange woman and he did not understand the workings of her mind.

'Very well, I will accept your wager,' he told her.

'Had I been a man I would have trained the Dillon horses. I picked Captain Bagnall's horse. It is mine and that is why I bet on it.' She turned on her heels. For Maud Dillon this was the day when she would prove to her brother that she understood horses better that any member of her family. She had first seen the mare at Ballinasloe.

72

Tadhg Mor, the Piper, Elinor and Kevin made their way to the square. Tadhg Mor carried Kevin through the crowd on his shoulders. They made their way to the far end of the square and took up a good position where they could watch the horses gallop across the field and enter the town from the direction of Kilmaine. At two o'clock the bell sounded on the square. The crowd pressed against each other, craning their necks for a better view.

The Piper looked across the open space where the horses would thunder past them. He saw vague, moving outlines and tried to make them more precise by narrowing his eyelids. He often did this to test his failing vision but week by week it became more difficult to impose outlines on shapes. Blindness was coming like the shortening of days, almost unnoticeably. Frequently his eyes wept and mucus formed on the under eyelashes. He often thought of the dark years which lay before him, when all vision was sealed from him.

But for the moment his mind was filled with delight, wondering how the horses were managing the high walls, certain that Clasher would win. He would cheer the English captain when he crossed the finishing line.

'They're coming, they're coming,' the crowd roared. They could hear the thunder of horses and the excitement grew. Perhaps Clasher might not win after all; something might have happened to him along the course.

'Is Clasher in the lead?' he called to Kevin, high on Tadhg Mor's shoulders.

'Yes. He is three lengths ahead and still making ground. He is certain to win. Only Dillon's horse is close to him,' Kevin answered.

The pressure on the watching human line surged, horses' hooves louder and more menacing now on the cobbled square. Suddenly the Piper found himself thrown forward into the empty space, his hands snatching at the air in front of him as he went down. The iron hooves on the cobbles grew louder and he looked down the course at the approaching shapes, trying to cry out. But then the horse was almost on top of him, jumping over his kneeling form. It skidded beyond him and Captain Bagnall fell to the ground. The rest of the horses, avoiding the prone figure, passed quickly by to the finishing post.

An iron hoof had caught the side of the Piper's head and he had fallen again, profusely bleeding. Elinor ran forward to pick him up, but before she could reach him Maud Dillon was standing there.

'You blind fool! You have destroyed the chances of Captain Bagnall.' Her eyes were on fire with rage, blind to reason or compassion. She brought her long whip down heavily upon his body and face again and again, while the crowd stood about her in awe.

'Leave him be. He is not to blame. He is blind,' Elinor cried, rushing forward and grasping the hand of the woman. She threw her aside on to the cobbles and brought the whip down on to the Piper who had drawn himself into a foetal position, hands gathered about his head, knees in his stomach. With a quick movement Elinor threw herself on the body of the Piper and the blow intended for him cut through her light dress and marked her back. She flexed instinctively in pain and she knew that blood had been drawn on her skin. She did not cry out but looked up at the woman through the mass of hair which had fallen over her face, observing the twisted mouth and flashing eyes.

The woman raised her whip to bring it down again when she saw that Elinor was ready to spring upwards and attack her. She would have torn her eyes out with her bare nails. Maud Dillon became conscious of the crowd gathering about them, beginning to mutter under their breaths. They were cursing her, calling her a soldier's whore. She glanced at them and they fell silent. She let her hand drop, and trailing the whip behind her, went towards the winning post and Captain Bagnall, who was in a dark mood. He walked away from the presentation stand and towards the Barracks, Maud Dillon following him.

The crowd broke. They continued to mutter in small groups. The incident had its own interest. They were curious about the young woman and the giant who walked beside her, a head taller than any man at the fair.

The Piper lay dazed on the ground, his fingers pawing at the dust for his instrument. The blood continued to pour from the wound on his forehead. Elinor tried to comfort him.

'It is all right. Everything is over. You are bleeding but soon we will have you back to the hotel.'

'A woman beat me. Men will remember that I was beaten by a woman,' he cried.

She took her handkerchief and began to staunch the flow of blood.

'Take me away, Elinor. I am filled with shame. I do not wish to have the people stare at me. I feel so humiliated.'

'Will you carry him back to the hotel?' she asked Tadhg Mor, who came forward and lifted the Piper in his arms. The remaining section of the crowd parted their ranks as the giant passed through them, starting at his massive form, the ease with which he carried the frail Piper. 'That terrible woman has hurt my friend,' Kevin told his sister as he walked beside her. 'I should have rushed at her when she raised the whip but it all happened too quickly. Who is she and what right has she to do such a thing?'

'I do not know, Kevin. I only wish to return to the hotel and forget all that has happened. That woman has destroyed our visit to Ballinrobe.' She hurried along behind Tadhg Mor.

'Well, I shall never forget her. I will remember her face and I will remember her voice.'

He could not let the image of what had occurred leave his mind and was determined to find out more about this woman, slipping into a dark pub where men were angrily discussing what had happened. It was only here that they could give free rein to their feelings.

'It will not always be so,' one man was saying to a small group. 'Their day of reckoning will come. Believe me, men are gathering into secret societies, beginning to talk and plan. The landlords' day will come to an end like everything else. Revolution is in the air.'

Kevin was impressed by the man who was talking. His intelligent face and articulate speech was not that of a peasant or cottier. When he had left the bar, he asked one of the men who he was.

'That's Kievney, the hedge schoolteacher. He's keen and talks treason, so keep what you heard to yourself, young man. The Castle will have a few spies in the square and in the bars listening to everything that is going on. You cannot be too careful,' he was told.

Kevin O'Donnell did not understand what the word Castle meant but he did know what spies were. He felt that Kievney was a man of courage, and decided to follow him through the fair.

When the small, beleaguered group reached the hotel, her aunt could not believe the story which Elinor told her. She directed Tadhg Mor to take the Piper to a small room at the back of the hotel.

'I was whipped by a woman. There was no reason to whip me. It was not my fault. I did not deserve to be whipped,' he told Tadhg Mor as he drew off his shirt and looked at his body. It was marked with blue weals but the skin was not broken. He took a towel and sponged away the blood from a deep wound above the Piper's right eye.

In another room her aunt had washed the wound on Elinor's back where the whip had broken the fine skin, marking it with a line of blood.

'It is nothing that I would not expect from Maud Dillon,' her aunt told her when she heard what had happened. 'She is only a high-class whore who consorts with soldiers. She is ruled by pride and anger, like all the Dillon breed. They would sell their souls to the devil for a good horse. And of course there is the Parr dash in them, French Irish, Protestant and Catholic, an odd and strange mixture. They are at war within themselves.' She concentrated on the long wound, rubbing iodine on to the broken skin.

'Just as well you had your back turned. If the whip had cut your face your features would be marked for life. As it is the trace of the lash will remain on your back.'

Elinor winced as the iodine cut into the wound. She went over the events of the day as she leaned forward over the bed, hating the woman who had visited her anger so fiercely upon the Piper.

'That is all I can do for you. Until it heals it will be painful. That woman lays a blight on everything she touches. Only the captain can tame her and he despises her. There is much I could tell you about them. You live in isolation by the sea and you are out of contact with many things. Here in the town it is a different matter and important to know what goes on.'

'Then tell me. I wish to know more about the Dillons.'

They sat together in the room and her aunt told her about the

Parrs and the Dillons. She told her how the first Dillon had travelled from France and purchased his estates. She told her of Margaret Parr who came to have a mare covered and married the present owner of the house and about the children of the marriage. By the time she had finished, Elinor O'Donnell had a good knowledge of the lady who had whipped her.

That night Elinor visited the Piper. He was sleeping lightly and when she entered the room he cried out, 'No, not my eyes. I have little vision left.'

She felt protective towards him, putting her arms about him and holding him close to her body. He felt her young and firm breasts against his bandaged head.

'You saved me, Elinor. You saved me from the strokes and the humiliation. It was terrible to be whipped by a woman in public view. What will they say of me in the villages and the towns, the man who was whipped by a woman?'

'No, they will not say that. They know that she is a demented woman.'

She held his head tighter between her breasts and she felt at that moment that she was a woman giving succour to a frail and sensitive child. She kissed the glaucomose eyes and sealed them with her fingers, setting his head down gently on the pillows and drawing the blankets about his shoulders. She remained with him until he fell asleep.

That night as she lay in her bed she recalled how she had held the Piper's head between her breasts and kissed him.

Two days later they set off for the house by the sea.

# Chapter 8

Valentine Parr set the trap slowly, like a spider spinning a giant web. His mind was filled with dark pleasures as he watched Henry O'Donnell fail month by month. Folds of blue flesh had formed under his sad and confused eyes. His shoulders had bent under some invisible weight and he had the shuffling gait of an old man.

He could no longer live without rum, flying into fits of wild anger if a bottle was not at hand, cursing Tadhg Mor and his daughter for hiding it.

At night Elinor often visited her brother before he fell asleep, to talk of what was happening to their father. She was protective of him but Kevin was angry and ashamed. He wished that his father was dead and that they were living many miles from the house.

Each morning Elinor came into the kitchen and tried to put it in some type of order, washing the dishes and sweeping the floor, throwing the empty bottles on the large pile outside the door. Then she cleaned out the ashes and lit a new fire in the gloomy kitchen. Often her father was snoring on the long settlebed beside the window, and when she wakened him she only stirred him to anger.

Taking a bottle of rum in his hand he would stagger towards the sea and raise his fist in challenge against the waves, cursing and abusing them.

'I lay my misfortunes at your feet. It was a black day that I set out from France.'

He did not know how much he owed Valentine Parr, who seemed ever-present, a leer on his face, his men crowded about him.

After each game of cards, each cast of the dice, Valentine Parr produced his notebook and in the presence of his bullyboys had him sign it, his signature becoming increasingly erratic during the past year. He could not control his trembling hands to pour rum into a glass, so he broke the neck of the bottle against the side of the table and drank directly from it, careless of cutting his tongue as long as he drew the liquor into his body.

'Leave them lying there,' he told Tadhg Mor who wished to carry the bottles away. 'Others may have tombstones of granite but this is my monument, a tribute to wasted years, a wasted body and a soft brain. Parr has poisoned me the only way the weak could destroy the strong. Go, Tadhg Mor, to Parr's Protestant mansion and bring another case of rum to me. There is a fire in my belly and I must quench it.'

Tadhg Mor had gone to the back door of the great house and

78

made a sign to the servant girl that his master needed a case of rum. When he was there Valentine Parr carried it to him and placed it in the back of the cart. Then he produced his book and in the presence of the servant Tadhg Mor made his stroke. He never let Parr know that he could understand English, knowing that it was in his and Elinor's interest that he should appear mute. He calculated that Parr owned the estate now and everything on it and wondered when he would make his move.

Two years after he had been whipped in the square at Ballinrobe, the Piper came down the dusty road which led to the house. He noted the scent of the heather and the spring flowers. The tang of the sea was in the air and he knew that he was approaching the house. During the year his sight had failed. Objects had become grey and their outlines uncertain. Soon he would need a companion to lead him through the countryside.

He heard voices calling to him and stumbled forward excitedly. Soon Elinor's arms were about him and he felt the warmth of her body on his and was aware that she had become a woman in his absence. Her brother Kevin was beside her and he held him in his arms. They led him down the hill to the house talking excitedly, asking questions which he was permitted only to half answer before they asked another.

He was brought to the far end of the house where there was a small room set out for him, far from the kitchen where her father now lived his dissolute life. That night, after he had told them of his journeys through Mayo and Galway he set to playing his music, alternating between joy and sorrow. When they left him it was late.

He had placed his pipes on a rough table when he heard the sound of horses' hooves in the courtyard outside, accompanied by drunken voices. He knew that Valentine Parr, unable to sleep, had come to play cards or dice. He pulled the blankets over his head and fell into a light sleep. Towards morning he heard two men urinating against the wall and carrying on a drunken conversation which suddenly sharpened his mind.

'Parr won't leave the place without her. I'll lay money with any man. He's set to have her.'

'He could have taken her years ago. He owns the house and the lands.'

'Would you eat a half-ripe fruit?'

'No.'

'Well, she's ready to carry the bull now,' a voice laughed.

'He'd do well to marry her. She would bear good children and it's time that Parr settled down.'

They made their way across the yard and he listened to the sound of their heavy boots die away and a door bang. Suddenly he felt that he was surrounded by evil and wanted to rush through the house and warn Elinor. The bright dawn flooded the white-washed room. There was banging on the door as if someone wished to bang it down.

'Wake up, Piper. Parr wants to be entertained in the kitchen. He has little patience and it will be the worse for you if you don't hurry. Put on your trousers and bring the pipes with you.'

He hurried through the long corridor towards the kitchen. As he lifted the wooden latch on the door his nostrils were filled with stale, rough air.

'Strike up a tune, Piper,' Valentine Parr called to him as if he were a servant, 'the place wants cheering up. The captain is in a dark humour and needs to make merry. My men will set him dancing.'

'I'll not dance, I can't stand. Leave me be Parr. Haven't you enough pleasure with my wine?'

'Not half the pleasure I'm going to have before the night is out. Isn't that right, lads?' Valentine Parr laughed.

'That's right, Mister Parr,' his men answered.

'Then take the drunken bugger under the arms, lift him on to the floor and he can kick his feet about. Let's see the sea captain dance.'

Two men took the inert captain and dragged him into the centre of the circle.

'Play,' one of the men ordered.

The Piper took his pipes and filled the bag with wind, playing a slow jig. The captain's feet barely touched the floor as he made awkward steps to accompany the music.

'Faster! We're not at a wake. Let us see the captain put his best foot forward. I will be entertained,' Parr called out.

The Piper played more quickly. One of the men prodded the

captain in the backside with the point of his cudgel and he tried to dance to the speed of the tune, his feet loose and ludicrous.

Kevin heard the music and decided to go down and listen to the Piper play. He heard the rough voices of men shouting in the kitchen and looked in at the small window in the door, feeling his father's humiliation as the men lifted him on their shoulders and forced him to dance. He pushed open the door and rushed to the centre of the floor shouting 'Leave my father be. Don't you see he is not well. Do you have to make a fool of him?' They laughed at him, but as he moved forward to hit Parr a man caught him and drew him aside.

'Your father is a drunkard and Parr owns him body and soul, so keep away; Parr's pleasure will not be interrupted.' With that he pushed Kevin out of the circle into a corner.

But Parr had lost interest in Henry O'Donnell, and his mind dwelt on the beauty of Elinor. Now it was time for him to have his pleasure with her.

'Leave the fool be. I wish to see the young woman of the house dance,' he called out from his chair.

The two men who had been supporting the captain let him fall on the floor where he collapsed into a dull heap and began to sob drunkenly.

All eyes turned towards Elinor. She had been in and out of the kitchen all evening preparing food and carrying it to the men. She was aware that Parr's eyes followed her everywhere, looking at her as he might at a good animal. She knew his reputation with women from the village.

'I want the woman to dance for me,' he said again. Elinor was standing by her father.

'I'll not dance. You may come to this house and gamble and drink but I will not be a spectacle for you and your men.'

Valentine Parr would not brook such arrogance in a woman.

'Then your father will dance until his gut bursts,' he told her.

'Leave my father alone. He is not well and you have insulted him in his own house. Have you no decency?' She stood before her father protectively.

'I've had enough of this. Get her out into the middle of the floor and let us have a look at her.'

The men pushed her into the centre of the ring. She looked with scorn at Parr and drew her shawl about her shoulders.

'Dance for the company. Dance I tell you,' Parr roared.

'I'll not.' She shook her head.

'Then out with the father,' Parr commanded. She hesitated and said venomously, 'I'll dance Parr, but some day I hope I'll dance on your grave. Play a reel,' she asked the Piper. He began to play and she danced lightly on the stone floor. Her face was immobile. As she danced she began to hate those who controlled the destinies of others and could humiliate them. Turning towards her brother, she could see that he too shared her hate. Valentine Parr watched each movement of her body, lying back comfortably in his armchair. She sharpened his jaded tastes; he would have her tonight, the delight postponed no longer.

'Enough,' he roared. 'The dancing is over. Hold her by the arms and bring the captain to the table. I will have words with him.'

There was silence in the room as Valentine Parr put his hand in his pocket and took out a leather pouch filled with papers. He threw it into the middle of the table.

'Now, captain, you play the biggest hand of your life. In that pouch lies the deeds of this house and all bills you have signed for drink over the years. I own everything belonging to you and you owe me more money than you ever can repay. So we will play a final game. The deeds against the woman.'

'No, Parr. You are not as low as that. You would not take my girl from me. I couldn't do that,' Henry O'Donnell cried.

'Then you have nothing left to gamble. You win everything or you lose everything. You are a gambling man and we stand an equal chance.'

The captain put his hands to his face and began to weep, his mind in turmoil. He was bound to be lucky. Fortune could not always favour Parr.

'Five tosses of the dice and you have everything to win. Five tosses of the dice.'

The captain laid his hands flatly on the table and looked at the pouch of papers.

'Five tosses,' he said.

O'Donnell placed the dice in a tumbler and rolled it on to the table, scoring a six. His face showed a sparkle of delight. He looked up at Valentine Parr, who shook the dice and turned up two. Four times the dice was cast and twice the captain won and twice Parr won. Each cast it twice again and the score stood at four – four.

'And now, captain, we reach the final toss,' Parr said, handing him the dice. The captain shook it vigorously and cast his luck on to the table, turning up a five.

'Beat that, Parr. Beat that,' he said, banging on the table.

In taking the dice Parr knocked it on to the floor. He retrieved it and shook it, keeping his eyes fixed on his opponent. He cast it across without looking at the table. It faced up a six.

'He won the woman fair and square,' Parr's men called out. The captain vomited on to the table and fell sideways on to the floor.

'Get rid of him from my sight and clean up the mess. Bring the woman directly to the Lodge and I'll follow later after we've finished the best in the cellar, for I will not be returning here again. This shambles of a house must now go on the market.'

They led Henry O'Donnell away. Elinor stood in the centre of the kitchen, her body mute with terror. Parr looked at her as if she had been purchased at a cattle fair. Two men grasped her by the shoulders and dragged her from the kitchen. Kevin was terrified at the presence of so much evil. He knew now why the hedge school teacher preached rebellion in the Ballinrobe pub. The memory of what happened in the kitchen would never leave his mind.

The other men went down into the cellar and carried up bottles of wine and whisky, placing them on the table.

'The only decent things in the house, fine whisky, fine wine and a ripe woman. Open the bottles without delay and let us celebrate victory and possession. To our general health and intact young woman,' he called to the men. They called on the Piper for some more tunes and he played while they roared abuse at him.

Much later when they were drunk he left the kitchen and went to his room, shaking with fear. He had witnessed the most shocking scene and his mind was numb. Already Elinor was being led up the mountain road to the Lodge. He could hear the roaring of the

83

bullyboys as they caroused in the kitchen and called out obscenities. He tried to block out the sounds and began to weep.

Tadhg Mor had watched everything from the shadows of the kitchen. He knew that he could not take on Parr's men single-handed and he controlled his fury. While Elinor was taken from the kitchen by the two men he drew Kevin aside and with rapid hand-signs indicated that he should follow him to the Piper's room. When they broke in on him the Piper thought that they were Parr's men. Kevin explained to the Piper what Tadhg Mor's hand-signs meant.

'He says that Parr changed the dice for a loaded one. We must follow them and bring her back.'

'It is impossible to get close to the Lodge. They will guard all the roads and pathways. You have seen where it is positioned as we made our journey to Ballinrobe. If they were to see us approach they would kill us,' the Piper said despondently.

'Then you must lead us across the mountains. Blind men can move in the dark and find their way across difficult country,' Tadhg Mor suggested.

'Perhaps a little easier than others,' the Piper admitted rising from the bed. Kevin looked intently at Tadhg Mor's hand-gestures and tried to understand them exactly. When he was satisfied he nodded in approval.

'Then we approach the house from the mountain. Their flank will be unguarded. If we set off now and take some food we will have the advantage for they will not leave this house until they have drunk every bottle of wine and whisky which is to be had.'

'And what plans have you when we reach the house? You cannot rush through the door and rescue the woman,' the Piper questioned, dubious of the plan.

Tadhg Mor's signs became angry. Kevin translated: 'I am an island man. We do not lay out plans as you do. That is not our way of thinking.'

The Piper was surprised at Tadhg Mor's composure, the deep hate he harboured towards Parr well-concealed. Tadhg Mor signified that they must immediately set off for the mountains.

They moved rapidly along the road, Tadhg Mor holding the Piper's hand, his steps quick and anxious, his face rigid with anger. When the Piper protested he scowled and would not listen to his protests.

They passed up out of the valley and were soon crossing the rough heather. Below them they could observe the outline of distant islands on the horizon. They followed goat tracks through the brown heather just showing purple flowers.

Tadhg Mor did not relent in his pace, though the Piper and the boy complained that he was moving over the coarse ground too rapidly.

After three hours they approached the summit of the mountain. A fog had rolled in from the sea and fine rain wet their clothes, making them uncomfortable. The Piper began to lose faith in their plan.

'It is purposeless. We could get lost in the fog and fall over one of the ledges. I have been here many years ago and even on fine days one could miss a footing and slide over a precipice.'

But Tadhg Mor would not listen. He grasped at the granite boulders and pushed himself on through the damp rain, adrenalin coursing through his body.

When they reached the summit he paused, sitting on the brittle heather and ordering them to eat some of the bread slowly. The mist disappeared as quickly as it had come and they could see the Lodge below them, long and squat, with heavy slates and thick chimneys. It was surrounded by yew trees and only a goat track led from the upper wall to the mountain. This was the Lodge which people looked upon with fear. Parr had taken young women to this remote place and debauched them. It was said that Satan once appeared during a wild feast and played cards with Parr who bartered his soul against immortality.

Even from their position on the mountain the Lodge looked significant.

Tadhg Mor peered down, his sharpened eyes brought the house into clearer focus.

'Remember, Piper, that I am depending upon you to lead us up the path from the Lodge and across the mountain,' he signed.

'And what do you intend to do? Do you think that you can take on a small army?' the Piper asked, his teeth chattering with cold. 'What if we are caught? These are rough and brutal men. I know their reputation.'

85

Tadhg Mor looked at the sky towards the west. Night was closing in, and soon they could move under the cover of darkness.

'We will go now, when surprise and darkness favours us.' They emerged from beneath the shelf of rock and brushed the dry heather from their clothes. A lantern light in the window of the lodge set their direction, as they moved down the sinuous goat track.

Elinor was a prisoner in a great white room with a hipped roof. Her hands were firmly bound behind her back, the ropes cutting her wrists. She lay on the wide deal bed unable to move through fear. The journey to the Lodge was fragmented as she tried to recall it, but the memory of Parr's lustful eyes, his heavy satisfied jowl, dominated all other images. She knew she would lose her virginity to a man whom she had been told was rotten with syphilis. She would be tainted with the disease, soiled and untouchable.

Her two jailers sat in the kitchen, drunk from the wine they had carried to the Lodge. They discussed raping the young woman in the bedroom.

'Parr won't notice in drink. When we've done with her we can bind her legs again. We've humped the servant women before and devil a notice he took. Consider the pleasure. She's a woman I wanted ever as much as Parr.'

'We had better do it quickly for he could be here any moment and he would surely shoot us.'

They reeled along the corridor, supporting each other, but hesitated when they approached the door, certain that they heard a horse approach. They rushed back to the kitchen and waited.

'Our minds are playing tricks on us. The time is getting short and we will have to hurry.'

They drank more whisky and the raw warmth gave them courage, but this time they were interrupted by a horseman. He pushed open the kitchen door and asked where the woman was.

'Trussed up and ready in the great room,' they told him.

'Then guard the two approach roads. Parr will be here within the hour. I'll stand guard by the front door. Take the whisky with you to keep you warm.'

The three of them walked to the front of the house, carrying a lantern which the leader set on a small circular tower to direct Parr.

'Take up your posts at the end of the road and let no one approach. Parr will castrate you both if he is disturbed. I'll stand here.' They stumbled off into the darkness as the leader took up his position in front of the door.

Tadhg Mor, the Piper and the young boy lurked in the shadows, moving cautiously around to the window with the light. They looked in and saw Elinor on the bed, her hands behind her back.

'I hate them, I hate them,' her brother whispered.

Tadhg Mor nodded. Then he gestured, 'I want you to move round to the back yard and untie the horse when Parr has entered the house. It will distract the guard and I will get to him in time. I will deal with Parr and later I will deal with the guard. If this fails we will be in grave trouble.'

Time passed slowly and once the guard passed within ten feet of them.

Parr rode into the shadow of the lantern light. He descended drunkenly from his horse and reeled towards the guard.

'Is she ready for me?' he asked gruffly.

'Yes, sir. She is on the bed in the great room.'

'Well, she'll carry Parr tonight, Myles, and the next to have her will have a scratched article. Keep well away from the house and if you hear her cry don't come near.'

'Yes, sir,' the guard said and moved into the darkness. As Parr entered the front door Kevin moved quickly to the back yard, untying the horses and stabbing them with a knife he carried. They cried out in pain and galloped into the darkness. Immediately the guard shouted and followed them. Tadhg Mor and the Piper opened the kitchen door and padded quietly along the corridor.

Parr moved towards the young woman lying on the bed. He ripped open her bodice and exposed her full breasts. They were neat and firm as he had often imagined, and desire for her shook his body.

'I have put off this pleasure for many a year. I won you with a loaded dice when your father was too drunk to notice. What man

87

but a drunken sot would bet his daughter to regain bad acres and a tumbledown house?'

She looked at his face, loose and sodden with drink. Her life would now be destroyed.

'Kill me, Parr, when you are finished with me for I vow that I will not rest until I destroy you and your breed.'

'Enough of your talk.'

He hit her on the face, making her cry out in pain.

'I would have taken you pleasurably, bitch, but now when I am finished with you, you will feel not like a filthy woman but a filthy animal.'

He struck her again and tears ran down her face. He began to undo his trousers, looking at her while he tore at the buttons.

He swung around as the door shot open, and let his trousers fall to the ground. Tadhg Mor sprang forward and clamped his hand on his mouth, dragging him out of the room and into the kitchen. Parr's eyes were bulging with fear. Tadhg Mor felt that they would explode and the poison of the pupils stain his hands forever. He grasped the head and pushed it into the barrel of water, holding him there until he drowned.

Meanwhile the Piper undid the rope binding Elinor's hands. She threw her arms about him and wept.

'Oh, I had given up all hope. It was terrible and nothing will ever be the same again.'

He stroked her black hair and held her close to him and let her cry quietly.

'We must leave this place and go back over the mountain. You must have my coat.' He took her torn dress and knotted it under her neck, covering her breasts. She put on his coat and they left the room. Parr lay on the floor drowned. Tadhg Mor pulled up his trousers and put on his coat. Then he searched through the pockets and took out a bag of coins. He was going to place them in his pocket but decided against it. He searched the pockets again and discovered the loaded dice. He handled it to Elinor. She looked at it in the palm of her hand, wanting to fling it away but something prompted her to keep it.

Tadhg Mor bid them remain silent, taking an iron bar as he left the kitchen. The guard did not see him approach in the darkness.

He knocked him unconscious and placed Parr's money in his pocket. They moved quickly up the mountain, the Piper leading them, Tadhg Mor carrying Parr's body on his back. When they reached the edge of the corrie lake he lifted the body high above his head and threw it into the darkness. A moment later they heard a splash.

Henry O'Donnell sat alone in the house, surveying his life. He had gambled his own daughter on the cast of a dice and lost. He tried to banish from his mind that Parr would soon ravish her, but the image returned.

He could not face his son and daughter again. He took his pistol and looked at it several times, but he lacked courage. He left the house and the sound of the sea in his ears gave him some comfort. He would return to it again and it would cleanse the memory of all that had happened. He reached John Kelleher's small boat in the cove, and drew it down to the sea. When it was afloat he jumped aboard, raised the small sail and headed out to sea.

When the small group finally reached the house at early dawn they found it deserted. They checked every room but could find no trace of Henry O'Donnell. They went into the back yard and along the sea-shore but there was no trace of him anywhere.

Gathered about the kitchen table they tried to decide where the future lay for Elinor and Kevin O'Donnell. They decided their aunt in Ballinrobe was the only person who could give them advice and sort out their problems.

## Chapter 9

On receiving Elinor's letter her aunt set out immediately from Ballinrobe. She was quick to grasp what had happened and decided to stay at the house for a few days.

They had searched everywhere for Henry O'Donnell but he was nowhere to be found. John Kelleher told Elinor that his boat was missing and she wondered if her father had taken it and sailed south. She took her horse and travelled many miles along the coast.

Her aunt set about examining the papers left behind by her brother. He had left the house and lands in Elinor's name. The forty acres would realize some money but the house was fit only for demolition.

It was decided that Elinor and Kevin should come with her to Ballinrobe, where they would have rooms at the hotel. There was a room for Tadhg Mor above the stables and he could be employed in the yard, seeing to the horses.

During the days which followed the police searched for Valentine Parr. The guard gave his evidence but failed to state that Elinor had been in the Lodge or that Parr had come to rape her. Neither could he account for the purse of money found on his person.

When Parr's body was finally discovered, the lacerations to the face and the body suggested that he had fallen over the edge of the precipice in a drunken stupor and drowned. The case was closed but the valley people suspected that Tadhg Mor had something to do with his death. For the peasants the name of Valentine Parr stood for all that was darkly evil in the land system under which they worked and no one mourned his passing.

A fortnight later Elinor, Kevin and Tadhg Mor visited every corner of the house before they turned the key on its silence and dereliction. Elinor mounted her horse and Kevin and Tadhg Mor sat on the cart loaded with their possessions. On the crest of the hill they looked back on the house and the great strand. A wind had freshened the waves in the bay and they carried white foam on their spines. They stayed there silently for some minutes then moved down the hill and away from the sea.

Elinor O'Donnell found it difficult to submit to the discipline of her new life, pining for the sound of the waves, the free spaces of sea and island. The social moods of the town were confusing. She often went to the small rooms where Tadhg Mor lived above the stables and spoke with him. He too felt lost in his strange surroundings.

90

'I am sorry I took you from the sea, Tadhg Mor. You should have returned to your own island and found happiness there fishing. This is no place for one like you,' she told him, holding his rough hands.

'I remain with you. I vowed never to return to the island and our fortunes are bound together. Do not think of the house by the sea and all the life about if it is gone. Had you remained there you would have always been a wild, unbroken woman whereas here you have a chance to become a lady and will adjust to the ways of the town. There is no going home, there is no home to go to.'

Her aunt was of the same opinion. Each Saturday she brought Elinor to her office and drew up a list of orders for the coming week. It was hard, disciplined work but she was paid for it.

'You have been with me now two months,' she told her one evening. 'I have watched you carefully. Perhaps you think that I am too hard on you but I have your best interests at heart. You work well, you have confidence in yourself and you know how to behave. But you need finish. I have arranged that you meet Madame Avery, an old French lady who will give you the polish you require.'

The French woman was small, neat and spoke with precision. Each gesture was formal and measured and her English was old-fashioned. She had worked for forty years at Castle Wilder, educating two generations of children in her fine ways, until she disagreed with John Wilder's wife who came from London. Taking her savings, she left the house in a fine anger and set up a small school in Tuam for young ladies.

'Teach her deportment and some elegance. She needs finishing,' Elinor's aunt told the old lady as she introduced her niece.

Madame Avery sat on an armchair, supporting her hands on a silver-tipped cane and directed Elinor to walk up and down the room.

'You must walk like a lady. You have the hump on your back like a small mound, as if you carry the weight of the world on your back. Now walk with a book on your head and walk and walk until your neck is straight and your manner elegant. Your gestures must be neat and precise. If you wish to walk through the halls of the county houses then you must use your height for effect.'

Sometimes she left the room and went into a curtained alcove. Elinor would hear the clink of a glass and later Madame Avery would return to her armchair, calling out, 'You must walk like a lady.'

She was like a small drill sergeant. Elinor felt like rebelling against her and her discipline.

'No, no,' she would cry, 'lift your head and don't look at the ground. You are not a serf. Look ahead of you. Practise. Practise. You will get it in the end.'

One day Madame Avery abused her in French. The remark sparked anger in Elinor and she retorted in French. Madame Avery was delighted.

'You speak excellent French. Why did you not tell me this before? This makes it all so different. Now you speak French to me always and ever.'

When Madame Avery spoke in French it was filled with exactness and idiom, almost as if her mother were present in the room. A bond grew between them and she looked forward to her weekly journey to Tuam, eager to learn all that this woman could teach her. She felt that she was paying back her mother some debt she owed and perhaps making up for the harsh, lonely years she had spent by the sea.

Madame Avery introduced her to French literature choosing classical works from her small library. She sat beside her, carefully explaining the form and purpose of each literary work.

'I have tried to explain such works to others but they do not understand. They have no feeling for fine things. Barbarians. But you have French blood in your veins and this is your inheritance. It will help you to look upon all things with the French mind and remember that it is a sceptical mind. Always read particularly the poets like Ronsard, Villon and many others. And Voltaire and Rousseau give you the two sides of the French mind. Keep them by your bed.'

And when they became friends she found that there was a good reason why Madame Avery sat on the armchair and supported herself with a cane. She had a supply of brandy hidden in the alcove and during the day she would retire behind the curtain for a drink. When Elinor became aware of this she always brought a bottle for her.

'Ah, you have discovered my little secret,' she said, when Elinor presented her with the first bottle. She could sip it openly before her while Elinor went through her various gestures and paces and later read for her.

'Oh, but I was a gay young thing, my dear, though you might not think it looking at me now. My neck was not always like the goose's leg, and how I could dance!'

She stood up and tried to do a small dance but fell into Elinor's arms and had to be brought to a chaise-longue where she rested.

When she left Madame Avery after two years Elinor had been changed into a sophisticated woman, certain of her presence in any company. She had also developed a taste for French literature and fine manners. She continued to live and work at the hotel. It was a period when she was given an opportunity to observe the world, its politics and social grades. She listened to the conversations of the judges who arrived for the assizes as they sat by a blazing fire drinking their port. She became familiar with legal idiom and the ways of the law, its absurdities and contradictions.

She impressed people who met her, becoming well-known in the town. Men looked at her when she passed along the street and women wondered about her mysterious past. They were curious, too, about the mute sad-eyed giant who often accompanied her.

In her mind she carried the scars left by Valentine Parr's brutal attempt to assault her and could recall each moment at the Lodge vividly. She feared the intimate presence of men and remained aloof from them, particularly the landowners who frequented the hotel. She questioned the power that many of them wielded over their tenants, knowing that they could evict whole villages if they so wished. Yet at night, dressed in smart clothes, drinking the finest wines, their conversation was pleasant and their manners without fault.

When her aunt felt she was ready she introduced her to the management of the hotel. She learned how to purchase the best cuts of meat and top quality fish. She watched the servants at work in the laundry and helped them. She pored over books on cookery and learned how to set out the tables with cutlery and china. Her aunt opened the ledgers and explained how the entries were made.

'Every night, even if you are falling asleep and your muscles aching you must sit before the ledger, set down how much you paid out and how much you took in. The day you slacken is the day your business fails. And remember, every farthing must be accounted for.'

Her face was always rigorous when she sat down to enter the expenditures of the day. When she closed the ledger she looked for a moment at its leather cover, tapped it with her fingers and went upstairs to bed.

'Remember that you must be discreet. Never divulge to anyone what goes on in an hotel. You will find the landowners, the lawyers and the officers drunk and disorderly. You will see fortunes gambled away on the gambling table, you will find men in the company of fashionable whores. You must keep tight-lipped. If I were to set down on paper all that I knew concerning certain respectable gentlemen of the county and certain ladies I could demand a king's ransom.'

Elinor was now seventeen years of age though to an observer she looked much older. She had grown taller during her time at the hotel and already her beauty had become known throughout the counties of Galway and Mayo.

She began to enter a pleasant part of her life. Sometimes she took the coach to Galway and spent the day shopping there. The city was attractive, with its square, medieval streets and wide expanse of quays bearing ships from all over the world. Perhaps some day she would open an hotel in Galway, she thought. It was a large city and could run a successful business. It would be pleasant to live close to the sea again.

Life changed suddenly. Elinor did not suspect that her aunt was so ill when she left the office one night. She had been working over the ledger and complained of pains in her chest. Elinor suggested she should go to bed but she replied she would not change a life's habit for a pain. Next morning when Elinor entered the office she found her aunt dead, her face lying on the open ledger as on a pillow.

She arranged for the funeral and walked behind the cortège as it wound its way through the town to the walled cemetery, her face firm and expressionless. When she returned to the hotel she locked the door to her aunt's office and wept. She had no relations left in the world other than her young brother and her only friend was a huge, quiet man who had once committed murder in order to protect her.

The will, when it was opened that evening, was in her favour. Not only did she come into possession of the hotel but a large sum of money set aside by her aunt. There was also a bequest to pay for Kevin's education.

When Elinor awoke the morning after the funeral she suddenly felt that she now carried a heavy weight of responsibility and wondered if she could carry on as her aunt had trained her. And then she reminded herself that she was a young woman of wealth, well-trained and well-prepared. She banished whatever doubts she carried in her mind, dressed herself quickly and swept through the hotel. She checked every room to make sure that the servants were at work. Then she went into her office and set about ordering the provisions for the week. A new period in her life had begun.

When the meal was over the gentlemen retired to the gaming tables. Elinor supervised the occasion with a little uncertainty. The Hunt club had been boisterous. Many glasses lay smashed on the floor and some members had slid under the table and fallen asleep but there had been no rough behaviour. That evening she called Tadhg Mor aside and asked him to wait close at hand in case he was needed.

When Maud Dillon and Daniel Parr arrived for dinner she was surprised because previously they had never frequented the hotel. As she went forward to welcome them, the women's eyes met. Maud Dillon did not recognize her. Captain Bagnall had returned to England and now she lived with Parr at one of his houses. Men turned their heads when she entered a room, fearing her wild presence.

It was during a card game that she began the scene, becoming increasingly agitated as she played. She had placed a considerable sum of money on the table and already knew she would lose.

'These cards have been set against me. I know they have not been correctly shuffled. I have sat down with swindlers.'

Elinor was instantly aware that Maud Dillon was going to create trouble. She noted that there was a pile of sovereigns in the centre of the table and calculated that there were at least one hundred there. The room fell silent; the men's faces waxen in the candle lights.

'I have heard your accusation,' Elinor began coolly. 'I know these gentlemen about the table and I do not doubt their integrity.'

'Yet you doubt mine?' she asked jumping up from the table and knocking the cards to the floor.

'I believe that you are a liar and a cheat,' she said firmly. As Elinor spoke she vividly recalled the day this woman had brought her whip down on the Piper's face and her own back. She could have been more savage in her reply but restrained her anger. Maud Dillon's hands began to tremble in rage, the pupils of her eyes to dilate. No one had ever addressed her so brazenly before and she could have torn out the eyes of this dark-haired young woman standing rigidly before her. In her madness she felt that she had met her before but could not recall the occasion.

With a quick movement, Maud Dillon grasped the brass candle-holder by the neck and swung it at Elinor's face. But a heavy hand gripped her wrist, and she could not move. Wincing in pain, she looked up at Tadhg Mor standing above her.

'Take your hand off me, you filthy imbecile, I will have you whipped,' she raged, clawing at his face with her free hand. Tadhg Mor caught the hand as it came towards him and held it. Maud Dillon screeched at him in a demented voice, her eyes rolling in her head and her head swivelling at the neck. Tadhg Mor held on impassively until she emerged from her fit. Her madness had burned out the anger and her body was limp. Tadhg Mor turned to Elinor for instructions.

'Throw her on to the street where she belongs. I shall see that her money is returned. I will not entertain such filth at my hotel. Never come here again.' She spoke with taut passion.

Maud spat at Tadhg Mor as he carried her towards the door of the gaming room which was quickly opened by one of the servant girls.

'I will have vengeance on you. No one crosses a Dillon and is not scraped,' was her final cry as she was thrown out. She fell on her back, the churned mud sticking to her dress. As she looked up she saw Elinor standing at the steps of the hotel, throwing a handful of sovereigns in her direction. Where they fell a group of men fell on their knees and began to gather the money from the mud.

'Get away from me. You are a pack of mad hounds,' she cried flaying at their faces with small hands, her blows completely ineffectual.

Elinor O'Donnell stood watching her humiliation then turned and swept into the hotel. Maud Dillon mounted her horse and rode into the night.

There was a babble of low conversation as she returned to the gaming room. All eyes looked towards her but she seemed unperturbed by what had happened.

'A table has been disturbed,' she told one of the servants, 'have it set out again so that the gentlemen may continue their game.' In her office, she put her head on her arms and began to tremble. She felt a hand press on her shoulder and looked up to see old Sir Harry Christian looking at her.

'Beware. Maud Dillon is a dangerous woman and will hold this against you until the day she dies. The Parrs will never again enter this hotel. Henceforth you must be on the alert.' There was a humane expression in his old face.

'Do you know why I lost my temper with her?' she asked.

'No,' he answered, looking keenly at her.

'From the lash mark she left on my back. She once whipped me in the square when I tried to protect a friend. She did not recognize me tonight.'

'I understand your aunt banned her from the hotel some years ago. There is a mad streak in her and you must now be careful and keep a watchful eye.'

'I will, Sir Harry. Thank you for your caution.'

'Now I must return to my port and my cards.'

Alone in her office she drummed on her desk and reflected on what she had done.

Three months later John Dillon rode into the town of Ballinrobe, arriving early for the election. There were two candidates, James Cosgrave of the Parr faction and Robert Gore of the Repeal Movement. Robert Gore was John Dillon's man and he intended to speak on behalf of Gore in the square. His physical power, his fame as a sportsman and drinker and his clever speech drew even the Parr supporters to listen to him.

As he looked at the warehouses of the merchants and the offices of the professional men, he knew he had a hard campaign on his hands, with little hope of dislodging Cosgrave in favour of Gore. Cosgrave had received the patronage of the county and his father had been made High Sheriff. He was a handsome shrewd man, and had made a name for himself in the House of Commons. There were certain traits about him which John Dillon admired but he sided with Gore because he wished to test Daniel Parr's position. His mind burned with fury when he thought of his sister cohabiting with one of them, darkening their name. He was aware that the men who shook their cap in greeting towards him knew also that his sister was now with the opposing faction.

He was keen to meet the new mistress of the hotel. He had heard of her great beauty, her fiery temperament and the manner in which she had removed his sister from the hotel.

He had written the week previously asking for rooms at the hotel. When he entered the courtyard a large, mute man took his luggage to the first storey. As soon as John Dillon had settled in he sent for a bottle of whisky and set out his papers on a desk, working for an hour on some ideas which had been passing through his mind. When he set aside his work he continued drinking until the bottle was empty.

That evening when he emerged from his room he felt sullen and depressed, a state of mind brought on by the whisky. He had arranged a meeting with Henry Turner concerning a horse he wished to buy.

As he went down to the dining room he saw a tall woman coming towards him and gazed thoughtfully at her. She had a distinguished appearance, her lips were full, and her hair fell in full black masses to her shoulders.

'Permit me to introduce myself,' he said as she approached, 'My name is John Dillon. I shall be staying for a week and may

98

return at irregular hours. I hope I shall not disturb the good order of the hotel.'

He felt that his words were too formal and that he should have been better prepared to engage her in conversation.

'I shall give you a key and you can let yourself come and go as you desire. If you wish to have meals served in your rooms I shall arrange it. I'm afraid that I was not here to welcome you when you arrived but I had business to attend to in Tuam.'

There was something almost too perfect about the manner in which she spoke. He looked at the lines of her face and body and was stirred with desire.

'Thank you. I must meet an acquaintance now,' he said, his mind still confused.

He was about to go when she asked, 'I believe that you have come to the town for the final week of the elections. You side with Mr Gore?'

'That is correct.'

'Then you are free to use the rooms for your friends and agents, although I believe you have little chance of winning.'

'And you are plumping for Gore?' he asked.

'No, but I am against the Parrs and the power they wield. Daniel Parr controls almost two counties through his man. He seems to have power over every policeman, jury man and squireen in the country,' she told him in a hard voice.

'And this power should be broken?'

'I do not wish to be under any obligation to servants of Parr and while the present candidate is elected to office I feel that I am unprotected by the law.'

'Then he is your enemy, this Parr.'

'Not Parr alone, anyone who uses power in a corrupt fashion.'

'I see.' He nodded his head thoughtfully. His senses and mind fired by her presence. 'I shall remember what you said.'

He bowed graciously as she made her way towards the kitchen. She reflected on their meeting, and his handsome, intelligent face. She knew that he was one of the finest horsemen in two counties, recklessly taking high walls at steeplechase meetings.

When she saw him much later that night he was completely drunk, raucously singing a hunting song.

'Typical of Dillon,' she heard one of the men remark, 'drinks too much, rides too much, too ready to be angry. Well-educated and knows how to debate, could have a great political career.'

Dillon collapsed on the floor and Tadhg Mor carried him to his room.

Next morning he apologized for his behaviour, and asked that his horse be brought around to the front of the hotel. After a hearty breakfast he left at ten o'clock for a nearby town where he was to address a meeting.

During the next three days his life followed a similar pattern. He returned to the hotel late in the evening, became very drunk but rose fresh and left the hotel after breakfast. He was always impeccably dressed. Elinor could never be certain if she liked or detested him.

The final rally took place before the hotel. All afternoon men carrying banners and placards arrived from the country and grouped in the square. John Dillon, who had been standing quietly at the hotel bar with Robert Gore and his agents, left his table and walked on to the steps of the hotel. His supporters formed a firm line behind him. From the window of her dark office she watched as he stepped forward after the loud applause. With a quick gesture he silenced the crowd and began to speak. His rich baritone voice seemed to reach out over the square and fill all the corners.

'We will have the victory and we will have the land. Men will plough the fields certain of crop and tenure down the long span of the years, their generations strong and vigorous continuing after them. With the land will come the power and the dignity that every son of Adam is born into. Man will have his birthright, the possession of the soil.' There was loud applause from all corners of the square. After a few minutes he continued, 'Parr's poison will be cleansed from the land and neither his breed nor generation will last. You will see them dispossessed. The estates walls will be breached, the deserted houses will become the habitat of foxes and the chimneys nesting places for the black raven; the syphilitic Parrs and their dandy women will go the way of all their flesh. If the rot does not eat them gut and balls, then time will have its way with them.'

He continued speaking for an hour and when he was finished the crowds cried out, 'Dillon is our man. He should speak for us in Parliament. He'll lift the rent and the taxes from us, and the day will be ours.'

They lifted him on their shoulders and carried him around the square, men stretching out to touch him.

As Elinor looked at the procession she realized how powerful he could be if he could control his wild habits.

When the crowds had broken up and gone to the public houses he returned to his table, where men came to congratulate him.

'We will give Cosgrave a fair run for it this turn,' they told him. 'You moved the people tonight. They would have burned Parr out. You could have turned them on the military barracks and they would have taken it.'

'Tomorrow they will have forgotten what we said, blown from their minds like chaff taken by the wind. No, our day has not yet come, but we must keep up the push.'

He became drunk later as he had most nights, falling across the table and having to be carried to bed.

Next morning one of Parr's men delivered a challenge to a duel. Elinor brought him the news.

'And so I have offended a Parr. Good. Well, let's have a duel. Life has been exceedingly dull without any excitement for the last two months,' he told Elinor when he had read the note.

'You do not take this challenger seriously?' she asked, alarmed.

'I am a gentleman and would be a coward, mocked by Parr for the rest of my life to refuse a challenge. Of course I accept. Let us meet the bearer of such a challenge.' He walked into the foyer.

'Come here, fellow,' he said to the servant. 'Did you bring this message?'

'I did,' he said curtly.

John Dillon caught him by the neck of his coat, threw him on to the street.

'Tell your overlord that the challenge is accepted. I shall meet him tomorrow by the river bank close to the bridge, and we shall see who is the better man, Parr or Dillon. The duel will be fought with pistols. Now off with you.'

All that day he was morose and spoke little. He drank firmly until finally he fell asleep on the table.

'You cannot fight tomorrow. You are in no condition to go,' Elinor told him when he woke.

'What is life? If I die now it will put an end to misery. Eventually I will have to die and why not on a glorious morning, with bird song about me and a river flowing by?'

'But you have so much you can live for, so much you can do,' she argued.

'What have I to live for? A son who will be master of a small estate?' He spat out the words sarcastically.

'You treat life cheaply because you do not appreciate life or its obligations. You have never been poor, uncertain, threatened. If you cannot think of yourself, think of others. Think of the fine thoughts in your speech last night. You could be a parliamentarian if you so wish.'

'I have only one wish, woman,' he told her drunkenly.

'And what is that?' she asked.

'To hump you,' he told her roughly.

She left the room, detesting him and yet anxious for his safety.


Tadhg Mor and Kevin lay in the grass and looked down towards the river bank where a low mist covered the ground, like a mysterious sea. Lightly formed bushes looked fragile as a spider's web. The air had the touch of velvet. While they watched the air became dry and a little warm, the images certain and local.

'Their hatred was bound to boil over into a duel,' Kevin said to Tadhg Mor. 'There is no love lost between the two families. Dillon can outshoot him and is accurate so why has Parr challenged him? I have seen one of them die and another will be no loss; they are a bad breed.'

Tadhg Mor with rapid gestures told him that he held too many angers in his heart and that it was not a good thing. The head should rule the heart.

Tadhg Mor had watched Kevin grow out of boyhood. He would not attend to the solid wisdom of Tadhg Mor whose gestures told him that he must be careful in his expressions. The Piper had put too many hates into his heart and reason would never fully prevail.

The silence was suddenly broken by the approach of carriages which drew up at some distance to each other. Men in frock coats and tall hats walked quickly towards each other. The seconds checked the pistols and moved away as Daniel Parr and John Dillon stood back to back. At a signal they began to walk away from each other with formal, measured steps.

The two figures on the hillside watched spellbound as the gap between the men widened. They stopped and turned to take aim. There was a puff of smoke from the pistol barrels, the late sound of fire. For a moment both men faced each other, then John Dillon slumped to the ground. Daniel Parr handed his pistol to his second and left abruptly in his carriage.

'Did you hear the second sound?' Kevin asked. 'The ball hit steel!'

Tadhg Mor nodded in agreement. They rushed down to where John Dillon lay, his second and driver kneeling beside him. A ball had torn his shoulder and blood was flowing from the rough wound.

'He's a scoundrel,' John Dillon told them weakly, 'an absolute scoundrel. I'm certain he was wearing armour. Did you hear the ring and see him falter?' he asked.

'Yes, it was obvious that he was wearing something over his chest,' Kevin answered.

'I know he was. I aimed directly at the heart.'

His face was ashen with pain and blood seeped across his shirt.

'Raise him slowly and we will bring him back to the hotel. He needs immediate attention,' his second told them. Tadhg Mor lifted Dillon and instead of carrying him to the carriage, walked up the hill and through the back streets to the hotel.

Elinor was waiting anxiously for some news of the duel when they arrived.

'Is he dead?' she asked her brother. Dillon's eyes opened: 'No I am not dead, but sleepeth, as they say, on the tombstones.'

'Bring him upstairs to his bed. I will send for the doctor. The wound will have to be cleansed.'

Elinor went with her brother into the office and asked him what happened, a note of anxiety in her voice. He could see that she was attracted to John Dillon.

'Were you very worried, Elinor?' he asked, a suggestion of a smile on his face.

'Of course I was anxious and worried. He is after all a guest at the hotel,' she told him, 'but tell me how he was wounded. Everybody said he was an accurate shot and Parr stood no chance?'

'And Parr did stand no chance if it had been a proper duel. If justice had been done Parr would be dead now. He was wearing armour and I heard the sound of the ball on steel. No wonder he was so confident. They are a family without honour. If I had pistol I would have shot him.'

'Control your anger, it will do you no good. Mr Dillon has lost a great amount of blood, I hope he will be well.'

In the mean time the doctor arrived and removed the lead ball from the shoulder, cauterizing and binding the wound.

'He must rest here for three weeks. He has lost much blood and an infection could spread into the body. If it does, you change the poultice to draw out the poison. These duels should be forbidden; death will come soon enough without sending it an open invitation. I will return tomorrow to see his condition.'

Elinor looked down on the weak, pale face, the eyes seemingly full of shame. He did not look as though he desired to live. He had suffered humiliation at the hands of a Parr.

In his carriage Daniel Parr quickly took off his shirt and removed the steel plate from his chest. He looked at the fresh dint, made by Dillon's accurate shot. By rights he should be dead. He bundled the torn shirt and steel plate together and hid them in the carriage, directing the driver to take him directly to Ballinrobe. He spent the day in another hotel drinking. As he sat there men peered through the window at him, gazing in awe at the man who had taken on John Dillon.

'A Parr has the beating of a Dillon. He will never live it down and it will swing the election to Parr's man. Dillon will never face him again.'

It was only later, after the election, that the rumours began circulating. Men began to whisper in the pubs that Daniel Parr had worn armour and that the ball had torn his shirt over the heart. Opinions remained divided on the duel.

Two days later Margaret Dillon arrived at the hotel in her carriage. Though small and bulky she was a hard, impressive figure. Elinor introduced herself but Margaret Dillon was not interested in conversation, asking that Elinor show her to her son's room.

'Could I have some privacy with my son?' she asked authoritatively, and Elinor immediately left the room.

Margaret Dillon looked angrily at her son. His face was drained of any colour.

'I believe that you cannot be moved for some time. Better if you were in your own room where we could give you proper attention. It is high time you changed your ways. Bad enough riding madly across the countryside drunk but engaging in a duel with your first cousin! Do not deal with the Parrs; they are dangerous. I am one of them and I know. Time you said goodbye to this wild career and married some woman of fortune and looked after your own estate. I'm surprised that your brother was not up to his neck in the whole affair; when will you both ever learn?'

'I was provoked. I should have killed him but he wore armour on his chest,' he protested.

'Typical. Be warned of the Parr's treachery. You have learned a hard lesson. Good day.'

With that she was gone. Downstairs she went into Elinor's office and gave instruction concerning the care of her son. She left the hotel as briskly and firmly as she had entered.

During the two weeks which followed, John Dillon slowly recovered from his wound. He became irritable and called for books which he read rapidly. He ordered drink to be brought to his room and when she refused there was an angry exchange between them.

'Do you refuse to bring me drink?' he asked her furiously.

'Yes,' she said stubbornly. 'You are in my care and the doctor has forbidden you drink.'

'He is a quack and you are a gaoler. Bring me drink or I will drag myself out of this bed and make my way downstairs.'

She gave in, watching him pour the whisky into a glass and drink it rapidly. By evening the bottle was finished and he banged on the floor for another.

When the carriage arrived to take him home she felt lonely at his departure. He looked weakly at her, affection in his eyes.

'I shall miss your company,' he said laughingly. 'I hope to see you again. You are a kind and considerate lady.' She watched the carriage turn and make its way across the square. Later, sitting in her office, she recalled him reading poetry to her, quiet and seemingly at peace with himself.

# Chapter 10

Margaret Dillon had spent the morning in her office going over the accounts with her manager. Every shilling spent on the estate was accounted for in the ledgers, thicker and more formal than church missals. Her writing was clear and she took pride in the columns of figures running down each ruled page. Before she finally ended each book she wrote a terse history of the year without flourish and excitement. She felt proud of her achievements: the estate was the best run in Mayo and Galway and her tenants were well-fed and clothed.

Before she left the room she looked at the large map of the estate. Each year it was redrawn and she set out the fields which were to be cultivated and those left for grazing. She planned the vegetable gardens and always experimented with new seeds brought from England. She even calculated how many trees should be felled in the forest and how they should be cut at the saw mill, an exercise which gave her pleasure.

Her body had become heavy with the years, her face doughy and without character. She had raised a family and improved the estate beyond recognition. Although time had been unkind to her appearance, her eyes were sharp and her mind decisive. Her estate gave her deep pleasure, a sense of importance in the scheme of things.

When she entered her carriage, her manager mounted his bay mare and rode alongside. The tenants anticipated her inspection, knowing that nothing escaped her keen eye.

They passed the edge of the lake at a slow pace. She looked at the forty-acre field she had created from scrub land and furze, a monument to her tenacity. It was fertile, the stalks of wheat green and soft, moving in erratic waves beneath the wind. She stopped the carriage and gazed at the dense mass of healthy stalks, knowing that when she returned from France the huge field would be buff stubble. She would have it top-dressed with lime and manure, seeding it with clover.

She visited all the fields and gave instructions to her manager who rarely added to her suggestions. She did not welcome advice in these matters, certain of her knowledge. This was her estate and she had shaped it, made it profitable.

The wheels of the carriage were muffled on the forest paths. The dappled light fell on the brown floor of dead leaves and branches. Some of the trees had gained full stature and must soon be cut. She felt no mystery in the woods and the small sounds of animals went unnoticed.

She visited all the outhouses, gathering her large frock about her as she examined the cattle. Her final visit was to the stables to see that they had been cleaned and aired. Her eye for a horse was almost as keen as that of her son. No expense was saved on these animals. Each morning they were led from their stables and exercised on the runs. During frosty weather when the ground was hard as metal plating, they were exercised on the forest paths. It was said that she thought more of her horses than her tenants.

At the house, the servants were packing clothes into huge trunks for the journey to France. There was subdued excitement; soon they would be free from her sharp eye and enjoying the lax discipline.

In his library Robert Dillon made his final preparations for the journey to Paris. His brother George had died some months previously and his son Edward had inherited the estates and warehouses. Edward had been well trained by his uncle to continue the family business in France and Robert Dillon felt pleased that his son fitted so well into French life. He was now a very wealthy and independent young man.

That evening at dinner he was in a bright mood. He had one of the servants bring the finest wines from the cellar to celebrate their departure. The lines on his face seemed less tight as he spoke of his early days in Paris and the period spent with his brother in the mountains. Sometimes he broke into French, stating that the English language did not carry the right lightness of touch. He quoted poetry easily to demonstrate his point.

'Enough of all this cultivated talk,' his wife said stolidly from her end of the table. 'I hope the estates and the accounts will be in good order when I return. I have given firm instructions to our steward and I have laid aside a sum of money for expenditure during the period.'

For a moment his face registered some pain but he brushed the remark aside and continued talking. His wife left the table and went to make some final arrangements with the servant girls, aware that they were becoming giddy in anticipation of her departure. She wondered if she should remain at Dillon Hall, but knew she had to visit Paris and see the possessions inherited by her son. She took great pride in the fact that her children carried French blood in their veins. It placed her a step above her family. Her brother's children could never boast of such lineage.

She had built her life on hard work, leaving her husband to his history and literature. He knew little of the world of the beast, soil and seed. He was an ineffectual drone, removed from the heavy presence of life.

Next morning, very early, a light mist still on the lake, the carriage with all its trunks drew away from the house. Their sons Matthew and John stood on the steps and the servants lined the avenue, waving to them as they passed. After their departure a great sense of relief spread among the servants and their sons.

The months which followed were wild and free for both of them. John Dillon had fully recovered from his shoulder wound and was eager to return to the hunting fields again. The quiet dining hall was soon occupied in the evenings by several squireens of the locality. After an arduous day, following the ragged hounds across the countryside they were both hungry and thirsty.

The wildest week ever spent in Dillon Hall began soon after their parents had left. Bartley Gaynor was called up from the woods by John Dillon. He came late in the evening when the tenants had finished their work and were making their way home to their cottages. He was dressed in torn clothes, patched and gathered about him with a rough belt. His eyes shone out from a heavily red-bearded face and there was always the smell of unwashed sweat about him. He rarely left the woods during the day, moving through the roads and villages only under the cover of night. Solitary years in the woods and by the lakes made him almost animal in his instincts.

His allegiance was to Dillon Hall and its owners.

'What is your wish, master?' he asked when they met in the yard.

'Bartley, you know the woods and thickets more than any other man. Tomorrow we are going for hunting. Could you stop the holes for us?' he requested.

'Indeed, I will, sir. This very night when they are searching their prey I will plug every earth between here and the boundary.' Bartley Gaynor did not take kindly to foxes. 'They were born sly from their tails to their snout. I better be on my way, your lordship. I have a long night's work before me.' He turned to go.

'Would you accept a shilling for your labour, Bartley?' John Dillon asked, searching for a shilling in his pocket.

'I have no truck with money, my lord, the very root of all evil. But if you would pardon me for asking, my lord, you could leave some heavy boots and trousers bundled up under the bridge – they would be of service to me.'

John Dillon asked him, 'Do you feel lonely in the woods, Bartley?'

'That I can answer straight, my lord. Ever since the day I built my hut in the wood I never looked very much to the company of man but to that of the animals. My mother, God rest her, berated me for a whole month at the door of my hut but no budge would I make. I'm disowned by my own but that is no great matter. You see, my lord, I'm free and have no truck with people, were it not for yourself and your father. I'll go now and plug the holes. If you could see your way to leaving the parcel under the bridge, I'll collect it. Good day, my lord, and I hope the fox gives you a run for your money.'

John Dillon shuffled into the dusk and reflected on what he had said.

Bartley Gaynor could smell a fox on the wind like the hounds.

'Tomorrow, my friend, you will run for your life for there will be no burrow where you may hide. May you be savaged as you savaged the hare and the rabbit. May the blood run from you as the yoke has run from the pheasant's eggs.'

That night he passed easily through the countryside, blocking up all burrows where the fox could take refuge. He chose for destruction a fox which lived close to the wood. For several years he had failed to trap him. It was a long night's work but at morning light he felt certain that he had settled his scores with an old enemy.

He listened for the sound of the horn calling through the wood. In the cobbled yard the squireens had finished their stirrup cups. There was the barking of dogs released from the kennels, the horn again and then the thunder of hooves across the lawn to the lake edge. He listened to the sound and felt that the fortunes of the old fox would now take a final bad turn.

For John and Matthew Dillon the excitement of the chase was like heady wine. Matthew, however, could control his excitement. He did not swing between moods of elation and despair like his brother. The previous evening they had sat before the great fire talking of steeplechases and point-to-point meetings. Their knowledge of horses was not only drawn from the land about them but also because they read every book which came to hand. The Dillons owned some of the finest English sporting prints, particularly those of Townely Stubbs. They always hoped to breed a horse as great as Eclipse, a chestnut with a white blaze and stocking who had never been beaten, making a fortune for Denis O'Kelly. They played with this idea over their wine. With a fortune they could buy an estate and devote their lives to the breeding and training of horses, far aware from the dour presence of their mother.

But following the hounds across rough ground they thought only of securing the brush. The delight of movement, the even light of the morning, the horses spread out across the field with their careless riders, all filled their senses with animal delight. Tom Kepple rode beside them, swigging brandy from a silver flask. His face was red from rough living, and he wore a tall silk hat, a soiled, red-tailed coat and yellow breeches. He was the most reckless rider of the field and had broken several bones during his career.

He led the field for an hour leaning backwards and forwards in the saddle by an old instinct. They gave him the lead until the fox scent was taken by the dogs. The bugle sounded across the fields and horses and riders became alert. Ahead in a clump of bushes on a light hill the fox made a dart into the open field, the hounds giving chase. The fox, sensing immediate danger, ran for a flock of sheep grazing close to a gate. They scattered in every direction and threw the hounds off the scent. The huntsman blew his horn and called the dogs to order. They followed him through the gate and soon they recovered the scent. By now the fox had entered a hazel wood. There was immediate confusion, as men wheeled their horses this way and that, looking for a path through the trees, their faces and hands cut by the branches.

'He's a smart one,' John Dillon told his brother as they saw the hounds' confusion.

'Trust Bartley to pick out a wily fox for us. He knows each one in the locality. Let us move on to that wide space beyond the wood. We are certain to pick him up there.'

It took them twenty minutes to make their way through the wilderness of the wood, some of the horses already showing the strain. Beyond the wood they reformed behind the master hunts-man, finally picking up the broken scent. There was nowhere the fox could take refuge, but if he reached the far bank of the river then he could elude them.

The fox's ears picked up the sounds of the dogs and horses' hooves. He had used up too much energy in his first rush and now his heart was pounding. There was no copse in which he could find a small breathing space, so he pushed forward towards the river. It was a long mile to run and his old limbs were smarting, his breath was coming in short bursts. He gasped for cool air. He slipped through a sheep gap in a stone wall and rushed towards the river. The first dog was upon him just a hundred yards short of the river, snapping his leg and throwing him forward. As he rolled on the open sheep ground the others were about him, their teeth tearing at his body. Three horsemen sailed over the large stone wall, the Dillon brothers and Peter Blake. They jumped from their horses and, scattering the dogs, John Dillon took his knife and cut off the large brush. Blood covered his hand as he held it aloft for the approaching riders to see.

That night at Dillon Hall they stuck the brush in the candlestick and set in at the centre of the great table. John Dillon had summoned the Piper from Ballinrobe to play for the company. It was a savage gathering. Great cuts of meat had been spitted in the kitchen and turned all day over the open fire until the rind was crisp and brown, the meat succulent. The cellar was opened and baskets of wine placed by the wall. All night they drank and sang, the candle smoke filling the room with a heavy dry smell. When the morning came they closed the shutters and banished the presence of the day. Men slept on the floor or under the table and woke in a drunken stupor after a heavy sleep. With shaking hands and loose faces they began to drink again. The servants set more meat to braise on the iron spits while men staggered out into the cobbled yard to urinate openly and grasp the fresh air. Others vomited and returned to the feast which lasted three days. When it was finished they dragged themselves from the room, mounted their horses and set off to hunt another fox.

When Mrs Mangan entered the dining room she wept openly. Linen had been stained with wine, fine delft broken on the floor and some of the silver forks looped into horseshoe forms. The smell of excreta hung over the room.

'Oh, what got into them at all? Where did they get the wild streak from, the mother and father they have. I reared them from the cradle and watched them grow into two men of intelligence and education and yet they would let such a type into this house. God knows what the mistress will say when she returns.' She called two of the stable men, ordering them to open the windows and clean up the dining hall.

The fox hunting continued for two weeks. The huntsmen moved from house to house in the vicinity, hunting by day and drinking through the nights. The two brothers were finally carried home in a coach, bearded and filthy, their faces ashen and grey.

Matthew soon recovered from the weeks of recklessness. He washed, shaved and presented himself in the dining room for breakfast. He read the papers, wrote some letters and set out to examine the estate. He quickly returned to the routine of the house and did not mention the events of the past weeks.

A dark lethargy set into John Dillon's mind which made thought and action impossible. He stayed in his room for a week, his sunken eyes staring into the fire for hours on end.

He thought frequently of Elinor O'Donnell during these depressing days, her face and figure sharp and immediate to him. He recalled her voice, her carriage as she walked before him, her intelligence as she engaged in conversation. Of all the women he had ever encountered this was the one he wished to possess. He would invite her to the house; perhaps her presence might cleanse it.

Ever since they had crossed the Irish Sea and landed on British soil Margaret Dillon felt at a disadvantage. She was aware that her clothes seemed out of fashion and that her accent was déclassé. On reaching London this was more apparent. The circle in which her husband moved was marked by gaiety and wit. For hours she had to sit patiently in some ornate chair listening to flighty conversation, mute and embarrassed. Having been educated in England, the atmosphere of the elegant rooms suited her husband and she understood in some dim way why he had withdrawn from the life of a county landlord. In this privileged society his talk was full of confidence and finesse. He spoke with a cultivated London accent engaging circles of young women in conversation while she reflected on the years she had worked on the estate to bring it into profit, the long days spent supervising the labourers in the fields. She detested London as she would soon detest Paris.

On their journey to Paris she steadily gazed at the French landscape, noting the rich earth and small villages set like islands between cultivated fields.

But when they reached Paris she again felt the limits of her education. Her husband seemed to gain new vigour from seeing the landmarks and buildings that he had almost forgotten. As they entered the heart of the medieval city he became quietly excited, and at Ile de La Cité his imagination was filled with the cries of the revolution. At the Conciergerie Marie-Antoinette had been imprisoned to await her trial, her beauty and power gone. The mystique of royalty had been destroyed when they took the Queen in a common cart to the guillotine, reviled on her way by the mob from the gutters. At thirty-eight she looked haggard and old. Robert Dillon determined to examine the room in which she was imprisoned and follow her journey to the guillotine at his leisure. And he must go to the Bibliothèque Nationale in rue de Richelieu and examine several manuscripts and documents. He could spend the rest of his life in this city, stimulated by its history.

Robert Dillon was interested also on the effects of the Revolution in Ireland. They would be slow in coming and perhaps not so drastic. The landowners of vast estates in Ireland took little or no interest in such things but the ideals which destroyed Marie Antoinette could destroy them also. The destitute and the poor would not benefit. It would be the middle men, those of small property, who would take advantage of the ideals.

After two hours' journey south of Paris they could see the Dillon château rising up from among trees. Robert Dillon had followed the current political movements of France, and thought the new king suitable to the times. He had no flaming passions and had the politeness of a merchant rather than of a prince, which suited the temper of the times.

At the château a liveried servant came down the steps to open their carriage, their son Edward and his wife Lise coming through the open doors to greet them. They led them into an elegant room with great ornamental mirrors.

Margaret Dillon looked at her son's slim, well-bred wife. She could not speak English but she prattled along in French giving her mother-in-law the sense that she did not belong in the place. Even her son seemed to have completely assumed the French ways and she wished she was at home on her own estate. Her husband had broken into French as soon as he entered the house, leaving her to sit in rigid silence on a brocaded chair. Edward turned to her, talking of Ireland but she detected an air of detachment in his polite interest. She felt that she was talking to a stranger.

The next four months passed slowly, though her visit to the estates in the Loire Valley gave her great satisfaction. She travelled with her son, who left her there to journey further south making arrangements with the vineyard owners for the purchase of wine.

Her contact with the earth took her mind off the stylized life in Paris. The château was surrounded by the aromatic barns with their huge oak hogshead and she watched the vines being weeded and trimmed during August days. All day the men worked among the dry pathways, while about them the black grapes began to turn colour. In September the vintage began and the men drew large cartfuls of grapes into the sheds and the fermenting vats. Here women in bare feet broke their caps, their skirts hitched to their waists. She walked about the vineyard and the timber sheds with excitement; the process was not unlike the harvesting in her own estate. She picked up some simple French words with a peasant accent and learned something of the taste and quality of wine. At the beginning of November, when they were dressing the fields with grape skin and deep ploughing the new plantations, she left reluctantly for Paris.

Robert Dillon enjoyed the delights of the city and through his son's contacts with the various ministeries he could obtain direct access to files and manuscripts, hardly touched since the Revolution.

Late evenings were spent with his son discussing political ideas which had been growing in his mind for many years.

'Europe will never again return to the medieval world of the monarchy. America and France have seen to that. Those who pine for kings and queens, like some of our Romantic poets and writers, are living in a fool's paradise. The world is expanding in every direction and I can see the merchants and industrialists flourish. I only celebrate the past.'

'And what of England?' Edward asked.

'It too has passed through a revolution when Cromwell had Charles I beheaded. I cannot see that monarchy shaken again. You can also accurately predict that as the new middle-class secure political ground in England they will develop a taste for wine,' he told his son, laughing.

'I have anticipated such a mood. Each year our trade doubles. I have secured export and import licences for London and it is a lucrative trade.'

He continued to be surprised by his son, his knowledge of men and affairs seemed far greater than his own. He had a shrewd certainty which seemed to inform everything he did. He was not aware, however, that his son belonged to the British Secret Service and that his frequent trips to London had more purpose than that of business. He was on intimate acquaintance with members of the French government and he could judge the temper of the city from their conversations. He was also familiar with the private lives of many of the government's officials, aware that their indiscretions could be used against them. He could also bring back Home Office information and spread it in the city. If it became known that he traded secrets he could forfeit his trade both to London and the French colonies.

When the time came to depart in early November, Robert Dillon felt reluctant to return to Ireland. The constant rain, the poverty of the people, the despair which seemed rooted in the earth would bring on dark moods rendering him powerless to compose his ideas or set them down on paper. He was saying goodbye to a culture in which he would have been happy.

She had washed slowly, she had combed her hair with delight and put on a cool blue dress. She had accepted John Dillon's invitation because she wished to see Dillon Hall. She had heard much of the racecourse, the woods and the islands on the lake.

She took a certain pleasure in this man's company, recalling many of the peaceful hours they had spent at her hotel when he was recovering from his wound. When he was sober and not in a dark mood he could be excellent company. Now his eyes were bright as he explained the history of many of the estates and houses which they passed.

John Dillon was aware of the clean body beside him, the stiff blue dress, the dark hair combed and ordered. Her face seemed to have an inner glow, the mind possessing its own secrets. There was a privacy about this young woman which he could not know.

Her image had returned again and again to his memory during the days of hunting and drinking when all decent restraints had been cast aside. While staying at Galway he had been to the soldiers' bordello. There, with the smell of thick perfume, the open abandon, the memory of Elinor O'Donnell had haunted him.

The carriage entered the drive. They passed by the lake, catching the quiet light of evening. Elinor O'Donnell watched the birds breaking through the reeds as they settled further out on the water. The islands were silhouettes, mysterious on the water. The grooms were leading the horses up from the lake where they had been drinking.

There were lights burning in the hall and a servant was waiting to take her cloak. The dining room was set out for supper, a formal occasion which she enjoyed. Mrs Mangan was surprised at her dignified presence. She knew how to handle the cutlery and the Delft.

When supper was finished she sat and conversed with John Dillon before the fire. He later showed her his father's library, explaining that he was engaged in an historical work which occupied most of his time. She was shown Margaret Dillon's office where the accounts were calculated and the affairs of the estate planned.

'Certainly the two rooms provide a strange contrast,' she remarked.

'They represent my parents' attitudes and interests. My mother would not be happy in the library and my father would find no comfort in this office. But my mother is most content here, going over her accounts and making the arrangements for the estate,' he explained.

He took a lantern and showed her the stables, set around a cobbled courtyard.

'It is a very well-run place, I can assure you. If one were so inclined there would be no reason to leave the estate. I know that my mother must be quite unhappy in France.'

In the drawing room he opened a bottle of wine, explaining that it had come from their estates in France. She appreciated its excellent quality but could not afford to carry such a fine stock in her cellar.

It was late when she left and darkness had descended upon the estate. The moon was in the east and cast a path of silver on the lake. The scent of heavy dew came up from the wide lawn. When she returned to the hotel that night and reflected on all that had passed she felt a warm attraction for John Dillon. His manners

117

had been flawless, his conversation had never lacked interest and he had not touched her. Had he touched her, she would not have accepted his invitation to ride through the woods with him on the following Saturday.

'Take caution, Elinor. Look for another. There is a dark strain in the whole lot of them,' Tadhg Mor told her the next day. 'I have seen it. They fear neither God nor man and they fall easily into excess. I don't know why you are taken by this man. You have seen the bright and dark side of him and he will not change now. Perhaps a settled life might reform him. If he took a greater interest in politics he would have more on his mind than riding after every fox in the county and carousing in bordellos. I have ears. I hear everything that is going on.'

'I cannot give counsel to my heart. The bright side of his nature is delightful. He is intelligent and civilized,' she argued.

'And what of the dark side of his character? He cannot drain the poison from his blood. It cannot be like other poisons. I know your aunt would advise you against any contact with the Parrs and the Dillons.'

She sat on his bed close to the attic window, the evening light catching her hair. Tadhg Mor sat in his armchair, smoking his pipe. From his window he could look out over the town to where the mountains rose up out of the flat lands. The strong bond between both had been made firmer by the years, each knowing the intimate thoughts and worries, of the other.

'I thought that you did not take very greatly to the landed gentry,' Tadhg Mor said.

'Some I like. Sir Henry Christian is a decent man and so are many others but the name Parr frightens me. That fear will never leave me as long as I breathe.'

'And what would you do if you were mistress of a great house?' he asked.

'I do not know,' she said pressing her arms around her knees and drawing them towards her.

'Well, consider it. For some day you will marry well and may find yourself in a county house. You were not reared to live in a cottage or a middle man's house.'

'And what of love?' she asked laughing. 'Am I to marry a man I do not love?'

'I've seen many a woman on the island marry out of harsh necessity. She learned to love her man and wept when he died. The nature of people doesn't change between the island and the mainland.'

'And you would have me marry into a county house?'

'Yes. That's where you belong, not in miserable lodgings. Then you can change things. Not like your brother who will find himself in jail some day. Already his head is buzzing with hate and revolutionary thoughts. Keep an eye on him for he is hot in his ways.'

They fell silent for some time aware of bird song from the trees. Elinor considered all that had been said by Tadhg Mor.

'I am not certain of love, Tadhg,' she said directly after some reflection. 'When I come into the presence of some men my heart seems to freeze. I recall the terrible journey I made from the Lodge and I recall those dreadful men and the abuse they hurled on me. Sometimes at night I jump forward in the bed and scream out, thinking that I am going to be raped. I can never clear the memory of that out of my mind. I enjoy their company but when they place a hand upon me I feel threatened.'

Four months later John Dillon asked Elinor to marry him. During the autumn their days together had been happy, and he had never been drunk.

She considered her position for a week. She had seen him in his dark moments and knew that he could quickly descend into raw and irrational behaviour. Above all she wondered if she were capable of having a passionate relationship with him. She had almost decided against marriage when an encounter took place which changed her life.

119

# Chapter 11

Margaret Dillon listened sullenly to her son. She sat in her deep armchair, her eyes on his face. She noted every nervous twitch and tick. She was thinking that the fair promise he had shown as a child and a youth had come to nothing.

She had returned from France to discover that the house had been abused by squireens and their hangers on. The wine cellar had been depleted and her sons had overdrawn on the bank to the tune of one thousand pounds. Her anger was deep. All her married life she had given care to the estate, watching over its fortunes and its profits. She had bought bankrupt farms and estates and annexed them to her own. In her four months' absence she could see the deterioration in the walls and drains; even the woods had become untidy. If she died, it would quickly return to wilderness like many of the estates in the county.

Her son finished speaking.

'I have listened to you at length. I have not interrupted you so do not interrupt me.' She placed her hands flatly on the arms of the armchair and spoke in resolute voice.

'You seem to be taken by this woman from Ballinrobe. Marry if you will, but you will bring no hotel owner near this house. Are you a fool to be trapped by the wiles and beauty of a young woman? Why should a girl of eighteen wish to marry a man twice her age? Have you reflected that perhaps she might be more interested in property or in rising above her present situation? Men may marry for love but women have other things in mind. What do you know of her background; a commoner and certainly not county? There are many fine women with money and estates you could marry, and you will need estates and money if you wish to pander to your tastes.'

'I love this woman. Does that consideration not carry any weight with you?' he protested.

'Love has nothing to do with the matter. It is not love, it is infatuation. You would look a fool marrying a young common woman. Who would have you to their house with a common woman? You spring from a French family who can trace themselves

120

back to royalty. Very few in the country can boast such lineage. The Parrs are well established and have been honoured for their service to the Empire. You wish to marry a scullery maid. I'll not have it. She will not enter this house while I live and she can expect no gift from me. I have said my final word and I will not talk further upon it. The matter is closed.'

'But mother. . .' he protested, coming forward towards her. She held up her hands.

'The matter is closed,' she repeated, rising from the chair and leaving the room.

John Dillon stared after the small, heavy woman who dominated the estate and the lives of her children. He was angry with his mother. She had a resolute will and her mind was settled on her crops and her animals and her rents.

He went through the kitchen to the stables, saddled his horse and set off through the woods. Much later he emerged from the woods into open countryside. He reduced the speed of his horse, proceeding upland towards the hills. He dismounted, looking down at the estate spread along the lake. He could make out the woods, firmly crossed by wide breaks, the extensive fields, green and beige. And at the centre of the estate the house itself with its outhouses, saw mill, brewery and stables, the mill for grinding oats and barley. Apart from the rest stood the hanging house, where pigs and cattle were slaughtered for the estate, the blood and entrails spread on the land as fertilizer. Nothing was wasted by Margaret Dillon.

She had brought him here as a young man, telling him how she had crossed the mountains to meet his father on business. They had stopped at this spot and wondered at the location and great beauty of the estate.

'Here I set my roots. I have lived the better part of my life in Dillon Hall. I made it a rich inheritance,' she had said to him. He remembered her words as he looked down on the estate. His brother would inherit everything, his other brother possessed vineyards in France and warehouses by the Seine. He had been born unlucky.

Margaret Dillon could not banish from her mind the thought of a common woman marrying her son. She moved quickly about the outhouses, giving unnecessary directions to the servants and was out of breath when she returned to her office. She locked the door, sat in her swivel chair and gazed at her account books. 'Thank heaven I have an older son who is stable and with some interest in the estate. And to choose an hotelier for a wife.'

She recalled the young woman at the hotel with black hair running down her shoulders, her carriage firm, her manners polite. The old woman muttered to herself, 'She belongs to the middle lower class and has no place in the great houses. She should marry her own.'

All day, despite her activity about the estate, Elinor O'Donnell's face was before her. That night in bed, she had to leave aside the book she was reading and reflect upon her position.

She was growing old and even to turn in bed was slow and cumbersome. There was a deep pain in her hip which the cold weather aggravated. Phlegm gathered in her chest and she had to hack it loose with racking coughs. She had watched animals grow old and now as she took stock of her body she realized that she was decaying. Her life was as active and regular as a religious and it centred upon the estate. The thought of her son marrying a domestic stirred thoughts of mortality within her. She could not die with this affair unsettled.

Before she fell into a painful sleep she determined to confront the hotel owner at Ballinrobe.

Margaret Dillon's actions followed directly upon her thought and next morning she had her carriage drawn around to the front of her house. Wrapped in rugs and with a stone hot water bottle on her lap she set off for Ballinrobe.

The sight of her estate in autumn, when it was resting after the fertile summer, made her more determined that the young woman in Ballinrobe would not be part of it. Her mind was grim with anger but she drew herself up and steadied her thoughts. Looking out of the window she saw they were passing through a village of windowless mud cabins where the smoke escaped lazily through a hole in the roof. The filthy children carried an impoverished and hungry look as they ran beside the coach. She ordered the coachman to go faster.

Suddenly the horse shied and she was thrown sideways on her seat. When she drew herself up the whole village crowded around the carriage, shaking their fists at her.

She drew open a small hatch and called to her drive, 'Will you please hurry forward.'

'But the child?' the driver questioned, his face white with fear.

'What child?' she asked.

'We ran over a a child.'

'Is he killed?' she asked firmly, the crowd now beating on the back of the carriage.

'I do not think so but it appears that his leg is broken. They are carrying him to one of the cabins.'

'Did you have to be so awkward? You knew that I wished to be in Ballinrobe by midday.'

The hungry faces looked at her with large glazed eyes. They were barefooted, their limbs almost fleshless, seeming to belong to a strange and foreign species, one with an ever-increasing population. The land could not sustain them; every acre was tilled in order to set potatoes, even the wet and grim mountain moorland. They lived on the margin of life and each day brought a hungry challenge to them.

She got out, setting her heavy form firmly in the circle of peasants and staring at them. They became silent, knowing her and her reputation. In the small cabins they had heard stories of the ferocious Parr woman who had whipped a man tied to a cart and pushed hardened criminals beyond their endurance.

The child lay at the door of his cabin and she examined the leg, the broken bone pressing against the skin. The boy's face was ashen. She took some money from her purse and handed it to the father who grasped it with a sullen face.

'Have the leg set and splinted,' she told him gruffly. 'I presume you know some healer who sets cattle bones. And keeps your children off the side of the road when carriages are passing by. The boy could have been killed.'

They followed her at a distance and watched her mount the carriage steps and close the door, cursing her under their breaths. As the carriage left the village their cry rose to a futile fury.

As she lay back in her seat she began to consider the village through which she passed, not unlike many others in Connaught. Each year they seemed to grow more populous; the poorest land was drawn into cultivation and the potato was the staple diet. If a blight should come to destroy the single crop there would be no way to feed the people.

The land improved as they approached Ballinrobe, the fields larger and regular. Cattle browsed calmly on the grass and massive trees secluded the estate houses.

She observed the hotel as she approached, taking a new interest in it. Situated at the western end of the square it stood out among the other buildings, the bright whitewash glowing in the light. Railings ran along the front of the building and a portico covered the entrance.

She made her way up the steps into the foyer of the hotel, calling imperiously to a servant, 'Could you tell the owner of the hotel that Margaret Dillon of Dillon Hall would like to speak to her.' The place smelt fresh, the paint work and the ceilings well maintained. The brasses were burnished and the floor carpet had been renewed. The servants were busy about their work, wearing clean linen bibs over blue dresses.

Elinor O'Donnell moved briskly down the corridor, her expression strong. Her black hair carried the sheen of blue steel. Margaret Dillon was impressed by her presence; she could not brow beat or confront her openly in the foyer. She felt that this strikingly tall woman was a challenge to her.

'Could we talk in private?' she asked in a dry voice.

'Yes. In my office.' Elinor directed her into a small room beside the foyer, a comfortable, intimate place, not unlike her own office at Dillon Hall. She noted the ledgers and the accounts neatly arranged in piles indicating an exact mind. She knew that she was in the presence of a formidable opponent.

'What is the nature of your visit? I am sure that it is not a social call,' Elinor said directly.

Margaret Dillon began in a haughty voice. 'You are perhaps aware of the history of our families. On my husband's side we can trace our line back to Henry I. We have belonged to a very distinguished French family, which is something quite unusual in Ireland. On my own side, which is the Parr side, we have strong

124

connections with several notable English families.'

Elinor looked at the round, dour face, which carried no trace of joy. She wondered where the preamble would lead.

'As you are aware, the Dillon estates will pass to my eldest son. My son John possesses an estate of two hundred acres of frugal ground and he will not inherit any further property. He is a man of ability and married into the right family could make something of his life. I have promised him the sum of five thousand pounds on the day he marries a woman of my approval. I can assure you, young woman, that if he marries you he will not receive that money.'

It was a hard, direct statement and made by a woman who thought only of her estates and the placement of her family, her eyes narrowing as she coldly made her point. Elinor O'Donnell did not betray any emotion as she looked at the fat, overdressed woman.

'You believe that your son wishes to marry me?' she asked.

'Most assuredly he does. I object firmly to his choice. I told him that he was infatuated by your youth. He is approaching middle age and he is hardly the proper choice for a young woman.'

Elinor's first instinct was to laugh, then as she reflected she began to grow angry.

'I presume you have further objections to me other than that of my youth,' she said.

'Most certainly. Like should marry like. We are landed people and I expect that my children will marry into landed families. You do not belong in the same class. I do not know what family you belong to. I have made some enquiries and believe me, I cannot discover anyone who knows about you. So you understand my position very well. I see you are a sensible young woman and you would not want to jeopardize John's chances of marrying into a good family. I presume you have now gathered the purpose of my visit.'

Elinor O'Donnell was amazed at the arrogance of the woman. All the county families came to the hotel for the various occasions. She knew them on an intimate social level and did not feel inferior to them. Now this woman sitting before her had tried to demean her and fired by controlled hate she began, 'You may not

125

know who I am but I know the earth and the seed from which you are drawn. You belong to the loins of dour Cromwellian soldiers, regicides who have no lineage. You dare to sit before me and call the Parr name noble, when I know the dark side of your history better than you do. Even to this day your own brother demands the rights of the Lord on the young women of the estate, and your dead brother debauched women in his lodge in the mountains. He destroyed my father. I remember him riding into our yard with his bullyboys, demanding the hospitality of the house. Your brother cheated my father out of everything he ever owned and brought about his death.'

Margaret Dillon rose to leave but Elinor O'Donnell grasped her hand and forced her to remain seated. 'And you know how he brought about my father's death? He played a false dice against him. My virginity was the collateral set up against the old debts. So I know the Parrs and the noble quality of their lives. I know who you are and yet you dare come here to my hotel and tell me that I am inferior to you. The day will come when your line will disappear from this landscape and no one will every know who the Parrs were.'

'I do not believe such an outrageous story. Only an unhinged mind could believe what you have told me. You have invented these things,' Margaret Dillon's voice was shrill, but she felt uncertain of her position. She regained control of herself.

'You have no proof that such a thing ever happened, no proof whatsoever. I will not have my late brother so ill spoken of.'

Elinor O'Donnell looked at her in firm anger.

'I have proof if you wish to see it.'

'I do,' the old woman vehemently replied.

'The proof is here.' She opened her hand to reveal a yellow ivory dice.

'A dice?' she asked incredulously.

'Yes. I will roll it three times, and each time a six will face upwards.'

She placed the dice in a small tumbler, shook it and threw it on to the table, turning up six. She cast the dice twice more and the same thing happened.

'If you look closely at the dice you will see your brother's

126

initials cut into the face carrying one. He used it against my father. So you see Margaret Parr, you belong to a race of thieves and cheats. You have tried to diminish me but you cannot for I have a feeling that we will meet again. I ask you to leave my hotel and if you refuse I will have you thrown into the gutter as I did your daughter.'

Margaret Dillon did not move.

'You know something then of my brother's murder?' she asked.

'Murder? I believe the coroner brought in a verdict of drowning. Is that not so?'

'That is the official version of what happened.'

'We must keep with the official version. After all we live under British law and must abide by it. When it speaks it does so with a balanced and unbiased voice. It is not a loaded dice.'

'Marry my son and I will cut off any monies that might come to him. I will have him beggared before I will acknowledge you. If you think that you can win against me then you are greatly mistaken.'

'I have won our first encounter, Margaret Parr. What the next encounter shall be I do not know. Our meeting is at an end.'

'Indeed it is. But do not be too confident; I have legal powers over my children. You wish to marry, then you marry a beggar-man. Not a penny of my money, not an acre of my land shall be yours. Your schemes will crash about you. I do not think we will have any occasion to meet again.'

She drew open the door and with a last dismissive look left the hotel. She had no wish ever to meet Elinor O'Donnell again. If her son married her, outside a two-hundred-acre estate, he would have nothing to sustain this ambitious wife. No commoner would ever enter Dillon Hall.

Elinor O'Donnell sat at her desk, shaken by her conflict with this arrogant, dull woman.

She knew she would marry John Dillon. Despite the difference of age she felt some love for this man. He possessed two hundred acres of land, a house and the Dillon name. She knew his wild reputation, she had seen him drunk on the floor and listened to his incoherent vulgarities. But beyond all that he had some strange nobility and attraction that she could not define. This vague attraction and the arrogance of Margaret Dillon had set her on a course of events which would change her life.

At their next meeting Elinor O'Donnell told John Dillon that she would marry him. She travelled to his house on the small estate and saw that it needed to be refurbished. The fields ran down to a lake and the long house and outbuildings stood among great sycamore and oak trees. She brought a cabinet for her collection of books and other pieces of her own furniture. She walked the neglected fields and decided that the land could only bring in a small income. She would continue to manage the hotel; Tadhg Mor told her she must keep her independence. He pleaded with her not to marry John Dillon.

'He is one only for the military whores and low women. He drinks too hard and will never love you. He'll have you and throw you away, because his tastes have been spoiled. Pick a young bright man; it will break my heart to think of you lying with a Parr.'

'He's more of a Dillon than a Parr. He is a man with ability. I have seen him sway the crowds with his words. Some day he could be elected to Parliament and perhaps do something for those who are dispossessed. I've made up my mind. I love this man and I will take my chances with him.'

'I cannot accept it but your will is your own and I'll be beside you always.'

'You will come and live in a small house on the estate which is by the lake, surrounded by a small copse of silver birch and hazel. You can plant a garden there and you will always be close to the house.'

Kevin was surprised when he heard the news. He put his arms around his sister and they held each other for some time.

'You deserve to be happy. Our lives will go in different directions now.'

'You know that you will always be welcome to stay with me at the hotel. There will always be a room for you.'

'Thank you, but I must make my own life and my own decisions. I hope that your husband lives up to the high ideals he preached from the steps of the hotel.'

'I know he will,' she told him confidently.

128

Kevin was fifteen years of age and had moved to Galway where he lodged with a printer called John Higgins. While not attending school he helped him, setting type in a grimy room where the air was heavy with the smell of ink, paper and molten metal. Already his mind had been politically formed and he knew he wanted to be a journalist. His vision of Ireland would lead him down dangerous paths.

Two nights before her wedding she retired to her room and was sitting in front of the fire. Winter was coming and the frost had already hardened the night ground and formed rime on the windows. She looked into the glowing embers and reflected on the step she was about to take.

She was startled by a knock at the door. When she opened it she found the Piper standing outside.

'Come in,' she invited, 'I thought that you were somewhere in Mayo.'

'And so I was. I heard the news at a fair. Men wondered who you were, so I sat in a corner and composed a tune for you. I bring it as a wedding gift.' His eyes were grey with glaucoma, his steps faltered as he came into the room. He stretched out his hand.

'Let me show you to a chair,' she said, leading him to a seat beside the fire. He took out his pipes and set them on his lap. She listened to him play, looking at the sadness in his face, and she remembered how she had once protected him from the whiplashes of Maud Dillon. She had run to him the night at the lodge when Valentine Parr had tried to assault her and he had thrown his arms about her nakedness.

These memories flooded into her mind as she listened to the music he had created for her. When he was finished he placed the chanter on his knees and looked forward, his eyes focused on no certain object.

She was deeply moved by the music and remained silent.

'I hope it pleased you,' he told her. 'It came very quickly to me from some lonely place at the back of my mind. I do not know why it should be lonely but that is the form it took and one must follow one's inspiration.'

'It pleases me very much. It is one of your most beautiful airs. All beautiful airs are touched with sadness.' He was the most

129

gentle person she had ever met and perhaps this was the reason for the strange physical affection she felt for him. He was tall and well formed, his mind intelligent and alert. His touch was kind when she held his hand.

'I'm sure I have disturbed you but it was my wish to bring you this tune before your marriage. I wished to celebrate your beauty. As my eyesight fails I recall it frequently. It is a constant image in my mind.'

'You flatter me. You have seen more beautiful ladies at the fairs and the big houses,' she laughed.

'None as fair as you. I have watched you grown into beauty. I wish you every blessing as you enter marriage.'

He took her head in his hands and kissed her forehead. Instinctively she threw her arms about him, laying her head on his shoulder and weeping. He held her for many minutes and no words were spoken. Then he took his pipes and prepared to leave.

'No matter what happens I will always come to you and give you comfort,' he told her ominously.

Two days later John Dillon and Elinor O'Donnell were married at the Augustinian Church in Galway. Her brother and some others from Ballinrobe were present but none of John Dillon's family attended. By this act he had cut himself off from them. There was a sense of emptiness in the church as the priest gave them his blessing. They signed the register in the small sacristy and then made their way down the aisle. Elinor had once dreamed of a large wedding, surrounded by friends and well-wishers, but this was a small ceremony with strangers as onlookers. She felt sad as she walked through the porch and out into the sunlight.

They held their reception at Quinn's Hotel in Ayre Square. The conversation was fragmented and the guests were uncomfortable in the presence of John Dillon. It would have been a a lonely gathering had not some of the Galway Blazers arrived for drinks. When they heard that John Dillon and Elinor O'Donnell had been married they ordered the best wine in the house to be brought to the reception room, and the company soon became boisterous, toasting the couple again and again. John Dillon began to get drunk. Elinor Dillon's new husband neglected her, sat with the men and recalled days at the hunt. Later he sang coarse songs for

130

them and ignored her plans to leave. When he collapsed on the floor Elinor had the coachman drive them to the house she had refurbished.

When she awoke the next morning she recalled the dreadful first night of marriage. She looked at the purple-veined cheeks of the man sleeping beside her. He could not respond to the gentle words she had spoken in his ear, but pushed her arms away and moved on top of her body. His breath was heavy with drink, his language and actions rough. She could not respond to him and pushed him away. He cursed her and then fell asleep.

It was a dark discovery. He became morose and drank more heavily. One night as she undressed he looked at the beauty of her unapproachable nakedness, the full breasts with fresh nipples, the rich, flawless thighs, the black pudenda, the tapering legs.

'Our marriage is over before it has begun. We will never have children. I should have married a woman with some experience, not a virgin. You have cut me off from my inheritance and you will fail to give me heirs.'

He hit her with the palm of his hand on the side of her face, the sharp sting making her fall back on the bed.

He left the room in silence, taking a lantern to the stable and saddling his horse. He rode into the night, on his way to a gambling house in Galway.

When she had recovered from the blow, she dressed herself and reflected on all that had happened. She wept briefly then drew herself up; she would not be beaten down by a Dillon or a Parr.

She drew on her warmest cloak and walked down to the lake, staring across the cold, placid waters. On the far shore she could make out the lights of Dillon Hall.

# Chapter 12

Elinor Dillon rode to the hotel each morning by the lake path. She felt alone in the new world of marriage and there was no-one she could turn to for help.

Tadhg Mor watched the change in her face and manner. She went about her business in the hotel in a daze and he did not intrude on her privacy with questions. When the work about the yard was finished, he retired to his room, lit his pipe and began to read. He waited for her steps on the wooden stairs but she never came, keeping whatever troubled her to herself.

It was known at Dillon Hall that the wedding had taken place but it was not spoken about openly. They knew that Elinor Dillon had moved into the small estate and that John Dillon was drinking in his usual haunts in Galway. It was obvious that something serious was the matter. The marriage would not be a success, Margaret Dillon assured herself.

The first months of marriage had nearly destroyed Elinor Dillon but she tried desperately to build up the shattered wall about her heart. Twice she had been beaten by John Dillon after he had arrived home drunk from Galway. Impotent in her presence he took the whip and brought it down upon her back: 'The common women of Galway can stir me and this precious wife of mine leaves me frigid. There will be no issue from this marriage. I have lost everything to a scullery maid.'

Another night he threw back the sheets and looked at her savagely. He grasped her nightdress and tore it from her body. He would ravage her as he ravaged the whores he bought. She was his property to do with as he pleased. He was shocked when she produced a small pistol from beneath her pillow and pointed it at him.

'I will not have your filthy hands ever touch my body. I will not be beaten and I will not be humiliated. I will not be blamed for not bearing children. You will have your children. Your sister whipped me, your first cousin tried to rape me and your mother dispossessed me. I will not suffer any more humiliation.' She held the pistol close to his head.

132

He tired to bring his incoherent mind into focus.

'You would not dare raise a pistol to your husband,' he said in a firm voice, trying to gain control of the situation.

'It is raised against you. One more move towards me and I shall shoot you through the forehead.'

'Then I shall leave the house and return to Galway. I may not return again.'

'That is your choice.'

He left the bedroom in a rage, banging the door and crossing the yard. Then she heard him ride across the cobbles and down the avenue towards Galway.

Two weeks later she brought him home from the city.

One Sunday evening Robert Dillon put down his pen. He had finished a paragraph and he was pleased with its content. He sat at his desk and considered what he should do with his evening. He rang the bell and ordered the groom to saddle his mare.

He set off into the woods, his mind preoccupied with the daughter-in-law he had never seen. He had remained silent while his wife raged against her but he made some enquiries from a trusted friend in Ballinrobe. When he heard their opinion he was satisfied that his son had married a woman of some merit and decided that he would make a call on her.

He approached the avenue of the small estate with some trepidation. He detested family quarrels and he did not wish to get embroiled in the present situation. He reached the small, gravel semi-circle in front of the house, dismounted and knocked. The dull sound followed through the house as he waited nervously. The door was opened by a young woman of great beauty in a fresh linen dress.

'I'm afraid I have intruded upon your privacy. Let me introduce myself. I am Robert Dillon.'

She was surprised at his appearance. In old age he was handsome, a direct contrast to his wife. His gentle manner was that of a well-bred gentleman. She recalled all that her husband had said about his father.

'John is not at home at present,' she said slowly, 'but do come in. You are most welcome. May I take your coat?'

He laid it on the side table and she led him into a comfortable room with a glowing fire. She directed him to a chair.

'You can see the Hall from the bow window,' he remarked.

'Yes. At night I can see the windows lit up.'

'Well, if you look at the right window on the second storey you will know that I work there.'

'Yes, I know the window. It is always the last light to go out.'

'That is correct. And indeed I'm the last one to rise in the morning. Sometimes I forget about time. Some book or other takes my interest and I read till morning. Quite a useless life they tell me.'

'Not from what I hear. John told me you write a great deal and have embarked upon a book,' she said, drawing out the conversation.

'It is of no importance,' he answered dismissively.

They had established a relationship which was important to Elinor. She felt no longer cut off from Dillon Hall.

'I must apologize for not attending your wedding. I received your letter of invitation but my wife would not agree to go. I think you know why.' He looked at her keenly.

'Yes. We had a stormy meeting. I do not think that we can ever be friends.'

'That is rather tragic. I would like to have my family call to see me,' he said, sadness in his voice.

He formed a pleasant impression of her, accepting her invitation to stay for tea. They sat at the bow window and continued their conversation.

His friend in Ballinrobe had described the young woman accurately. She was well-mannered and intelligent, possessed of a strong character and remarkable beauty.

'I'm afraid John will not return tonight,' she told him directly.

'A quarrel?' he asked.

'Yes.'

'These unfortunate things occur and for both your sakes I hope it will blow over. But whatever happens will not effect the friendship we have built up between ourselves. You are part of the family now.'

'I appreciate both your visit and your kind remark,' she said warmly.

When it was time for him to go, she accompanied him to the hall and helped him with his coat. They stood talking at the door for some time as if he were reluctant to say their farewells.

'Let there be no rift between us. My son is most fortunate to have married such an accomplished woman. Night is coming on and my groom will have informed the house by now that I have gone missing. Men will be searching the woods with torches for me. Because I spend my time writing in the library they feel that I am incapable of taking care of myself. If I may I would like to visit you again. I think that we have much to say to each other.'

'I would be delighted to have your company,' she told him.

'What day would suit you?' he asked courteously.

'Sunday. I am always at home on Sunday.'

'Very well then, next Sunday at three o'clock.'

He returned as promised, bringing her a present in a long velvet box. It contained a heavy diamond necklace.

'It belonged to the French side of the family. It is quite old I believe, and was always passed down to the woman of the house. Please have it in token of my regard for you.'

'Then I must keep it hidden from view for as you know I shall never properly belong to the family,' she told him sadly.

'No, wear it if you wish. I believe that one of my ancestors wore it at Versailles.'

He watched her face as she placed the necklace around her neck.

'I have never been given anything so precious,' she told him.

'And why is that? I am sure you must have had many admirers,' he asked, gently probing her past.

'I lived by the sea for many years, taking care of my father and mother. Not a very interesting life; I'm sure you do not wish to hear about it.' She tried to sound light-hearted.

'You are my daughter-in-law. Everything about you is interesting.'

'Everything?' she said, looking sharply at him.

'Yes.'

'Then I do have something to tell you which may trouble you, perhaps even make you ashamed of me. But I will tell you and you can make up your own mind.'

'I assure you that I am a man of discretion. Perhaps I too have something to be ashamed of,' he said enigmatically.

It took her a long time to tell her story, sometimes hesitating, looking into the fire, particularly when she described how Valentine Parr had tried to rape her. When she was finished she looked up to see his reaction but there was no expression of surprise on his face.

'What you have said will remain with me. Your friend was justified in his action. It was indeed a terrible experience.' There was silence between them for a while and then the conversation turned to some other subject.

On his third visit he repaid her trust in him by revealing the secret he had withheld from his wife. He told her of his visit to France as a young man and the journey he made with his brother into the mountains.

'It was on that occasion I learned that if a Dillon woman gives birth to a girl there is a certain chance that she will have some strange quirk in her nature. My daughter is strange, as was her grandmother and others in France. I have kept this from the others. Not even my children are aware of this strange defect, but be warned of it.'

'We have traded our secrets,' she told him, 'but tell me more about your work?'

'Oh, my work on Marie Antoinette. I met her once riding through the forests of Saint Cloud, and was taken by her beauty and her manners. At Versailles I used to watch the carriages drive through the ornamental gates and across the acres of cobblestones for some state occasion or other. I have followed the course of her life ever since.'

'Some day perhaps I may have the opportunity to read the manuscript?' she suggested.

'It is very long and cumbersome, running to some four thousand pages. I keep it locked away in a large iron chest. I should have made a second copy for if it were destroyed a lifetime's work would be brought to nothing.'

They spoke of many things during these meetings and Elinor Dillon felt that she had become part of the family.

Her husband did not return to the house and she felt increasingly isolated. One Saturday night she heard the sound of horses in the yard and rushed out to see if her husband had come back. Instead she

136

discovered Tadhg Mor had brought the Piper to visit her.

'I shall leave him to play to you. He insisted that he should pay you a visit,' Tadhg Mor told her. 'I must return to Ballinrobe.'

She showed the Piper into the main room.

When they were sitting before the fire he took out his pipes. 'They tell me that this estate is lonely and that you are lonely too. I will play for you and perhaps some of the music will come back into your voice.'

'How do you know these things?' she asked.

'I listen well. While I was eating in the hotel kitchen I heard the servants talk among themselves. They are observant people.'

He played a gentle air to her, filling the room with enchantment. She listened to it in awe and when it was finished began to cry.

'Why does the lady cry?' he asked. 'Did it not please you?'

'It pleases me very much.'

'Shall I continue?'

'Yes. It reminds me of the days by the sea. And when it is done will you recite the story of Deidre of the Sorrows?' she asked.

After the music he began to recite the story as it had been handed down to him. When it was over there was silence.

'Is there anything wrong?' he asked.

'Oh yes, there is. There is no love in my marriage and there is none but you I can speak to. I have been beaten and humiliated.'

He put his arms about her shoulders and she wept while he stroked her hair, his fingers fine and sensitive.

'What is love, Piper, and where does one find it?'

'I do not know. Once only did I find love with a woman. She was my wife, fair-haired and fair-skinned. We whispered all the endearments of love and then three weeks after our marriage she was thrown from her horse on the avenue leading to our house. I raised a tall obelisk to her on the spot where she died and I left my house and lands to become a piper. I have never been content or happy since.'

'Tell me of the joys of love and of its deep pleasure.'

'Do you wish me to tell you of these intimate things?' he asked.

'Yes.'

'Then come to me and I will tell you,' he said with a trembling

137

voice. 'You are a woman now and need to be told of these things.'

She sat on the floor and put her head and arms on his knees. He approached her body subtly, playing with her hair and face, whispering endearments in Irish. Tremors began to sweep through his body as he felt her shoulders and arms. He drew her up and kissed her.

'I have loved you all your life, Elinor. Did you know it? Could you not hear it in the music? It is always in the music. Now you are in my arms and I shake with delight.'

'Teach me the secrets,' she said. 'Let me know some joy.'

The Piper made love to her that night, love that was quiet and rapturous. She did not believe her body could take such pleasure in the man beside her.

Next morning he left with Tadhg Mor who had returned to bring him to Ballinrobe. All that day she felt a strange content within her body. She had become a woman and discovered the secrets of the flesh. She returned peacefully to the hotel on Monday.

There was a letter waiting for her from Sir Harry Christian and she decided to go immediately to the Brass Castle in Galway, Tadhg Mor escorting her.

She was familiar now with the city and enjoyed the sights of the trading streets, its waterfront and warehouses, its masted ships.

The Brass Castle was set on the peninsula facing the harbour. It was an eighteenth-century barracks which had been abandoned by the army. The derelicts, prostitutes and thieves took refuge there now. It was three storeys of grey limestone with small, grim windows, built around a quadrangle where the refuse was heaped in rotting middens. Fever often broke out here, killing the weak and infected. No one went near the building or left it while the fever ran its course. When it was over the bodies were buried in a communal pit close by the wall, then more derelicts took the rooms of those who had died. It had its own shebeen where only raw poteen was served. The prostitutes at the Brass Castle were old, their faces carrying the ravages of venereal disease. None of the soldiers ever ventured near this building.

Tadhg Mor looked at it curiously. Respectable people rarely approached its gates; it was a colony to itself with its own laws and dictums.

'I feel eyes have watched our approach for the last half hour,' Tadhg Mor said. 'I am sure that behind these small windows they are whispering and wondering why we are here.'

'What draws him to this wretched place?' she asked.

'The mind is a dark place. I have heard strange things at the hotel when drunken men confide in each other. They have made my hair stand on end at the evil that is in this world. I hear but I do not understand.'

They entered beneath an arch which was more like a wet tunnel, dismal and without light. The horses moved through the mud and emerged into a quadrangle. Children with adult eyes approached them.

A terrible stench caught their nostrils; Elinor thought it could be a metaphor for hell.

A broken-down soldier propped up by a crutch saluted them and shuffled away.

Tadhg Mor kept a sharp eye on all the doors leading on to the quadrangle, aware that their only escape would be through the gateway. After some time a rough, middle-aged man followed by a woman in a loud dress approached.

'We don't take kindly to strangers here. They break in on our privacy. We leave the outside world to them and they leave the Brass Castle to its own ways. So state your business and be on your way.'

He spat in front of Elinor to show the depth of his disregard for her.

'I'm seeking a man called John Dillon,' she said directly.

'He might be here and then he mightn't be,' a prostitute said in a brazen voice. Ladies did not often come to the Brass Castle and she wished to rile her. 'Of course you ladies of leisure don't take care of your husbands now, do you? Why, I believe you are the very lady couldn't be humped. Too clean, too sweet and your husband had to make his way to the Brass Castle to get the affection he couldn't get from his wife. Carrying the silver pistol, are you?'

'So you know my husband then?' she said, keeping a tight rein on her patience.

'Oh I know him. I know him in ways his wife never knew him.

139

Strange things men get up to. Of course, it costs and your husband was low in sovereigns when he arrived here. So, lady, if you are not willing to hand over twenty sovereigns for his board, I'm afraid that you may not see him again.'

'It's thirty sovereigns, lady,' the man added quickly. 'Not only has he enjoyed the company of our finest ladies, he has also been treated to our finest wines.'

'Bring him to me and I shall pay you,' she said.

'No, lady, you go and fetch him yourself. You see he's been drinking now for two whole weeks and I'm not certain he knows his own name.'

Others had emerged from the door, enjoying the baiting the lady on the horse was receiving.

'Very well. Lead us to the room. When I am sure that it is my husband I will pay his debts.'

They dismounted and followed the man and woman. They opened the door of an old prison.

She cried out when she saw her husband. His clothes were torn, his face bearded and his body soiled. He cowered like a frightened animal in the corner of the room as if he were afraid of the light.

'How long has he been in this condition?' Elinor asked.

'A week, maybe ten days. Yes, come to think of it, it was ten days. Could not keep him in good drink, he became boisterous and dangerous, so we had to put him in the prison. And of course we had to give him drink to keep him quiet. He called out through the bars like a caged animal.'

'And you did not send for help or enquire who he was?' Elinor said severely.

'Well, lady, once you come down here to the Brass Castle you keep our laws and no one here wants truck with the outside authority. We are what you might call a country to ourselves, a democracy,' the man said.

'Tadhg,' she directed, 'take him out of that cesspool.'

Tadhg Mor lifted John Dillon and carried him through the crowd to his horse. He rested the body behind the saddle and bound it to the animal. Then he returned to the door of the prison.

'I carry only twenty sovereigns with me,' Elinor told the leader. He looked suspiciously at her, the crowd about them becoming unfriendly.

'She distinctly said she had fifty sovereigns on her,' the old prostitute said. 'Why we would never have released her man had we known she had twenty. She has played us false.'

Tadhg Mor took the twenty sovereigns from Elinor's purse and with a wide sweep of his hand spread the money across the courtyard like evil seed. It glinted for a moment in the air then fell among the middens. The crowd followed its flight, then broke from the rough circle and went in search of it. In the confusion, Tadhg Mor hit the leader and knocked him to the ground.

'You have murdered Shaver,' the prostitute cried out, but no one paid attention to her.

Tadhg Mor helped Elinor on to her horse, then quickly mounted his own, making a dash for the gate guarding the tunnel. A man tried to close it before they were through but Tadhg Mor stooped down and tore him from the door, dragging him through the gutter and into a pool of filth.

They were out into the clear air, the scent of the sea in their lungs. The day was bright and the waves with white crests came evenly ashore on the strand.

When they reached the end of the bay, they discovered a small cove.

'I will wash the filth from his body,' Tadhg Mor said. He undid the rope, stripped off the filthy rags and plunged the semi-conscious man into the sea. The cold water stung John Dillon's mind into some type of coherence. Tadhg Mor plunged him beneath the waves, washing the grime and filth from his body. Then he carried him ashore, dried him and put on clean clothes which he had brought in a saddle bag.

'Man in his naked condition carries little beauty,' Tadhg Mor said as he placed him again behind the saddle.

They rode as quickly as they could through the countryside, keeping away from villages and towns. Six hours later they approached the small estate and by now John Dillon was raving, calling out for drink. A sweat had broken out over his body and he began to tremble.

'Thank you, Tadhg Mor,' she said when they entered the house. 'I do not know what I would have done without you. You have been with me through all the terrible moments of my life.'

'It is the darkness they talk about, the loss of innocence. The whores leave a man without taste and now he will never drink from clear water.'

'Then what shall I do?'

'You know what you must do and you will do it. Experience makes the mind as hard as iron. I will be always by your side, and for me you can do no wrong.'

They were strange words; she wondered if he knew she had lain with the Piper.

'Enough of talk,' Tadhg Mor said. 'I have seen this happen before and I know how to deal with it. I do not wish to have you close at hand until he becomes sober, so go to the hotel for a week.'

When she left the house, Tadhg Mor strapped John Dillon to the bed where he began to rave, calling out for drink. He drew on all his strength to tear off the leather thongs but Tadhg Mor only gave him mouthfuls of water. For three days John Dillon's imagination was assaulted by strange creatures who could chew on his substance. On the fourth day his mind and body became calm and on the fifth day he woke.

'What has happened?' he asked confusedly. Tadhg Mor remained silent, looking angrily at him. He undid the leather thongs but Dillon was almost too weak to sit up. Tadhg Mor brought him milk and buttered bread and signalled him to eat. Dillon rose from the bed and looked at his reflection in the glass, his face blotchy, rough with hair stubble.

He asked Tadhg Mor to leave him, give him time to think. He tried to bring the recent past together but could not gather in the images. He remembered being forced out of a hotel in Galway and making his way to the Brass Castle. He remembered an old whore laughing at him but then there was a blank. He looked at the leather thongs and the marks they had made on his wrists and feet. He called to Tadhg Mor.

'Did you go to the Brass Castle?' he asked.

Tadhg Mor nodded.

'And did my wife go with you?'

Tadhg Mor nodded again.

John Dillon returned to his room, his humiliation complete. He stared out of the window beyond the flat lake to Dillon Hall which he would never possess.

Matthew Dillon had not encountered his brother John since his marriage. He felt that he should have followed his mother's advice and sought a woman of property, someone from a similar background. Matthew had settled into a pleasant life. His brother had made a fatal mistake and would have to make do now with two hundred acres of land and a young woman who owned a hotel. He had disgraced his class.

Matthew Dillon had spent the night drinking in Tuam with some of the propertied young men of the country. He did not hurry home and twice he almost fell asleep on the saddle.

His mind was clear as he looked at the countryside about him. He did not possess his mother's pagan attachment to land but he did admire the layout of the country estates, their copses of trees, their parks where horses could be exercised, the cattle grazing in the pastures. He noted how the poor had moved on to the impoverished ground on the mountain flanks, taking what sustenance they could from wet, boggy soil. They were pale as ash, their arms and legs weak and brittle.

A bad winter followed by a wet spring could starve them out. The country always seemed to be on the verge of a famine; many peasants had become beggars, moving slowly along the roads in hungry groups.

He had little sympathy for them and could not understand his father or brother when they spoke of the rights of man. His mother had expressed a wish for him to marry; she would then hand over control of the estate to him.

As he neared the estate he decided to take a short cut home through the Convicts Field. The stone wall presented a formidable hurdle which his horse could take at a push. He lined him up with the wall then kneed his horse forward.

The animal failed to take the limestone wall, throwing Dillon from the saddle. He fell forward on to a rock with a jagged edge.

143

Bartley Gaynor found the body. It was obvious to him that he had bled to death.

'The field has been avenged,' he said simply.

The workers carried the body across the field and through the woods to the house. Robert Dillon and his wife looked on in silence as the men brought the body of their son into the hall and laid him on the great table. His face and hands were chalk-like in death.

Margaret Dillon made the immediate arrangements for the funeral. The Requiem Mass would be said in the chapel and his body carried to the family vault in the woods. That night she sat alone in her office. The tragedy left her mind dull. Her hopes for him had been great. He would have settled into the house, married a county woman and established the family in another generation. Her plans had failed and she suddenly felt old.

After much thought she found that she had no other alternative now than to deal with Elinor Dillon. Anger shook her when she thought that this woman of no breeding might rule the house as she once did. But when she reflected on the wide and fertile acres, the vast woods with their oak and ash, the fields which she had reclaimed, she knew that this woman could carry on the work and perhaps extend her achievements. She had presence and force and did not submit to another's will. They would have to meet and she knew that hard words would pass between them.

In his study Robert Dillon's despair was complete. He recalled the last time he had spoken with Matthew, over some trivial matter or other concerning his fishing rods. He had intended to spend a day with him on the lake fishing for trout, a pastime they both enjoyed. He could be certain that Matthew would have everything prepared for the occasion. He was the most dependable of his children, and he had looked forward to the day when he would bring a wife to the house. Man was the plaything of the gods and life had no logic. He drew out his days, ate, drank, slept, was stirred a little by intellect and then descended into the earth. It did not matter any more. And then he thought of his other son and his wife. Perhaps Elinor might now come to the house. He had grown attached to her. He would wait to see how his wife would act.

The Requiem Mass was celebrated in the small oratory. The air was thick with the scent of incense and candles. Many of the neighbouring landowners had come for the funeral, remaining in the hall while the Mass was in progress. They talked quietly among themselves, their murmurs concerning the future of John Dillon. It was common knowledge that he had been banished by his mother for marrying Elinor O'Donnell. Many of them were familiar with the gossip circulating in Galway, how his wife had rescued him from the Brass Castle and brought him home on horseback. They had watched both as they arrived for the funeral and were impressed by the presence of the young woman. She held her head erect and showed no outward sign of emotion.

Elinor Dillon knelt with her husband in the front prie-dieus. She felt that fate had drawn her back to Dillon Hall and during the chanting of the Dies Irae she wondered what lay in store for her. She was with child, telling her husband that it had been conceived after he had been carried home from the Brass Castle. He could not recall the occasion and he would never question the paternity of the child. If he bore suspicions he never declared them.

After Mass the coffin was carried down the avenue and through the woods, the long line of people following behind. Late autumn was approaching and leaves lay on the path. The procession passed close to the tranquil lake, quiet and windless. The coffin was brought down the steps of the mausoleum and placed with those of other Dillons. The family returned to the house as the masons proceeded to block up the vault. Margaret Dillon had expressed the desire to meet her daughter-in-law privately.

They sat opposite each other in the estate office. Elinor looked at the older woman as she eased herself into her chair, her face displaying dour sorrow; Matthew had been her favourite child. She would continue with the business of living as she always did. The solemn chants of the church, the thuribles and the incense had been offensive to her grief.

She looked sullenly at Elinor, aware that she would challenge anything she might say. There was a small tremor in the old woman's voice when she began to talk.

'You know my feelings for Dillon Hall and my expectations for my son Matthew. I have built this estate with my time and my mind and my energy. When I arrived here forty years ago the land was nothing. When I look about this room I see my life's work, inscribed line by line in the ledgers. I made the Dillon's prosperous. If there is money in the bank it is because I put it there with sweat and toil and I feel that it is mine to dispose of. I even visited their estates in France as a young woman and made certain that my son would one day inherit my brother-in-law's property. Like a general I planned each move but the last move did not come to fruition. Now I have to turn to you.'

Elinor did not take her eyes from her face while she spoke. A certain respect stirred within her.

'What if I do not accept your offer? I have lived without the Dillons and the Parrs for most of my life. Perhaps this estate should now collapse about you. Why should I take on the responsibility?'

'I have said nothing concerning the responsibility of the estate. I will not hand over the responsibility of the estate to anyone. I alone know how to run it. I could not accept a new authority in this house. You have not listened to my conditions,' she said testily.

'I do not have to listen to your conditions. I come here on my own conditions,' Elinor began angrily. 'It is time you passed over the running of the estate to a younger woman. I have the experience to run it and I have respect for it. I have gazed at this house from the far side of the lake like someone standing outside the gates of Paradise. There is no one else you can turn to.'

'What are your conditions?' Margaret Dillon asked wearily. The loss of her son had made her vulnerable.

'I move into the main section of the house with my husband. I have control of the servants and all matters relating to the finances of the estates. I wish to have complete knowledge of all bonds and ledgers and legal matters. I will accept your advice on most matters but all final decisions remain with me.'

'No. Never. I will not hand over my estate to a young upstart of a woman,' the old woman protested, rising stiffly from her chair.

'Sit down,' Elinor told her. 'I have accepted your insults. I will give you one hour to consider my offer. I shall walk in the avenue.

146

When I return I hope you will have come to your senses.'

She left the room, feeling a strange new power. An instinct told her that she would come into possession of the Dillon estates, that she would be lady of the house.

When she re-entered the office the old woman had a hopeless look in her eyes. She had obviously been crying at the humiliation she must now endure.

'I accept your conditions. The lands need all your attention. There is much to be done and it is a huge undertaking. My only request is that you sell the hotel; remember you are now a lady. Accept that condition and I will accept yours. The house and lands will pass to you. I will be here to advise you. But you must be tolerant with an old woman and the usages of time.'

'Very well. I will dispose of the hotel. It would be an encumbrance to me. I will have papers drawn up, transferring the house to my husband and I. Soon we will have an heir to these estates. I must leave now; there is much that I have to attend to and you have a son to grieve. Good day.'

She felt the taste of triumph. Her children would inherit the wide acres, the grand house. The sea and the white strand belonged to another woman and another memory.

The next three weeks moved swiftly for Elinor and John Dillon. The sudden responsibility that had been placed on her shoulders gave her a new urgency. She arranged for a solicitor to come from Galway and legal documents giving control of the estates to both her and her husband, were formally drawn up and signed. John Dillon's attitude changed towards his wife. He had watched her sit with the lawyer while she examined each clause of the agreement. What she did not understand she asked her husband to explain as they sat together during the autumn evenings. Together they rode through the estate and she became familiar with every field and wood. He felt proud of his wife. Not only was she beautiful and young but she had all the practical talents possessed by his mother.

She entered the house as mistress in October, when the woods were rich with colour and the lake had a clear sparkle on its surface. She had the family carriage sent to the house to pick her up.

'I intend to ride up the avenue like a new owner come to take possession. I have suffered too much both at your hands and the hands of the family to feel either compassion for your mother or any sense of humility. I will not bend to Dillon or Parr; my servitude is over,' she told her husband when the carriage arrived.

A new sense of purpose had entered her life. She was nineteen years of age, yet she looked much older.

Her husband rode beside her on his black horse, still uncertain of himself since his experience at the Brass Castle. Three weeks of his life were a blank and he could not recall what had happened.

When they reached the crescent in front of the house the servants and the tenants were waiting for them, dressed in their best clothes.

John Dillon opened the carriage door for his wife. She was introduced to each person on the estate, then formally entered the house to take possession. Robert Dillon came forward to meet her, placing his hands on her shoulders and kissing her warmly. She knew she had an ally in the house.

The shift of power at Dillon Hall did not go unnoticed by the Parr family. The conditions set down by the young woman were known in all the county houses.

'I have lived to see my sister pushed aside,' drawled David Parr, 'and by a young woman whom I'm told owned a hotel. The Dillons have fallen on bad days when a young woman of no background or breeding controls the fortunes of the house. I feel that we shall hear no more of them. The family will disappear as quickly as it arrived.'

He sat in the drawing room with his son Daniel, his face despite his age still sharply intelligent. His life had been a success. His family were growing up about him and his eldest son had a determined grip on the affairs of the estate.

'I do not think that John Dillon will further engage in politics. The man is a drunken sod who takes his pleasures with soldiers' women. Probably riddled with the pox by now,' Daniel commented.

They drank a toast to the declining fortunes of the Dillon family.

In this they had underestimated Elinor Dillon. The Hall exercised the same power upon her as it had done over Margaret Parr many years previously. The estates were certainly well cared for but Elinor found the servants had become careless about the house. The silver was tarnished, the curtains brown with years of soot, the kitchen where the food was prepared filthy.

She ordered all the servants to appear before her. She visited each room with them and explained in an authoritative voice what she expected from everyone. The dusty carpets were carried on to the lawn and beaten; the curtains taken down and washed in great tubs.

'Open the windows, let air blow through. The place needs freshening,' she told them, lifting up one of the sashes to demonstrate her resolution.

It took her fortnight to make the improvements. During that time everyone on the estate discovered that the house had a new mistress.

# Chapter 13

Winter came early in 1845. Elinor Dillon looked at the first fall of snow from her bedroom window. It came out of a grey sky, which hung low over the landscape. Soon she could see only the park beneath the window. At night when the lamps were lit, the flakes outside the window caught the glow and turned to gold.

Each morning she visited Robert Dillon before he settled to his work. She discussed with him what she had read and he listened, impressed and charmed by the young woman who had taken charge of the estate. She enquired about his work and became acquainted with the manuscript notes carefully arranged in huge volumes.

'It will never be finished you know. The subject is too broad and too serious,' he confided. 'I should have been less ambitious.'

'Of course you should be ambitious. This work is important. Even I can understand why you must continue,' she said firmly.

It took her three weeks to read the manuscript and become acquainted with Robert Dillon's handwriting. She read the work, folio by folio, and returned it to its place when she was finished. Some of the political ideas she did not immediately understand but she did enjoy its wide sweep and the characters who passed through its pages. Robert Dillon was eager for her opinion.

'I know that it is a wonderful book and I believe in it. I know each character. I know the rooms through which they passed. I have felt how they hated and loved. It has engaged my mind for three weeks. I can offer you no greater compliment,' she told him in admiration.

'You make me eager to finish it,' he said with unusual zest.

He took a sharp interest in all that she was doing about the house. When she needed advice about legal matters she now turned to him. He was shrewd in his assessment of events and people, looking beyond the estate walls to what was going on in the larger world. She listened eagerly when he told her the histories of the neighbouring estates and she became acquainted with all the fine details of the social web in which she would live.

'They have all something to hide. Do not be put off by studied manners; most of them are of yeoman stock.'

She discovered that he enjoyed gossip, wanting to know what was happening in the kitchen and on the estate.

He urged her to visit France with the enthusiasm of a young man. 'Your mother was French and you speak with a good accent. You must visit Paris and walk through the parks and the forests. The great châteaux still bear their former splendour. It will give you some idea how life was lived before the Revolution.'

'We intend to go there when my child is born, at the beginning of summer. We will take a coach all the way from the coast to the city. It is a promise made to me when I first met John.'

'Then I wish I could go with you,' he sighed deeply as an awareness of his mortality passed through his mind.

'I must leave you to your thoughts. I shall call on you before dinner and see how your work has progressed.'

Margaret Dillon only gradually relinquished her hold over the estate, her pride preventing her from yielding up her possessions and power so easily. Elinor insisted that the ledgers should be explained to her and she poured over the complicated pages until she became acquainted with every fact and figure. Her admiration for the old woman grew greatly but they could never become friends. There had been several scenes where the two women challenged each other in the presence of the servants. It was obvious to them that the young woman had taken firm command and that their best interests lay with her.

Her happiest days in the house were during that winter. She felt the child stir within her and looked forward to its birth. The relationship with her husband was detached. When she looked at him, she recalled the filth and degradation to which he had once succumbed. He seemed to forget that terrible experience, drinking heavily again, spending nights away with the soldiers' women.

Her child, a boy, was born in March, the delivery easy and without distress or pain. The first one to lift the child from its cradle was Robert Dillon. He looked at the small face, deep in the swadling clothes. He felt stirred at the fragile presence of the child. In his hands he held the continuance of the Dillon blood and name. With the unnamed child rested the fortunes of the house.

Margaret Dillon was less enthusiastic. She watched the baby being bathed, examining every line on its body. A strange suspicion that the child did not carry Dillon or Parr blood darkened her mind. She kept the suspicion to herself; there would be continuance of the name.

At the end of May they decided to set off for Paris.

'We will be away from here for some months. I must read every book on France in the library. We will plan the route together,' he told her excitedly. For hours they pored over the maps laid out on the library table, consulting travel books and guides to widen their knowledge. She saw her husband become in his enthusiasm the man she remembered at the hotel. Perhaps he would resume his interest in politics and his great talents might not be wasted.

The journey to France was a new experience for Elinor Dillon. When the carriage passed across the Shannon she felt the journey had begun.

In Dublin, they boarded a three-masted ship, rigged with buff-coloured sails which took them to Wales. She felt the sea rolling beneath them, listened to the crying of the wind and was reminded that her father had been a captain and the sea part of her blood.

The journey to London took four days. While her husband visited the Houses of Parliament she set out to discover the city for herself, hiring a cab and asking the driver to take her along the Strand. She was overwhelmed by the great population of the city.

She travelled by barge down to Greenwich, gazing in awe at the dome of St Paul's, the spires of innumerable churches, the movement of merchant ships drawing the wealth of the world into the city. Great brown warehouses stood by the waterfront, where gangs of men, numerous as ants, loaded and unloaded ships. It was a huge, energetic city which controlled the destinies of half the world.

After a week they journeyed to Dover. She was taken by the fertility and order of the land. The soil was a pale-yellow loam, and would run easily through the hand like sand. Here and there were hop fields and, always close by, the strange-shaped oast houses. They passed through fine pasture land on roads that were smooth and handsome.

The English farmers had an independent gait and expression, certain of their position in the landscape. John Dillon explained to her the laws under which they held their land and she compared them with the high rents and doubtful tenure under which Irish tenants lived. She began to question the rights of certain Irish landlords to own their lands.

When they boarded the ship at Dover she felt she was about to pass out of the influence of England and a strange sense of freedom filled her mind. Many passengers were French-speaking and she immediately engaged in conversation. When they discovered she was Irish they asked, 'And do they all speak French as well as you, Madame?'

'Oh no, my mother was French. She spoke French to me as a child.'

'Then you are one of us. We do not mix very well with the English. They refuse to learn our language and we refuse to learn their rough tongue.'

When she saw the buildings of Calais rise out of the doubtful

152

horizon she felt that she was returning home. She began to cry.

'It is strange but I feel I belong here, that this is my second country,' she told her husband.

She knew now why her mother insisted on speaking French with her and longed to set foot on French soil.

When she stepped on to the pier her lungs were filled with the strange scent of tar, timber and leather. She looked about her at the houses with their dutch roofs and wooden shutters. A gaunt fortress protected the city from attack by sea.

They stayed at the Hotel de France at the Place d'Armes. It had a restrained and elegant façade, the tall windows leading to balconies from which they could watch the square beneath. The bedroom was clean and uncluttered and the warmth of summer filled the place.

They spent the day visiting the town, enjoying the strange mannerisms of the people whose gestures seemed as important as their words. The dining-room windows were open to the square and they could watch the night activity of people who sat about tables and engaged in lightly quarrelsome conversation.

The wine they had drunk at dinner made her dreamy and soft. She thought perhaps she might make love to her husband but when they were alone in their room, the memory of the Brass Castle flooded into her mind and sensuality died within her.

Next day they set out for Paris, travelling at their leisure, breaking off at various towns on the way. Four days later they reached the capital.

They made their way through the Bois de Boulogne towards Ville D'Avrey, a quiet town on the edge of the city, set between two long hills. The road through this town led towards Versailles. Within a day's riding distance from this small town lay La Celle de Malmaison, where Josephine had lived and where Napoleon had spent his last days before going into his lonely exile. St Germaine was in the neighbourhood as were the woods of Saint Cloud, where Robert Dillon had talked with Marie Antoinette.

They passed through ornate gates hung on staunch pillars which a peasant shut behind them. They felt that they were entering an enclosed place. The avenue to the house led between formal trees, erect and trained. In the distance they could see the outline of an eighteenth-century building, designed to please the eyes. As they neared the house, the trees gave way to impressive classical gardens, geometric hedges, flowerbeds and a maze of alleyways. The château itself had been inspired by Mansard. Each relief and window was restrained and there was a delicate play between all the parts.

They looked in awe at the façade; Dillon Hall was bleak and featureless in comparison to this château. A liveried servant rushed down the shallow steps in front of the main door to greet them.

'You have been expected for some time now. I'm afraid Monsieur Edward Dillon attends to business in the south and it will be a few days before he returns. He bids me make you welcome. Madame Dillon is riding in the forest but will return at two for lunch.' He clapped his hands and immediately another servant appeared and took their baggage.

'If you follow me I shall show you to the right wing of the house which has been set out for you during your visit.'

Elinor thanked the servant who was surprised at her fluency in French. They followed him into a large parquet hall with a marble staircase leading to the first storey, observing the beauty of the interior as they ascended. Everything was so different from the English style of architecture: the ceilings and doors bore light plasterwork, touched with gold leaf, and the paintings were bright and without severity. When they reached the room they looked at each other in wonder.

'The descriptions given by your father are weak in comparison with the house itself. It is larger than I expected the more palatial,' Elinor Dillon said to her husband.

'It belonged to a royal prince who lost his foolish head during the Revolution. My uncle was a practical man who enjoyed the comforts of life and took pleasure in tangible things,' he told her.

'All this could have been yours,' she said, looking at him. 'By right of succession it belongs to you. It is a place of immense beauty and wealth. It was meant for you and you would always be happy here.'

'One cannot change the past. I did not follow the rules. My way of life at the time the decision was made was more suited to the bogs and racecourses than to running a French estate. My brother seemed a most suitable choice at the time.'

'Would you have liked the soft life of a French château?' she asked him one morning.

'Of course I have thought about it, but I made all my mistakes at the wrong time. I have read my uncle's letters to my father. He described precisely what person he wished to take over these estates. Edward fitted the formula. He was chosen and educated for the role.'

'Well, I think they made the wrong choice,' she declared vehemently, looking at his fine head and intelligent eyes. She put her arms about him, feeling a rare pity and understanding.

He stroked her hair, looking beyond her shoulder to the gardens below. His wife was correct; all this could have been his.

'Perhaps I am unlucky,' he said. 'I wonder if I should have come at all. My French is faulty and I express myself awkwardly.'

'Of course you should have come. You will enjoy the château and Paris itself. We can ride together in the forests. Your father has told me all about them and I am eager to see them,' she said encouragingly.

'Both of us could have been happy here, Elinor. I know it in my heart. Our life would be free of the constraints of living in Connaught.'

She let him weep quietly, pushing him gently away when there was a knock at the door and a servant entered with refreshments.

After they had eaten, he took her hand in his. 'Did you know there is a codicil to my uncle's will which states that if there is no issue from my brother's marriage, these estates will revert to our son?' He said it in a thoughtful way, as if the sight of the château stirred some thoughts of ultimate possession in his mind.

'No. I did not know that. Your mother never told me.'

'Perhaps it will never happen but they have been married now for some years and have no children. Our child is the only issue from my generation.'

For a moment she wondered if he doubted her fidelity to him. It remained as a scruple at the back of her mind but she assured herself that there was no way he could suspect that the Piper had been the father of her son.

At three o'clock Louise Dillon returned from riding through the forests. She was a slender, confident figure and they could see the strong wrist with which she controlled the horse. Elinor gazed intently at her face and even at a distance she could see her arrogance. When the servant helped her off the horse she did not even acknowledge his presence.

She met them two hours later after a rest. Her body and her features had the hard qualities of diamond, her gestures were precise and dismissive. As she approached them in a light satin gown, Elinor felt badly dressed. Her clothes were more suited to the hard climate of Connaught.

'You are welcome. I hope you shall have a pleasant time here.' She spoke in slow French, hoping that they would understand her.

'Thank you for your hospitality. My husband and I are delighted to be here,' Elinor began, impressing her hostess with her fluency. Louise Dillon's initial hauteur softened a little.

'Have you my husband's passion for horses?' she asked, embarking on a subject which was obviously of primary interest to her.

'Yes, both of us have a great interest in horses. Dillon Hall has produced several winners and my husband is reckoned to be one of the finest horsemen in Connaught.'

'Then you will have to see our stables. We once bred horses for Napoleon's generals but now we are interested in racehorses. We have had several winners at Chantilly.'

The conversation continued in a brittle fashion until she excused herself, saying she had to attend a reception at Saint Cloud. They decided to walk in one of the avenues which radiated from the house.

'And what impressions did she make upon you?' John Dillon asked his wife.

'Trivial and remote. She is obviously from some important family or other and has a very high regard for her own whims. I think she felt obliged to entertain us but to her we are inferior strangers from the edge of the world. She did not even enquire after your brother's death.'

'I have rarely found you so sharp or less charitable,' he told her, placing his arm in hers. It was evening and the wind was soft, bearing the scents of the dry forest floor.

'It is a delightful and soft culture,' he said, after they had walked in silence for some time.

'One feels that the Revolution of which your father writes so passionately never happened,' she reflected as they passed into a formal garden.

'There is a new aristocracy in France now. They are the bourgeoisie and I can assure you they will never permit a revolution again. Napoleon's soldiers marched to Russia for all this. My uncle made a fortune from his wars and purchased this château and these lands. They are as corrupt, perhaps more corrupt, than those they replaced. The French aristocrats were spoiled children, whereas these are calculating men who will not let their possessions slip easily from them. Inequality will always remain, there will always be a gatekeeper at the lodge to open and close gates.'

'But your father believes that there will be such a revolution in Ireland. It may not be as bloody but some day the great estates will be divided up,' she told him.

'So we must take warning.'

'Yes. I believe that he is correct.'

'Are you becoming political?'

'I am learning about politics. Your father is a wise man in his own way.'

'I know. He is also a dreamer. He needs somebody to put his ideas and his thoughts into reality .'

She was surprised at how astute and cynical her husband could be when his mind was clear.

Each morning two horses were brought to the front of the château with food and wine carefully placed in the saddlebags. They spent the day pleasantly discovering the woods. They left the estate and rode to the small village inns where they ate under awnings in the squares.

They expected Edward Dillon to return every day. He had sent a message from Limoges explaining that he had been detained by some wine merchants. He was waiting for them one evening when they returned from a trip to Versailles.

He threw his arms about his brother's shoulders and they patted each other on the back. Elinor noted that Edward did not bear any resemblance to John, as if he had been born into a French family.

'This is my wife,' John Dillon said, introducing Elinor. He was surprised both by her beauty and youth. He looked intently at her for a moment then kissed her on both cheeks.

'But come, there is much you have to tell me,' he said, leading them up the shallow steps. 'I wish to hear of my brother's death. It shatters one's belief in one's own immortality. It brought back our childhood together on the lake and in the woods and much that I thought I had forgotten returned to me. But let us speak of pleasanter things. How would you like to spend your leisure moments, Elinor?'

'I should like to go to the paddock and look at the foals,' she told him.

'Good. And I shall make it interesting for you. I have not given you a wedding present. Pick out one of the yearlings. There are twenty in the paddock. The yearling of your choice is yours. I have a ship sailing to Galway and it will be delivered at the dock for you.'

She felt such a present was a patronizing gesture of his wealth. He had also offered her a challenge and she would accept it. She knew that he was interested in her, guessing that probably he had received a letter from his mother concerning her marriage. She would have to prove her own worth.

She tried to determine the nature of his character, finding him dismissive, even remote. He was aware that already a child had been born to them who would control the destinies of the Dillons in Ireland and perhaps some day in France.

She did not realize that he had been sharply taken by her beauty. There was an expression in her eyes which deserved to be respected, and he found her company interesting. Her thirst for knowledge seemed endless and she took fresh pleasure in everything about her.

As she walked down towards the paddock she could not know that the fortunes of Dillon Hall would depend upon her choice of yearling.

They were all strong-boned animals, every line suggesting good breeding. She watched them cavort for two hours. Her father had put her on a horse as a young child and she had an instinct for a good animal. She rested her arms on the fence and looked keenly at them. It was late in the evening that she became aware of their personalities, and that one stood out from all the others. He had a finely chiselled head and neat nostrils. Above all his eyes were intelligent.

She opened the gate and went across the paddock to the yearling. He turned shyly away from her but he noticed all her movements. She took some corn she had scooped from a barrel and offered it to him. He turned towards her and licked it from her hand. While she patted his forehead he began to nuzzle her shoulder affectionately. There was an understanding between them. She took him by the mane and led him up the path and around to the front of the house.

The two brothers broke from their conversation, rising from their chairs.

'This is my choice,' she said simply.

The next three weeks passed quickly between visits to Paris and a journey to the south. They stayed in the Château of Vouvray and travelled through the famous vineyards from where the Dillon wealth was derived. John Dillon rose every morning before daybreak, washing in the barrel in the yard filled with grape scents. Before Elinor sat down to her breakfast he had already spent three hours riding through the countryside. He took a keen interest in the work of the vineyard and on one occasion spent all day working with the men. He bronzed under the southern sun and had the healthy appearance of a labourer. And at evening he sat with the men and drank their wine and ate their bread.

Elinor had many happy memories of the south of France. She recalled later the innumerable fires in the vineyards at night. Men set out stoves and spent the night keeping them alight in order to ward off the dangerous frost which could destroy the young crop before it had flowered. She remembered the peasants dancing as they passed through a village at night.

Edward Dillon reserved his greatest display of wealth for the final night before their departure, throwing a lavish party for his bourgeois friends. They were polite, refined and informed. Their gestures were restrained, their clothes expensive and they belonged to a new age. They represented the merchants and the professional men of France. Edward Dillon was at ease in this company. He introduced Elinor to the men, surprising them with her beauty. She danced happily to the music of an orchestra but noticed there was one person who did not seem to belong there. He had a lame step and the expression of a conspirator. Edward Dillon took him to his private office for an hour and when they emerged it was obvious that the lame man was carrying correspondence in his pocket. He left in a carriage bound for Paris and Edward Dillon was pleased by his departure.

John Dillon left the château with reluctance. His brother clasping him in his arms for a moment before they said their final goodbyes. He turned to Elinor, an expression of affection in his eyes.

'You must come again. Do not let this be your last visit. You have taken to France and I know that I have taken to you. Let me know how the yearling performs.' He kissed her, not on the cheeks as she had expected, but on the lips.

Elinor continued to look back at the château as the carriage went down the avenue. Outside the railings, she had the coachman stop so that she could take a final look at it.

'Have no worry. We will return. I promise,' John Dillon told her.

'I have spent the most delightful days of my life here,' she said.

## Chapter 14

Daniel Parr considered the evidence. It was not only circumstantial, it was also incredible. At the time he had accepted that his brother's death was accidental; now he had to decide if he had been murdered.

'I want you to try and remember every detail of what happened

160

on that night,' he told the man who stood before him. He had been one of his brother's bullyboys who had fallen on bad times. His face was gaunt and it was obvious that he was hungry. Twice he had been in jail for petty larceny.

Holding the rim of his cap tightly between nervous fingers he went over events of that night. It was obvious to Parr that he could not have left the Lodge. There had been somebody else present that night.

'And you have no idea who attacked you?'

'No, my lord, but he came up from behind and gave me an awful skelp on the head which knocked all the sense out of me. The trace of the wound is still on the back of my head if your lordship would like to examine it.'

'I have no desire to see the back of your head. I believe you,' Daniel Parr said irritably.

'Whoever they were they came from the direction of the mountain. They must have been able to see in the dark for you could easily get lost there at night. And another strange thing that didn't make much sense to me. The barrel of water in the kitchen was turned over. I've been thinking a lot about it and I thought I would come and tell your lordship what I knew in the hope that he might be favourable to me,' he ended obsequiously.

'Have a meal in the kitchen but keep this matter to yourself. You may stay in the Hoban cottage and we will find some work for you. You may go,' he said dismissively.

'I'm most grateful to your lordship and if anything else comes into my mind, sure I will come and tell you. But the belt rattled my head and I'm not the better of it yet. Sometimes I see double,' he said plaintively.

'That will do. Good day.'

'I often wonder if the young woman had anything to do with it,' he muttered, moving to the door.

'What young woman?'

'The woman they brought to the house that night, the sea captain's daughter. He was going to have his way with her.'

'And where is this young woman now?' he asked, his eyes narrow with interest.

161

'I don't know. But when I got back a little of my sense she had left the place.'

'Why did you not tell me all this before?' he asked sharply.

'Sure, we agreed among ourselves not to say a word about the woman. It was not a thing you would want known.'

The man returned from the door, knowing he had caught Daniel Parr's interest and that if he played with a faulty memory it might be of some value to him.

Left to himself Parr got up from his chair and walked to the window. He was sure now that his brother had been murdered. He wondered where the young woman had gone. He immediately contacted Damien Egan, the Galway solicitor who was favoured by Daniel Parr and carried out much of the military legal business. He required him to discover who the young woman had been.

Six days later he received a long letter giving him every detail which he needed. Her former name had been Elinor O'Donnell and she was married to John Dillon. He found it strange that she was protected by a mute called Tadhg Mor. He discussed the matter with his son.

'The evidence points to them. She saved the man from the sea and he keeps a vigilant watch over her. It must be true. Should the case be reopened?'

'No. It will serve no purpose. Your brother was a burden around my neck and his death was welcome to me. But remember that a Parr was murdered by a Dillon and when you have the opportunity of revenge, make sure it is hard.'

Johnny Appelby had worked for the Dillons for fifty years. He had been their principal jockey and had broken several bones during his steeplechase career. Now he lived in a small, two-roomed cottage at the end of the estate, on the edge of activity. Each day he came down to the stables early in the morning and made his way from one door to the other, looking at the horses and calling out their names. He had an uncanny knowledge of their temperament and could communicate with them.

He kept a close eye on Tony Buckley, the shy young stable-hand who suffered a speech impediment. The others often laughed at him but Johnny Appelby had watched him groom the horses, handling them with gentleness. Starting with the hocks he would curry every hair on the horse's body in a slow curved motion. Then with a rub rag he would wipe the dock, ears, head and eyes, always moving with the hair of the horse. The most nervous animal became compliant to his touch. But it was when he swung himself up on a horse that he was transformed, his eyes intelligent, his manner certain. When he took a horse to the Round Field for training he showed his instinctive ability.

Elinor Dillon had watched Johnny Appelby working with the horses. He had a small body, a sharp head like a bird, and a limp. She asked Robert Dillon who the old man was who smelt of horses and was always in some stall or other looking at the animals.

'I knew him as a young man and I have great affection for him. He has courage and understanding of an animal. He could have won every steeplechase in Connaught but he was drunk more often than sober during the races. My wife banished him from his position as head of the stables because of this weakness. He is on a small retainer's pay. I often meet him on my walks. He still believes that he can train a winner.'

'And can he?' she asked.

'I believe he can but he will break your heart. He will work religiously for a month and then he will take to the drink and turn up a week later full of gracious apologies or with some unbelievable story about the death of a relative whose wake he had to attend.'

One day she encountered him in one of the stables, sitting on a bundle of hay with a bottle to his mouth. As soon as she entered he jumped to his feet, rubbed his mouth, looking at the blue bottle in surprise.

'It's my chest. The hayseed tears my chest and if I don't have a drop of medical aid I can't do a decent day's work,' he told her.

'And did you obtain the medicine at the medical hall?' she asked, suppressing a smile.

'What do they know about medicine? This medicine was handed down in our family for ten generations and it has never failed. I have no truck with the medical hall and I have never been in one all my life. That is why I'm so healthy,' he argued.

'I've come to you for advice,' she asked directly.

163

'Advice,' he repeated, taken by surprise. He assumed his most important air.

'Then, Lady Elinor, you have come to the right man. If Lady Margaret had taken my advice then indeed we would have had more winners to our name. But no. I was relegated and a heart scald it has been. I am at your service with the best advice there is.'

'I know all about you,' she began.

'Most of it lies,' he interjected.

'I know all about you,' she began again, 'you have a bad reputation with regards to drink but many think very highly of you as a horse trainer. Now who do you think is the best jockey in the stable?'

'A young lad named Tony Buckley. You wouldn't give him tuppence to see him walk or try his hand at sport but he's the one to bring home a winner,' he told her. 'He knows what the horse is thinking like I did myself when I was his age. And he never abuses a horse. He has the nature for the animal.'

He was pleased that she had sought out his advice. Margaret Dillon had treated him like the lowest servant but this young woman had a different manner of handling men. Now he felt he might re-instate himself at the yard.

When she returned from England she sent Johnny Appelby and Tony Buckley to Galway to bring the horse home. She took the old man aside before their departure and talked severely to him.

'Upon my solemn oath, Lady Elinor, but not a drop of drink will pass my lips until I have delivered the horse to the stables.'

When they took delivery of the horse at Galway they both felt that they had seen nothing like him before in their lives.

They walked him through the city, one at each side of the head, the same idea was going through both their minds.

'Of course we don't have to be home for three days,' Johnny Appelby suggested, sniffing.

'Lady Elinor will have our lives. Remember you promised to behave.'

'That I did, but that promise was made concerning drink. Now it's my considered opinion that this horse needs some light exercise and then should be stabled up and fed. I know a man this side of Tuam who has a good stable and strange as it might seem a good

164

paddock and some fences and he wouldn't be beyond giving us a saddle if you get my drift.'

'Too well I get it and I don't like it,' Tony answered fearfully.

'Trust Johnny Appelby.'

They brought the horse to the farm, watching him with appraising eyes.

'He's a certain flyer. I'm thinking to myself that we are looking at the winner of the Chester Cup. It's a race I always had set my heart on but no horse had the heart or the temperament for it. Given the right training he'll leave the field behind.'

That evening while Tony Buckley groomed the horse, Johnny Appelby broke his promise. He disappeared with a friend to reminisce about the old days and when he reappeared he was well and truly drunk.

'Now we will all be in trouble,' the young boy complained.

'My constitution couldn't take the shock I got when I saw the horse. Sure if it were a normal horse I'd be normal.'

'That's a lame excuse.'

The boy was troubled by nightmares. He was riding the horse at a high fence when it fell awkwardly and broke his neck. People were blaming him for the accident and Johnny Appelby was beating him with a large cudgel. He started awake, sweat soaking his clothes.

The next day he approached the horse, placing a pad on his back and sliding the saddle forward. The keen eye of the horse observed his movements, then he bucked and threw the saddle off his back, surprising the boy. He left the saddle on the ground and patted the horse on the forehead, holding its nose in his hands. The horse nodded his head slowly up and down, enjoying the comfort of the touch.

After some minutes he took the blanket and the saddle and placed them on the horse's back. He secured the strap and mounted. What happened next was amazing both to the boy and Johnny Appelby. The horse with some inner instinct began to run around the paddock. Rider and horse seemed to move in the same rhythm, and at great speed. Johnny Appelby checked the pace against the field posts, and knew then that the horse possessed extraordinary powers.

'Pegasus is the name for that horse for he is quick as the wind. I'd swear on St Patrick's Bible that's the fastest horse I've ever seen draw breath. Should we try him on jumps? I feel he would take them as easily as a bird.'

'No,' the young boy said, rubbing the horse down carefully. 'I'm not going to take him across a jump until Lady Elinor tells me to. If she knew that we had him saddled and in the paddock running it would mark the end of us.' Johnny Appelby walked about the horse while he groomed it, looking at each line and muscle.

'He will bring fortune to the house properly rode and properly backed. Had I my years back again, lad.' He sat down on a stump of tree, and knowing this was always the opening to his long stories, the young boy let him talk.

It was late that evening when they entered the stable yard at Dillon Hall. The labourers had left and only some of the maid-servants noticed the arrival of the horse. They were about to bring him into his stable when Elinor arrived.

She had the young boy walk the horse about in a circle, looking at the animal with a careful eye. He had grown lean from the journey but would quickly regain weight. His eyes shone with intelligence and she felt that he recognized her.

'And what do you think of this horse, Johnny Appelby?'

'Oh man, he's a right flyer. He's a Pegasus surely.'

'But how can you say he's a Pegasus if you have not seen him run?' she asked shrewdly.

'I have a way of looking at a horse walk, Lady Elinor, to know the way he'll run.'

'Did you run the horse?' she asked sharply.

'I had to, Lady Elinor. When I saw him in the quarantine in Galway and looked at him I knew that I was looking at the best horse ever bought into the Dillon yards. I had to test him. I'm sorry.'

'And what did you find?'

'I may drink, Lady Elinor, and I break my promises. I have pulled horses because I've laid bets on the side but I know a good horse when I see one. This is the greatest horse I've ever seen. He was born to run and born to win. You picked a champion when you picked him. When the young lad mounted him, sure they took to

166

one another. I've lived to see the day when I'd bring such a horse to Dillon Hall.'

His face was serious and there were tears in his eyes. His life had been devoted to the horses and stables and his knowledge had been born of long experience. She considered Johnny Appelby and the boy for a minute.

'How fast is he?' she asked.

'Like lightning. There is none faster.'

'Then no one must know,' she said slowly. 'I am placing you both in charge of this horse. He will be trained in the Round Field so that nobody knows either his speed or his temperament. You will not tell anyone about his training. For the moment you have brought an ordinary horse to the stables. Can you both keep that promise?'

'Yes, Lady Elinor,' they said together.

'Johnny Appelby, you are now trainer of Pegasus. This may be the greatest year in your life. If I find you drunk or talkative then you will never enter this stable yard again.'

Her voice had the stern ring of authority and he understood that she meant what she said.

'I'll give up the drink and stay sober until after the race. I'll make the promise on my mother's grave.'

When Johnny Appelby left the yard, it was deep summer twilight, the air rich and heavy with the dust pollen. The woods were quiet except for the hollow cooing of pigeons, the sound of their wings through the branches as they took quick flight.

In his cabin he drew up his armchair to the empty fire, his memory filled with the voices and images of the past. He recalled the neglected years at the stables when Margaret Dillon would not let him near the horses. Now he was getting a second chance. He drew off his clothes and went to bed, the thunder of hooves ringing in his mind.

The Round Field was set in woodland, some miles from the estate. Around the edge was a run some twelve feet wide where horses sometimes did their training before a flat race. Now it was reserved for Pegasus.

The kitchen staff and some of the labourers wondered why such secrecy surrounded the new horse or why Johnny Appelby, so long banished from the stables, had suddenly become a trainer again.

'The mistress has little sense letting that scoundrel near a horse,' Mrs Costigan told the labourers when they gathered into the long kitchen for their dinner. 'He'll be all grand notions and talk and there will be no standing him at all.'

'And the young fellow will have airs. Imagine Mrs Buckley's scut put in charge of a single horse,' one of the stable boys complained. 'We are ordered to have nothing to do with the horse. With Johnny Appelby and the scut Buckley who can barely pronounce his own name in complete charge of the horse there is no chance of him even getting near a starting line. And no one can tell me either his dam or his sire. If Lady Margaret had the running of the place Johnny Appelby wouldn't be let within an ass's roar of the yard.'

Johnny Appelby knew of the hostility towards him and remained silent. He was sober and both he and Tony Buckley had the horse groomed and saddled before the house was awake.

When the horse and rider began a slow canter around the edge of the field, Johnny Appelby could only see the animal's head and the boy's arched body. It had a visionary quality that held him in awe. Only the thudding sounds of hooves coming off the bend shook him from his reverie.

They both realized the horse's temperament was almost perfect.

'He must have some fault,' Johnny Appelby said the first morning they led him into the great field. He discovered that he hated soft ground. His feet seemed to stick to the surface of the track and there was no spring in his legs. But when they tested him on the hard course he seemed to barely touch the ground. When they put him to the test they knew that there were few horses to beat him.

'He has a great heart but we must not extend it. We'll teach him to keep with the others until the last furlong. When you give the word and ease him forward, that will be the moment when he must run like the wind and he will be faster than any other horse I know.'

A week later Elinor Dillon visited the Round Field, elegant on her grey horse. She watched Pegasus during his final run and smiled with delight when she saw his performance.

'Well, Johnny Appelby, did I choose well?'

'None will come near him, but we cannot race him in any race. The first time will have to be at Galway because if news of his speed gets out, every penny on the course will be on him.'

'Why do you think I brought him to the Round Field and want you sober until the race is over?' she asked. 'Nobody, not even the men in the yard, must know of his speed. You must keep him in training for six months.'

'He'll be in fine fettle, Lady Elinor. This is my last chance with a great horse; I feel that I was born for these months.'

Autumn passed into winter, but Johnny Appleby barely noticed the frost arrive or depart, his mind was always on the horse. In March when the great lawn was a yellow flare of daffodils, he knew it was time to test the horse in Galway.

They set out five days before the races, walking the horse the forty miles to Galway in easy stages, putting up each night at a farm with a paddock. Each morning Pegasus had a light training and then they moved out on to the road. Their final night was spent with James King, a recluse who reared pointers and setters and spent his lonely days in the Curragh marshland. Two men and the boy gathered around a peat fire anxious for what the next day would bring.

John and Elinor Dillon had taken a room at King's Hotel on Ayre Square, settling in the day before the race. At eight o'clock their carriage took them to Ayre House for the annual ball. It was an occasion when the Connaught society was seen to its best advantage. When Elinor entered the ballroom, there seemed to be a pause as men watched her walk to their table. Even the women were struck by the beauty of the hotel owner who had married John Dillon, placating their jealousy with the thought that she was their social inferior.

When the Parr party arrived it was evident that there could be trouble. The old man strode vigorously across the wide maple floor followed by his son and Maud Dillon. After dinner the orchestra began to play and the couples moved on to the floor. Daniel Parr could not take his eyes off Elinor Dillon.

*Was this woman the cause of my brother's death?* he thought to himself. He noted that she seemed to have learned the social graces and could carry herself well. During a waltz with her husband, he deliberately bumped into her and she fell forward on to her husband.

'A fallen lady,' he cried out in a loud voice. She steadied herself and came forward to where he stood.

'Did I hear you correctly?' she asked.

'I merely stated that you were a fallen lady,' he said in a haughty voice, 'who has found herself in company beyond her station.'

She hit him with the palm of her hand and he staggered backwards, his mouth open in surprise.

'How dare a reprobate insult me,' she cried indignantly. 'One of the Map Cap Parrs who thinks he can strut through Connaught as if he had some divine right to the possession of all lands and all people. He is merely a Cromwellian spore is an evening suit.'

'Enough, Elinor,' her husband said, trying to draw her away. A circle had formed about them anxious for the excitement and scandal.

'It is not enough. Others may fear Parr but not I.'

'You shall regret this, lady. You have made a grave mistake,' Daniel Parr called out.

'I have made no mistake and I have no regrets. I challenge you to a wager. What odds will you give me on my horse?' she asked.

'Ten to one,' he said, angrily. 'Your horse is untried on any course.'

'If you are so certain of winning, give me fifteen to one,' she challenged.

Daniel Parr was hesitant but could not back out of the wager.

'Very well.'

'Then I bet a thousand guineas on Pegasus.'

'Your money is already lost,' he sneered. 'A Dillon could never outrun a Parr horse even without weights.'

'The bets are taken, the challenge is set. We will meet at the races.'

She left, followed by her husband and immediately the story of what had happened passed through the hall. Within three hours it was known all over Galway, giving excitement to the night and an anticipation of the next day and its outcome. An unknown woman who owned an untried horse had challenged Daniel Parr

170

in the Galway plate. In the hotels and taverns no other subject engaged so much attention. Nobody had seen or heard of the horse Pegasus.

At their town house the Parrs considered the challenge. The bets had been placed publicly and their pride was at stake. Daniel Parr had been vicious towards the servants since he came down to breakfast. Twice he went upstairs to change his clothes for the race meeting. His father considered the bet and he wondered if this woman had some certain knowledge of which they were unaware. He knew the form of all the other horses in the race. One or two night have given an outside challenge but the Gold Plate would certainly be his for another year. But perhaps he had underestimated Elinor Dillon. He reflected that this woman was the cause of his brother's murder. Beneath her calm and young exterior there was cunning and strength. The feud which for so long had favoured the Parrs could quickly go against them. A dangerous opponent had entered the Dillon ranks.

'We must get to the course and see the form of this Pegasus,' his son said crossly.

'It would show weakness. That in itself would be a victory for the Dillons. No, preserve your dignity. There is no way this horse can win. The woman acted in anger. I pressed her into the challenge.' He spoke confidently but within himself was uncertain about the result of the race.

At the racecourse the crowd cheered the passing carriages, filled with wonder at being so close to those they feared. None was more feared than the Parrs.

'God bless your lordship,' one of his labourers cried out, 'and may that Pegatry only see the tail of Silvia. God bless your lordship and may good luck shine on you and the winds of prosperity blow in your face.' But when the carriage had passed the labourer cursed him in his heart.

Finally the Parrs reached the patron's enclosure. They made their way to the second storey of the stand where they had a sweeping view of the race and the lands beyond stretching as far as Lough Corrib.

'How do you fancy the chances of this Pegasus, my lord?' Thomas Severn asked.

171

'None at all,' he said firmly. 'I have not seen the animal and neither has anyone in the field. All the horses are in the paddock and this marvellous beast has not arrived. I wonder if he is the figment of this mad young woman's imagination.'

He might have continued talking but there was a loud shout from the crowd. Suddenly all eyes were turned towards the paddock entrance where a horse was being led in by Johnny Appelby. A young insignificant-looking jockey sat in the saddle. But then people looked at the elegant horse. His head was held high and his lines were perfect. Daniel Parr was shocked.

'Where did they buy her? How was I not informed that such an animal existed?' he asked angrily of his father.

'How should I know? He has not raced on any Irish track and he is not in the sale book.'

'Then this young women has set a trap for us. He looks like a winner to me.'

'But he has not been tested.'

'Does he have to be tested?'

'Quickly get a word to the jockey. Let him use his stick to blind the rider. Tell him to cut at his eyes.'

The message was sent to the jockey as they made their way down to the starting post. Excitement was mounting and everywhere men's eyes followed Pegasus. They were sharp judges of a horse and this young horse had the qualities of a winner, making the rest look like jaded hacks.

They lined up at the post, the horses edgy and reined into obedience by the riders. The line broke and reformed. The horses' eyes were wide with urgency. Tony Buckley patted Pegasus on the neck and did not see the Parr jockey bear down upon him. With a quick swish he cut at the young boy's face, drawing blood from the forehead, which streamed into his eyes. He tried to wipe it away from his face but could not see the judge to know when he drew down the flag. When the signal was given he remained confused. The horses were thundering down the course in front of him. He wiped away the blood and saw hooves cutting up the sods before him.

'Now Pegasus, move for I'm no good to you. Move and win for Lady Elinor,' he cried. He sat grimly in the saddle and gave the horse free rein. Pegasus started off down the field a length behind. it took him some time to gain his stride and find his position. The crowd immediately dismissed his chance; he had been an outsider from the beginning. They wondered what all the fuss and rumours were about. They urged on the Parr horse as they pressed against the rail. At even money he was a certainty and it would be a bad day for the bookies. As the horses settled in to their stride, Pegasus moved up and caught the last horse.

What happened next was spoken of at the Galway meetings by generations of racegoers. The crowd kept their eyes on the Parr horse, a length ahead of the field. Tony Buckley wiped the blood again from his eyes and took stock of his position. He knew that Pegasus was penned in and could not move forward. He saw an opening and drew him out from the main body, knowing that he was losing precious seconds. Pegasus felt an urgency and a challenge. He must run as he ran in the Round field. He quickly accelerated into full speed and the crowd turned to the outsider. He was making a challenge. Perhaps the rumours were correct.

The other horses seemed stolid as Pegasus moved forward, passing horse after horse. He remained on the outside, distinct from the others who hugged close to the rails. Now the crowd were calling to him, the Parr horse out of favour. He was already leading when they entered the straight. The Parr horse was ahead, breathing heavily, slowing a little like the rest. Pegasus never lost his pace, hearing the acclamation of the crowd as he passed the stand. He was twenty yards ahead of the Parr horse. The crowd roared and threw their hats in the air.

Daniel Parr watched grimly as victory turned into defeat. He could feel that the crowd were in favour of Elinor Dillon.

'That horse will have to be destroyed,' he said. 'I have been humiliated and deceived.' He ordered his coach and left the field.

The victory was total and sweet. Johnny Appleby wept, taking a bottle of whisky from his pocket to celebrate. Everything he had ever dreamed of had happened.

'He won the race on his own,' Tony Buckley told Elinor. 'The Parr jockey blinded me and I never saw the race. I held on and let the horse do the running.'

'Never you worry. You took the right decisions. I watched you move out from the middle of the field. Had you failed to do so you would have lost. Pegasus would not have been able to show his true quality. You were made for each other and will ride him again when the time is ripe.'

On the stand the owners were crowding around John Dillon congratulating him on his victory. He felt proud of the horse and of his wife.

'We have not heard of this horse before, John Dillon. You certainly sprung a surprise upon us,' they told him.

'I cannot accept the credit. My wife picked the horse and the trainer.'

'Then we must meet this lady of yours.'

Elinor Dillon made her way up to the stand as men rushed forward to congratulate her. Her name was now on everyone's lips.

That night at Ayre House she accepted the Galway Plate. No Parr was in attendance and she did not feel challenged by them. She moved easily across the floor with a variety of eager partners, knowing that the ladies were staring at her from their seats. This was her moment of triumph and she was going to enjoy it. She was now securely mistress of Dillon Hall.

Daniel Parr had to honour his bet, delivering fifteen thousand guineas to the bank before leaving for his estates, his mind bent on revenge.

Elinor was toasted all the way home to Dillon Hall. Bonfires had been lit at crossroads and on hills and the countryside was wild with excitement. The first potato stalks were showing on the ridges. The destruction of Dillon Hall was growing in the fields.

# Chapter 15

Elinor Dillon sat before a fire in her room, reflecting on the challenge which lay before her. She knew that the famine would be widespread. Each year there was a partial failure and the reports coming in from all over Ireland gave little comfort. No parish or estate would escape the black rot as Death stalked the roads and villages. She would have to prepare for what would surely happen.

John Dillon was aware of the threatening hunger and for some weeks had been making plans for the estate. He had met other land owners who wished to protect their tenants, setting up a Relief Committee. He had been elected chairman and for three weeks had been going from village to village appointing people who could give him information on the progress of the famine. His mind had been active and intelligent until the night he went to Galway. He visited the soldiers' women and drank heavily. He returned, smelling of the brothels, and tried to make love to his wife. Next morning he could not recall what had happened.

The people thought the rot came from the sky. In many fields they had watched the potato stalk flourish and then overnight it failed. Men and women sat on the fences of their decaying gardens smelling the stench which filled the air like rotting flesh. Where the stalk was healthy men quickly dug their fields and pitted the tubers but they carried the rot in their core. There was a stillness in the fields and by that September of 1846 it was obvious to all that a terrible famine would sweep the land and that men, women and children would die.

Already in June of that year some cottiers had sold their animals and furniture, pawned their clothes and headed for the ports of Galway and Westport. Here they found three-masted ships and avaricious captains who could carry them on the perilous sea voyage to America. Those who remained were faced with complete starvation. Not only did the ships in the harbours take on board emigrants but many of them carried grain from Irish warehouses to England. This export of wheat and barley continued during the whole year. The only source of life was being carried across the sea.

By November people began to die. Many of them left their roods of land and joined the other starving beggars on their way to the towns in search of food. Others closed their doors and died quietly in corners, drawn together for mutual heat. Nothing would save two million people.

The lands of Connaught suffered the greatest loss. In the small acres and bogs to which many had been pushed by the great estates, the failure was total and final. Only food brought through ports could save the people, yet the government at Westminster seemed unable to grasp the size of the disaster.

Elinor Dillon rode with Tadhg Mor through the countryside in October, visiting the mountain areas and the isolated villages. They passed people with skeletal bodies, thin imploring fingers and childish voices asking for food. On one occasion they passed through a silent village, where only a mangy dog growled at them, the air heavy with decaying corpses. At another village the rats had entered the low cabins and picked the flesh from the dead bodies. There was even a rumour that a woman had eaten her young.

'It is horrible. No picture or word can describe what is happening. It is a plague and there is nothing I can do about it, Tadhg Mor. The countryside will become a green desert.'

'Fit for sheep. Some of the landlords will stand by their tenants but men like Parr will see it as visitation from Heaven. It will be in his advantage,' he replied sourly.

'I do not understand.'

'Men are bothersome, they cause trouble, they have children and they have mouths, but sheep and cattle grow fat and can be sold into the English market and they can reap a fine return. When all this is finished and the lands are as silent as a calm sea, sheep will flourish on the hillsides and cattle on the plains.'

'We cannot let that happen. What can I do Tadhg?'

'Accept the dark turn in the times. You cannot put your shoulder to the tide and push it back. It must come full and then it will ebb.' He spoke with finality.

'No. I will not accept that. There is a brighter fate. I possess a large amount of money. I will buy food for the people. I will not have them starve and have the mark on my conscience. I do not think about the death of Valentine Parr. He was vermin and deserved to die but these people have done no harm except that

176

they were born in the wrong place at the wrong time,' she cried angrily.

'Then you will beggar yourself.'

'Very well, I'll beggar myself. If necessary I will go to the banks and raise money but I will not have people in the districts starve.'

'If you are so intent on using your money then use it well. I know that the seas will be soon too dangerous for shipping. Charter a ship at Galway and bring in flour from America. Many people will survive the winter but if the crop fails again as it well could, then you will need your flour.'

'I will invest all my winnings in flour. The horse has been lucky for me. Perhaps this is the bright side of fate.' There was an intense energy and determination in her face.

It was dark when they reached the edge of the estate and they could barely make out the fields on either side of the road. As they passed the Great Field she turned to Tadhg Mor and made a strange comment.

'That is a perfect field and yet every time I enter it I have a hostile feeling. It does not want people.'

He hesitated before he responded.

'Perhaps it is hostile to the Dillon family. I have heard the servants whisper and talk and at no time more than after the funeral of Matthew Dillon. There is a curse on that field and they believed his broken neck was in revenge for the death of two Galway prisoners who were brought to tear out the heather and whins to make it fertile. Margaret Dillon rode up and down the field on her horse urging the men to work beyond their strength. That is why it is a hostile place.'

'Do you believe such a story?'

'I believe in fate and in revenge. I believe that this field requires another Dillon death before the curse is lifted. It does not belong to the family.'

They felt silent for some time, both caught up in their own thoughts. As they approached the stable she reined her horse.

'Tadhg Mor, I have a favour to ask you.'

'You know, my lady, that I would die for you,' he said directly.

'I have not heard from the Piper for a very long time. I saw him play at a street corner in Galway. He looked poor and his clothes

177

were shabby. He could not survive these terrible times. Find him and bring him to the house where I will take care of him. He is too gentle and well-bred to last very long in the city or in the countryside. Find him and bring him here; he is part of me.' There was a softness in her voice which stirred him.

'Tomorrow I will set out and find him,' he said simply.

'I shall give you some money. You may perhaps find that it is necessary.'

As Elinor Dillon crossed the yard she was aware of Margaret Dillon's eyes watching her from an upstairs room. She had been pushed aside by the young woman, a shift of power made final by the victory of Pegasus at Galway.

Robert Dillon was unaffected by the spreading famine, remaining in his room, writing quickly and trying to get the first draft of his biography finished. Elinor continued to sit with him each morning and he looked forward to their conversations. She did not tell him of the desperate hunger which was wearing down the people, whittling the flesh from their bones. His sole interest was in the last days of Marie Antoinette, awaiting her trial in the Concierge.

That night Elinor Dillon resolved to beggar the estate rather than have one tenant go hungry. She had come from these starving people and she would not stay aloof from them in their hour of misery and want.

The Piper decided to move to the towns. He had listened to the conversations in the village shebeens. Where men talked only of the potato failure. As he moved through the narrow lanes he could smell the stench of potato rot in his nostrils. It held the air and tainted the land. He had been hungry before, drinking milk and eating cold potatoes in cabins where he had spent the night piping to dancers. Now the humour and song had departed and he was banished from cabins. Frequently he had to take refuge in some sheep hut or on the protected side of a ditch. The cold seemed to enter the marrow of his bones.

He recalled his youth, remembering his young wife. His impulse to leave his land and travel the roads of Connaught had been foolish. He must go to the towns or die in the countryside.

But soon the towns were feeling the pinch of hunger.

The music he played was sad. His mind was filled with sorrow and his vision blurred. Soon he would be locked in the prison of darkness with no hope of light.

He had visited Dillon Hall once since Elinor had become mistress. When the bad times had overtaken him he became gaunt, his clothes threadbare and his shoes patched. He would not appear before her impoverished.

In September he made his way to Galway, enjoying some patronage from the pot houses. They were low dens, crowded and stale, the floors slimy with spit. His music was drowned by the loud conversation as night approached.

'Play on, Piper,' the pot-house owner would call, 'entertain the customers. Cheer us up with some jigs and reels. The country may be starving but we have not lost our hearts yet.'

Finally he was no longer welcome at the drinking houses. His body was filthy and even the sleeve of his coat had worn so thin that his elbow showed through. He tried playing at street corners but the children stole from his box. In desperation he pawned his pipes for ten shillings, aware as he left the pawnshop that he had no dignity, that he was now one of the hungry mass and would have to beg.

He starved for five days, then one morning he drew himself up and decided to make his way blindly to the workhouse. He hired a young boy with the promise of twopence to lead him to the gates. Along the way he heard lamenting voices and shuffling feet about him. They were pushing and shoving him and when he fell on the ground somebody walked across his back. When he reached the workhouse the gates were closed and he clung to the bars, begging admittance.

'Wait until tomorrow. When we have buried the corpses there may be room for you. Forty died last night and we took in a hundred today. There is an end to the bins of meal,' an attendant called from inside.

He had reached the final humiliation, unable to gain entrance to the workhouse.

Tadhg Mor passed through the sullen, silent countryside. Men and women, bent like foraging animals, clawed the fields in search of some healthy tuber. Many searched the woods for berries and nuts

179

while others ate grass. Everywhere he inquired through gestures and written notes for the Piper and always received the same information; he had moved to the big towns.

Tadhg Mor knew that he must begin his search in Galway and it was here he picked up the Piper's tracks. Some days earlier he had pawned his pipes and had been seen begging at the corner of Ayre Square. The trail ended there until he offered a guinea reward at one of the pubs and discovered that he had been seen on his way to the workhouse.

He wept inwardly at such news, having known the Piper in his finest days as a handsome man welcomed at the great houses for his music. He joined the miserable crowd of hungry beggars seeking their final refuge in the workhouse. They were beaten aside by a man on a cart carrying the dead to a mass grave. Tadhg Mor looked to see if the Piper's body was among them and was certain that it was not. He took the workhouse gatekeeper by the collar and pushed a rough note in his face.

'Did a blind man ask to be let in?' he inquired.

'There was a blind man here yesterday but I don't know where he has gone.'

Tadhg Mor moved out through the crowd, not knowing where to seek.

And then he saw him, lying in a ditch, away from the hungry crowds, dying quietly. His eyes were closed and his face turned to one side resting on cold moss.

'Oh Piper, why did you let this happen?' Tadhg Mor groaned. 'Did you not know that you had friends. The door of the house is always open to you.'

He took the giant's hand and felt it weakly.

'Why did you come? How did you know I was here?'

'Elinor sent me. I have travelled all through Galway looking for you.'

'Your quest ends at the workhouse gate. Have I not fallen on bad times, times against the makers of music.'

Tears ran down the sides of his face.

Tadhg Mor lifted the light figure in his arms and carried him through the city streets, anxious to get him into a warm bed and bring him hot broth. He did not notice the people staring as they observed the strange sight of a huge man carrying a starving beggar in his arms.

He arrived at a small hotel beyond the Spanish Arch which fronted the harbour. It was a peaceful place where the Piper could recover his strength.

He carried him up the stairs and stripped him, washing the filth and smell of hunger from his skeletal body. He knew how much the Piper hated filth and had always kept his body clean. He placed him between linen sheets, drew the blankets over him and brought him broth. He took each spoonful like a helpless child.

'I have not eaten for five days,' he began. 'My head is light and I cannot hold down hard food. I had reached the bottom of the pit and knew it when I no longer took an interest in washing my body.'

When the Piper had fallen into a deep sleep, he left the room and returned to the pawn shop to buy back the pipes.

In a drapery shop he brought proper clothes, the most expensive shirt, knowing that the Piper liked fine linen close to his skin.

Four days later, when some of the Piper's strength had returned, Tadhg Mor brought his horse to the front of the hotel. He mounted and drew Piper up behind him. They left Galway by the Quays where an emigrant ship was taking passengers abroad for America. It would be the last journey outwards. On its return it would carry flour for the Dillon Estate as cargo.

# Chapter 16

Dorothy, the daughter of Gerald Parr, had been influenced by her three aunts, spending her days reading extreme religious tracts. Her hatred of the Popish religion was never in doubt and she kept in constant contact with Exter Hall, imploring them to send their missionaries to the west. A seminary had been established in Tuam but it remained empty. On the small estate of Carrydoon, she had built a model Protestant school and engaged a school mistress to teach the children but this building also remained vacant. Even the slated houses she had built for those who would change their religion had not been occupied by the wretched tenants.

Now that they were hungry she decided to make a move. She set out one morning in her coach, followed by a large cart of food which was guarded by eight riders.

'They will accept it, never you fear,' she promised her brother Daniel, who had no interest in her activities. 'But they will have to fulfil one condition. They will convert to the Protestant faith. They may not want education or slated houses but they want food. They will not die for their faith.'

Her hopes were dashed. All day she went from cabin to cabin, enticing them with promises of food.

'I have more food than you will ever need. Is it not a pity that I have to return with a laden cart? Where are the priests now that you are needy? They do not carry food to you as I do. Have they built comfortable houses or set up a new school where your children can read and write? Ask yourselves these questions.'

She took some of the meal and threw it to a few starving hens who gobbled it up. The hungry looked at the precious food on the mud of their small yard.

In one village they attacked her, tearing the bag of grain from her and eating it. Her mounted protectors fell upon the starving people beating at their heads and backs as they shoved handfuls of food into their mouths. She fled from the village with her dress torn, screaming at them.

'My brother will have his vengeance on you. Let us see what your well-fed priests and bishops can do for you when the eviction brigades descend upon the valley. You will be damned in hell and will die on the side of the road without a miserable roof over your head. You will be hunted off the land within a week.'

Daniel Parr listened to her account of the incident, both amused and angry. However he did see the authority of the Parrs had been challenged. They had given him an excuse to evict them. He could flatten the houses and walls and turn it into a sheep ranch which would turn a decent profit. He set out a week later with his crowbar brigade.

Elinor Dillon heard the story from one of the tenants and was shocked by the injustice of what she had heard. She knew that Protestant missions had been set up in the wild districts for many years, having little success. She knew also that the missionaries had to write glowing reports to London giving the numbers of new converts.

'We have nothing left your ladyship, except the faith, no food, little clothing, and the winter will see the end of many of us. But we will not barter the faith for a ladle of Parr porridge or soup. We know how you treat your tenants. Come to our help, lady or we'll surely be evicted,' a tenant told her. She looked at his gaunt face and her mind was filled with fury.

'Send word as soon as Parr's men are seen approaching and I will do all I can to help you. But now I must sit and think about this matter.' When the man had left she reflected on what was about to happen. She had been the victim of a Parr's whip lash and a Parr's lust. She looked out of the window. The days were shorter and colder. It was obvious that many would die during the cold months. She saw the figure of Tadhg Mor approach, carrying the Piper on his horse. Her heart warmed at the sight of him and she rushed down the kitchen steps and across the cobbled yard to greet him.

His face was spare, the eyes sad. He had become quieter.

'Thank you for sending Tadhg Mor,' he said simply. 'I would have died had he not come.'

She threw her arms about him and hugged him, his presence giving her simple joy.

They settled him into a comfortable room in the yard, removed from the other buildings and set aside for visitors if the house was full. He sat before the glowing fire and told them honestly all that had happened to him.

It was only later as she lay in her bed and reflected on his humiliations that she began to weep.

Daniel Parr rode a grey horse and was followed by soldiers and bullyboys he had hired to carry out the work of destruction. They were a sinister frieze of moving figures on the landscape. From early morning the tenants had been warned that they were

183

approaching, signals being sent from hill to hill. A strange inevitable silence settled over the heather and rock, broken only by the sounds of wheel rims on stone and horse hooves. When they stopped for a rest, Parr turned to his men.

'We will destroy the villages first. That will tear the heart out of them. Burn everything including the thatch and the furniture. Let them know that they have been visited by Parr vengeance.' They smoked their clay pipes, drank mugs of whisky and looked senselessly at the ground. They carried no vengeance and felt no guilt. They were hired men paid to do a job by the landlords.

Kevin O'Donnell followed at a distance, intent on what was happening. He had ridden from Galway as soon as he had heard news of the coming eviction. He was a reporter on the *Galway Tribune*, influenced by Republican opinion through his editor and reading revolutionary literature when he could find it. His mind was on fire with new ideals.

The soldiers bore down on the village, clearing it of people, then the bullyboys went from house to house, setting fire to the thatch. Immediately afterwards they set up their tripod and slung a battering ram beneath it. When it had gathered momentum it crashed into the gable of a house and brought it tumbling down. Villages became mounds of smoking rubble.

Every image was scored on the young man's mind; the smell of the smoke drifting up the hillside towards him, the bleak famished landscape brown with rough heather, the frightened huddles of people crying with despair.

The whole land system was wrong; the tenants had no rights. There seemed no way to right the evils he had just witnessed except through violence.

He promised himself, *Some day I will settle this account with the Parrs. They may forget what they have done today and it may be of little account in their eyes but I will never forget.*

All day he followed the course of the evictions, as Parr left the landscape scorched and empty. The cold winds blew down the flanks of the mountains, cutting through the miserable garments of the tenants who stood in confused and huddled masses.

Having driven the people as far as the lake shore, Parr stood on a hill surrounded by his soldiers and addressed them in his hard voice.

184

'You are now trespassers on this land which reverts to the Parrs. If you return to your holdings you will be whipped within an inch of your lives. Sheep will crop where you planted your miserable potatoes and grazed your mangey cattle. You are the vermin of the earth. You insulted my sister and now you have reaped the revenge.'

The Mad Woman of the Hill came forward and called up to him: 'Parr of the Bastards, you have set us on the way to die. You have destroyed hearths and homes and blackened the land. But the hand of fate will throw the dice against you. I put the curse of the mad on you and yours. May you rot in hell's fire and may your children come twisted from the womb.'

Daniel Parr was about to turn away and begin his journey home when he saw a horsewoman and a huge man ride along the lake shore. They were shadowy figures but soon they became firm. He recognized Elinor Dillon and wondered where she had come from.

A cry went up from the crowd as she rode towards them. They were silent as she turned towards Daniel Parr.

'So you have had your day of destruction. You have thrown the weak from their holdings. Sup well tonight and feel satisfied. But know this: they did not sell their souls for your mess of pottage. This deed will be long remembered and your name will be infamous.' She cried out in a strong voice, an imposing figure on her white horse.

He quickly returned his horse and directed the soldiers to follow him. Even in the dusk Kevin had recognized his sister, but he did not move towards her. He listened to every word she had said.

The cold, famished people looked with expectation towards Elinor. Their silence was a plea for help and she knew that she could not abandon them to the cold of winter. Once she had been diced for on a deal table. Her heart did not belong with the landlord class and she could not look at these people with a callous eye.

'Line up behind the horses,' she told them, 'and follow us. I will not have you starve. I will bring you to a place protected from the landlords.' The confused people fell into a line behind her, moving along the sandy edge of the lake in family groups. They were without possessions and had little hope. Kevin O'Donnell was moved to tears as he watched them.

By morning over a hundred people lay on the hay in the stables at Dillon Hall. A huge cauldron was carried to the yard and placed on a blazing fire. Meal was poured into the boiling water and the hungry were served.

Margaret Dillon looked out of her window at the confused crowd, and furiously confronted Elinor.

'What is this I hear? You have taken the tenants from Parr's estate and brought them here. Have you not read the ledgers? We cannot sustain them. This estate is not encumbered like others because I have a vigilant eye upon it. Will you beggar us by bringing every pauper in the country on to our lands?'

'Where will I send them? Should they die on the road?' Elinor retorted.

'Yes. That is their fate. Either that or let them go to the work-house or to one of the relief committees. I will not have them on the estate.'

'It is my estate.'

'By default. It was never my wish to let you near these lands. Never. And where will you house them?'

'I am settling them on the Great Field.'

'No. Not the Great Field. That is mine. I had scrub and whins torn from it to make it fertile. I drained it and had grass sown on it. It is my field, I tell you. I will not have peasants break its surface and plough it up. You have set out to destroy my life work.' She raised her stick to bring it down heavily on Elinor Dillon's head. She caught it in mid air and forced the old woman back on to her chair.

'The land belongs to me. The times are mine and I must make the best decisions that I know. People must live.'

'I will bar the gate. I will ride out with a gun and shoot the first one who enters the field,' Margaret Dillon said, her heart beating wildly in her chest.

'Stay in the house, woman. I will have you forcibly carried home if you so much as go near that field.' She left the room, and the old woman went to her office, her mind in turmoil. She began to talk to herself, opening the pages of a ledger which related to

186

the Great Field. The entry in the ledger read: 'The Great Field is now finished, consisting of eighty unbroken acres. It is seeded and in spring I expect a good return. According to my calculations it will fatten seventy bullocks every year.'

She stared at the vivid lines, recalling the days when she was mistress of the land, when the earth was more precious to her than a virile husband.

Elinor Dillon led the dispossessed tenants to the Great Field. They were ranged along the fence and the land was shared among each family, stakes marking the perimeters of their holdings.

'I wish to have no ditches break the field. You are free to dig the earth and build simple cabins. Go to the saw mill where you will find timber, to fashion roofs and doors. You are also free to take the dead wood for your fires. I will make what food I can available to you. If there are problems I wish to deal with one spokesman. I will now leave you to your work.'

They set about making quick shelters by the long wall, taking branches for small scalps which were warm and sealed. Two days later they began to build a village in the corner of the Great Field, thirty houses which would be protected by the woods from the harsh winds.

Margaret Dillon did not answer the call to dinner. The servants knocking on the office door several times received no response. In anger she left the house and made her way to the Great Field. She would beat the starving peasants from her acres. Rain penetrated her clothes but she paid no heed, limping down the path with the aid of her stick.

One of the tenants found her wandering in the woods, shaking with cold. He went for help, and she was wrapped in a blanket and brought back to the house.

But the cold had penetrated her body and pneumonia followed swiftly. She died several days later, anger still on her face.

'The field has claimed its second victim,' Tadhg Mor said when he heard the news.

Dillon Hall was in mourning for several days. Servants walked quietly about the house and even in the vaulted kitchen they talked in hushed tones. It was difficult to believe that the woman who had dominated the estates for so many years had died. Robert

Dillon was sitting in the library when they brought him news of her death. He hurried to her room where the local priest was calling out the Latin psalms of repose. He joined in the soft chant.

That night she was brought to the small family chapel and candles set alight about her coffin. Next morning the local estate owners drove to the house in their carriages to pay their respects. Maud Dillon arrived for the Requiem Mass, walking directly to her priedieu and kneeling stiffly. She remained aloof during the ceremony and funeral.

When the vault of the family mausoleum was sealed Elinor Dillon invited Maud Dillon to return to the house. She looked directly at her, a snarl on her lips.

'I do not accept invitations from scullery maids. You do not belong here and neither does your child. I believe some of my mother's jewels come to me; have them sent to Daniel Parr. My mother was a Parr and she made this estate. I have no wish to remain longer than I have to.'

She mounted her horse and rode through the woods.

That winter the frost and the snow were severe. The land was hard like steel and the sharp spades could not make a dint on its surface. By January the meal had failed, and the sheep were brought down from the hills for slaughter. The cattle were bled and the tenants drank the blood. By March they had to slaughter the cattle and it was felt that the horses might have to be killed. Each day somebody brought news of death. People were found dead by the side of the road, their mouths stained green with grass. Others lay on black ridges where they had clawed down into the earth looking for potatoes. In other places whole villages died. Every day was a challenge to Elinor Dillon. She checked all the resources of the estate, every morning looking towards the east. The sun was beginning to rise earlier and heat was softening the land. The cold north winds gave way to soft winds from the south-west. Seed began to grow in the earth.

When the food began to fail in March, Elinor Dillon went to a merchant in Galway and purchased twenty cartloads of corn for two thousand pounds. She spent nights pouring over the ledgers which showed their bankruptcy, wondering how long she could hold off the debtors.

It was during this dark time that her second child was conceived. She sought comfort from the Piper at night in the warm loft room, banishing thoughts of the famine during these short hours.

'When this is all behind you, you will be strong,' he told her. 'We never know when we have lost and when we have won. You have saved the lives of many people. Fate must look favourably on such a deed.'

'We will see,' she said, her mind and body exhausted.

For John Dillon the famine was a half-certain nightmare. He returned to the house after a week spent in Galway, drunk and filthy. He fell into bed, remained there for two days and then set out again as if bent on self-destruction. He sobered a little for his mother's funeral but thereafter continued as before. Sometimes in anger, he questioned his wife about the Great Field and the debts she had accumulated. The greater part of the time he lived in a haze of drink which blinded him to the terrible events about him.

In March something happened which was to change his life. He left the brothel early in the evening, setting off on his horse across the mountains, certain that he knew all the passes and paths. The moon cast a shadowy light about him.

He was set upon in a lonesome valley. The assailants faces were blackened with soot and he could see only the bright eyes and sharp teeth. They dragged him from his horse and three of them held him while they gathered about the frightened animal and ripped his throat open. A dark red jet of blood shot on to their clothes. They cupped their hands and drank the blood like animals. They cut the animal open and fed his entrails to hungry dogs. They cut shreds of meat from the body and ate it raw, a mad, satisfied look in their eyes. When their hunger was satisfied they became more rational, dismembering the animal into large slabs of meat before setting out into the hills. When they left others came and took the head and legs. When there was nothing left for them to take they tore the clothes from John Dillon's back and searched for money to buy food. Finding nothing they released him.

He was deeply drunk and the splintered images made up the

189

sequence of a nightmare. He blundered up through the valley following a narrow path, three times falling on the ground and vomiting sour drink. He travelled all night, tearing himself on briars and falling into unsuspected pools of water. As the grey dawn broke in the sky he came over the hill and looked down on the estate. Johnny Appelby and the stable boy found him exhausted in the Round Field when they took Pegasus for his early-morning ride. They carried him to the house where he raved for two days. Then a fever set in and it was felt that he might die. When he emerged from his illness his hair was grey and he was weak.

Finally the ship arrived with flour from America, the whole operation costing ten thousand pounds. It supplied the tenants of the estate with food for ten months.

'What shall you do now?' Robert Dillon asked from behind his writing desk. He had followed everything she had done from his room and had not attempted to give her advice.

'I do not know. My mind is exhausted and I am with child,' she told him.

'I am happy for you.'

'I will leave as inheritance to the children a bankrupt estate,' she told him wearily.

'Perhaps not,' Robert Dillon told her. 'There is one desperate chance. I have been down to the Round Field and I have seen Pegasus. He can win one great race at high odds but you must have him heavily backed. Place every guinea you have on him.'

'That is very dangerous advice,' she said, placing her hand on his.

'During desperate times you take desperate measures.'

'Do you believe we should take such a gamble? I trust in your judgement. I will do as you say,' she said.

'Yes. But bring the horse to England and enter him for the Grand National. That is the only race worthy of him. I know the measurements of the course. Build them in the Round Field so that you go prepared.'

'Could we really build it in the Round Field?'

'Of course you could,' he said, looking keenly at her. 'You encouraged me to continue my book and I encourage you now to build the Aintree course.'

She reflected for some time.

190

'I agree with you. If we are to survive then this is the only possible way open to us. I will have to speak with Johnny Appelby.'

On an April day when the worst of the famine had passed, Johnny Appelby smoked his pipe on the fence and looked at the wonderful horse. All during the famine he had brought him each morning and evening to the field, watching him grow in power. The muscles in his legs had hardened and he no longer feared the soft ground. Johnny Appelby had not noticed the ravages of the famine; he lived only for the horse. Now the fortunes of the Dillon Estate would depend on his care and judgement. He was not aware of this on that April day.

## Chapter 17

They sat around the table and looked down at the plan of Aintree Racecourse. It consisted of fifteen jumps built to proportion by the carpenter, set out on smooth green baize. Beside each jump they placed the number of horses which had fallen at each race. Blue markings of chalk showed the water jumps.

'Are you certain that all these heights and distances are correct?' Elinor asked the two men.

'Certain,' Robert Dillon said. 'Anything else I may doubt but not the fences of Aintree. I was there in '39 when Captain Beecher came a cropper at the sixth fence. That was the very first race across the four-mile course and it started two hours late. Lottery had been the come-up favourite, going from nine to one to five to one. If I remember correctly it was Lord Sefton who lowered his starters flag. He stood right here.' He pointed to the start, marked by a white line. His memory seemed to sharpen as he looked down at the model of the course. He could remember the movements of each of the seventeen horses. They listened intently to his commentary, knowing that upon the accuracy of his memory depended a lot of the decisions they were about to take.

'Daxon was in front and he took the first railed hawthorn jump before the others had got up to a gallop. They had to cross ploughland and that took the sparkle out of Daxon's gallop, just couldn't negotiate the soft ground. Beecher went into the brook at this point, jumped too early. Then Conrad could not take the canal turn. The turn has to be watched: swing out into the middle of the course and keep full gallop. By now several of the horses were riderless. The second circuit is always easier because the horses have been around it before. Lottery was the horse and Jim Mason the man on the day. He romped home. I had favoured the Irish horse, Rust, but he let me down. I once had the ambition of owning the winner of the National – maybe now is our chance.'

He had let the excitement of the race carry him away. He looked at his son, still weak and gaunt-faced. There was a sharp interest in his eyes.

'Tell me, Father, what are our chances of winning? We could hold the horse for another race and take a more cautious course. Aintree is so uncertain. You cannot be sure of the outcome.'

'You are never certain of any race. Anything can go wrong, that is why men place bets on outsiders in the hope that something will go wrong. This is the great race to win. This will bring you glory.' He was excited again, some strange fire burning in his mind.

'We are not seeking glory,' Elinor told him.

'I know. Build the course. I have read accounts of each race run on the track. I will take you through each one until you will be certain of what lies ahead. The house will be saved or lost on this race.'

Elinor spoke seriously, 'I have always trusted your wisdom and I will order the course to be built. We have six weeks to prepare for the race. Fortunately Johnny Appelby has kept the horse in training all during the terrible times. He lives only for a final victory.'

'He was at Aintree with me the day Lottery won; he knows the course better than I do.'

'Then it is decided,' John Dillon said firmly. The gamble they were about to take stimulated him.

Next morning all the men from the estate and the new villages were summoned to the Round Field, the carpenter and Johnny

Appelby taking command of the work. They set out the fifteen hurdles, each properly spaced, each the same height as that at Aintree. They dug trenches beyond some of the hurdles, breaking for bread and milk at midday. Many did not understand why they were erecting such a complicated course but others quickly gathered from what Johnny Appelby was saying that this was the replica of a great course in England.

'Pegasus will carry the fortunes of the house on his back,' the carpenter told them that evening. 'Do you think that the lady is building the course without a purpose? Watch carefully.'

They had been warned not to go near the field for five weeks but each day some of them hid in the woods and watched as Johnny Appelby and Tony Buckley put the horse through its paces.

Pegasus did not take easily to the course. He could sail over the smaller fences but when he came to Beecher's Brook he refused to take it. Johnny Appelby had a foot removed from the fence, gradually building it up to its correct height. It took him three weeks to create confidence in the horse, until he knew every corner, every level, every height. Six weeks to the day he was ready to travel to Liverpool.

Daniel Parr had observed the fortunes of Dillon Hall closely during the famine. The new woman, who had taken the place of his aunt, had strained the financial reserves of the house. Debts must be weighing heavily upon her and he believed there was no way that she could honour them in the bank. She had humiliated him at Galway and taken fifteen thousand guineas from him. He would not let the memory of the humiliation out of his mind and waited for the day when he would settle the score with her.

He was informed by the directors of the bank in Galway that the Dillon Estate was already in debt to the sum of twenty thousand pounds. They had been more than lavish to their tenants and the dispossessed during the famine. Daniel Parr urged the directors to place the Dillon Estate in liquidation but was told that the woods had been set down as collateral against the debts.

'Then we will have them cut the trees. We will leave the place as bare as a plucked pheasant,' he told the trustees. Despite his threats they did not wish to move immediately against the estate.

193

But time was on his side. Other estates were encumbered by famine debts and he watched landlords sell out their estates and move to England. A new breed of landowners took possession of the estates, determined to squeeze the peasant of his last farthing. Soon the Dillon Estate must come on the market and when it did he would outbid all others in order to take possession of it.

His plans were thrown into confusion when one of his men, who had been spying on the estate, came to him with surprising information.

'It's impossible; I have never heard anyone going to such trouble over a race before. You mean that they have built an entire racecourse?' he asked in disbelief.

'Not a word a lie, my lord. I crept through the woods and looked for myself and I saw the great horse Pegasus. Declare but he's a bird, and he takes the big fences as easily as he takes the small ones.' What plans had the young woman? Why build a racecourse on the grounds? His man was reliable and intelligent. He asked him to describe the racecourse further.

'Fifteen fences, sir, and water jumps and a grand turn at the eighth fence. Twice he went round the course. The size of the fences varies. The sixth was the toughest.'

The man roughed out the course on a piece of paper and when Daniel Parr studied the drawing he knew immediately that they had built the Aintree racecourse at Dillon Hall.

'They are going to race the horse at the Grand National. Imagine the winnings! Nobody in England is aware that such a horse could win. It could run at twenty to one. Four thousand guineas properly spread on the course could make them a fortune.' He scratched his temple. 'But then where would they get so much money? They are broke.'

He was grim when he contemplated the drawing. This woman was beginning to make inroads into his mind.

'The horse will have to be destroyed before it gets to Aintree. If they win the Grand National it will establish the family here and in England and I cannot permit that to happen. It will also guarantee that not only will they pay their debts but that they will return a handsome profit.'

*　　*　　*

Daniel Parr's man moved through the woods, familiar with the night sounds. He had poached the Parr rivers and stolen hens from his roosts. He had never been caught despite the best efforts of the bailiffs. Now he had been drawn into the service of Parr himself, given ten sovereigns and promised twenty more when he had accomplished his task.

He moved along the dark path to the stable yard which was empty. He crept across to the south side and began to count. When he came to the seventh door he stopped and listened, there was only the breathing of horses. He lifted the latch and entered, taking the knife from his belt. One quick cut to the hamstring and the horse would be rendered useless.

But Pegasus sensed danger. He smelt the acrid smell of stale sweat, the whole stall seeming to pulse with danger. He whinnied and kicked at the enemy as he bent towards his legs. He knocked him into a corner and pawed at the body fiercely. The man screamed with fear.

When the grooms arrived they discovered the terrified poacher cowering in the corner of the stall.

'Get him away,' he screamed. 'He'll do me a danger.'

Johnny Appelby arrived later. Immediately he saw the knife on the floor. He picked it up and would have plunged it into the poacher's chest had he not been restrained.

'Tie him to the stalls. I have ways of dealing with one who would maim horses. Pull down his trousers and let me at him,' he roared. 'I'll do to him what he would have done to the horse, the blackguard.'

The two grooms trussed him against the rails of the stalls and tore off his trousers.

'No,' the poacher shouted. 'I'm only a paid man. It was only worth thirty sovereigns to me. Blame Parr. He put me up to it. He said that the horse had to be destroyed.'

'The old fellow or the young fellow?' Johnny Appelby asked.

'The young one, but one is as bad as the other. They say the horse is going to win a great race.'

By now the poacher was white with fear. His eyes stared and he began to cringe. Johnny Appelby cut the ropes about his wrists and he fell on to the hay.

195

'You are lucky I didn't geld you, for gelding you deserve. You have no heart. But you have given us warning. No Parr will come close to this estate or these stables.'

From that night until the morning the horse set out for Aintree, he was guarded by armed men. They moved through the woods as he exercised in the Round Field and they walked before and behind him as he made his way along the paths.

For the long journey to Liverpool they decided to walk him across Ireland, staying each night at stables where he would be lightly exercised. Tadhg Mor, Johnny Appelby, Tony Buckley and John Dillon would accompany him all the way. Elinor Dillon would remain at home.

She stood at the door of Dillon Hall as the retinue moved down the avenue. Beside her stood Robert Dillon, his arm on her shoulder. He had followed each day's training, worried that he would break a bone or tear a muscle. He had discussed the matter with Johnny Appelby on several occasions. He also wondered if the horse was being pushed too hard. He could grow stale and lose his zest for the course.

Robert Dillon went to Athlone twice during the training period. On his return the second time he produced three thousand guineas. He did not explain how he came by money, even to Elinor.

John Dillon rode ahead of the small group, carrying the guineas. It was the upper limit of the amount his father could borrow and he knew that the fortunes of the house could fail and his saddlebags be empty on his return. If the horse lost, then the woods would be felled and the outer farms and sheeplands sold.

He did not question his wife's decision to bring in the tenants from the Parr estate. He felt that her strength would carry them through.

He had lost his taste for the low women and wild drinking and despised himself for having ended up in the Brass Castle with its human derelicts. He refrained from drink now, except an occasional glass of wine. To drink spirits was a call back into the hell from which he had just emerged.

He looked at the landscape they were passing through. The sight of hunger lay everywhere. Men, women and children roamed the roads, dragging their possessions behind them on carts. Corpses lay on the side of the road in Connaught and when they stopped at the hotels in the towns he listened to harrowing tales.

He considered what his father had often said about revolutions: they did not come from the peasants but from the professional men, the thinkers. They could bring down the whole rotten system, but the bitter seeds sown during the famine had yet to show their flowers.

He had abandoned his former beliefs. Now, seeing death and despair at every turn of the road they travelled on, he realized that he must return to politics in a serious way. At the hotels he began, retiring early to his room and reading avidly.

It was the young boy who first spotted Parr's men at Athlone. He had an alert eye.

'I tell you I saw them before. They were in Galway the day of the races. One of them took the order to the jockey before the race. There is a gash on his cheek, and it's not a face I would forget.'

They entered a tavern and the young boy followed them, knowing he would not be recognized. He sat close and listened to their conversation. When he returned to the hotel he was trembling with fear.

'The horse must not get to the course. They were told to murder if necessary. If they cannot maim him they will poison him.'

'They were very forward in their conversation,' Johnny Appelby said, scratching his head with his finger, 'but we must not tell the master. We'll deal with this our own way.'

Two nights later, at Mullingar, the men struck. They had watched the horse being stabled and knew where to go. Quickly they gagged the horse and bound his legs. Then with vicious delight they cut his tendons.

Next morning they watched the hotel. Very early, just as sunlight was pouring into the streets of the town and drying the wet dust, a stable boy rushed from the yard crying out: 'Pegasus has been destroyed. Somebody has cut his legs and he'll not run in Liverpool now. Call the peelers.'

'That's the music we've been waiting for. You have heard it yourselves, lads. Let's track home with the good news, but keep out the way of the peelers.'

When John Dillon looked at the gagged horse, its eyes bulging with fear even in death, and the sodden straw where the blood had coagulated, he felt ill.

'Who could have done such a terrible thing to a horse? They should be hanged.'

'The Parrs did this, sir. We didn't wish to trouble you but we knew they had some plan afoot and we did not know when they would strike. That is why we muffled the hooves of the horse and brought him to a paddock outside the town. We have done the same every night since we left Athlone and they have tailed us since Castlereigh,' John Appleby told him.

'But I should have been informed of these things.'

'Well sir, we felt that you had enough responsibilities and thought we should handle it in our own way. The three scamps are on their way back to Parr with the news. We watched them make tail this morning after they heard about the horse. I think the way to Liverpool is safe now.'

John Dillon had seen corruption and evil at the Brass Castle, but had not seen such a savage and heartless crime before. He turned away in disgust and sat on a chair in his hotel room for a long time, looking at the wall. His mind could not cope with the callous action of the Parrs. He thought again of the horse so brutally savaged and it cast his mind into despair. When they set off next day, he did not speak to any of the others, but went on ahead, his eyes set dully on the dusty road. In Dublin he stayed at the Shelbourne Hotel and left the men to stable the horse on the quays. His isolation broke when he boarded the ship and felt the bracing sea air in his lungs.

The rest of the journey was uneventful. Pegasus was brought down into the hold of the ship and Johnny Appelby and Tadhg Mor stayed with him during the journey. When they brought the horse up the gangplank at Liverpool they were greeted by a forest of shipping masts, huge red-brick warehouses six storeys high, and the constant motion of men and winches. They passed up along the quays and watched the steamships, with huge funnels and black plumes of smoke, move towards the mouth of the river and America. But most surprising of all was the strange engine which hurled along, faster than any horse, on shining iron lines. They gazed in awe at its vast bulk and bullish power.

John Dillon was amused at the expression on their faces as he led them up from the docks and through the city towards Aintree.

They had arrived two days before the race, enough time to study the course and bring Pegasus to the peak of his form. He had travelled well and did not show any strain.

They checked the odds and found him at twenty to one, not among the favourites.

While they were settling in at Aintree, Elinor sat on the balcony at Dillon Hall. The air was warm about her, the stars lustrous. Somebody was moving by the lake with a lantern, a swinging censor of light in the great darkness. The woods about her were haunted with the mystery of the night.

She felt the baby move and reflected on the lands about her, how they would belong to her race. Some hard instinct had made her take decisions that were secret to both herself and the Piper. She had been unfaithful to her husband but he had failed her at the beginning and she lay some of the blame upon his shoulders. Since the famine she no longer shook at the responsibility she had taken upon herself. Her purpose has hardened. She felt certain that the horse would win, despite the hazards of the course. She had gone over and over it in her mind. One wrong step and the horse could break a bone: it was not something she wished to contemplate again tonight. She stayed on the open balcony long into the night, wishing to be alone and above the land. She had the sense that the land itself was more potent and lasting than love, that it would sustain the generations not yet born. She felt part of its being and life.

While the others settled in for the night John Dillon's work was about to begin. He ordered a carriage which brought him to the Owner's Club in Liverpool, where he had been once with his father. He had bought new clothes for the occasion and when he handed his coat and hat to the doorman he felt that he was in familiar surroundings. The candelabra shed its muted light on the parquet flooring and the second-rate portraits of landowners and merchant princes stared down at him. He entered the gambling room with a confidence which he had not possessed for a long time, intending to play out a charade. He had to be accepted by men of wealth and substance to whom the loss of five thousand guineas was of little significance.

They sat about tables playing cards, glasses of brandy beside them. They were heavy and full, their faces marked by pleasure and plenty. Many had made their money from coal and iron. He ordered a bottle of wine to be brought to the gaming table and bet liberally on the fall of the dice. Luck was on his side and on three consecutive occasions his combinations fell face upwards. Their attention was drawn towards him.

'Damn fine luck you are having. Have you some secret that we do not possess?' a gentleman who had lost ten successive throws of the dice asked him.

'I expect so, sir. Fortune seems to have favoured me since I reached England.'

'Am I correct in thinking that you are Irish?' a portly figure at the end of a heavy stump of cigar enquired.

'You are indeed correct. I brought with me an Irish horse which I believe may win the Grand National.'

He spoke in a deliberately loud voice, and watched their interest. They were anxious to know who this stranger was.

'I don't believe I've got the name,' the same man said.

'Dillon. John Dillon.'

'Not the Dillons of Dillon Hall, surely. Why, I believe I know your father. Is his name Robert?'

'Yes. He was a member of this club many years ago. He had some winners here.'

'And good winners they were. I am George Quennell. Thirty years ago I raced against your father at Leamington. Now of course the races are more professional. I heard he writes books now and has lost interest in horses. I did beat him on one occasion but it was bad luck on his part. Had to put down a fine animal. And what horse have you brought to Aintree?' he asked, pursing his lips.

'Pegasus. He is running at odds twenty-five to one but I'm

200

willing to bet twenty to one that he wins.' The challenge was in his eyes and his voice.

'I have not heard of this horse. Severus is best favourite and then Option. Pegasus, mmmm. Usually there is a buzz about the place when an outsider sounds promising.'

There was a controlled babble of conversation.

'You will take twenty to one?' someone asked.

'Yes. And I will place challenges about the club. I will bet in lots of two hundred guineas.'

The older members thought that he was too loud and certain.

'I think your confidence is badly placed. How many races has Pegasus won?' Sir George Quennell asked.

'One.'

'And you have sufficient confidence to bring down the odds? I think you are being foolish. Do you realize that everyone will wish to bet against you? Can you honour your bets?'

'Most certainly. I believe I can cover any bets that you gentlemen would like to place. I think Pegasus can beat the best that England can set against him.' The members set down their bets readily. He smoked a cigar as he casually signed thirty betting slips at twenty to one. The signatures were witnessed on the green baize table. When they were placed in the safe he ordered champagne for the company.

'Well, gentlemen,' he said, raising his glass, 'let me toast your good health and our bets. It is a privilege to be at Liverpool and I can assure you of a victory.'

'To victory,' they responded. Men were eager to meet this gentlemen from Ireland who had set them such a generous challenge. They sat about him and questioned him concerning his horse. They learned that he had been brought from France and trained at Dillon Hall. They told him that no horse with such little experience should attempt such a difficult race. His chances of winning were impossible; some even felt honour-bound to cancel the bets.

'No, gentlemen,' John Dillon was emphatic. 'The bets are laid and there is no going back on our deal. If I am to lose I am to lose. Let me lose graciously. The bets remain.'

John Dillon did not look like a man who would cast money to

the wind yet there had been news from Ireland that many of the estates were heavily in debt. Opinions about the mysterious horse began to change; perhaps he might be a challenge to Severus and Option. It would certainly make the running interesting. Before the night was finished fifteen more bets were placed with him, his mind clear as he signed each note. His casualness however belied his anxiety. If Pegasus lost he could not honour his debts. By the standards of the club he was no gentleman.

At three o'clock they began to leave the club. John Dillon watched them wrap themselves in cloaks against the night, mildly drunk and in a happy mood.

As he was about to rise from his armchair a waiter placed a bottle of champagne before him. He looked up and saw Sir George waddle towards him, his face as rich as plum pudding.

'Join me in a final bottle of champagne. I do not sleep very well. I keep late hours, I drink too much and my doctor tells me I have been dead for five years. I detest being alone. Prefer to die at the club than in my own bed.'

He lowered himself into a leather armchair, ordering the waiter to pour the champagne. His eyes sparkled as he watched it flow into the tall glasses.

'To your victory, John Dillon. You know I am beginning to believe that you could win the National.' He lifted his glass in a toast.

'To victory,' John Dillon smiled.

Then Sir George put his hand on the younger man's arm and said conspiratorially, 'The bets have been placed and sealed in the safe. Now you must know something about this horse that nobody else knows. I have heard them calling you foolhardy and boastful but I do not believe it. Would you satisfy my curiosity?'

'You will not divulge what I tell you?' John Dillon asked, leaning towards Sir George.

'As a gentleman. My lips are sealed.' His eyes were large with curiosity.

John Dillon told him the story of Pegasus and he hung on every word.

'Incredible,' he said softly when he had heard the story. 'You have gladdened my heart. I look forward to the race tomorrow. I shall drink here until dawn and then I will bet on Pegasus. I have not had such an interesting night in a very long time. You have given an old man much pleasure.'

'Good night,' he said, as John prepared to leave. 'If I do not meet you after the race then give my regards to your father.'

'Yes. Indeed, Sir George.'

He left the club and made his way through the morning light, realizing that he had over extended his bets. He stood to lose six thousand pounds or win one hundred thousand. He had played his best hand and now everything depended on the outcome of the race.

# *Chapter 18*

Johnny Appelby slept all night above the horse in a rough hammock suspended from the rafters of the stables. He lay on his back, his fingers knit over his stomach, satisfied that he had done all in his power to bring Pegasus to full form. He recalled all the hours and days of training at the Round Field. Now he would set the horse against the best in England. On a small ledge beside him lay a cocked pistol; he had no intention of letting anyone into the stables.

He awoke early and checked the horse, leaving the stable to wash himself in the wooden cask of water outside the door. The mist lay light on the flat countryside, the trees unsubstantial and half-created.

When Tony Buckley arrived Johnny Appelby had brewed some tea, boiled himself two eggs and was eating a rough wedge of cake.

'Never could get through a big racing day without a full breakfast. I raided a farmhouse yesterday evening and came away with two good British eggs.' He was munching contentedly. Tony Buckley was white-faced.

'I don't know how you can eat on a day like this and disaster facing us if we don't win. My stomach is twisted like a knotted

203

rope and I hadn't a wink of sleep. I hope I don't fall asleep going over the fences. When I did drop off I dreamt the course was built with limestone jumps ten feet high. My head is still reeling.'

'Well it's sleep you need, so up into the hammock. The smell of the hay and the dung will set you to sleep and I'll take care of the horse. I'll call you later.'

He hoisted the young rider into the hammock and talked to him while he combed down the horse. A little while later he heard him snoring. He saddled the horse and took him for a light canter through the countryside. The fine mist wet his face, the light thuds of the hooves on the ground were like muffled drum beats.

When the sun was well up he returned to the stable, to remain there until two hours before the great race.

All day the crowds gathered, men and women arriving in long carts drawn by plodding horses to take up their positions beside the fence. They opened bottles of cider and drew cheese and bread from cloth parcels. Closer to the stand, men of more substance drew up their carriages so their wives could have a comfortable view of the race. Huge tents with banners waving above them already drew the drinking men, bookies, three-card-trick men, pickpockets and bawds.

There was colour and confusion about the course. By one o'clock the owners and the members of the club had found their way to the stand. It had been built solidly of brick and stone like the city itself. From an upper deck people had a total view of the fifteen-fence course. John Dillon sat with members of the club. His father had been familiar with many of them and he found himself at home in their company. Only a slight tightness about the lips betrayed the fact that his body was taut with nerves and apprehension.

Already, news of the previous night's betting at the Owner's club had added spice to their conversation. The man stood to lose five thousand guineas on a horse that was a rank outsider. The odds on Pegasus stood at twenty-five to one, and the horse had had only one outing at Galway.

'Are you willing to risk more bets on Pegasus?' Lord Clare asked. He was attended by two ladies who were obviously better-class whores.

'I'll wager for each lady and for myself,' he said. He was a rotund, red-faced man, slightly drunk and proving an embarrassment to everyone in the select rooms. John Dillon signed the bet slips, hoping that no more drunken lords would come his way before the race.

He looked anxiously at his pocket watch and began to sweat.

The twenty-nine horses made their way to the paddock and he craned his neck to see the red colours of the Dillon Estate. He picked out Tony Buckley getting his final instructions from Johnny.

'Don't rush the first fence. No matter what you do hold back and keep to the outside edge. The same applies to Beechers. We have been over that fence forty times so there should be no difficulty. Don't get boxed in. Keep safe and at the edge. The victory will be in the final romp home. Keep him comfortable until the final few fences then let him rip.'

'I feel sick. I don't know if I'm up to it. Some of these jockeys seem to know what they are about and have faces hard as shoe leather. If only I had slept well last night.'

'It's the toe of my boot in the backside you need. Here you are and the quality of England looking at you and the whole of the estate with bets on you and you complain about sleep. If you don't ride the race of your life I know what I'll do with you. I'll take a whip to you and leave marks on you that you will carry to the end of your life.' He started cursing and it was reported later that some English gentlemen objected to his language so he proceeded to curse in Irish.

He was the last to leave the field. From the edge of the paddock he watched the parade of horses, casting a cold eye over each one. Three could present a challenge; Matthew, Chandler and Peter Simple. The others were well-trained, of good stock but showed no sparkle. He began to be worried, about the horse and about the young country boy who carried the fortunes of a house on his back. Nothing was certain at Aintree. His confidence began to weaken and he took off his cap, twisting it in his hands.

The horses came under starter's orders. They moved nervously and anxiously on limited ground, waiting for the flag to fall. When it fell there was a surge forward, the thunder of hooves on the torn turf. They were spread across the field and Tony Buckley could only see

205

the rhythmic movement of animals and jockeys, moving forward like a river of colour. Some were already crowding towards the inner fence, finding positions.

He kept Pegasus back at the edge of the field, feeling the eager strain on the reins. At the first fence he watched horses and jockeys rise easily, tear sprigs from the top of the fence, rest for a moment in mid air then move downwards, like roughened water at a fall.

He took the jump slowly and with caution, keeping well to the back of the field. Two horses had fallen and one had broken its back. The other fences lay ahead, each a dangerous hurdle. The horses had settled into their place, Gardener taking a comfortable leading position close to the fence. The next four fences claimed no casualties until Beecher's Brook rose up before them. He could see it from far down the field, its menacing height, its lurking danger beyond. He began to sweat: would Pegasus refuse it? They had practised him on this fence more than any other. It loomed up and he could feel fear in the horse. The animals about him cried out at the obstacle. And then the horse was carrying him over, prepared for the rise beneath him. Two horses fell alongside, throwing him into confusion. He almost slipped from the saddle as the horse landed. He threw his arms around Pegasus's neck, holding on grimly. He must not fall and let Lady Elinor down. When he was easy in the saddle again the horse took up speed and brought him up with rest.

'The horse has more bloody intelligence than the jockey,' Johnny Appelby called from the roaring crowd but his voice was lost in the excitement. He had thrown his cap on the ground and jumped on it with anger.

John Dillon's fingers twitched then Tony almost fell at Beecher's. Both the jockey and the horse seemed too inexperienced for the course. But then Tony Buckley recovered, Pegasus built up speed to gain lost ground and he felt proud of the animal. The spectators had not as yet noticed the Irish horse.

'Chandler for winner if he keeps the pace,' they commented about him. The horses took the canal turn cautiously, moving on towards Valentine's Brook.

Pegasus had settled into the race, some instinct telling him that he had to contend with horses equal to his own speed. He moved forward on the outside and gained distance. People in the stand began to ask the horse's name. The fences came easily to him but ahead lay the Chair and the Water Jump.

He had been born to win and a deep instinct told him that he had been bred for this moment. He jumped Beecher's with a little difficulty, hating the useless height of the jump and the shortened drop beyond. He was uncertain on his feet suddenly, and almost slipped on to his knees but Tony Buckley was crying in his ear.

'We are nearly there. Fly now for me as you flew across the meadows. Don't let me down. You can do it.'

The crowd said later that Pegasus had done a remarkable thing. Three fences from home he drew on all his powerful strength and began to run quicker than he had done before, moving easily over the fences, drawing closer to the favourites who were making the only running. On the final flat it was a straight romp home. The crowd called out to Pegasus to give a final effort. Matthew was ahead by a whisker and Pegasus felt challenged by his proximity and went ahead this time to win.

The field and stands were wild with excitement. How had they not heard of this marvellous horse before? He had the perfect character, lifting his head with pride as he passed the crowd, making Matthew seem like an unfinished horse. Tony Buckley was confused as the people wheeled about him, tapping him on the thighs, and slapping Pegasus on the flank.

'Did I win?' he asked somebody.

'By four lengths at the finish. It was never a race at the end. The horse had a great heart.'

Johnny Appelby made his appearance.

'Make way for the trainer,' he called. He had fought vigorously and kicked shins to get through the crowd, but this was his glorious hour and he was going to enjoy it. He took hold of the horse's reins and led him to the enclosure.

'We won, Johnny. I can't believe it. It's a dream. How did I do?' Tony Buckley asked.

'The first time you landed at Beecher's, I nearly wet me trousers and I said next time I put that young fellow on a horse I'll glue his backside to the saddle. I declare that the horse took it easy while you climbed back on to the saddle.'

'He ran the race himself. I was talking to him all the way, saying the things I used to say in the Round Field.'

They were almost isolated now in the enclosure, a young boy with spots on his face, an old stable hand with a crooked slant to his shoulder, an elegant horse and the owner, John Dillon. There were tears in his eyes when he shook hands with Johnny Appelby and the boy.

'It was all in a day's work, sir. We took on the best and won.'

'We engaged the fates that preside over our destinies, Johnny,' John Dillon said.

'Maybe we did, sir,' he replied and then the crowds were about them again. The people had taken the horse to their hearts and they all felt popular and loved.

Elinor looked at the clock, following the hand as it moved like destiny. The National was about to begin. Then it was over, she calculated. They had lost or won. She left the house and made her way through the small pathways to the Round Field. The jumps having served their purpose looked neglected. She walked from jump to jump, trying to imagine what it would be like to take a horse across them in a race. She would have to wait restlessly for three or four days for the result.

The horseman raced along the road from Ballinrobe, having waited anxiously all morning for the coach. When he received the news he let out a huge hurray, startling the other passengers. He jumped on his horse and rushed from the town, his heart pounding all the way to the New Village. He rode through the single street calling out, 'We won, we won. The odds held at twenty to one. I have it from *The Times*. We are saved. Pegasus romped home. Spread the word.'

There was excitement as they poured on to the muddy street. The horse had saved their lives. They would survive the famines to come and they would be rooted in a single place.

'Where's the mistress?' the messenger roared as he rushed into the kitchen. 'We won all before us. It's in *The Times* of London. Four lengths ahead of the favourite.'

'Show us it on the paper,' they told him.

'It's in the middle page and I'm instructed to bring it directly to Lady Elinor.'

'She is at the Round Field. Bring it to the old man. He also waits for the news.'

He ran up the stairs, and knocked on the door.

'Sir, Pegasus is a winner. He led them all. It's in the paper.'

'Did you tell the mistress,' he said.

'No. She's in the Round Field. I'll go immediately.'

Robert Dillon took the ruffled paper. With the control born of discipline he flattened the paper and looked at the racing results, taking in the description of the race. Pegasus had been perfect all through. He had run as he had been trained. The old man wept, looking out of the window at the great lawn, the lake and the eternal mountains.

'Take the news immediately to her. She has saved the house, the land and the people.'

But he was not the first to bring the news.

Elinor Dillon stood at the centre of the Round Field, a still figure, heavy with child. She looked at the woods, green with the leaves of summer and she breathed the scent of the wild flowers. The news might be a day late and she must wait anxiously. As she stood in the field, people began to pour in through the gate.

'We have won, we have won,' they called.

They were about her, thanking her, feeling part of the victory. She had brought them safely through the famine and settled them on land. Their money had been placed on her horse and it had won.

Later, when the newspaper was brought to her, she read it to them and they repeated each sentence after her.

'Now I wish to be alone,' she said later. 'I have not slept for the last few nights. There is much I have to think about.'

They melted from the field as quickly as they came. In her mind she accepted the victory and the new destinies of the house. She must now carry it forward into the prosperous years.

# Chapter 19

All morning the people arrived from Ballinrobe and the other towns, gathering along the roads which led to the estate. News had been brought by coach that Pegasus had reached Castlereigh and would arrive some time in the evening.

News of the victory had spread all over Connaught. Men began to recall the Dillon luck with horses and when the question of pedigree arose men thumbed through stud books looking for Pegasus's sire and dam. He was a mystery who seemed to have appeared suddenly from nowhere. Gradually, through rumour and fact, the romantic story of his arrival in Ireland and his training in the Round Field began to emerge. Sir Harry Christian had saddled his horse and ridden directly to Dillon Hall to congratulate Elinor on her victory. His face as always was ruddy with port, his gait awkward on bowed legs. It was only when he heaved his corpulent body on to his horse that he was in his true element.

'I came to congratulate you. We showed the Lords of England that we still have a good eye for a horse in Connaught. They say that you trusted his training to Johnny Appelby and set a young unblooded jockey in the saddle. It has the makings of a long story at the club. Heard all sorts of rumours so I came to see for myself. Must say that you are blooming. Can't say the same about myself, up to my neck in debt. Just couldn't turn hungry wretches from the door during the famine. Expect the debtors to come knocking any day now. Could be reduced to penury, my dear. If I can't have my port and brandy and a stout cigar and follow the hunt then life is not worth the candle. Might put a quick end to it all. But do tell me the story of the horse and my curiosity will be satisfied.'

She brought him brandy and port and when he was heavily settled in one of the armchairs she told him of her visit to Paris and her choice of Pegasus from a field of others.

'He had intelligence and spirit; I could build up trust in him. I knew that Johnny Appelby would bring him to prime form. This would be his last chance at training a great horse.'

She told him how he had been trained each day during the worst months of the famine in the Round Field.

'All that I can understand, but damn it, Elinor, Aintree was no place to bring an untried horse. Have you ever been to Liverpool? It is the most treacherous course in the British Isles. Why bring him on such a long and hazardous journey? There must have been some good reason for taking such a decision. When you could have run him at the Curragh.'

'At what odds?' she asked.

'You could have got six to one,' he said and then reflected. 'No, you would have to go four to one. People would have spotted that he had the makings of a winner.'

'Precisely,' she said, watching his reaction. 'At Aintree we could get twenty to one. Who would suspect a horse on his second outing to romp home five furlongs ahead of the field?'

He began to nod his head and mumbled to himself. He emptied his glass with a gulp and she replenished it. He grasped it in his pudgy hand and looked at her.

'I still say that it was a dangerous decision. I've seen the finest of horses put down after the race.'

'We had foreseen the problem,' she said, stimulating his curiosity.

'You cannot foresee the problems. I have been in racing too long and I ought to know.'

'That horse knew the Aintree course before he ever got to Liverpool. Follow me and I will show you something that might interest you.'

He gulped back his brandy and she had their horses brought to the front of the house. When he entered the Round Field he did not immediately recognize the course but as he made his way along the line of fences it became clear. He rode towards her excitedly.

'I see, I see, I see. The Dillon intelligence. You set out the Aintree Course on the estate. No wonder you were so certain. In a hundred years from now racing men will sit down and tell the story.'

He was pleased with his discovery and pleased that he had witnessed where the great horse had been trained. He had much to tell his friends, a story he could stretch.

'I must have my best mare covered by Pegasus, if you could see

211

your way to facilitate me. She's a marvellous mare and I might breed a winner.'

'It will be my gift to you when the time comes.'

He said goodbye excitedly in the centre of the field and rode off on his heavy mare.

She was not to see him again and Pegasus never covered his mare. When the debtors moved in he was forced to sell his estate. He watched his hounds being auctioned off to the Parrs and one by one his horses were brought from the stables and bids taken. That evening he visited each stable, still carrying the smell of horse sweat and dung. Dressed in his hunting coat and favourite cap, he stood there, remembering all his winners and losers. They found him next morning on the cobbled yard, a pistol just beyond his hand, a large ball-hole above his ear.

Bonfires were lit at the crossroads and on the hills but they could not catch sight of the horse.

A horseman carrying a torch galloped excitedly down the road. A great cry went up and filled the night.

'They are coming, they are coming,' the people called.

Two lines of torches began to move along the lake road, lighting up the figure of John Dillon leading the horse. Behind Pegasus rode Tadhg Mor and then Johnny Appelby, borne on the shoulders of the crowd. Then came Tony Buckley in his colours. It looked like some pagan festival procession.

The general voice of the crowd rose up and moved through the gates of Dillon Hall, passing beneath the branches.

Elinor and Robert Dillon watched the procession move towards them, the lights of the house shining out in the darkness.

The servants threw up the window sashes and looked down on the crescent in front of the house. The men were forming a flaming edge about it and into the semi-circle walked Pegasus, sensing the importance of the occasion, feeling sure now that he was on certain ground.

John Dillon ran up the shallow steps of the house and placed his arms about his wife. They held each other affectionately for some moments and then he turned to his father, tears of joy in his face. He rested his hand on a silver cane and his shoulders were hooped.

'The house has been saved,' he said simply.

Elinor came down the steps and the crowd fell silent. She had saved their lives, feeding them through the famine and earned them high returns on Pegasus and their feeling of gratitude was almost tangible.

The horse came towards her and placed his head on her shoulder. She caressed his long mane, pressing her cheek into his neck.

Already she knew how much he had realized for the house. The land could be restocked, the estate added to and some of the joy, destroyed by the overbearing presence of Margaret Dillon and the famine, restored. She looked at Johnny Appelby, putting her arms about his small sparrow shoulders. He wept also.

'I can die now, not that I intend to. You gave me the chance to train a great horse when the rest thought I was too old and too drunk. We took on the greatest and the best and beat them. I'm ever at your service, lady, until I die.'

It was a long, emotional statement and he sniffed when he was finished and bent his head. Then she turned towards Tony Buckley who was standing shyly with the crowd. She took his face in the palm of her hand.

'I knew you could do it. You were made for Pegasus.'

'And he for me, Lady Elinor. Sure, didn't he wait for me at Beecher's when I almost took a tumble and when I was settled back again away he went like the wind.'

Somebody called out that three cheers should be given to Lady Elinor and the communal roar filled the night as the servants from the windows joined in. Elinor went towards her husband and whispered something in his ear. He moved forward into the light, raising his hands for silence. The murmur stopped as the crowd waited for him to speak.

'Tonight when the torch lights brought us home to Dillon Hall I felt that it was a new beginning. We have come through much and we will not easily forget what has happened. I watched our representatives to Parliament raise no voice to protect the people in the House of Commons. They are helpless fools who do the command of others. I have passed through Ireland on the way to Liverpool and I have seen how badly this province has been treated by a heartless government. But that will not be so in the future. A Dillon will stand in the House of Commons and cry out against the doers of evil, the tyrants in their great houses, and against the men who make the laws.'

His voice had the cadence of an orator and a cheer rose from the crowd. He looked down at the faces beneath the torches, recalling the days and nights he had spent holding men's attention in the great squares and the mean streets. His life would be meaningful if he could take a serious interest in politics. Only then would the past be truly dead.

'But while I speak of the future I must dwell on the recent past. Had it not been for my wife Elinor and the confidence she had in this horse the estate would be encumbered and the Dillon name lost for ever. On her young shoulders she has carried the estate through the greatest difficulties that it ever had to face and now we can look forward to long prosperity. She has given us the gift of life and time.'

'And now to celebrate the victorious return of Pegasus we invite you to the stable yard. Porter and whisky have been carried from Galway this very week to give substance to our joy. And may you find the road crooked going home tomorrow morning,' he finished in Irish, his mind falling into the idiom of the language. A great bonfire was lit in the centre of the yard. The bungs in the porter barrels were knocked loose and frothing drink spouted into willing jugs.

The fiddler from the village drew out his instrument from under his coat and sitting on a chair close to the fire began to play. Soon the crowd was a mass of dancing figures and even Tadhg Mor, who had stood so solidly by, danced when Elinor drew him out of the shadows into the circle of light. As they danced Tadhg Mor and Elinor remembered days by the sea-shore when the Piper played to them and they danced in the sand.

'I must take care of myself, Tadhg. The child is within two months of its birth,' she panted, as the ring closed in about them and the crowd began to dance again.

Her husband was also dancing. She had forgotten his immense talent for life, his delight in movement. She felt a little tired and decided to retire within the house for a while.

As she walked up the broad stairs to her room she found Robert

Dillon standing at the bow window looking down at the yard.

'Are you not tired?' she asked, standing beside him. She put her hand about his waist and placed her head on his shoulder. It was a comfortable, intimate gesture. She had grown to love this old man during her time at the house. He had the best qualities of a gentleman and was delicate of manner and conversation. Unable to face the ravages of the famine he had listened to her in his room and backed each decision she made.

'No. Tonight I am not tired, Elinor. Tonight I am elated. I am reminded of a warm night some fifty or so years ago in a small village in the south of France. My brother and I had gone into the mountains and we stopped off at country inns each night. We often danced to the tambour and the pipes and perhaps they were the only times I felt natural and happy. Tonight I am reminded of these things. The people are happy and they dance. This night will be remembered while the house stands. No other woman could have done what you have done, not my wife, not any other woman. Come with me to my room, I have something I wish to give you.'

She took his arm and led him up a flight of stairs. In his room manuscripts lay on the table. She had watched them being shaped into final order during the famine year and felt that he would finish his life's work now.

He went to one of the bookcases, took a key from his pocket, unlocked a door and threw it open. Then he called her to his side.

'Now attend very carefully.' His face was serious as he drew out a set of books one by one and placed them on the ledge of the cabinet.

'To the eye this seems to be the back of the bookcase with some brass studs, five in all. In fact you will find that they run right across the back panel, but watch the manner in which I press each stud and remember the sequence.'

She watched carefully as he pressed the studs in an odd sequence.

'Have you followed my movements?' he asked.

'Yes.'

'Then try and push aside the panel.'

She pressed the studs in the given sequence and they moved under the pressure of her thumb. She heard a faint click within the panel, then pushed it aside to reveal an iron safe and a large key beside it. She turned the key, and opened the door.

'The possession of this safe I entrust to you. You may examine the jewel case and then I shall explain the documents to you.'

She drew out the silver jewel case carefully. Inside on a cushion of velvet lay a jewelled necklace, the stones catching the candlelight.

'I put these up as collateral against the three thousand pounds I borrowed,' he told her. 'They belonged to Marie Antoinette and were a gift from my brother many years ago. He bought them cheaply at the time of the Revolution. Sometimes when my style and inspiration failed I have taken them out and studied them. Place them about your neck.'

Nervously she took them from the velvet cushion and placed them about her neck, instinctively turning to the mirror to see herself. She felt it strange that a girl from the sea edge should now wear the jewels of a dead queen.

'They suit you,' he told her, 'perhaps better than the queen who wore them. You will find her name stamped on the clasp. I do not know how much they would fetch on the market; many thousands of pounds I believe. They are the final currency of the Dillons and must never be sold unless the debtors are knocking upon the doors. Nobody knows I possess them. They are yours now.'

She placed the diamonds in the silver box and gently slid it on to the safe ledge.

'The papers are of much greater importance. My father was a very shrewd business man, something which I am afraid I never inherited from him. He set aside certain sums of money in banks in France, Germany and England. A banker called Kellerman looks after this part of the estate. He is old now and his son will soon take over the business. This money has never failed. It is in gold and has been moved from country to country when war was imminent. Only the bearer of this document has access to it. Use this money before you sell the jewellery. I do not know how much has accumulated as Kellerman and I have not met for many years. Next time you are in London you can visit his son.'

She looked at him in surprise; he had told her secrets of which the rest of the family knew nothing and given her access to a very large amount of money.

'Why did you not tell me these things when the famine was raging?' she asked.

'I told you I would find money. I brought the jewels to Athlone and used them as collateral. Had the horse lost, the jewels would have paid my debts. Are you angry?'

'A little. Such knowledge would have saved me sleepless nights.'

'I know. But you were hardened by the experience. In handing over this information to you I have given up my only remnant of power. You will also find in the safe my father's and brother's final will. They are dated and witnessed. As you know my son in France has no issue so the estates may pass to your children. Let us return to the festival. I wish to look down upon the merriment a little longer.'

She kissed him affectionately on the cheek.

'You gave me a queen's necklace and I was angry. Forgive me, please, I was ungracious. Thank you very much.'

They returned to the bow window and looked down on the excitement in the yard. The bonfire now burned with a firm core, dancers whirling round the flames. The kegs of porter were far from emptied.

People staggered slowly through the estate, singing raucous songs, cheering their new prosperity.

For Daniel Parr the story of what had happened at the house and in the yard was a cause of blind anger. He listened to the foolish peasant describe how he filled his guts with meat and porter.

'What exactly did he say in front of the house?' he asked, shaking the man.

'I can't be clear about it, I had so much to drink, but he said something about running after the House of Commons and he cursed the Parrs and everything they stood for, as far as I can remember.'

'You are unreliable, it sounds too audacious. Where will he find support in an election?'

'I know nothing about these things, sir. I came as fast as I can as

217

you always give me money when I bring news.' It was an unsubtle reminder that information cost money.

'Take this and be on your way,' he said, giving him five shillings. 'Had you been more accurate I would have given you a sovereign.'

He felt restless: all his plans seemed to have failed. Had things been different he might now possess the estate. Already there were rumours from Liverpool that John Dillon had bet five thousand pounds with takers at twenty to one. It meant that the Dillons possessed more ready capital than the Parrs. He was pitted against the new generation of Dillons and the enigmatic woman who had married into the house.

Two months later Catherine Dillon was born. She was a strong healthy child and her birth was greeted with joy. She had been conceived during the darkest days through which the people and the estate had passed and her arrival marked the beginning of a new departure. Bonfires were lit on the hillsides and on the lake shore to mark the event. That night Elinor went on to the balcony and looked at the reflections of the fires on the quiet lake. The house and lands were now doubly secure.

# *Chapter 20*

Kevin O'Donnell had followed the eviction parties across the Parr estates, watching whole villages turned away from their miserable acres and set wandering aimlessly down the roads. They would eventually find their way to the workhouse or perhaps emigrate to England and America. They were tenants without rights, ejected when the harsh rents fell due. It was the cries of the children and the sight of a thatch taking fire which he would recall when he reached America.

He followed Daniel Parr like a lonely conscience across his estates, noting every gesture and movement.

'Fine and powerful writing but too full of wind,' was the editor of the *Galway Observer's* verdict on his first articles. He was an old, thin-faced man with a high-domed head. Steel-rimmed glasses were pressed on his nose, leaving a raw mark when he removed them. 'And don't make classical references to the dawn. That is strained and foolish. I want to hear people cry, I want to feel the thunder of the battering rams against the frail gables and I want to smell acrid smoke from wet thatches. So go back and write it again.'

The young man was angry and frustrated; five times he changed his article before it was set into the metal casing. He read it as the compositor slotted it into place on the third page. When it was peeled off the printing drum, he took the wet page in his hands, reading it carefully to himself. It was clear: he did hear the thunder of battering rams.

The editor called him aside.

'I am pleased. You have the gift of style and observation. Some day you may be an eminent journalist but you will have to work hard at your trade. What looks easy and sounds simple needs consummate skill. But be careful; I notice revolutionary feelings turning up in your lines. Despite your personal feelings, they must be toned down and kept private.'

'If I possessed a gun I would have shot Parr or one of his henchmen,' he said, anger showing in his face.

'This is not a time to talk openly of what you feel. Spies are planted in each town and if they hear rebellious talk they will have you thrown in jail, maybe transported on a trumped-up charge. Such is the present justice. They must keep the peace until the desperate famine has passed over. It is thinning their enemies, making their problem easier.' He spoke in a hard voice which frightened Kevin. His eyes were cold and sharp.

'Then what shall I do?' he asked.

'I have watched you. You have a quick temper and will blurt out what is on your mind. I wonder if you can be trusted.' Kevin did not answer but wondered where the conversation was leading.

'There may be others in the city who share your sentiments, who have their own plans and strategies. Maybe they burn with hatred also.'

'What do you mean?'

'I have watched you for eight months, O'Donnell. Do you think that I have no hates? I do, but they are hates of a deep kind, based upon rational thought. I have sat nights in my little room poring over the works of Locke, Voltaire, Tom Paine and a thousand others. I have smelt revolution in the air. We will not always be a slavish race, touching our caps to the landlords, paying unjust rents for land and property and kept from the great offices in the land. We have to break with London, we have to be free.'

He spoke like somebody possessed of immense passion, a bright light in his eye which belonged to the mystics.

'Where can I find these young men? I have reason to hate those who control our lives.' He remembered the dark night on the mountains with Tadhg Mor and the Piper. He could still recall the sight of Valentine Parr entering the room where his sister was secured for his pleasure. He had stood by while his body was thrown into the dark lake.

'Tonight meet me here. Make sure that you are not followed. I will take you to some friends of mine.'

It was dark when he made his way along by the quays. A mist hung over the water and the street, concealing images in mystery.

His mind was exalted. He was young and he had found a master who was certain of his vision.

He was writing something in the printing room which he quickly concealed when Kevin entered.

'Is it so late?' he said. 'I did not feel the time pass.'

'Have you eaten?' Kevin asked.

'No, I'm afraid I forgot. It sometimes happens when I stay on at my desk.'

He took off his glasses and knuckled the weariness out of his eyes. Then he put on his cap and coat and both left the office.

Kevin noted that they seemed to pass through the same streets several times as if to shake off some unknown pursuer.

'You can never be too cautious. The city is riddled with informers who would sell their father's blood for a few shillings.' His hands were deep in his pockets and his back stooped as if to make himself insignificant.

Eventually they arrived at a small row of thatched houses. They went into the kitchen where an old woman knitting by the fire nodded her head. They entered the only other room in the cabin.

220

On the trampled earth floor stood a large double bed with brass fittings and beside it a table and two chairs.

Young men sat on the side of the bed or on the floor. The editor sat on the chair, taking notes from his pocket and placing them in front of him.

He lectured for an hour on the fundamental rights to property, quoting from the political thinkers, searching through his notes for the proper quotations. The final five minutes of his speech stirred the young men. He found justification for the use of arms against the landowners and those who possessed too much wealth.

'Remember that the laws are made and exercised by those who possess the wealth of the country and wish to protect it. To that end and that end only are laws drawn up. You cannot change these laws; you have to destroy the system which created them.'

Discussion followed at length. The editor's mind was alert and he drew the young men into his way of thinking easily.

Kevin O'Donnell attended these meetings each week. They gave him substance for his beliefs. He was convinced that the ownership of the land was the key issue in the long struggle for Irish freedom. No nation could be formed without people possessing solid rights to land. While Parr could evict people at his whim, things would never change. He began to think of revenge, sure that justice was on his side. Eoin Kearney, also in the group, often walked home with him after the meetings. Kevin painted vivid pictures of what he had seen at the evictions.

'It's killing he needs,' Eoin Kearney said with youthful conviction.

'I have thought of it. It would be a warning to others.'

'We would need guns.'

'Guns can be easily had. I know an old rebel who would gladly lend us two. We could rid the land of Daniel Parr, if we were properly placed in a ditch and knew his ways.'

Without the knowledge of the others they set to discover if there was any pattern to Daniel Parr's life, questioning a man from his area when he came to Galway for the markets.

'He's well-guarded except when he goes to hump the Kelly woman on her estate. She has had a bastard by him and he is greatly taken by her. Sometimes twice a week he rides out of the domain at evening to have his roll with her. Otherwise he never travels without men attending. But be careful of him; the Parrs have nine lives.'

When they took the long guns in their hands they were excited by the power they carried.

'You must get your first shot in. There will be no time to reload,' an old rebel told them. He brought them to the sand dunes beyond Salthill and trained them in the use of arms.

'You are competent enough, but remember it is a different thing when you have a man in your sights or you are under fire. Don't let the bastard escape because if you do he will come after you with a vengeance and will bring you to ground.'

Kevin was eighteen years of age, Eoin a year younger. They felt lonely and insignificant lying on the wet moss.

'I'm feeling weak in my stomach,' Eoin said. 'I hope I can hold my aim when I get it trained on him.'

'We only get one chance remember, so make your ball count. Go for the heart.'

'What if he hasn't a heart?' Eoin asked in feigned humour.

'If he has balls he has some sort of a heart,' Kevin said in return. Their ribaldry gave them confidence and reduced their fear of Parr.

They had picked a good position. It overlooked the road and they would have a clear view of the rider. In the event of failure they could escape into the woods and take shelter there.

It was only as they lay and waited that they realized the magnitude of their task. And then it was too late to run. They heard the sound of hooves and watched Daniel Parr approach on his black horse. He appeared a menacing figure, in his frock coat, a ruff about his neck. He was trotting a shade too fast for a firm aim. They took their guns from the grass and took aim. Eoin in his excitement shot too early. The old rebel had cautioned him about this mistake. Instantly Eoin rose from his position and rushed towards the forest but by then Parr has seized the opportunity. He faced his horse up the bank and charged after the retreating figure. Kevin could hear Eoin cry out in fear as the horseman drew down upon him. He was about to climb over the fence and escape into the woods when Parr blasted him at close range. A gout of blood spat from his back and he lay dead on the ditch. Parr turned his horse. Kevin waited until he was almost upon him. Then he released the trigger, hitting Parr firmly on the leg and knocking him sideways. Throwing his gun aside he fled to the woods. He knew that he had not killed him and must move quickly. The horse's head had covered his heart and he had to discharge the gun into the exposed leg. His heart was pounding and he tore his limbs and clothes on the briars and brambles. Five hours later when darkness had fallen he left the woods and walked across country towards the Dillon estate. Next day he slept in a small scalp in the side of a ditch, the reeds drawn over him for protection.

Early next morning he arrived exhausted at the estate. He lay concealed in the woods and watched all day. It was three o'clock when Elinor took her walk along the forest path. She was pensive when she came in view and he could see that she was heavy with child.

'Elinor, Elinor. Over here among the undergrowth. It is I, Kevin.'

She shook herself from her reverie.

'What is the matter?' she asked. 'You look frightened and exhausted. Your clothes are in shreds. Where have you been?'

'On a desperate mission. I tried to kill Daniel Parr. Instead he killed my friend at close range. He was only a boy and I can still hear him screaming like a young animal. When Parr turned and charged at me I shot him in the leg. I'm on the run and I need help.'

'Will you come to the house then. You can wash and have new clothes. We can make arrangements for your escape.'

'No, not to the house. I must stay in the woods.' He was trembling with fear.

'Then follow me.' He followed as she went ahead into the wood, and she noted how tall and firm he had grown since they had met a year ago. He spoke to her of the past and she gave him a quick summary of all that had occurred at the house.

'I can never forget the evictions and the famine. One helped

223

the other to destroy people,' he said. 'I will carry these memories with me to America if I ever get there.'

'Remember all the landlords are not as black as the Parrs. Several of our friends have become bankrupt. When the famine has passed they will have to sell their estates and the new purchasers will wish to have their money returned with interest.'

'It is the land system which is wrong. The whole structure will have to be changed. Men will never die again in fields and ditches.' He talked nervously and at speed.

They moved deeper into the wood. The light barely seemed to enter here and their direction was uncertain. Bartley Gaynor appeared behind them from the shadows.

'Well, Lady Elinor. I heard you mention my name further back. What good service can I do for you?' He had a shaggy head of hair, a matted beard and his clothes were colourless with age. His eyes were sharp, familiar with the shadows and secret places of the wood.

'My brother has shot one of the Parrs and needs to be hidden. I expect they will have soldiers combing every corner of the countryside soon.'

'Have the Parrs hounds, Lady Elinor?' he asked sharply.

'Yes. I'm sure they have.'

'Then the woods will not be a secret place. I could scent your brother's body downwind like the dogs. We must act quickly. I'll go with you to the yard and you can give me clothing for your brother. Then I'll foil the dogs. I'll prepare something for Mr Parr.'

When he returned with the clothes he took Kevin to a stream.

'Strip off and wash and throw your clothes on the far bank. Then put on these fresh garments and return to my hut. I have business to do and I must do it quickly.'

Daniel Parr drew himself up from the ground, his thigh seering with pain. Anger surged through him. He had been remiss; he should have carried a brace of primed pistols. There was a cap on the ground and he put it in his pocket. He dragged himself towards the boy he had shot and saw he was dead. He pushed over the body and looked at the youth's face.

'A boy, a mere boy,' he said in disgust. He pulled himself on to his horse and rode the ten miles to his estate, his leg hanging loose. He was certain that he had seen the man who had escaped before. But his leg ached and he could not define the image.

By the time he reached the lawn in front of the house, he had lost a large quantity of blood. He fainted, falling on to the grass.

Some time later, he regained consciousness. The ball had been dislodged and his thigh was heavily bandaged.

'Release the dogs. There is a murderer loose in the woods,' he called. His father looked down at him, his face tight with fear and anger.

'I will lead the dogs,' David Parr said. 'You are too weak to move. Tell me where to pick up the scent and I will take the dogs and the men across the countryside until I find him.'

Daniel Parr had them bring his frock coat. He took out the cap he had found and gave it to his father.

'The dogs will find the scent on the cap,' he told him.

It was too dark to start the search that night so they waited anxiously until dawn. At first light they released the dogs into the woods, their mouths wet with angry saliva. Men rushed forward after them. When they were in open country on the far side of the woods, Parr rode forward and took up the chase. The dogs ran ahead as they did at the hunt, yelping with anger. They lost the scent at a river but on the other side he took out the cap and helped them pick it up again.

When evening fell they were moving towards the edge of the Dillon estate. If necessary he would ride across their lands in pursuit of the criminal.

The dogs hesitated at the wall of the estate. They were confused and ran in many directions. It took them an hour to pick up a direct scent. It seemed very strong and the dogs rushed forward toward the quarry. David Parr rode behind them at a distance, allowing them to savage their prey.

He saw them enter a culvert in the side of the hill. He listened to the booming sound of the dogs as they ran along the channel, then only the remote sound of barking and silence.

David Parr listened grey-faced. He ordered one of his men to dismount and enter the culvert.

'What if I come to harm, sir?' he asked anxiously.

'You will come to no harm. Just be careful.' The man crawled into the cave and returned ten minutes later.

'It's most extraordinary, sir, but the dogs plunged to their deaths. The cave leads to a ledge and I dropped a stone over it and counted. It took four counts to take it to the bottom. I listened and could hear water rushing by somewhere in the dark. They have been carried out under the hill, sir.'

'We have been tricked. My dogs were deliberately lured into that cave. Perhaps several men are involved in this plot to murder my son. Let us return to the estate. Tomorrow I will call out the soldiers and the police. I'll not rest until the culprit is brought to justice.'

As he rode home he wondered if the woman at Dillon Hall was implicated in the act. She was a strange woman and he was filled with anger towards her.

'That woman has something to do with my son's injury. She will not rest until he is dead. She carries the old hates,' he told himself.

Bartley Gaynor chuckled to himself from the edge of the wood. He hated the Parrs and they had fallen into his trap. He had saved Kevin O'Donnell's life.

For two days the soldiers and the police combed the Dillon Estate. Kevin lay beneath the floor of Bartley Gaynor's shieling. Twice he had heard soldiers question Gaynor.

'I'm a poor man, sir, and you are welcome to examine my noble abode. I have been gutting a pig and his insides are inside on the floor.'

They looked in the door to discover the rotten carcass of a pig, his guts protruding from a long cut in the underbelly.

'Sure, I boil up the guts and make soup when I'm hungry. If you want a drop of blood to drink you may take it.' He took a dish of blood himself and put it to his mouth. They almost vomited and ran from his presence.

When the soldiers and police left the area Bartley Gaynor removed the rotting pig and took up the floorboards. He peered down into the darkness.

'Did the air get down to you?' he asked.

'It did, as well as the smell. I'm nearly poisoned,' Kevin said wearily.

'It was the smell that saved you. No dog could smell you with that rotten pig's carcass above you. The danger is over but you will have to stay here for some time. They will have their eyes on the ports and their spies will be everywhere. Shooting a Parr is a most serious offence.'

For several months he lived within the confines of the woods. Bartley Gaynor taught him to live off the land, to move in the darkness and see objects which normal people could not see.

Kevin's editor's confinement was not endurable. The solitude of his cell, the hunger and beatings drove him mad. He cried out to be released into the light; he asked for a book that he might read. In the end he began to give speeches and knock his head against the padded walls. David Parr would not have him released despite the governor's plea for clemency. One night he hanged himself with his belt. He was buried in an unmarked grave and his printing shop and press smashed to pieces. Children found lettering and ink in the rubble and made print marks on their hands and faces.

# Chapter 21

During Kevin O'Donnell's months in the woods he had little contact with the events of the world outside. He did not realize that his attempt to take revenge on Daniel Parr was only part of the general discontent in Ireland and in Europe. Some great revolutionary wave seemed to pass across the continent in 1848, the discontent stretching from Palermo in Sicily to Ireland. In January of that year the people of Palermo had swept on to the streets of the city in open rebellion against Ferdinand of Naples. The same protest followed in every city in Italy. In Paris barricades were thrown up in the city streets by the working class. Even quiet Switzerland had a revolution which left it with republican forms of governments. In the German states the ferment was deep and consistent.

In Ireland young men set up confederate clubs, reading the works of John Mitchel and Thomas Davis. All were intelligent, brave, and willing to endure exile and prison for their beliefs. Many formed secret societies bound by oath. The rebellion of the young Irelanders ended in a humiliating skirmish in a cabbage garden at Ballingarry, led by William Smith O'Brian. James Stephens, a young man of twenty-four who had been with O'Brian, fled to Paris. There he set up revolutionary cells while he supported himself translating Dickens and teaching. In time he founded the Irish Revolutionary Brotherhood.

The talk of revolution went on even in the quiet cloisters of the seminaries. Father Croke openly supported the popular revolutionary movement and Father Kenyon of Tipperary organized the young men into clubs. But to the young man in the Dillon woods these ideas and movements were of little account.

Frequently he recalled the death of his friend, remembering how he had cried out in boyish fear. He had made the fatal mistake and turned his back on the enemy. The next time he faced Parr he would be well practised with a gun and the landowner would not ride away to the security of his mansion.

Often he explained to Bartley Gaynor that some day all men would be equal before the law. Bartley found the idea both ludicrous and humorous.

'Faith, when you get rid of Parr and his kind then you will have other tyrants to take their place. If you aren't under one type of a tyrant then you are under another. That's why I choose to be alone here in the woods. I'm like that man Robinson Crusoe, monarch of all I survey and my rights there are none to dispute and I leave it at that.'

'These are established tyrants,' he told the old man, who seemed to treat all his ideas as folly.

'So you say. It's a young man's dream. Didn't Moses take his people out of Egypt in the old days and if my memory serves me right they wanted to return to slavery and plates of gruel and they refused to obey the laws forged for them by God himself, and Moses chiselling them down as quickly as he heard them. That's

228

the sort of people you are up against. If you know the nature of the beasts of the forest you know the nature of man, for not only does he look like an animal but he has all the same qualities inside him.'

They engaged in these long conversations as they sat in the cabin at the end of the day cooking a rabbit or fish. Bartley Gaynor seemed to foil all his arguments by quoting from the habits of animals.

'The great advantage of living with the animals is that you get to know their constant habits. They never change. But man wants and wants like Mrs Elliot who fell into money and wanted three skirts and a fancy hat although she was brought up on potatoes.'

In September his sister came down into the woods, carrying a bundle of clothes, some papers and a large supply of money. They sat together on a fallen tree trunk, shafts of sun coming through the wood canopy and filling the spaces with misty light. He observed her sister, her face full with mature beauty, her body strong and confident. There were light lines on her forehead from worry and responsibility.

'You have to move tonight. If necessary you can stay in safe houses on the way. David Parr has died and the hunt has been called off for the moment. His men have returned to the estates and I expect that the military will give him a regal funeral. There is a ship sailing from Galway to New York in five days' time. The captain is sympathetic to the cause of the young Irelanders and you will find others on board who share your feelings. You will be met in America and taken care of by friends of the movement. Remember that you have been identified and that there is a price on your head. If you are captured you face hanging.' She wept a little when she had finished speaking.

'Don't cry. All is not over. I will return again and we will be only separated for a short time.'

'Tonight go to the far gate. Tom Lydon whom you know, will be waiting for you. He will remain with you until you reach Galway. Goodbye until we meet again.'

They threw their arms about each other then she drew away from him and fled up the path.

He washed in the river, trimmed his dark beard with scissors and waited for darkness to descend on the woods. He talked with Bartley Gaynor.

229

'I believe America is a big place and to ride from end to end would take many months. I heard it once said that there are forests there with mighty and large trees old as the world itself. It would be too big for me and too wide. I know my kingdom and I will remain in it. But remember if you ever return, find your way into the woods. I will always be here.'

He walked with him to the edge of the trees, moving quietly through the pathways, their ears sharp for movement. At the gate Tom Lydon was waiting for him. He climbed on to the cart and they moved forward into the night. Tom Lydon filled him in on all that had happened during his months in the woods. It was only when the dawn was breaking that he could observe the countryside. The ravages of the famine were still upon it, the fields bare, the small cabins empty and silence everywhere. They rested for a night and a day, then joined the other carts making their way towards Galway. They carried large trunks and looked stolidly in front of them as if they had no feeling left for the land.

'We are safe here. The police and soldiers have been withdrawn to Galway. One Parr dead and another poisonous weed to take his place. Well, I hope he rots in hell with all those who went before them, for they were never any good either.' The driver took his pipe from his mouth and spat a jet of saliva on to the dry road to give emphasis to his words. 'Some of the landlords went bankrupt to feed the people. But Parr had his day. I have looked at his new sheep runs and I remember that they once carried large families. He threw them out, to roam the roads on the darkest and coldest of nights. They say the old bastard died screaming. I hope he did, a pity you didn't put a bullet through the head of the son; that would have been something. They have a song composed about you and they sing it at the fairs. I'll give you a bar or two.'

Kevin O'Donnell listened to the simple ballad composed about him and recognized the Piper's tune. He wondered if he had written the words also. They had his stamp upon them. It had been the Piper who first stimulated his imagination many years ago and it was because of the Piper that he was passing down the road to Galway.

When they got to the city they were halted by two soldiers, young men with soft frightened faces. They waved the train of carts past.

They approached the wharfs by a back road which led through low, huddled cabins, holed to permit the grey turf smoke through. Wizened old men sat outside the doors and caught the autumn sun, content with the day and untroubled by young men's dreams.

That night he stayed in a small hotel close to the quays, three other men of his age sleeping in the same room. They were secretive and kept to themselves. Kevin placed his money in his stockings and drew them on over his feet.

Very early next morning a sailor came knocking at the hotel door.

'The four for America, the four for America,' he called out. They quickly rose from their beds, washed in the barrel outside the kitchen door, ate some rough bread and followed the sailor to the ship.

They spent the day hidden in one of the stifling hot holds, and became acquainted in the narrow space. Each one was a wanted man.

Only when the ship passed out into the broad bay did they come on deck to have their last view of Ireland. Galway was a city in grey silhouette. To the south lay the shallow hills of Clare, purple in the evening light. To the north lay the rough landscape of Connemara and the pointed Bens of Connaught. Gradually the city began to disappear, then the smaller hills, and finally the massive mountains of Galway and Mayo. Before them lay the wide sea and America.

# Chapter 22

David Parr's head lay on embroidered pillows. The aquiline face, Roman nose, the glitter in the eye, made him a fearful presence. Servants moved quietly about his bed and in the hallways. No cart passed in front of the house, no wheel crushed or slipped on stone. Cattle lowed sadly on the lawn and then fell to grazing. A quietness descended upon the estate where the leaves had changed to burnt colours and hay lay in buff reeks. The apples were heavy and ripe in the orchards and the bees had become lazy.

Drowsy air came through the open windows, lifting the light gauze curtain. The cool breeze on his hot forehead brought him some relief from the fire which consumed his body. Shafts of pain like tiger's nails clawed his stomach and his abdomen. He bore the pain stoically until it became too powerful. He began to cry out in a long, piercing scream for help.

Later there would be hours of peace when the enemy within seemed to have retreated. He would lie silent, turning his head towards the window, looking out over his vast possessions. They had been handed to him by his father, they were in good shape and he would hand them on to his son. His mind was easy; no troubled conscience, no doubt as to his decisions and actions. They had been taken in the cause of his Queen and for the sake of his family. Now it was time to relinquish his rights to life.

In the villages and towns men waited for his demise. He had been master of life and death, sweeping tenants from their lands when they were no longer profitable and setting sheep to graze on wide tracts made up from small holdings. In his youth he had claimed the rights of the lord on all the women of the estate and villages. His feudal sense had been strong and firm and as he lay dying they cursed him in the hardest manner they could, hoping he would roast in the inner limits of hell and his testicles spiked on its gates. The servants brought news each evening of David Parr's descent into death.

'It is like a fight,' one of the servants said. 'You think old Parr is finished and on his way. But he comes back from the struggle a little weaker each time. He will not die easily. He no longer talks; the gates to his senses are banging closed on him and he's locked inside his body. His son sits beside him night and day looking at his father's face.'

David Parr did not believe in an afterlife. It was a clerical scheme set up to chain the minds of the poor and keep them subservient. He hated the Church of Rome more than any institution and would have gladly helped to destroy it.

'It is the great whore of Babylon,' he had told his son. 'And remember that it is set on establishing itself in England again. Its tentacles stretch out across the world and it has an ear in all courts and in all parliaments. The Pope and the Jesuits never sleep; they are always busy planning darkly in the back rooms. I have seen it happen here in Ireland. O'Connell was the Pope's man. I remember when no priest would dare perform his Latin sorcery but now they do it openly. Watch them. Watch their educational system. The old days are slipping away. And watch the land. It is set down in our names but political change could sweep it from our possession.'

It was a theme that had obsessed him all his life and now as he approached death he returned to it again and again. He recalled the act of his sister, forsaking the Protestant faith for the Popish Church.

'Her heart was never with them. You cannot change a Parr. She turned for one reason and one reason alone; the possession of land, and for that I admired her. But she did receive the wafer and the bishop poured oil on her head.'

He began to reveal to his son the inner secrets he had kept from him during his life. He was a man whose power stretched from Dublin Castle to the ministries in London. He was a master spy, with a wide network of contacts. The contacts were made out in forms of five, each name with five names branching out from it. These again carried five more. The whole network must have involved over two hundred people. He explained to his son how they were paid and how they operated, setting out the procedures for recruiting members.

'In this system people are not acquainted with each other. Only the central figures are known to me and I meet them rarely. They send their reports to me, I sift them for value and send them to Dublin. Some practical information I hold for myself. It is important to have files on your friends and your enemies so that you can always press them into your service. I have had the Dillons researched and have even contacted one of our best men in Paris to look them up. You will find strange contradictions in the reports. Make what you will of them. You will also find a bank report on their lodgements which I do not believe to be comprehensive. They must have money at other banks, perhaps in England, but I have not been able to trace it. You will find eyewitness accounts of John Dillon's visits to the whorehouses of Galway but unfortunately the evidence is not signed. The woman he married is well documented. Makes interesting reading, as do some suggestions concerning the legitimacy of his two children. Nothing, mind you, that can be proven or disproved, but there are strong indications that they belong elsewhere. I will leave you to read the files.'

Daniel Parr felt power grow within him as he read them. The details had been accumulated over the years, the work of a thorough mind. The files were arranged in two different colours, red denoting the personal possessions of the Parrs.

He spent a considerable amount of time sorting out the large file on the Dillons. It was spread through several folios and he meticulously arranged it so that it fell into sequence. In a ledger he discovered other information which he copied out and placed in a special file. He wanted to know every intimate fact about that and pored over the details while his father lay dying. Two strange facts emerged. The family branch in France was also defective in the female line. One of the Dillon women had hanged herself in the stables at the Hall, the evidence of the death lying before him in signed statements. By default she had been buried in consecrated ground. The same madness was evident in Maud Dillon. She was his mistress and it explained much of her behaviour. Information had been gathered concerning John Dillon's visit to the whorehouses in Galway and his weeks at the Brass Castle. Daniel Parr read the lurid accounts of his encounters with the women there, an eye witness to John Dillon's roughest pleasures. The second interesting fact concerned Elinor Dillon, whose origins were traced to the house by the sea. A strong suggestion had been made in a recent entry that she was present when Valentine Parr was murdered. It was further noted that the giant who always stood by her had perhaps murdered his uncle.

Having read the file Parr gave instructions that Maud Dillon be removed from her house on the estate. He had his men take both her and her possessions to the main gate. She sat there for some time on her chest and considered what she might do. After reflection she set off for Galway. She felt that she was growing old.

grey streaks were appearing in her red hair, the lines in her neck were deepening and her skin was dying. Sometimes she scratched the back of her hand with her nails and looked at the dry flakes come away. She felt that she was ageing on the bone.

She cursed her own family, not the Parrs. Then she cursed the young woman known throughout the province as the saviour of the tenants. The story of the horse Pegasus had turned into a legend. She would have her revenge on the jumped-up hotelier.

The old man struggled within himself, isolated from the rest of the world. Only his eyes moved and he could no longer scream out in pain.

He died as the sun set over the forests. His son closed his eyes and left his body to the servant women. When the new master left they stripped David Parr, his skeletal frame holding no reverence for them. They laughed at his nakedness and tickled his shrunken parts.

'As limp and as little as the fifth tit of a cow,' the fat-faced woman commented as she washed his testicles. 'Well, all his bother and much of our bother is over now. There was many a young one he got with that shrivelled piece.'

'Keep your voice down. Have you no respect for the dead? If the new master hears you laughing you will be out the back gate on your head. And the bother is far from over. The new master is as bad as the old fellow any day. I heard yarns about him and women that would make you blush. He has queer and crooked ways.'

'Tell us about them,' the other urged, raising suds on the corpse.

'And give scandal and bad example? But if I told you what I heard it would shock you red.'

While they washed the corpse and drew on the shroud she told the women what she had heard.

'And three women in the bed with him?' the fat woman asked. 'Well, I declare. I never heard the likes of it in my life. And him wearing bloomers?'

'So they say.'

'I don't understand now and I'll never understand. But we better get this bugger in good order for I'm sure they will be laying

235

him out in the grand finery with his medals and swords.'

When the body had been shrouded they withdrew from the room, their faces serious, their backs bent low in respect. They retired below stairs to talk and gossip with the other servants.

He was laid out in his ermine robes in the hall, his medals and regalia beside him. All day the gentry arrived in open coaches to pay their respects. They stood for some time before the figure and then talked with Daniel Parr. They were the middle rich come to pay homage to the new master as well as say goodbye to the dead one. Daniel Parr would have both parliamentary and political power. For the merchants he could decide whether their tender would be accepted by the workhouse guardians or by the quarter masters in the barracks. He listened to their commiserations with a certain disdain before dismissing them.

It was different when the five lords arrived within the hour, as was their practice when one of their circle died. They were men upon whom the safety of the Province depended.

They were treated to a sumptuous dinner that night served on Sèvres porcelain and carrying the symbols of their private society. Daniel Parr was now a member of this company and as he looked down at the men eating at his table he was struck with awe for not only had they powerful connections in Ireland but their power stretched to England. His father had placed in his hands files on all these men as double protection, and during dinner he tried to recall the notes he had read on each lord. In name they upheld the law yet each one had broken it in his own interest. One had sold information to the French, another had acquired money from the slave trade and smuggling. A third had defrauded the army of several thousands of pounds, a fourth took his pleasures with young boys and the fifth had a child by his own sister.

'We must show our force at the funeral. For that reason your father must be carried to Galway and set out in the military chapel. Then he can be brought triumphantly home to the family mausoleum. Dark and sinister forces from a new class are gathering against us. We must let them know that they are set against a mighty force,' Lord Musgrove told them when they were drinking

236

their brandies before the fire. He spoke with a gruff voice full of certainty.

'I have made all the arrangements. There will be troops in each town and village we pass through, each spick and span and armed.'

'The cortège will be led and followed by military bands,' Daniel Parr told him.

'Good. We must impress the populace. A good parade always induces new recruits to come forward. Taken by the brass buttons and the uniforms. Best recruits are Irish, as Wellington discovered in the Peninsular war. Our voices will have to continue to be heard in the future. Revolution spreads like a plague. It is scarcely fifty years since the monarchy was destroyed in France and less than thirty years since Napoleon placed his family on half the thrones of Europe. The union must stand. We have to watch these well-educated Young Irelanders. We must root out those who will spread the seditious seed.'

The lords followed the cortège to Galway in their gilded coaches, flanked by armed soldiers who surveyed the crowds for likely assassins.

After the funeral services were carried out at the military church the coffin was brought along a different route to the family vault where David Parr was interred with his ancestors. Daniel Parr returned home for a late supper with his wife and two children and then retired to his room where he continued to study his father's files and correspondence.

Next day he rose early, ordered his horse and rode through his wide estates. He was in total possession of everything about him and felt proud of the achievements of his ancestors. The responsibility of the estate now lay with him.

237

# Chapter 23

John Dillon was now thirty-seven years of age. His hair was grey and his face in repose carried lines of sadness. His illness had left its mark upon his character.

He appeared a strange, spectral figure as he moved about the estate, sometimes so abstracted that when men saluted him he failed to hear them. He would stand on the edge of the lake and look at the sheen on the water or listen to the sound of the wind in the stiff sedges. The mystery of the lake entered his mind. The islands with their tufts of hazel and sally had an air of secrecy. Hermits had once settled there and built their corbelled huts of thin limestone slabs.

He was preoccupied with politics following the parliamentary reports eagerly. The Irish Members of Parliament made few contributions to the debates at Westminster. They were disunited and uninterested. Daniel O'Connell had been a force for Repeal before the famine. Men had flocked to his meetings but they did not have the backing of the Church or the radicals of England. John Dillon believed that the particular interests of Ireland were not being well served. If the country were to prosper, if fair laws were to be enacted, then the Irish members must be welded into a united party. Tenants must be compensated when they were turned out of their holdings and absentee landlords should be subject to a special tax. All this could only be brought about if the Irish members had a united voice in the House of Commons.

He discussed these ideas with his father at dinner. Each conversation turned eventually to horses or politics. Elinor Dillon was soon caught up in the conversation. She could see that her husband was eager to enter political life. He was vigorous in his argument for a united party.

'But you cannot get them to unite. They will unite in Ireland but as soon as the party trumpets blow in London they will take the same old line as they have done on every previous occasion,' his father told him.

'They they must sign a pledge before they are elected to form a united party, enabling them to bargain with a strong hand. They

238

could hold the balance of power in the House of Commons.'

'And who can bind them together?' Robert Dillon asked.

'I believe I could help to bring them together.'

'But first you must get elected.'

'I intend to. I stated the night when we returned from Aintree that I would enter politics. I have given it considerable thought and I know what I am about.'

Elinor put her arms about him and kissed him. Politics would give him a central interest in life and she felt the excitement growing in him.

The two children, Peter and Catherine, filled the house with laughter. The family had come into the third generation. It was said that the boy carried John Dillon's features and the girl would be like her mother. They had a small carriage and pony which was led about the lawn each day by one of the estate workers. Sometimes he took them to the islands in a rowing boat and they would picnic in a small bay, splash in the water or try to catch some minnows in a fine net.

Politics took John Dillon to the other houses in Connaught. He knew that several of the landowners agreed with his ideas and wanted security of tenure for their tenants. Many of them had almost gone bankrupt during the famine and they laid the blame on an indifferent Parliament. Often he was away for a week at a time but he always brought back some gifts for the children. They watched for him from the drawing-room window, running out of the main door and across the lawn towards him, falling in their excitement. He would gather them on to his horse and ride with them to the stable yard.

His relationship with Elinor was tranquil. His illness had neutered his sexual drive. He took delight in her naked body as she moved about their bedroom. He would touch her breasts and thighs, stroke her skin, yet he knew that she was unattainable. He wished to take her with passion but he was frigid when he lay beside her. Neither could Elinor respond to him. She loved him in a way that she could love no other but knew that they would never form any physical union. He had brutalized her when they were first married and the scar was always there when he touched her. They never spoke of the problem, aware that something stood between them which neither of them could remove.

They walked each day down to the Round Field to watch the horses in training and discuss the problems of the estate. He trusted her judgement totally and told her of his fears at appearing in public again.

'I remember you as a young dark-haired man outside the hotel, enthralling even your enemies. You know what they said. No Parr would dare mount a platform in a town if you were speaking for the opposition.'

'That was years ago. Can I still find the words and phrases that will capture their attention?'

'You were given the power to sway crowds and you have it still. There is so much good you could do,' she argued.

'If you believe in me then when the time is ready I will make my move.' She moved towards him and put her arms about him.

'When you are ready I will be by your side.'

'I do not deserve you, Elinor. Without you this house would be in ruins and the estate the possession of the Parrs. The tenants would be scattered and the trees felled. I could have been kinder to you during the troubled and doubtful days but what has been done cannot be changed.' He spoke sadly.

'Those days are past. We are different people now.'

'These are idyllic days and I hope that they will last. Is fate going to be kind to us?'

'I do not know,' she said. By now they had reached the oval field and their attention was drawn to the horses.

Tentatively he began to commit his thoughts to paper. As he saw the words on the page his political ideas took firm shape. It was obvious that the Act of Union would not be repealed in the near future but there were much more immediate problems to be faced.

'I am tired of Repeal,' he told his father at dinner. 'The Union with Ireland and England cannot be easily broken. Perhaps if O'Connell was a young man we might indeed have stood some chance of shaking the establishment. We have come out of the famine and we subsist on the alms of the world. The government must be pressed to support the people.'

'Then continue to pursue your feelings on paper. Have the courage of your convictions and fight with the pen. I have only reported history but you must fight the present battle. My own political ideas have changed. I believe now that the French Revolution had to happen. And the very same thing will happen here,' he told his son with certainty.

'Are you preaching revolution, Robert Dillon?' Elinor asked him in surprise.

'I am not preaching it – I'm predicting it.'

'You quibble, father,' John said.

'No. This Industrial Revolution has changed the wealth base and the middle class which is emerging will not be easily put down. Their voice will soon be heard in the House of Commons. We forget that all the great families were established by buccaneers and merchants. There is plenty of revolutionary material about for young men to read; there is no way the old order will hold.'

'Except in Ireland,' John Dillon said.

'That I would question. I cannot look into the future but there is a shift in thought. Perhaps it might be better to remain with Britain. We have no tradition for governing ourselves.'

'You have changed your opinions late in the day, Father.'

'My opinions have been changed for me,' he said mischievously.

When dinner was over he would rise, smile and say, 'Well, I must unfortunately return to the eighteenth century.'

'It is only now I realize that my father is a most perceptive man,' John Dillon said when his father closed the door.

'But then you have not read the manuscript. It is full of political ideas. He has set you a challenge and you must take it up. Try your ideas out on the public; it will help to clarify your mind.'

'I may not write as elegantly as my father but I will set down my thoughts and send them to the papers. Let us see what friends we will make and what enemies will rise against us,' he told her.

His first article to the *Galway Tribune* was against Repeal.

'Repeal is dead, interred with the famine victims. Ask the weak and dispossessed if they seek Repeal. They will say, "Feed us. Give us the tenure of a small plot of earth to plant out seed, raise our

241

young. Then ask us about Repeal. The fat and corrupt men of the Repeal Movement will neither invite, entertain or consider these ideas." '

He did not have to wait long for a response to his first article. As he rode through the streets of Tuam men rushed from their shops and abused him. He stopped his horse in the square and addressed them.

'You are the gombeen men who survived the famine. You have full faces. Bring me those who are dispossessed and without substance. Let me listen to their voices and I will heed their requests. Let me hear the voice of the landlord who has gone bankrupt for the sake of his tenants and I will follow his counsel, but not the merchants, the priests and the Archbishop himself. Let him have his Repeal. Give me food for the hungry, money for the dispossessed.'

'Traitor who would serve the cause of the Crown,' they cried.

'You have served the cause of the Crown well. You have not cried against taxes. You pursue your own interest and will always follow the interest of the middle class. Repeal is dead.'

He drove his horse through the crowd and they drew aside and let him pass. He felt his old courage return, knowing he would be able to face the crowds and address them from any platform. His mind was free and he owed allegiance only to himself.

A week later he had a visit from John Brown, a landlord from Cong. He was a man with sagging jowls and eyes which seemed to be always wet with mucus. His rough appearance belied his character.

'I have been reading your articles for some time. I'm afraid some of the classical allusions escape me but I do like your style. It is hard and blunt like Cobbett's. I agree with you on Repeal and so do most landlords who were broken by the rates during the famine. The Repealers are a corrupt lot; give me a liberal any day who does not promise the people bread and games but sets down fair promises. The banks are trying to foreclose on me and I am stretched. Given two years to shake the financial weight off my neck I would be able to run a proper estate again. I'll side with you in the next election against the Parr faction and the Repealers, but I need your protection and so do many others. Here are the

242

signatures of eight others who would back you. They will bring in the leaseholders to vote for you so you stand a fair chance of being elected to Parliament.'

He took a document from his pocket and handed it to John Dillon. He noticed that the eight signatures were small landlords, hard put to survive the post-famine years. Their backing would give him a certain amount of power to take on Parr.

He looked at John Brown, sitting on the edge of the fine chair, uncomfortable with its fragility.

'We will walk across the land if you wish and talk about these matters.' They left the house and walked towards the ploughed fields.

'This I can understand,' the landlord said, pressing the heel of his boot into the earth. 'I can fight and die for this. I have worked my acres and no tenant died on my estate during the famine. I went to the banks and raised money for I would see no creature die. I had them live in my own house and I killed my horses to support them. But eaten gruel is soon forgotten,' he added sadly.

'And have you spoken with the bank managers?' John Dillon asked.

'I cannot talk with these men. They are clean-faced like the judges and solicitors and live off the flesh of others. In nightmares I see them riding up my avenue with bailiffs and soldiers ready to take possession of everything I have.'

'And so it has been since the beginning of time. The lawyers confuse the issues and the bankers fill their pockets with gold,' John Dillon told him.

'Then will you stand with us? Can we put your name forward in the next election?' he asked anxiously.

'Yes. You can tell them that I will stand with them against the Parr faction and against the Repealers.'

They shook hands on the promise and continued to walk, their minds turning to the crops that would be raised in the broad field. John Brown took a handful of clay.

'This is the base of life, the only thing worth fighting for.'

John Dillon's articles were taken up by the *Freeman's Journal* in Dublin and his name became fashionable. His style had hardened and he abandoned his classical imagery, drawing similes from the

243

solid world about him. He spent more and more time away from home, travelling across Connaught addressing political meetings. On some occasions he had to be escorted from the meeting rooms for fear of violence from Repealers. Others admired his courage and many agreed with his arguments.

In 1851 the Repealer, John Rawlings, died. They were at breakfast when the news reached Dillon Hall. John looked at his wife and father.

'You know what this means; a by-election.'

'Yes,' said his father. 'You have been waiting for it long enough. It will be a tough struggle. O'Connell's name still carries weight.'

'I know. Had Rawlings conveniently lived for another year or two I would stand a better chance.'

'That may be so. But you will have to test the times and the only way to find out how you are regarded is to go forward as an independent candidate,' his father advised.

'I may lose.'

'Of course you may lose, but at least you will have made your mark. This government is not going to last forever. You must be seen on the platforms.'

'We have no time to waste. I will summon John Brown and the others to the house. We will make plans for the election as soon as possible.'

It was soon known on the estate that John Dillon was to stand for election. It became the subject of much debate at the public houses. Opinion was already split in the district.

Two days later the small landlords began to arrive on horseback at the house, scraping their feet on the irons before they entered the hall. They drank warm punch until most of the members had arrived.

Elinor Dillon looked at the landlords gathered about the long table in the dining room, impressed by their presence. They were men of independence, each one letting his thoughts be known. The first man to speak was Martin Loftus, his voice anxious and gritty.

'I have been through hard times. I have seen my neighbours go to the wall during the last few years. I have no time for Repeal of

244

the Union or for any grand changes. I'm here because I believe you understand our needs.' He paused for breath. 'As I understand it, you wish to lift the burden of taxes from us. Well, how do you propose to do that?'

'I would argue that the tax concessions given to British industry and agriculture should be abolished. There should be no import taxes placed upon us when we sell into Britain,' he answered.

'And what can one voice do in Parliament?'

'It can make itself heard. Better one voice than no voice at all.'

'I'll back you because there is no one else to back and I'll read everything you say in the House of Commons if you are elected,' he said dourly.

The others were more practical and understanding. John Dillon let them have their say then made his own statement.

'We can at most muster two hundred votes. It will be a close run between the Parr candidate and the Repealer. During the next election Repeal will not rate a vote, so we prepare for the next election. We need wide attention and we can get it if we have the tenants with us. We must promise them fixity of tenure. Men cannot be kept miserable and uncertain. It may not be the general feeling at present but it will come. Any tenant who works his land and improves it deserves to have a strong right to it. It is natural justice, and in the end natural justice will prevail. If he is not given fair treatment then he will have recourse to arms.'

The men talked among themselves, some disagreeing with him, saying he did not understand tenants. If they were given any concessions they would seek for more.

'Perhaps we are sowing the seeds of our own destruction with these promises,' one landowner told him. 'Tenants will think that we are soft in our minds and they will band against us and make heavy demands. I see a cauldron of trouble and we are adding logs to the fire.'

'There is no other direction we can go. Your titles to your land are firm. You must fight for fair rates and in turn demand fair rent. We must defend our own rights and the rights of the tenants,' John Dillon told them. 'We are not saying that they should own the land. We are merely saying that they should have pay.'

'How many agree with John Dillon? How many will back him

in the next election?' John Brown asked. 'Those for, put up their hands. Remember this is the only candidate we have in the field.'

They all agreed to back him and the next hours were spent in strategy, calculating how many freeholders could be relied on to vote for Dillon. They made a list of those who were doubtful, in order to approach them and try to swing them their way. John Dillon would have to make his presence felt by speaking in every town and village in the constituency, and the campaign must begin once he had been nominated.

'I hope that we are wise in our decisions,' John Brown said when the meeting was finished. He walked with Elinor Dillon to the stables to see the first crop of foals sired by Pegasus. He scanned them with a careful eye.

'Well?' she asked.

'Good. They are all good, but I do not see a Pegasus among them. The strain is very rich and you will have winners, but none of these will win the Grand National.'

'I know. I have watched them now for three months. None of them has all the qualities. But some day he will sire another winner. Turning to more serious matters, what do you think of my husband's decision to enter politics?'

'He is the best man we have, but he is too honest, too reasonable. He will make our voices heard but he will carry a heavy burden on his shoulders.'

'Should I dissuade him?'

'No. He is alive, his mind is bright. Already his articles are causing a stir. Mind you, not all landlords agree with him and I think he believes the common man is more honourable than he is but he will be a voice for the future. He could have a dull life here or he can wage war against a sea of troubles. Let him sail into the storms.' He looked at her directly. 'But you will have to be with him. He needs a woman beside him as well as a political agent. It can be difficult when you face a hostile crowd from a platform. I have followed eight elections and I know the temper of the people. There are nights when the mind is light at the thought of victory. There are other times when you feel like giving up.'

'He would never have entered politics but for you. How well do you know him?' she asked.

246

'We rode together when we were young men. I remember his tenacious character. He had courage then and I think he has the courage again. We need change in Connaught and he could bring it about. The House of Commons needs a new voice; John Dillon has the voice.'

'I will remember all that,' she said. He mounted his horse and rode out of the yard.

John Dillon was filled with admiration for his wife during the campaign. She was beside him when he spoke in town halls and village squares. Her presence and beauty made men look at her in admiration when she entered a room.

His mind was tired and overstretched as he came to the end of the campaign. He had travelled across the county of Galway, making speeches on open platforms and accepting the ridicule of the Repealers and the Parr faction. He had decided, even before the results were declared, that he would run in the next General Election. He was certain he would gain a seat then. Men were changing their allegiances. A strong Irish party could swing the balance in a weak Parliament.

'We must weld Members of Parliament into a united party. It must be given some cause and I believe I know how it can be achieved,' he told his wife as he set out plans on a sheet of paper.

'This may well exhaust you. It destroyed O'Connell. You must moderate the demands you make upon yourself.'

'When I grow weary of it all I will take a boat and spend a week on Church Island away from all the turmoil and live like the Hermit Killian.' He smiled at the thought.

When the votes were counted John Dillon succeeded in obtaining 215 and Daniel Parr's man was elected, giving Parr two men in the Commons who would do his bidding.

'It was a brave attempt,' his father told him when the excitement was over. 'You did exceedingly well. Parr may have two men in the House of Commons but it will be different the next time. He will have to run against you himself.'

'What should I do now?'

'Go abroad for awhile. You can always learn from a visit to London and Paris. The estate can run itself and I am sure I can solve any difficulty which may arise,' he told them.

They were both excited at the idea. Three weeks later they set off for London, intending to spend a few days there and then travel to France.

They reached Edward Dillon's château in the summer. Workmen walked slowly through the ordered gardens attending to the small hedges and flowers. A fountain splashed into a broad scallop-shaped basin, the water running from shell to shell and then through the lawn until it ended in a large artificial pond which was set among a vista of old trees. The horizon was uncertain in the haze.

A servant took their luggage from the back of the carriage and showed them to rooms set out for them. When they were woken that evening they sat down to a light lunch of fine meat and wine. Neither his brother nor his wife were present at the château, both having engagements outside the city.

'And what shall we do, now that we are masters for a day and night?' John Dillon asked as he finished his wine.

'Let us ride through the estate to see what changes your brother has brought about during our absence.'

'Very good. I cannot think of anything more relaxing.'

They spent a delightful day together and continued on their own in the château for some days before Edward Dillon returned.

They often set off for Paris as the sun was rising. The summer dust was damp and the air fresh. Sometimes John Dillon left the coach at the Tuileries and walked towards the Louvre. Before parting they always arranged to meet at some café or other.

As Elinor Dillon was passing through the rue Honoré a letter was pressed into her hand. She glanced behind her and caught sight of a scabbed, rough face. For a moment she was going to cast the note on to the ground, feeling that it was soiled. On opening it she was surprised to see that the note addressed her by her first name, that her brother's name was mentioned and that somebody named James Stephens wished to meet her at the Irish College.

She made her way through the Latin Quarter, asking for directions from the hungry students who congregated at the cheap cafés. Passing through a network of streets behind the Sorbonne, she approached the heavy door at the college entrance. She knocked loudly, and after some time a black-robed seminarian opened the door.

'I have an appointment with a Mr James Stephens,' she said.

'I'm afraid there must be some mistake,' he answered, poking his lean head out into the street and looking up and down in a frightened manner.

She produced the letter which he glanced at before closing the door, leaving her standing in the street. Ten minutes later he reappeared.

'Enter,' he muttered secretively.

She found herself in a tranquil cobblestone yard and felt lost in the wide space. On either side the building rose four storeys to a mansard roof, the windows thrown open to catch some mild summer wind. She wondered how this building and its inmates had survived the French Revolution. Her thoughts were interrupted by the young seminarian.

'Follow me,' he said. 'The gentleman is waiting for you in the sacristy.' She was led into a dark chapel which smelt of candle smoke and incense. The seminarian directed her to enter a door beyond the altar. A man with intense eyes invited her to sit down.

'My name is James Stephens.'

'How did you know I was visiting Paris?' she asked.

'We have our own secret service. We have set up our network here and despite the continual eyes of both the French and English governments, we have our own methods of collecting information. However I will not burden you with such detail. I invited you here simply to give you some information which might be of interest to you. To begin with, your brother arrived safely in America. He has not written to you in case his letters are intercepted. He is safe and well and I believe working as a journalist.'

James Stephens's voice had a quality of certainty. The fact that he could give her definite information concerning her brother was worth her visit. She also felt that her brother belonged to some organization which perhaps might endanger his life.

'You know why he fled to America, I presume,' she said.

'We keep in touch with our American counterparts and I was

informed by them. Feeling is running high in America. Those young men who escaped the famine have felt the breath of freedom in that great country. They will not easily forget what happened to them and they burn with the desire for revenge.'

'But surely you did not bring me here to tell me all this. I hope my brother stays free. He did a foolish thing and his companion died for it. But what can be achieved from America? He should have a free life now and should not engage in Irish affairs,' she told him directly.

'The fact that he is Irish means that he will always take an interest in Irish affairs and you cannot prevent him from doing it. I asked you to come here to inform you that your brother-in-law is a British agent.' He was watching for her reaction as he spoke.

'That is a strong accusation,' she replied.

'He carries information to London on all the Paris activities. We have checked with our London sources and I know this to be true, so be careful.' With no emotion in his voice he added, 'I simply warn you against him.'

'Surely you do not suspect that he is spying on you? How would he be able to discover anything about Irish exiles in Paris?'

'There are others who attend to that, obscure men who live in the dark lanes of the city. But a time may come when it will be his business to carry information concerning Irish revolutionaries to England. Things will become dangerous for us and perhaps for him, so listen carefully to his conversation in case it may be of use to us.'

'You cannot think that I will spy for you,' she said incredulously.

'We think that your husband may some day help our cause. I have followed his articles in the *Freeman's Journal*.'

'I think, Mr Stephens, that you underestimate my husband and any interest he may have in your organization,' she said angrily.

'We need a new voice in the House of Commons and he could be that voice. But this is in the future. I am giving you this information so that you can be on your guard. Listen well to your brother-in-law; observe his attitude. If I have been direct and presumptuous then forgive me. Good day, Mrs Dillon. The young seminarian will let you out by the side door. I suspect that this building is watched and we must be careful.'

He rang a bell and the seminarian escorted Elinor across the courtyard and out of a side door. She walked through the narrow quarter down towards the Pantheon as if she had emerged from a dream. Later, as she sat at table with her husband and his brother, the conversation turned towards politics and she recalled what James Stephens had told her.

'I presume that Ireland is at peace,' Edward Dillon observed.

'At peace?' his brother repeated, uncertain of the purpose of his question.

'Yes. I read in some French journal that there was insurrection in some cabbage patch in Tipperary and that the insurgents fled before the police.'

'I think that it was more than an insurrection in a cabbage patch. The mood of the country was such that, had the conditions been different, there might have been a general uprising. Young men are angry at what happened during the famine. It has left a dark stain on people's minds.'

'Then you think there will be further troubles?' Edward asked.

'That depends entirely on the British government. They did not seem to learn from their mistakes,' his brother answered.

'And what are your feelings in the matter? You have a political voice in the country now.'

'I believe that an individual has rights, rights that cannot be taken from him. The people have endured too much and next time they will not tolerate the easy and detached attitude of the English government.'

'Then you believe in rebellion?'

'No, I believe in a revolution. Revolutions succeed, rebellions fail.'

'And you would be party to this revolution?'

'No, for the moment I believe in constitutional change. I believe that a united Irish Party in the House of Commons could swing things in Ireland's favour. I still think the voice of reason could prevail.'

'Yes, reason should prevail. But will it? I believe that many of the insurgents are in Paris. They are caught up in thoughts of rebellion and certainly do not believe in constitutional change.'

'I was not aware of that,' John told him.

'So the rumours of the city have it. Paris is now the refuge for every rebel in Europe. They gather at the cafés and discuss rebellion.'

'Then Europe may take flame, and kings and lords look carefully at their positions,' John said.

'You believe that a handful of malcontents can shake the political power of Europe?'

'You need a single flame to set Europe on fire and perhaps that flame is in the cafés and hovels of Paris. It happened before and it may happen again.'

'I do not think that this revolution could be carried to Ireland.'

'A king who lived a short distance from this château lost his sacred head, and the divine right now belongs to the people.'

'Then you are a revolutionary at heart,' Edward laughed.

'No, I read the signs of the times.'

They had many discussions during their stay and when Elinor and John Dillon started out on their return trip to Ireland she had much to reflect upon as they watched Paris disappear behind them. It was obvious that her brother-in-law's sympathies were with the established order of England. She wondered how true James Stephens's words were. Would Edward Dillon spy upon his brother?

# Chapter 24

Robert Dillon made his way falteringly from his bedroom to the library. He read *The Times* until eleven o'clock when he sat before his desk and looked at the sheets of manuscript set out neatly before him. He always arranged the following day's work before he retired.

He had reached the final chapter. Marie Antoinette was dead and the bloody Revolution was consuming its own. Paris was wet with the blood of Danton and Robespierre and lesser men who had gathered at the Convention. The Paris scenes filled his imagination and seemed more real to him than the daily routine at the Hall. He dipped his pen in the ink well and began to write.

'It was a rotten season. The end had come to all things cherished by an old way of life which had its roots in a dim medieval past. A queen had been executed. An epoch had drawn to a bloody close.' All the strands of history, all the political turmoil and all the raging passion must be brought together in his final comment. He believed that the very same forces which had brought down the French aristocrats would destroy the estates of Ireland in the future. The seed of their destruction was already in men's minds.

He continued to write slowly, setting down his pen when he felt tired.

When Elinor came to visit him that evening she found him sleeping in his chair, his face seemingly lifeless and dry as parchment. She was about to leave the room when he awoke.

'I dozed off, I'm afraid,' he apologized.

'And how did your writing succeed today?' she asked.

'Well, I think. For two days I have sat at this desk and looked at a blank page, lacking the courage and strength to begin the final chapter. Today some old feeling for the work returned and I made a start.'

She drew up an armchair to the globe of light and began to read the five pages of manuscript. When she had finished she saw that he was smiling.

'It is splendid writing, strong and simple,' she said. She rose from her seat and put her arms about his shoulders.

'I have loved you, Elinor, more than all the other women. More than my wife, more than my errant daughter. For you have a heart and a mind that are warm and free. No richer gift can be given to any woman. Without you I would never have come to the final chapter. If I should die will you see it through the press?'

'Of course I will. I am well enough acquainted with it to know where every page is. Do not worry concerning its publication. It will be placed with the other volumes in your library,' she assured him. She kissed his forehead.

'Remember, you have been a father to me. When I first entered his house it was a hostile place and I could feel dislike everywhere.

I was an intruder from the lower social circles. I know what was said concerning me in the other big houses, in the mud cabins and in the towns: I was a woman in search of a fortune. But I did not come here in search of a fortune. I came here because some strange fate arranged these things.'

'There is such a fate. I believe it works for us and against us. We can never see its pattern but it shapes our end. It works through everything, the animals, the earth and within us. Our destiny was fixed: how could a single racehorse save the destinies of a house? Why does a great famine sweep the land, destroying the innocent and leaving the owners on their estates?' he asked thoughtfully.

He took her hand in his. His eyes were wet and there was a slight dribble from the edge of the mouth. She noted that this body was cold and that there was a slight tremor in his voice.

'But do not think of these matters. They are best left to the philosophers. There is no answer to the darker side of life. Do not let it kill the laughter and the dancing; you will grow old quickly enough. Life flows by like the stream through the wood.'

She looked at the lawn, a few trees breaking the monotony of space. A servant was playing with her children on the grass.

The young horses were moving down towards the lake shore, Pegasus by now having sired twelve foals. She had mated her horses with care and yet the perfect goal eluded her. The horses moving towards the lake would fetch good prices at the fair of Ballinasloe. The estate was showing a profit. Many of the trees in the far woods were ready to fell. She would have them seasoned in the mill yard and cut into planks which would be sold to the merchants.

She was drawn out of her reverie by a young soldier walking across the lawn. The children rushed to him and he picked them both up and swung them around.

'Oh no, I don't believe it,' she said, looking more closely.

'What is the matter?' Robert Dillon asked, placing his pen on the desk.

'It is Tony Buckley. He has gone and joined the army. His mother brought him to me four days ago with tears in her eyes, begging me to dissuade him. But he would not be moved. He had seen the soldiers parade through the streets of Galway in their uniforms and listened to the band and talked to the sergeant major who painted a glowing picture of life in distant lands. He should stay with us at the stables. He understands horses and was happy here.' She watched the scene below on the grass.

Behind her the old man continued to work, writing with urgency, knowing that, if he did not continue, his book would never be finished. Then he put down his pen, asking her to help him rise from the chair. His body seemed as frail as chalk and the creative effort had made him weak. He fought for breath and fell back into his chair exhausted.

'Let me gain my breath,' he said in a humiliated voice. His eyes burned with determination as he tried to get up. He took his silver-tipped cane and they made their way to his bedroom. She rang the bell and Tadhg Mor came immediately. Gently they stripped him of his clothes and lifted him into bed, drawing the sheets up about him. He stared at the wall, his mind exhausted.

She returned to the library and placed the completed sheets with those of the final chapter. She counted the folios containing the rest of the manuscript: fifty in all. She knew every one as if she had written it herself.

The next day Robert Dillon did not rise, sleeping until midday and never moving from his fixed position on the bed. Tadhg Mor called her to see if he had died in his sleep but when they drew back the sheet and felt his heart, there was a slow old pulse still beating.

'I worked too hard yesterday,' he said when he awoke. 'Last night I had terrible dreams. I saw the library on fire and rushed to save my manuscripts but some invisible hand kept me back. I watched my work consumed by the flames and now I feel a power has left me.'

'Rest now, and we will bring you light food and some of your favourite wine. Of course you will finish your work,' Elinor said encouragingly.

News passed through the estate that the old man was dying. John Dillon was brought from Galway, arriving at the house four hours later. The old man spoke quietly to him but he was exhausted. The alarm had been premature and his strength returned. The rumours ceased and the estate got back to its normal work. One day the old man called Elinor.

'I would like to visit the estate, to see it for the final time. Do not flatter me by saying that my health will return when we both know it will not. Come with me and bring Tadhg Mor. He will carry me to certain places that are inaccessible by coach.'

Tadhg Mor now came and slept in a small room close to Robert Dillon's bedroom. The servants watched from discreet corners as he carried the old man down the staircase and out to the coach drawn up before the front door. Tadhg Mor mounted the driving seat as Elinor wrapped her father-in-law's knees in a woollen blanket and sat beside him.

He looked at the sweep of the lawn and the broad chestnut trees set to break the vast space.

'I played there as a child. My father built his house here because of the view. He told me that he stood on the hill and looked towards the lake and became enchanted by the prospect. It is as beautiful today as it was then.'

He fell into silence and watched eagerly as they moved along the lake. They reached a small peninsula of whin and rock and he asked to be carried to the narrow tip. When he was set down he turned to Elinor.

'When I was a small boy my tutor brought me here. He was a classical scholar and had been to Greece. On this peninsula we set up the battle of Marathon; I was all the Greeks and he was all the Persians. When the battle was over and I had won, I ran all the way to Athens which was our house and told the news of the victory to my father. That is how I learned my history, never for a minute realizing that all these battles were set up at a distance from the house so that my tutor could indulge in drink. On a summer's day he would draw a whisky bottle from his pocket and call out, "How hot the Greek sun is, burning my throat and parching my lips. Why, Alexander the Great, I must drink or we shall not conquer the earth." That is the great memory I have of the tutor who stimulated my interest in history.'

He looked at the small inlet, calm and tranquil.

'Old Parr never satisfied his wish to bring us down. Watch always for the winds of change and move with them. The times are changing, Elinor. This famine will not be easily forgotten and the young men in the towns will not endure the present systems. So shift with the winds. The children are healthy; I can see no defect in boy or girl.'

Suddenly she realized that he must know the children did not belong to Dillon stock. The house with its lands and beauty were more important than the legitimacy of her children. She put her arm in his and held him close to her. Tadhg Mor walked towards a small wood and left them to their privacy.

'You know so much,' she whispered. 'You seem to understand all things.'

'We are not stones but human beings. We may conceal our passions but the tempest rages in our minds. You need more love than you have ever been given.' He spoke looking directly ahead, avoiding her eyes. 'But enough of this. We must now visit the Round Field.'

At his request all the horses and foals were brought from the stables and allowed to run free across the open space. He watched the fluid movements of their bodies, the thunder of their feet on the dull surface of the field.

'Be the powers, me Lord, it's grand to see you out an' about again and looking in great shape and fettle,' Johnny Appelby said, approaching him. He had been slightly drunk ever since Pegasus had won the Grand National four years previously. 'I'd say, sir, you could get up on one of these horses and take the fences as well as you ever did. T'was only the last night and me with the quality at the Brewsters Arms and me telling how I trained Pegasus, that I told them that Robert Dillon took me into the stables and taught me all he knew about horses and put me on the back of my first mount and set me on my way.'

Robert Dillon was amused.

'You look as sprightly as ever, Johnny, and obviously enjoying the drop of whisky as much as ever.'

'They had me go to the priest to take this new pledge against drink which is invading Ireland. We all went along to the church and there was a strange priest who roared down at us. He made hell feel very near and very hot and put the fear of God into me.'

'And what of this hell?' Robert Dillon asked.

'Well now, it seems far away and not too hot and maybe it was never lit at all for I fear it's a way of frightening us and I'll take my chances. I'm past destroying women and I do no harm to any but myself.'

'And what do you think of the fine animals running free in the field?' Robert Dillon asked, changing the subject.

Johnny Appelby put his clay pipe in his mouth and studied them seriously. He pointed at one particular horse with the stem.

'That's a winner if ever there was one but he needs to build his leg muscles and sharpen his wit. He's a bit like Pegasus in his carefree ways. He moves like a horse belonging to one of the old Gaelic warriors.'

Robert Dillon looked intently at the horse. Everything which the old jockey had said was true.

'Has he been named, Elinor?' the old man enquired.

'No, but if you choose a name we would be pleased.' She had noticed the keen interest in his eye.

Many classical references came to his mind but he rejected them in favour of the name which would mark his last visit to the field.

'Call him Appelby's Fancy to commemorate a great human being.' There was a sound of celebration in his voice. Johnny Appelby was embarrassed.

'I'm obliged to you, sir, but it's no decent name for a horse. Call him Nightingale or Gold Dawn but Appelby's Fancy is a bit common.'

'It is a well-chosen name,' Elinor said, noticing that the old man was growing tired.

'I must go, Johnny. But tonight when you are drinking in Biddy Kelly's shebeen remember me and have a drink on me.' He brought out a sovereign and handed it to Johnny.

'God bless you, sir, and may good luck attend you.'

He watched as the old man was lifted from his seat and carried to the coach, knowing that he would never again see him alive.

The sun was setting when they reached the house, after they had visited all the places which Robert Dillon associated with happiness. Tadhg Mor carried him to his bed and he asked for Elinor.

'Quickly, fetch pen and paper. I wish to dictate the final pages

258

of the book to you. I have little time left.'

'But you are tired and should sleep.'

'I will have eternity to sleep in and I must set down the final pages,' he told her.

She brought fresh sheets of paper and he began to dictate slowly and evenly, his eyes closed. When they reached final paragraphs he sighed with exhaustion.

'The end must stand as it is, Elinor. I do not think we will have a chance to revise it.' A smile of satisfaction played on his face.

'It needs no revision,' she told him.

After he had gone to sleep, Elinor and John sat at his bedside throughout the night. At two o'clock the village priest gave Robert Dillon the last rites and sealed his senses with oil. He slipped quietly into death as the sun was rising over the lake.

The servants began to toll out the sad news on the farm bell. On the lawn Bartley Gaynor held his ragged hat in his hand in respect. Nature was taking its course as it took its course in the woods and in the depths of the lake.

That evening Tony met a servant girl in the woods. They made love on the moss floor, caught with the huge urgency of passion. Soon he would leave her to join his regiment on the heights above Sebastopol. During the harsh winter of 1854 the icy winds would cut into his bones as he lay in the mud without shelter and heat. He would die of exposure and starvation in December and be buried in an unmarked grave.

The funeral of Robert Dillon took place four days later, attended by the tenants of the estate and a few elderly gentlemen who had been acquinted with him in his youth. Many were surprised to know that he had lived so long and without significance.

# Chapter 25

Kevin O'Donnell watched the coast of Ireland pass beneath the eastern horizon. He wished that he were walking the streets of Galway instead of undertaking the long voyage to America. He lived in cramped quarters with three other young men, spending their days walking the deck and taking exercise. At night they talked intensely, wondering what lay ahead and who would meet them on the quays of New York.

Kevin O'Donnell made friends with Desmond Hogan. He had an easy, light-hearted manner but was sure of his own beliefs. He could quickly appraise a person's character and summarize it in a telling phrase. He walked the deck alone, his hands knit behind his back, his face tight with thought. He had spent three months in Ennis jail for carrying arms and escaped by feigning an epileptic fit. He had hidden in a garret for a month while the soldiers combed the town for him. Kevin O'Donnell felt secure in his presence but it was only halfway through the voyage that he told him of his failed assassination attempt on Daniel Parr.

New York was far bigger than they had ever imagined. Endless ships were moored close to South Street. There was the din of carts on the cobblestones carrying goods to the warehouses and the frenetic movement of people coming and going. The vast city, third largest in the world, claimed allegiance to no king or ruler, but to itself. Its buildings were high but here and there they could see the spire of a church or the heavy dome of a municipal building. While they edged up the river, steamboats discharging black smoke passed by. They anchored at one of the docks and two customs officers came on board to check the ship. They were followed by a doctor who pronounced the ship healthy and permitted the passengers to disembark. They moved down the gangway and felt the firm land of New York under their feet, pulsing with life.

'Well, what do you think of this great city boys?' a cabbie asked them. 'Is it not the first wonder of the New World?'

'I presume it is,' Kevin O'Donnell said, looking at the man with the bowler hat.

'You are expected by Colonel Morris and I have come to pick you up,' he told them, opening his cab door. 'Once I hadn't a donkey to call my own and now I have a fleet of cabs, an Italian woman in my bed and a house with five rooms. But step on board and I'll bring you up through Broadway and show you City Hall itself. And then I'll bring you to your Colonel Morris.'

He was jovial, taking pleasure in the city and in himself. He drove them along Broadway, a wide street with high brick buildings, the shop windows filled with goods and large signs and yawnings carrying proprietors' names.

'And that is Astor House,' the cabbie told them, pointing to a hotel opposite the City Hall. 'Finer than any hotel in Europe and filled with every type of water closet to wash yourself with. You could billet an army there, but sure it is only the quality that stay there. It was opened for business by Charles Stenson and there is scarcely a great man who has not inscribed his name on the register.'

'I thought that this was a democracy?' Desmond Hogan asked laughingly.

'Well it is, up to a point. The statesmen and politicians meet there and do their deals. I was in it twice and you could smell the wealth coming up from the carpet and staring at you from the large mirrors. The grand ladies were ravishing, ravishing, with their long skirts and plumed hats.'

Opposite the Astor Hotel stood the new Post Office and the Herald Office, the latter a conspicuous building of white marble, resembling a palace more than a printing house.

Kevin was interested in the offices of the *Herald*, remembering the squalid conditions under which they had worked in Galway. He felt that he would like to continue journalism in this city.

The traffic had become dense and drivers whipped their horses forward, calling abuse at those who got in their way. Men carried packs on their shoulders, others pushed loaded barrows, everyone anxious and preoccupied. The cabbie negotiated his cab through the confusion and they found themselves in a long street where the city was less chaotic. As they moved further west the street took on a settled urban look. The prosperous looking houses were detached and surrounded by walls.

'We are almost there,' he told them, reining his horse. 'This is the entrance to Colonel Morris's estate.'

They went through large ornamental gates, trees on either side of the avenue giving the impression that they were in the country. They emerged from the avenue and looked in awe at a huge house set in a wide lawn filled with rose beds.

'Kevin, do you remember the fine words you were reciting to us on the voyage to America? We hold these truths to be self-evident that all men are created equal. Well, I'm afraid I'm having my doubts. Nobody told the owner of this ranch that we were all created equal,' Desmond Hogan commented.

They laughed nervously. They had disembarked from a ship scarcely two hours previously, had been brought through the vast city of New York and were now in some private domain.

'This my boys, is where I leave you. Very few get such a view of the city their first day in America and very few are brought to the house of old Colonel Morris,' the cabbie said. 'You will be bedded and taken care of for a day or two which will give you time to put your thoughts together. He's a grand man but not to be crossed. He'll take care of your needs.' He whipped his horse lightly and set off down the avenue.

A servant girl took their baggage and asked them to follow her. They were led to a yard with outhouses where she showed them to a long room with several beds, looking like the interior of a barracks. The walls carried military prints and antique firearms and swords.

'I will ring the bell and summon you to the kitchen for food in an hour or so. Colonel Morris will meet you this evening when he arrives from the city. He is a punctual man and does things upon the hour,' she said and then left them alone, gazing at each other in some surprise.

'And who is Colonel Morris?' Desmond Hogan asked. 'He certainly will be an interesting man to meet. I thought perhaps that we might be met by some Irishman who would help us to settle in America. I suspect that there is more to all this than Irish patriotism, but in the mean time I'm going to enjoy a large meal. I had no appetite on board that ship but the New York air has sharpened it beyond a reasonable measure.'

'This is no time to talk about food,' one of the others said.

'This is the time to talk of food. We are not straying on the docks like many others and you cannot meet this Colonel Morris unless you have a full stomach.'

Kevin O'Donnell examined the prints and drawings on the wall, all celebrating notable American victories from the War of Independence to the Battle of San Jacinto. It showed Sam Houston leading his Texans against Santa Anna with the legend 'Remember the Alamo'.

A bell tolled in the courtyard and they left the long military room, walking across the cobblestones to the shining white house.

The kitchen was surprisingly sunny. In Ireland it would have been below ground level and filled with shallow light. Two servants kept the house, one the young woman who had shown them to their rooms, the other a large middle-aged negro dressed in liveried clothes. They had not seen a negro before and were amazed at the pigmentation of his face and his lustrous eyes.

'Just don't stare at him like he was an object in a circus. He is a human being just like you and me. Brought straight from the south and freed by Colonel Morris. He don't believe that men should be slaves and he's a union man,' the servant girl said proudly, as she placed large plates of food in front of them. They looked amazed at the beef and vegetables, never having been presented with such quantities of food before.

'Colonel Morris says all young men should be well-fed and muscular,' she added as she bustled about the kitchen.

'Who is Colonel Morris?' Kevin O'Donnell asked when they had pushed aside their plates.

'Shows you know nothing in Ireland. He is one of our national heroes. They have a statue of him in Texas and everybody knows him. Had his arm blown off at Jacinto, patched up in the military camp, and rode back into battle. That's why they have a statue to him in Texas. He has an iron factory now, down at the docks. He owns lots of property and is a mighty independent man.'

She never rested from her work while she talked.

'Now, you go and walk in the grounds and smell Colonel Morris's roses. They are the best in New York. He had them brought straight from England and France. If there is one thing that Colonel likes as much as marching armies its the smell of roses.'

They left the kitchen and went to smell the roses, discovering what the servant had said to be true. The huge garden behind the house was devoted to roses of every variety.

That evening the negro servant came to their room and said in a deep voice, 'It would be the Colonel's pleasure to meet you on the hour in his study, gentlemen.'

They followed him into a square oak-panelled hallway, feeling nervous and badly dressed.

The negro waited until the grandfather clock chimed seven before knocking on the door.

'The young gentlemen are here present, sir.'

'Bid them enter,' a strong voice ordered from inside the room.

They entered a room decorated with stuffed animal-heads backed by wooden shields. There were several cabinets lined with antique guns and the place smelt of cigar smoke and leather. The ceiling was ornamented with a large plaster eagle and military stands stood at each corner of the room.

Colonel Morris rose from his carved desk. He was broad-shouldered and well over six feet. His face seemed carved out of rock and his conventional clothes concealed the body of a soldier. The left arm of his coat hung loose.

'Welcome to America, gentlemen. Kindly take a seat,' he said, indicating the chair. 'I don't know your names. The reason that I invited you here is because you are young soldiers. I read the papers and I know what is going on in Ireland. I have set up a fund which helps young men escape from British hands. Obviously you know who I am; the cook tells every young man who I am. Most of what she says is true. I bring young men here to give them a start in this great country. I make an offer which they readily accept, seeing that I paid for their voyage to America. I pay them one hundred dollars if they join an Irish regiment which I have financed. You ask why I should finance an Irish regiment? Well, Wellington fought his peninsular campaign with Irish soldiers and they are the very best. I helped to weld America together. I was there when we fought the bloody war for Texas and I'm not going

264

to see this country torn apart again. You see this map of America,' he pointed with his cigar.

'Well, look to the South. Some day they will try and secede from the Union; the South is straining against us. I don't think I'll be going into battle again but I want the North prepared. The South rears good soldiers; they say that one Southerner can whack ten Yankees. We need professional soldiers to lead young recruits when the time comes. You could become these leaders. Some day you may be given the chance to return to Ireland with your experience. I leave the choice to you. You will be well-paid and fed and I will give each man who enlists a hundred dollars. If you have any questions, ask them. It's a free country.'

'What if we don't accept your offer?' Kevin asked.

Colonel Morris looked at him sternly, a flash of anger in his eyes.

'Nobody has ever refused my generous offer. You fought for a hopeless cause in Ireland, neither properly armed or trained. I make you a good offer. I brought you here, remember. You refuse and the cabbie leaves you where he found you on the docks. Think about it and give me your answer within an hour.'

They returned to their sleeping quarters to discuss the proposal. Three of them decided then and there to accept the offer and pleaded with Kevin to join them. A hundred dollars was more than they would earn in three months in New York and if they did not like the army they could leave it. Besides, they would be trained in the use of arms and they could return to Ireland if the opportunity was right.

'I believe in the cause as much as anybody,' Kevin said, 'but I will not be bought or bullied. The cabbie can bring me back to the quays and I will start out on my own. If I care to join the army I'll do so. I did not come here to be ordered about by a military tyrant.'

'How will you survive?' they asked.

'In my own way. I have plans. I passed by the publishing centre of New York today. I can do more with the pen than I can do with the sword. I will not be bullied by this loudmouth who thinks he owns us.'

'If that is your decision I will back you,' Desmond Hogan said seriously.

They returned to the colonel and gave him their answer. There

265

was anger in his eyes when Kevin asked to be returned to the docks.

'You owe me your passage money. The captain has to be bribed. It will cost you two hundred dollars. Have you that sum in your possession?'

'No,' Kevin said, uncertain as to what would happen to him.

'Then you may be declared an unwelcome guest in this country, be returned to Ireland and handed over to the British. We have had young men who did not accept my offer before and they ended in English jails.'

'We have accepted your offer and signed papers so we are entitled to three hundred dollars. We lost two hundred dollars to Kevin in a card game so now we intend to pay him back. Is that not right?' Desmond Hogan asked the others. 'And the strange thing, sir, is that I bear arms. I am a simple man and I have a simple aim in life and that is to kill my enemy when I know who my enemy is. Our friend must be let free. We have struck a fair deal and you must abide by it.'

'What type of arms do you bear?' the colonel asked.

'A colt revolver. I may miss the first time but I have four other chances which gives me a great advantage.' He produced a revolver from his pocket.

The colonel was impressed by his cool daring, seeing a potential leader who could think adventurously under pressure.

'Very well. I admire your courage. I promise your friend will go free and I swear it on these sacred flags. He will be returned to the docks tomorrow and you may now return to your billets.' Desmond Hogan did not like his manner or his promise, and when they returned to the dormitory Kevin was sweating with fear. He thanked Desmond for his support, asking where he had acquired the gun.

'If old Colonel Morris is willing to leave loaded revolvers about the place I see no reason why I should not borrow one. I picked it up on the way into his office. I never liked the arrangement but it was the best way out of Ireland. Colonel Morris is not interested in any Irish cause; only in his dream of America. I'll join his army and learn the craft of arms. Some day I may be able to put it to use in Ireland. I have no taste for working on the streets of New York.'

His humour had suddenly deserted him and he was serious. 'What will you do tomorrow when you are left at the docks?' he asked Kevin. 'You will have to begin all over again.'

'I have money to last me a fortnight and I have some ideas. The most important thing that the cabbie did was to bring us to City Hall. I was a reporter for two years in Ireland and I know something of the craft. I will see if I can find employment there.'

They talked late into the night, filled with optimism and convinced that one day they would return to Ireland and break the link with the union. Just as Kevin was about to fall asleep Desmond Hogan came to his bedside and placed the revolver in his hand.

'Use this tomorrow. I trust neither the cabbie nor Colonel Morris, so have your wits about you. I will see you again. Good night.'

The cabbie's mood was sullen as he drove towards the quays and there was little conversation between them. Kevin suspected that he had carried young men to British ships and had them transported back to Ireland. When they reached Broadway Kevin pushed the revolver in to the cabbie's back.

'What's that?' he asked in surprise.

'A revolver. It carries five bullets and each one has your name marked on it in capital letters. Do you hear?'

'Be dad I do sir. But sure, you are not going to kill me in the middle of New York?'

'I might. It is as convenient a place as any and might make a miserable life remarkable. Now, I want some information. Where were you ordered to drive me?'

'Down to the docks.'

He jabbed the gun into his back again.

'I'm not satisfied with your answer. Could you be more precise? Your life depends upon it.'

'It's the colonel that has me the way I am. He has me deliver young men to English agents. They are carried aboard ships and taken back to Ireland. Colonel Morris knows they are all wanted men and that is why he has the power over them.'

'Your honesty has saved your life. Leave me off here and disappear as fast as your horse will take you.' The cabbie followed his instructions and Kevin found himself back on the pier. He could easily have hired a cab and returned to the city centre but he felt that much more secure on the docks.

He went into one of the saloons, a grey, dingy place with straw on the floor. Sitting in small timber alcoves were men marked by rough living. They were a mixture of races – Irish, Scots, English and mid-European. The place was pungent with the smell of sweat and urine.

'What can I do for you, lad?' the barman asked. 'You are blocking up the door and that's not good for business.'

'I'm quite sorry, sir.' He went up to the long wooden bar. The faces reflected in the large windows were filled with the vitality of the city. Most of them seemed evil and though he had only seen one prostitute in Galway he was certain that the women, with slashes of red paint on their lips and exposing more breast than he had ever seen in his life, were in that profession. One brushed against him so that the large softness of her breast was pressed against his arm. He had not experienced sexual proximity before.

'Perhaps the young man would like an hour of pleasure with Rita?' she asked, a girlish smile on her face which did not belong there. 'Rita has her own room, very beautiful, and Rita loves young men.' He was beginning to sweat and her loud perfume was raw about him.

'Leave him be, Kate. Don't you see that he's wet behind the ears?' A man pushed her aside roughly and faced Kevin. She called out a string of curses at him, many of which were new to the Irishman.

'What in God's name are you doing here? Do you realize that every thief, pickpocket and fence has his eyes upon you and knows that you have just arrived. You have walked into a rat pit and some of these brutes would beat you to jelly without a second thought. They kill their prey and throw them in the river,' the stranger told him.

He looked carefully at the man who had come to his defence. There was a white sharpness in his eyes which indicated that he knew his way about the underworld of New York.

'Who are you and why did you take my part?' Kevin asked.

'I saw your face and listened to your voice and I know what is going on. I recognized your Galway accent when you said you were sorry. It is a word we don't use very often here. Now that I am here, would you like to leave the place or should we go down to the back where you would be less conspicuous?'

Kevin hesitated, afraid the man would rob him.

'No, I'm not one of them. My name is Liam Flaherty. Follow me.'

The gaslights glimmered weakly in the gloomy place. The voices were garbled and tangled. Finally they came to an empty space with two free seats.

'Ah, Mr Flaherty, and what can I do for you and your friend?' the barman asked.

'Give us honest whisky, Timothy. Nothing adulterated, nothing dosed, just plain, honest whisky. You know what I mean.'

He seemed to command respect. The barman brought him two tumblers of whisky and did not ask for money.

'Now tell me about yourself and how you found yourself in this pit. I'm sure you were warned against them.'

Kevin decided to tell this man everything which had happened to him. When he was finished Liam Flaherty took his hand and shook it.

'It would have been my pleasure to have been there. I read the papers. So you are the young man with the price on his head. I know all about Daniel Parr and I would have aimed straighter than that. We paid our rents to the tyrant's father and I came here to get away from the misery of living on potatoes and fish. Whenever I see a box of fish down by the quay I almost vomit. What are your plans, my brave rebel?'

'I don't feel very brave at this present moment. I was a reporter with the *Galway Advertiser* and I feel that I would like to take up the same occupation here. I have passed the *Herald* offices and was greatly impressed. There is so much to write about, but before I approached them I would need to have written a set of articles and this is about the best place to begin.'

'You think so?' he asked.

'Yes. It is full of noise and colour and character.'

'If you think that you can find a publisher for such articles I will bring you to places which will make your young flesh crawl. There are two cities here; one uptown and one by the docks. I will arrange a room for you this evening and set you up with pen and paper and you can write down all that you have seen. But in the mean time you remain here. This is my corner and you are under my protection. If you wish to leave, Johnny the Harrier will go with you.' He rose to leave then began to laugh. 'And to think that you knocked Lord Parr off his horse with a rifle shot. You should have murdered the bastard.'

Kevin sipped the whisky and wondered at the change in his fortunes.

'The young man requires new drink?' one of the barman asked in an obsequious voice.

'No. But could you tell me more about Mr Flaherty.'

The barman looked around, then sat beside him in the cubicle and whispered, 'He is the wild Irish man with the protection. Flaherty protects everybody but they pay Flaherty. If you do not pay Flaherty for this protection then your windows get broken, there is a brawl in your bar or it catches fire under mysterious circumstances. He's a big man down here. He knows everyone and everyone fears him. The ladies love him greatly I'm told, particularly the fine ladies from uptown. Strange man, Flaherty. A good friend, a bad enemy. The Hungarians tried to kill him once but he went and killed them all.'

Later he left the pub with Johnny the Harrier, who had a humped back and squint eyes. His head flicked involuntarily from side to side as they went along the vast quays.

That evening when he was tired of walking he returned to the saloon bar and took up his position in the lower cubicle. It was much later when Liam Flaherty returned, people making way for him as he walked past the bar.

'I have found you some splendid lodgings for the night. You will live in comfort and when you have four articles finished I will arrange a meeting with one of the editors of the *Herald*. Take your bag and follow me, my young felon.'

New York by gaslight was a strange and wonderful sight. The night life seemed to be as populous as that of the day.

'No doubt you enquired who I was?' Flaherty asked, looking straight ahead.

'Yes,' he said.

'Did you enjoy your day?'

'I never spent a day quite like it.'

'Well, tomorrow you sit and write of what you saw. A good friend of mine who owns a finishing school for the finest young ladies in the city will put you up for a few days. Feel free to come and go as you wish and charge all cab fares to me. Her name is Madame Rouge. She belonged to the French aristocracy and fled as a young girl before the Revolution.'

'You know some extraordinary people, Mr Flaherty,' Kevin said.

'The best and the worst.'

He was surprised at the gaudy splendour of the house. Inside he saw red perfumed drapes, nude statues and heard the sound of a piano playing the latest songs somewhere at the back of the house.

'*Vous êtes le bienvenu*,' Madame Rouge said in bad French when she was introduced to Kevin. He answered immediately in French which took both Madame Rouge and Liam Flaherty by surprise. She smiled.

'I'm afraid I have forgotten my French. It was such a long time ago when I left our château in France. One of my girls will show you where you can sleep.'

He was quite surprised at the arrangements for the finishing school. Several of the young women who passed him on the way to his rooms were dressed in light lingerie and he could not take his eyes off their bodies. The corridor smelt of heavy perfume.

'If the young man wishes any service I am willing to fulfil it,' a young woman said. 'I am here for pleasure.'

'No, thank you. I shall sleep now. Tomorrow I have to write some articles,' he told her. 'I am a journalist.'

'And what of the pleasures of the night?'

'I would like a cup of milk, please,' he told her. She left the room and returned much later with a cup of milk.

'Good night,' he said, as she left reluctantly.

Next morning he found he could write easily. The edge to describe what he had seen returned to him. He wrote each article four times.

271

At midday he had his meal with the young ladies, surprised to see that some of them were dressed as nuns. He asked them what order they belonged to and was told the Confraternity of Saint Sue of Le Havre. When the meal was finished he ordered a cab and visited the Bowery with Johnny the Harrier.

He spent three days in the luxurious room, breakfasting each morning with the young women, then going down to the docks to observe the life of that quarter. His mind was sharp and he observed the emigrants coming ashore with exhausted faces and confused expressions. He visited the cellars where many families took up their lodgings, strange lost people in a world they did not understand. He noticed their clothes, their patterns of speech, their modesty, their old world habits. Each evening he set out his thoughts on paper before he settled into bed.

One night somebody entered his room. He rubbed the sleep out of his eyes and saw Madame Rouge with a man standing over his bed. The man did not wear trousers but stood in his long johns.

'This is the sub-editor of the *Herald*,' she said. 'He would like to read your work. I will leave him with you and return in half an hour.'

The burly man sat down heavily on an armchair and looked at Kevin.

'You have powerful friends and in the very best places,' he said laughing. 'Let me read your work, young man.'

Kevin handed his articles to him. The sub-editor read them carefully.

'Who taught you to write?' he asked when he had finished.

'An old revolutionary I knew in Galway. He died under torture in prison. He was a frail old man.'

'Then he trained you well. You may not know much of life but you know your craft. I can use two of these articles. I do not know how you obtained such information on dockland but I suspect that it is Flaherty.' He looked at Kevin sharply.

'Yes. Liam Flaherty has helped me from the beginning.'

'Then I can use you. There are many things going on at the docks about which we know nothing. We need somebody who can get behind the scenes; it makes good reading. I will employ you for three months on the *Herald*, time enough to prove yourself.

272

He turned to go but at the door he asked, 'Do you know where you are?'

'In a finishing school for young ladies.'

'You are in my arse. You are living in the most exclusive brothel in New York.' With that he began to laugh until tears streamed down his face.

He felt humiliated and naive as he sat alone in the room. He had heard of the word brothel before and shady women had been pointed out to him in Galway. But he could not believe that he had been living in one for the past few days.

Liam Flaherty brought him to a clean apartment in upper New York the next day. The landlady was serious and kind.

'She is no Madame Rouge,' Liam Flaherty said, 'and she keeps honest people. You will have to make it on your own from now on. If you want information contact me.'

As he watched the disappearing carriage he felt apprehensive but no longer alone in the city.

# Chapter 26

The election came as a surprise. The great fervour for Repeal was dead and now it would be a straight contest between Parr, Dillon and a Liberal Independent. The excitement gripped the towns and countryside. Men fell into factions and in the pubs and at the fairs the issues of the day were discussed hotly.

'Dillon's time has come,' they called out as John Dillon passed along the road to Galway where he was to put forward his name as a candidate. A crowd gathered around the steps of the court house and choked the doors as he tried to get through. He was followed by the landowners who would bring in their tenants' votes. They pushed the supporters of Parr aside as they made way for John Dillon.

'Take your hands off a Parr man or it will be the worst for you. Daniel Parr will head the poll and put Dillon in his place,' a supporter roared as he was dragged out of the way by John Brown.

Inside in the court house the scene was as confused. People filled the hallway, talking and waiting for something to happen. It was hoped that the two candidates would arrive at the same time and that there might be a clash between their supporters. The reporters waited in quiet corners, biding their time.

John Dillon finally got to the registrar's desk and set down his name. The registrar dried it seriously with blotting paper and looked nervously at the door. He hoped that the peace would hold and wished he had asked for police protection.

There was a loud shout from outside the court house. Daniel Parr had arrived in his coach, flanked by ten horsemen. He made an impressive appearance as he descended from his carriage, taking some coins from his pocket and scattering them over the heads of the crowd. They cheered him as he walked up the steps, his men running ahead to beat a way for him with their whips.

'So you think that you can beat people into submission with your whips and bullyboys, Parr?' John Dillon said. 'Well, let me tell you the days of beating men are over. I will stand for each man's right and it is each man's right which will some day destroy you.'

The expression on Daniel Parr's face was tight. It was the first time he had run for election and he felt ill at ease in the rough company. It was his nature to be secretive and work behind the election scenes. Now he had to present his name as a candidate. He knew that the times were changing, that a new force was emerging in Irish politics. John Dillon was part of this change.

'I would challenge you to a duel but duelling is now illegal,' Parr said, reminding him of their last encounter.

'And so is the use of armour. It is well-known that you used plated armour at our last encounter. Now you are protected by the law.' John Dillon spoke loudly so that everyone present could hear him.

'You suggest that I am a coward and a liar?' he said angrily.

'It is known that you are a coward and a liar. I do not have to suggest it,' John Dillon replied.

Daniel Parr could no longer stifle his fury, and slapped John Dillon in the face with his leather gloves. Immediately bedlam broke out; it was the signal that the supporters had been waiting for. Tadhg Mor grabbed one of Parr's men, lifted him in the air and hurled him against the wall. He let out a scream and fell on the floor unconscious. Men used their bare knuckles and whip butts on the faces of their enemies. The chairs and benches collapsed on the floor and the ink and the paper was walked upon as men fought each other. Parr felt frightened at the turn of events and retreated to a corner where he was protected by three men. Tadhg Mor advanced towards Daniel Parr, dragging the men who stood about him away from their master. He put his hands about his throat and would have choked him had John Dillon not pulled him away.

'Don't soil your hands on him,' he called. 'He's not worth it.'

Daniel Parr rubbed his throat, trying to recover his breath.

The registrar left by a back door and ran to the police barracks. Constables had been drawn in from the small villages and were prepared for such disorder. They put on their helmets and charged into the square. At the command of the sergeant, they rushed into the registrar's office brandishing truncheons, beating back the milling crowd of supporters. Some they caught by their coats and threw on to the granite steps outside. After ten minutes some order was imposed on the room.

'Now, gentlemen,' the registrar said, clearing his throat and feeling the support of the police beside him. 'I think this can all be done with suitable decorum. Would the two gentlemen sign their papers and leave the building in peace. Certain procedures have to be followed in these matters and it is our hope that the election will be fought with decency and without corruptions.'

He was rising to his theme when Daniel Parr interrupted him.

'We have heard enough of your chirping. Let me sign the papers and be on my way. The stench of a Dillon presence is offensive to me.'

The order broke and there was an angry scuffle. The guards used their truncheons again and two men were dragged bleeding from the office. They were cheered as they were led away to the barracks.

'Blood nobly spilt,' somebody called after them.

John Dillon signed his name again, the first form having been trampled on the floor. He watched Parr set his name down on the

275

paper, feeling that they were signing a declaration of war. Both turned and left the room shoulder to shoulder. Men made way for them looking intently at their faces, Parr's cold and arrogant and Dillon's filled with fire.

'Three cheers for the Pope and the Pope's man,' somebody shouted at the main doorway when the two men emerged.

'Damm and blast the Pope and the Pope's agent, Dillon,' came the reply.

It was the signal for a general brawl. Those who had not taken part in the fight in the registrar's office felt that they had been deprived of an opportunity to show their hatred for the opposition. Men lined up in the square with their shillelaghs, a wide lane dividing the two factions. They waited while others joined them from the neighbouring streets, then with a wild cry they charged each other. Men savagely used the knobs of their blackthorn sticks and even women joined in the excitement. Taking off their long stockings they filled them with heavy stones and hurled the weights down on men's backs and heads. They wounded staggered away from the mêlée holding broken noses or cracked skulls. One man crawled towards the edge of the square where a woman rushed at him and brought a loaded sock down on his head. There was a loud crack as his skull was shattered and later he died in one of the side lanes.

John Dillon tried to prevent the fight by charging up the line before it began but his supporters roared at him.

'Out of the way. There are old scores to settle and you have no part in this. The Parrs evicted us during the famine and we'll have our revenge.'

He looked on hopelessly as they sought vengeance for old wrongs, a blood letting that had more cause than politics. The men fought for two hours and, when their forces were spent, hussars galloped forward, bringing the flat side of their sabres down on the backs of the bloody mass of men. Soon the square was deserted, the mud was thickened with blood. Broken shillelaghs lay in every corner and on the pavement the wounded groaned and took stock of their injuries.

Daniel Parr was sitting with his agents at a table in his town house. He would have to travel from town to town making speeches and he knew that he needed the protection both of his agents and his bodyguards.

'It is certain that you will carry the day,' one of his agents said, checking through the lists laid out on the table. 'We have checked the register of electors. There are eight hundred in all and we can count on three hundred. The rest will be divided between Dillon and the other independent.'

'That is not at all certain. Dillon has brought the small landlords in behind him. And we do not know how the towns will vote. Will the businessmen and the professionals come in with me or Dillon?' he asked sharply.

'They were Repealers but that is a dead issue. They have divided loyalties so it will be half and half.' He went through the names of merchants and professionals.

'We must induce them to vote for us. Make threats or promises to each man but bring in the votes. They vote openly and every vote will be marked. Threaten them with horsewhips if necessary. I must head the pole; I'll not have a Dillon declared before me. Is that understood? I have another political meeting to attend and will leave it now with my agents.'

The next meeting took place in his own house, the five most important landowners in Connaught gathering to decide on the temper of the times. They knew how serious the election was for the safety of the Union. Sir William Orme was the first to speak.

'I helped bring this country into the Union. We bartered Catholic Emancipation for the support of the Catholic hierarchy. We spent over a million pounds to bring the rotten boroughs with us and that came to fifteen thousand for every seat. Now this Union is under threat. I have read John Dillon's articles. He has a keen political sense and must be watched. Directly or indirectly he could bring our houses down about us. If the Irish members are welded into an independent party then they hold the power in the House of Commons. They can bring down governments, be they Conservative or Liberal, at their whim and every demand they make will have to be granted. Already Dillon is calling for land reform and rights for tenants and he seeks to have the Ecclesiastical Titles Act reformed and the disestablishment of the Church of

Ireland. Think closely on all these things gentlemen, and consider our position.' His face had a sad cast and he looked piercingly at each man as he spoke.

'Surely they can be bought out again,' Parr interjected. 'And if they will not be bought out with money they can be bought out by titles and sinecures. Each one of them has some weakness and we can play on them.'

'And where is Dillon's weakness or that of Gavan Duffy, or Lucas or Moore? They are all men of character. Sadlicr is weak and so is Keogh. Others might follow them, but it will not be an easy task. I have been in contact with London. Both the Liberals and the Tories are worried about this new development. We are certain that you will be elected but how many more of your political allegiance will be with you in the House of Commons?' Colonel Henry Gallen asked.

In the presence of these men Parr decided to speak the truth.

'No. I cannot see him beaten. Of course an accident could always happen. I have arranged accidents before which were to the advantage of the nation.'

'That would pave the way to chaos. We must find means to contain them, not give them a martyr. The last thing this country needs at present is a patriotic funeral. It would swing the sympathy of the people away from us. We must not damage our cause,' Lord Gerard French said emphatically. They considered their political position all that evening, counting how many freeholders would vote for their candidates. They planned how they would be brought to the polls and how the opposition votes could be intimidated.

Daniel Parr felt more hostile towards John Dillon than he had previously. A man who had been a drunkard and on the very edge of bankruptcy had been saved by his wife. He loathed her more than him, but he did not relish the thought of the election.

John Dillon felt that things were running in his favour when the young priests of the constituency began to come out in his favour. Many used the pulpits to canvass for him and one young curate, who had been trained in France, was particularly bitter in his attacks on Parr. He was an accomplished writer and regularly contributed letters to the local papers, stirring up resentment against the old political order.

John Dillon was uneasy when he was summoned to the Archbishop's palace in Tuam. The Archbishop had been a frequent visitor to Dillon Hall and had lengthy debates with his father in the library. He was a man of immense energy and influence and in no small way had caused his defeat in the last election. Perhaps he would now destroy the support he had among the priests.

He approached the palace. It was a drab, unimposing building, lacking any architectural value. The hall smelt of incense and candles and had a repressive ecclesiastical feeling. A gaunt young priest came to greet him.

'The Archbishop will meet you when he has finished his office,' he said in a low voice. 'Please come with me.'

He led him to the library. While he waited in the library, looking at the immense, boring volumes in Latin, he could find nothing that interested him.

Elinor did not share his respect for the Archbishop and was not in awe of his letter. They had discussed how he should confront the Archbishop if he came under attack.

'Tell him simply that he should mind his own business. He had no right to interfere in the last election and destroy your chances. You have more right to his allegiance than anyone else. Stand up to his challenge; his place is in the Church, yours in the House of Commons. In fact, I would not go near the palace if I were you,' she said, fiercely dismissing the letter.

'He is an old friend of the family. Courtesy demands it,' John Dillon replied.

'Fine friend he turned out the last time you needed support. Go if you think that it is proper and right but put your point of view and put it firmly.'

He was thinking of their conversation when the Archbishop came through the door. He was tall and heavy, bearing the appearance of a man who worked long hours in his study. One was aware of a strong presence in the room. John Dillon was prepared to challenge the Archbishop if necessary. He did not sit beside his desk but took an armchair beside the fire and indicated that John should sit opposite him.

'You are welcome. I know you are a busy man at this moment and am grateful to you for accepting my invitation to Tuam. I remember long and intense debates with your father at Dillon Hall. I believe he finished his vast work on Marie Antoinette?' His voice was arrogant and dismissive.

'Yes. He finished it four hours before he died. But I'm sure you did not bring me here to discuss such matters. We were opponents in the last election campaign. I wondered on my way here if it will happen again.' He spoke directly and with determination.

'No. I have read your articles and I believe in your cause. Nothing can be achieved unless you form an Independent party. It is in the air and I wish to let you know that you have my blessing. I will not come out directly in your support and I will not interfere with priests and curates who favour you strongly. You must play the independent card. In other words every candidate should make an election promise that he will form an Independent party. This is the time for one. You will hold the balance of power and with that you can achieve all your aims. And it can be done in a parliamentary and peaceful fashion.'

'And what will happen if we do not win and do not form an Independent party?' John Dillon asked, wondering what was behind his change of heart.

'The Parr faction will win the day and people will take up arms against constitutional power. I saw the aftermath of the '98 rebellion. I saw young men slaughtered in the small towns and I do not wish to see it again. Revolution is in the air and the seeds are blowing through Ireland. The British Parliament will have to grant concessions before it is too late.' It was obvious that he had given the matter much thought and that he was in possession of knowledge from all over the archdiocese.

John Dillon realized then that his power was growing in the province. If the Archbishop of Tuam had been impressed by his articles then they must have had a similar effect on other minds.

'It's a pity, my lord, that your ideas were not similar to mine during the last election. I could have done with your support then. Now I feel a little like Samuel Johnson when he wrote his letter to Lord Chesterfield. I have my allegiance to the Church but my political opinions are my own and I will not be dictated to.' There was no quiver in his voice.

'I do not seek to change your political opinions,' the Archbishop replied.

'Good. I will follow what I believe is best for the country. If a revolution comes then it is because there is something wrong with the whole system and people have grown tired of promises. I hope the Church has the wisdom to discern what is wrong and unjust and speak against it. You are protected by power; I am not.'

'It can be lonely in an archbishop's palace,' the old man said, trying to engender some sympathy from John Dillon.

'Then bring down the drawbridge,' he replied. The conversation continued for two hours, becoming pleasanter when John Dillon knew that he had made his ideas and conditions clear.

'I will not ask you to eat ecclesiastical food,' the Archbishop said as he walked with him to the main door. He shook his hand.

'I wish I could go with you to the hustings. They would excite my mind, perhaps even change some of my views. You lose touch with reality living here. I was more content when I was riding through Mayo and Galway as a young man, building up a strong church. I met the ordinary people and felt the joy of living. One word before you go. You will perhaps form your party but remember the old Latin tag, *divide et impera* – divide and conquer. The Irish Members of Parliament are greedy creatures. Goodbye and good luck.'

The young priest immediately brought his horse to the main door. As John Dillon left the palace grounds, he felt a new power moving through the land, like active yeast.

For two weeks he travelled the county with an escort of mounted men. They flanked his carriage, drawn by two swift horses as they went from town to town. The escort grew as the election gathered pace. Men assembled in town squares throughout the country to listen to John Dillon. His eloquence had returned, marked by maturity and seriousness. He held the mass of men below him by the power of his voice which carried to each corner of the square. Mounted on their horses about the platform the small landlords, some freeholders and a few priests watched for Parr's men.

'You can break the power of Parr as easily as you can break dry

281

timber if you band together. Do not be afraid on polling day when you call out your choice before the tally men. My men will be at each booth to afford you protection. You will have fair rents and fair tenure. The land will be yours,' he cried out.

His blazing words caught the imagination of men who feared Parr's insidious power. Already many of them had come to him privately to pledge their vote.

Elinor Dillon often went electioneering with him. As the coach passed swiftly across the countryside, flanked by a cavalcade of horsemen, she felt the old power within her husband. He had aged. His hair was now grey and lines furrowed his forehead. She had sat with the agents and counted the votes promised. Her husband could win with a comfortable majority.

They had rarely time to talk. It was only when the campaign was finished and the freeholders were being herded into the towns that they had time to walk in the woods.

'It seems such a long time ago that I saw you for the first time standing before a mass of men in Ballinrobe, effortlessly holding their attention.'

'That was speech-making. Now I feel conviction. I feel that we will form a strong Independent party in the House of Commons. All over the country the candidates are signing pledges that they will not join any English party and I think the pledge will hold.'

'I feel so proud of you. Even in England the papers have reported your speeches and some of them even wish you well.' They walked towards the Round Field. Only a few fences stood where once the course at Aintree had been duplicated.

'This field gives me joy,' he said, 'for it was from this field that both fortune and favour returned to us. Had you not trained the horse I feel that a Parr might be now walking this land. This is a sacred place.' She took his head in her hands and kissed him.

Parr knew that he had failed. He was taunted in the towns, people even throwing stones and rotten potatoes at him. He controlled his temper but behind the scenes he was making plans. He had called in his bullyboys two days before the elections. His freeholders were collected, placed in huge, cribbed carts and led like prisoners to Tuam. As they passed through the streets they were jeered at. It was feared that the Dillon faction might kidnap them and carry them off with their votes. Agents were placed in every booth to mark the way they voted.

The five freeholders set out from the village of Cashel, having settled the night before to challenge Parr and give the vote to Dillon. As they reached the head of the valley they were bundled into a cart and brought to the lake shore. There they were loaded on to a boat and at pistol point brought to one of the remote islands.

'You buggers can roar as loud as you like for Dillon, but you can starve there before you are discovered,' Parr's henchmen told them.

It was only on the election morning that Dillon's men discovered that there were at least forty men imprisoned by Parr's bullyboys at the Brass Castle. They rode furiously through Galway and out of the long sea road to the bleak building. Discharging guns they rode into the courtyard and released the men. Some of them were too late when they reached the booths. Their names had already been called but thirty plumped for Dillon.

For four days men entered the open booths and called out the candidate of their choice. Despite the threats of Parr's men, most had the courage to call out Dillon's name. It was obvious by the morning of the fourth day that he would head the pole.

Galway was jubilant. Men slapped each others' backs and some wept openly. All that night and next day people sat in the hotels and the shebeens discussing the results of the election. The Independent candidates had swept the country.

Men, women and children lined the roadways as John Dillon returned home in an open carriage. They were people who had little to look forward to, living in miserable mud cabins, eking out a meagre diet from poor soil. The children were subject to disease and many died young. As their new Member of Parliament looked at their eyes he saw that they believed in him and had some hope that he might change things for the better. They called out his name as he passed by and he felt at that moment that he could give them a voice in the House of Commons.

All the servants and tenants were waiting at the gate to the Hall, waving banners and flags. They followed him to the front door, and lifted him bodily to the steps. He stood before them and made a bright speech, then invited them into the wide hall to drink to his victory.

Later than evening John Dillon walked by the quiet lake, remembering that his father and his grandfather had found solitude and contentment here. He belonged now in the dark and knotted world of politics.

He looked up at the firm house on the incline. His children were playing happily under one of the trees. The horses were moving from the long field and he could hear the iron rim of a wheel locked in a rut, somewhere in the wood. He had finally come into his own.

# *Chapter 27*

As Elinor Dillon watched the young horse romp home to a convincing victory she felt excitement fill her body. She grasped her husband's hand during the final furlong, as the horse edged to the outside and found its stride. She had had her doubts at the beginning. They had raced him against the best horses in the stable but, like Pegasus, he seemed to have an over-easy attitude. It was only when he was pitted against unknown horses that a strange aggression seemed to possess him and he became eager to win.

'The strain has held,' she told her husband. 'We picked the best of the crop. He has the qualities of his sire.'

'And I placed a hundred guineas on him,' John Dillon said. 'I hope that it will be as fair for us in Parliament and that we can romp home in such an easy manner.'

When they reached the winners' enclosure Johnny Appelby had his arms around the neck of the horse. People laughed at the sight of the small man carried about the ring in so strange a fashion.

'I have lived twice,' he called to the jockey. 'The horse was named after me in the Round Field. I hope that there are racecourses in Heaven.'

At the club house the gold cup was presented to Elinor Dillon, the old men nodding approvingly at her beauty and style.

'It is given to few women to have the natural instinct to breed a horse of such merit,' Lord Dunraven said to her at the winners' table.

'I rode a horse when I was eight. I did not have the luxury of a pony which would be easy to control. Once I was placed on his back I felt an understanding between us and that has never abandoned me. Appelby's Fancy comes from pedigree stock, the best we have produced in years. The rest are firm and capable but they have not been given the extra quality which makes a winner. You need a sharp eye and luck to produce a horse like Appelby's Fancy,' she told him.

He was an old man with a white sunless face, his voice and gestures measured and austere. She knew that he owned a thousand acres of land in Armagh. His first passion was for fine art and he had spent several years in Italy as British Ambassador where he purchased many Renaissance paintings. His second passion was horses and these days he never left his estates except when new Parliaments assembled or for the great races which were held in England.

'But surely you are not interested in a woman's fancy,' she said, laughing.

'When that fancy is a top-class racehorse and when the woman is beautiful and assured and when her horse won the Grand National I am interested,' he said.

She told him the story of the journey to France and the wedding gift she had received from her brother-in-law. Because he was an old man she took time to describe all the details which surrounded her choice.

'What a charming story. Dumas would have written a worthy novel on the subject. A thoroughbred horse owned by a thoroughly well-bred lady.' He sipped his champagne slowly and thoughtfully.

'You equate horses and women,' she said.

'No, I equate women with horses.' He laughed. 'And that is why I am cynical. But tell me about Robert Dillon. I believe that he had embarked upon an impossible project. I knew him as a very intense and frail young man. Married a stumpy woman who ran

285

his estate. Did he ever finish his magnum opus?' he asked.

'Yes. I took the final dictation from him.' She described how she had sat by the dying man's bed and written the final pages of the manuscript.

'Did he ever explain to you why he chose such a fateful queen? I thought that he might have chosen a more serious subject.'

'It began as a romantic attachment but turned into a most serious work. And he did come to some definite conclusions,' she told him.

'What were they?'

'He believed that the estates in Ireland and the class which they sustain will fail. Perhaps it will not happen in this generation but it will happen.'

'You sound very definite.' He was watching the expression on her face.

'I feel definite about it. He explained his reasons thoroughly but perhaps he was wrong. Time will tell.'

'I wonder if we all shall fail like Marie Antoinette. I too ponder about these things. We have been established in Ulster for two hundred years. We formed our estates with great labour, nurturing them and building our fine houses. Yet they too could fail,' he said in a serious tone. 'But the South will fail before the North because we have a dour Scottish streak in us. Many of us are not thoroughbred and that helps.'

'Enjoy your champagne. Leave the future generations to deal with their own problems. Now I wish to dance with you. The music is in waltz time and I think I know the steps.' She spoke spontaneously, a smile returning to her face.

He led her on to the large maple floor, holding her in a stiff formal manner. He was pleased to have such a lovely woman as a partner, knowing that the eyes of the company were on them. When the dance was finished he led her back to the table.

'I'm afraid that I am out of breath,' he told his friends. 'I have let a young woman seduce me on the floor.'

He ordered a bottle of champagne and toasted the beauty of Elinor Dillon.

'What do you expect from this new Parliament?' he asked, suddenly changing tack.

286

'I am not a political person,' she replied smiling.

'You do not live with a political man and remain untouched by his ideas. I believe that we shall see a new Independent party in the next assembly of the House of Commons.'

'I believe that it has been mentioned in the papers,' she said cautiously.

'Then the Irish Members will have a new force.'

'That is true. My husband is filled with optimism. Most of the candidates have taken the Independent pledge.'

'Do you think that such a party can remain together? I believe that they may bring down the government but I can assure you that during the next administration they will be purchased. The Union was built on patronage and the Independent party will be destroyed in the same way.'

'You believe that it could be destroyed?' she asked anxiously.

'Oh, Yes. Her Majesty's Government will not permit itself to be destroyed by an Independent party, particularly if they expect too much too soon. They are very certain of themselves now but they are young in these matters.'

Elinor Dillon followed his eyes towards the dance floor. The light-hearted company waltzed happily, unconcerned by the burden of history on their backs. They belonged to the British order of things and they were not interested in the views of an Irish parliamentary party.

When she looked at Lord Dunraven's son she knew that she had never seen a more handsome man in her life. He was tall and moved gracefully through the waltz. His hair was black and thick, his face sharp and certain. He wore his evening clothes elegantly. Her eyes followed him about the dance floor, conscious that every other woman in the ballroom was also looking at him. When the music finished he excused himself and came directly to their table and spoke to his father.

He turned towards her. 'May I have the pleasure of the next dance?' Even before she accepted the invitation she knew that more than anything else in the world she wished to dance with this man.

'It would be my pleasure,' she said, her eyes bright with expectation.

287

Her silk dress rustled as they began to dance. People retired from the floor and let them dance, moved by the beauty and elegance of the couple. When the music finished they looked about them and found the floor empty. Then couples crowded on to the floor and joined them in a second waltz. She was aware of his body close to hers and the excitement of his touch.

'I watched your horse romp home to victory,' he told her. 'It carries your colours with distinction. Have you been very lucky with the foals sired by Pegasus?'

'This one was the best. I was in the stable the morning she was born. When she staggered to her feet in the sharp spring air I could see that her conformation was correct. I have had several failures. One is never certain with horses but we will have built up a good strain.' Their eyes were upon each other and they talked eagerly. When the waltz finished they were reluctant to return to their tables.

'Could I have the pleasure of your company in London?' he asked quickly before they parted. 'I believe you have come over for the opening of Parliament? I know the city very well and my coach is always at your disposal.'

'It would be my pleasure. I have only been to the city once before and I feel like a stranger there.'

'Then permit me to introduce you to its beauty and variety.'

She did not hesitate in her reply, wanting only to be in the company of this man. There was no logic to her motive, just a sensual hunger in her body.

That night as she slept beside her husband she considered her position. She tried to reason with her feelings but they would not be subjected to control. Again and again the features of the young man returned to trouble her. Even then she knew that she had fallen in love with him.

They moved down to London for the opening of the new Parliament. Already there was excitement in the air, the London papers speculating on the power of the new party which had been formed in Ireland. It could draw its attention towards Ireland when it should be dealing with its own affairs or looking towards the dangers on the Continent. There was a belief among the Irish members that they could make many demands on the new

288

government and push forward tax and land reforms.

Besides the preparation for the opening of Parliament the social life in London gained momentum. Elinor Dillon accepted every invitation delivered to the house they had taken for their stay. She looked forward to the Grand Ball as an opportunity to meet Lord Dunraven's son. Letters had passed between them since her arrival in London and she was eager to be with him again. She refused to entertain the thought that she was embarking upon a dangerous liaison.

John and Elinor Dillon climbed the wide staircase to the ballroom. Servants in livery stood at intervals like marionettes. Splendid chandeliers suspended from the ceilings each carried layers of tapers which caught the cut glass and broke it into a thousand small fragments of light. On all the walls were massive paintings depicting sea battles.

She wore a necklace and earrings of gold, enamelled and hung with cameos. Her black hair set in light curls and braids was held in position by two ivory combs and revealed her strong, well-formed neck and shoulders. Her light evening dress swept away from her waist in three tiers of light-green silk.

When she arrived in the city Elinor found it effortless to walk through the great corridors of the rich and powerful and talk freely with people. Even when the subject of politics arose she could enter easily into the conversation, Robert Dillon having prepared her well for such occasions. She met many of the political figures who had come to London to take their seats in Parliament. It was generally believed that the political system was in transition and that the Irish party would play a vital role in the new government.

They stood at the door for a moment and then moved forward into the great mass of people. The vaulted ceiling of the ballroom was carried on three-quarter Corinthian columns, and decorated with panels of intricate plaster work. The walls were hung with crimson velvet.

'I'm sure that you will have so many offers to dance that I had better take this opportunity,' her husband told her as the orchestra began a gentle waltz. Immediately the crowd moved on to the floor.

Her husband found the crowd oppressive and she knew that his mind was engaged in political matters. As they danced he took note of those present. Very few of the Irish members had been invited. He watched Daniel Parr and his wife, moving about at the edge of the crowd, uncomfortable in London company.

But Parr's sharp eye missed nothing. Already he had set plans in motion which could destroy the new party. Bribes had always succeeded in dividing the Irish and it was in his power to offer them certain positions of importance in a new government. Many of them could be offered small pensions. He had met with the young Lord Dunraven who had discussed the matter with him. Now it was up to the members to accept the bribes and he awaited the outcome.

John Dillon waved to Sadlier and Keogh. Both had taken the pledge not to accept government office. Sadlier was a compli-cated man. He had established a land company and a bank in Ireland. As a speculator he could be purchased if the offer was right. Keogh was an outgoing, charming man with an imaginative turn of phrase. His presence brightened any company and John Dillon had a special regard for him. There were some others whom he recognized but the rest had not been invited, being unacceptable to English society.

When the waltz was finished a young captain moved towards Elinor, asking her to dance. He had a fresh face and a direct smile. She accepted his offer and found him to be an accomplished partner.

Lord Dunraven caught her eye and her heart began to thump. He stood by himself gazing at her from the shadow of the curtains. She noted his expression on his face.

All day her mind had been upon him. As she moved through London she thought she saw him in some carriage or other or on horseback. They had not met for three days and during that time her heart seemed heavy at his absence. As soon as the waltz finished he moved towards where they stood, close to the orches-tra. He politely pushed the young officer to one side and claimed the next waltz.

'You have been in my mind and imagination for the last three days,' he told her. 'Everywhere I turned I seemed to catch a glimpse of you. I felt jealous when I saw you in the arms of the young officer.'

'And you were in my mind ever since I left you. London was uninteresting without you. Even the races could not stimulate me.'

She was caught up in the physical delight of his presence. The bright lights, the crimson wall hangings, the elegance of movement made the minutes with him memorable.

'You know that I love you,' he told her quietly. 'I loved you the first day I saw you at the races and listened to the music in your voice. I could not help it. I should have been with you but I had government business to attend to.'

'And I have been haunted by you. I have tried to banish you from my mind but you return again and again as if you were etched there. This is a dangerous position in which we place ourselves,' she said sadly.

'I must be with you. It is as simple as that. I know the dangers well. I am involved in the most important government business. I cannot have any scandal attached to our names.'

'We must be careful. I cannot be seen too frequently with you. We must move with great caution.'

'I have a private house at Greenwich,' he told her. 'We could meet there. It is down river and in beautiful surroundings.'

'I do not know where Greenwich is or how to get there. And for the next few days I must be at my husband's side. There is no way I can be with you,' she said urgently, praying that he would come up with some plan.

When the dance was finished the young officer returned and requested another dance. She refused and returned to one of the elegant seats at the side of the great ballroom, her heart in turmoil. While she was trying to rearrange her thoughts she noted that her husband was in deep conversation with a messenger who had entered the ballroom. They talked together for a while, then he called Sadlier and Keogh aside. It was obvious that some unexpected crisis had arisen.

'I'm dreadfully sorry,' he said, 'but I have been called away to a political meeting. I'm afraid I will not return to our lodgings until tomorrow evening. Some of the members have been offered bribes. The political agents have been up to their old tricks again. I will have to dissuade them from accepting, otherwise our party could be destroyed. I cannot leave you without an escort.'

But the young officer who stood close by interjected. 'As a gentleman and an officer it would be my privilege to escort your wife home at the end of the ball,' he said gallantly.

'Very well,' John Dillon said, and bowing to his wife turned and left the ballroom.

After they had danced together she returned to her seat. She turned to him and said directly, 'Thank you very much for your attentions but I already have an escort who will see me home.'

Lord Dunraven had realized something was amiss and sat down beside her. They talked for some moments and came to a quick and dangerous decision. He left the room and after some time had elapsed she made her way towards the door, moving slowly in order not to attract attention. When she reached the head of the staircase she grasped the folds of her dress and swept down the steps and out on to the pavement where his carriage was waiting. They threw their arms about each other and held the tight embrace as the carriage was driven down the Strand and Charing Cross to Westminster Bridge. Gaslights burned like magic lanterns along the streets. The tide had well turned and the river was moving down towards the sea. Lord Dunraven hailed a luxurious barge and they settled into a small cabin on soft cushions. The barge moved soundlessly down towards Greenwich. They looked towards the shorelights and the numberless masts with their spectral yardarms holding furled sails. They listened to the noise of bargemen calling to each other on the water.

When they reached Greenwich they disembarked and walked arm in arm through the darkness to his house set in a small garden.

All that night they made love to each other, hungry for the pleasure of their bodies. She held him tightly, again and again awakening his desire and calling out in pleasure as her body shook with satisfaction. Towards morning there was a little time to sleep.

She stood in the muted light naked, her breasts firm and luxurious, her thighs round and strong. His eyes followed her as she moved about the room gathering her clothes. His mind was obsessed by her presence.

As she moved up the Thames, relaxed with pleasure, she looked at the city under morning light. Ships carrying wide sails passed on their way towards the sea. On the horizon she could see steeples and domes arising above the city roofs.

She did not reflect upon her infidelity. She had been hungry for this sensual pleasure so long denied her and now her body felt like rich honey.

She hired a carriage to take her to her lodgings. When her husband returned he was tired and fell into bed.

Daniel Parr had spent the night waiting for Lord Dunraven, his mind filled with anxiety. He realized that John Dillon was drawing the doubtful members of the party back into the Independent ranks. He could have made them higher offers had he permission from Lord Dunraven. When they did eventually meet it was too late and the members of the Irish party could not now be bribed.

Elinor Dillon watched Queen Victoria and Prince Albert as they passed her on their way to the throne. The queen wore a silver crown and a diamond necklace. She was broad-shouldered, her skin like cream but her features plain. Sitting on her throne, her feet resting on a footstool, she delivered her speech to Parliament. Her voice was bright and imperial, almost carrying tones of disdain. When she was finished the stool was quickly removed and she rose, her ladies-in-waiting coming forward to take her train. She moved out of the House slowly, looking directly ahead towards the door.

John Dillon turned to his wife.

'And now the difficult business begins,' he said. 'You must return to Ireland and I will continue on here for some weeks. You can deal competently with the estates and my correspondence. We will hold out as an independent party as long as we can but I fear that some of the members may succumb to bribes. Daniel Parr made them some surprising offers. He is working behind the scenes and as yet I do not know how much power he possesses. I will have to keep a vigilant eye upon him.'

He came to the coach terminus with his wife. She waved him goodbye and settled herself into her seat, thinking of all that had occurred during her brief stay in London. She did not know when she would meet Lord Dunraven again.

# Chapter 28

Daniel Parr remained on in London when the members of the Independent party returned to Ireland for the recess. He had been a shadowy and insignificant figure during the sittings, watching from the back benches as John Dillon delivered his speeches on Tenants Rights to the House. His voice was powerful, his logic firm and he was popular with the members. Behind him he held the Independent party. It became obvious to the new Parliament that no government could afford to be held to ransom by Irish interests.

John and Elinor Dillon had been invited to the greatest houses in London, celebrities by the British upper class. They had produced several notable victories on the turf and the story of Elinor Dillon had the high air of romance. The *Illustrated London News* had carried a pen drawing of her and an article on her victory at Aintree. Furthermore she was declared the beauty of the season. Daniel Parr detested her arrogance as she swept past both him and his wife as if they were the lowest tenants on her estate. But beside the reports in the papers Elinor Dillon had been a remarkable companion for her husband. She could deal with people of all ranks on a free and friendly basis and carry on an intelligent conversation on politics and other matters. She had been remarked upon by several Members of Parliament who had met her during the social gatherings. Daniel Parr had to suffer her praise on more than one occasion.

'They come to London from a small estate; one a debauched drunkard and the other a scullery maid from a hotel,' he complained bitterly to his wife. 'The woman once had to carry piss pots to the cesspool and now look at her. She appears on the *Illustrated London News*. And who is in the illustration on the page opposite her? The Queen herself and Prince Albert. It is too much. And worse still, they were invited for a week to Lord Harrington's estates. Cost them not a penny, while I, one of the most influential figures in Connaught, have to stay in this cramped house and endure the stench and the filth of London.'

But while John Dillon and other members of the Independent

party held the centre stage he had been active behind the scenes in the shadowy world of intrigue.

One evening a letter was delivered to his address, an invitation to a certain Captain Curd's house. It did not specify the nature of the visit but insisted that he come alone, suggesting that his services were necessary to certain important interests.

At twilight the cab took him to the address. He was quite surprised that a captain could possess an imposing house set in its own gardens. The curtains were drawn and only slits of light suggested that the house was occupied. He noted that guards stood on duty and he was challenged when he approached the house.

He was led into a small room and sat down uneasily on an armchair, curious to know whom he was going to meet. He sat there for some time, aware only of the monotonous ticking of a clock. Then a door opened and he was invited into a large, panelled room. Gaslights lit a table around which five men were sitting. He was surprised at the company in which he found himself, recognizing members of the Conservative and Liberal parties. Some of them held high office in the government and had used the most abusive language towards each other in Parliament. He recognized Lord Raleigh sitting at the head of the table. Parr had delivered information to him concerning important figures in Connaught. He had cold, watery eyes which had always discomforted Parr. He looked at the five men who faced him with curious detachment and knew that he was close to the centre of the Secret Service.

'This is the gentleman from Ireland I have been speaking of,' Lord Raleigh began. 'He has carried important documents to our office and it is thanks to him that we have an almost total picture of the situation in the west of Ireland. He has given us dossiers on most of the leading figures beyond the Shannon.'

Daniel Parr felt like some hired servant as he listened to Lord Raleigh's patronizing voice. 'In fact it was one of his documents which set out in a clear fashion how we could achieve our objectives. He has a vast number of contacts and would perhaps better than anyone bring our plan to fruition. I presume, gentlemen, some of you would like to question him?'

295

They observed him closely as if he were some exhibit at a fairground. He realized at once that they had been discussing some plan before he arrived and had reached a conclusion.

'I am sure, sir, that you are aware of the present situation in Parliament,' one gentleman said directly.

'Yes, I am.'

'Could you give us your thoughts concerning the Independent Irish party?' Lord Raleigh directed.

'As you know, the Irish Independent party holds sway at present. They had to sign pledges before they were chosen as candidates. They will hold the balance in all future Parliaments if they stand together, and the longer they can disrupt the procedures of Parliament, the greater their power will grow in Ireland. You are witnessing a new political movement much more subtle than that organized by Daniel O'Connell. Even Sharman Crawford who represents the North is with them and believes that they can secure Tenants Rights for the tenants of the South. He is forward enough to think that they deserve to be franchised.'

'And is all this not inevitable?' Lord Raleigh asked.

'No. It will mean the end of the great estates. Eventually it will mean the end of loyalty to the crown in Ireland, if that can be contemplated. If the old property qualifications for the franchise are destroyed you will have a revolution as great as the French Revolution on your hands. It may not be as bloody but it would be as wide-reaching. My family have sacrificed their lives in each generation for this empire and I will not let my links with it be destroyed.' Parr's eyes were sharp and they took notice of him. He no longer felt inferior.

'And do you not deserve to fail as a class?' a voice opposite Parr countered. 'Would it not be better at this moment to grant the Irish their Home Rule to let them muddle through their own destinies. The country has become a burden to us. Many landlords went bankrupt during the famine, but others have brought unenviable reputations, taking the opportunity to extend their estates even at the height of the hunger.'

Parr controlled his anger, seeking desperately for a fresh argument.

'The famine could have been averted had the British Parliamen taken swift action. You knew it would happen. When it did you made no effort to avert it, when you could have prevented much of the hardship. It is not the cottiers or the hungry peasants you should fear, but the tenant farmers and the middle class. You grant the tenants rights and the middle class home rule and you leave your flank exposed. They can invite any enemy on to their shores and this country could be attacked from France and Ireland. Of course I wish to protect my class and my interests but in doing that I also serve the Crown.'

'Then let us hear your solution to the problem,' Lord Raleigh demanded.

Daniel Parr placed his hands flatly on the table and began. 'At this present time the Independent party is planning its next assault on Parliament. But even before it was formed it was weak, the divisions held together only by the promises they took before elections. You must buy the members out, that is the only way forward. Corrupt them. I can assure you that they are corruptible.' He let his last remark sink in and the others considered it. He looked at each one, knowing that he was the central figure in every plan they had hatched.

'How much would it cost?' a Liberal peer asked.

'Not a lot. It cost over a million to form the Union. I think that a quarter of a million can hold it. Of course more important than money is the desire for office and position. The Irish love positions even if they have no substance. I presume that I may be required to put this plan into action. If I proceed with it then I want one quarter million in the bank and I wish to have attractive offices at my disposal.'

'Such as?'

'Lord of the Treasury is a handsome bribe, as well as Solicitor General. And of course lesser sinecures should be available for other members who will come over to the government's side.'

The conversation became suddenly active. They talked rapidly among themselves and quickly came to the same conclusion.

'Very well. Give us a list of positions and titles you think you can use as bait and we will ratify them. You shall not meet us again. You are familiar with Lord Dunraven; he will deal with all these matters from this point on. As far as you are concerned this meeting has never taken place.'

'Yes, I have dealt with him and not with great success. The last miserable offers I made to some of the Irish members were derisory. I could not contact Lord Dunraven on the very night I needed him to grant me the use of several thousand pounds. Now I have to set out again and corrupt these men. It will not be an easy matter, let me state. And let me further state that I am not a menial.' Parr slapped his flat palm on the table to emphasize his position.

'I am about to set out upon a most difficult and secretive business. I know many of the members of the Independent Parliament and I know their weakness. Gentlemen, you have not asked me my price. For bringing about the destruction of the Irish Parliamentary party and thus saving you an embarrassing threat I wish to have conferred upon me the title of Lord. I am sure you can see your way to convince her Majesty that the time is now appropriate for the conference of such an honour on Daniel Parr. That is the deal. We are all up for sale today.'

They looked at each other in surprise.

'You seek a considerable honour,' Lord Raleigh remarked.

'And you seek a considerable favour. I think that you will get the best of the bargain,' Parr retorted.

'It will be attended to,' Lord Raleigh said. 'You may now leave.'

Daniel Parr rose from his seat and left the room. A cab was waiting for him in the darkness.

He would have to spend a further fortnight in London while there was so much business to attend to. He would have to arrange that large sums of money be deposited at various banks in Ireland so that he could draw readily from them. And he must make certain that he would be honoured for his actions.

He felt important for the first time since he came to London. He had been brought directly into the centre of intrigue and a vast sum of money had been promised to him. Knowing how easily many of the members could be bought he would turn in a handsome profit. And most important of all he would have his seat in the House of Lords. The family had reached the height of its good fortunes.

During the next two weeks Lord Dunraven met him and confirmed all the promises made at the meeting. They sat together and Daniel Parr went through a list of names set out before him. With a certain amount of pride he explained how each one of the members could be approached and corrupted.

'They must keep with the Independent party until I receive a directive. We believe that the life of the present government is to be short. It will be brought down when the time is ready. Then your candidates must back the next government. Most likely it will be led by Lord Aberdeen but this has not been made final. The announcement of your honour will be made as soon as you have delivered the Members of Parliament to us,' Lord Dunraven told him.

Parr's meetings with Lord Dunraven were formal. He was uneasy in his company and uncertain about his character. He had observed him move easily through the glittering society of London, his personality seemingly trivial and without consequence. When he sat with him privately, however, he knew that he was dealing with a clever, cold mind. He had on one occasion suggested that Sadlier could be assassinated if he did not accept the bribe.

With everything confirmed he left for Ireland, the excitement of intrigue in his blood.

For John Dillon and the members of the Independent party it was a time of optimism. With others he attended a banquet in their honour and spoke of the great future of the Party. He could feel power flowing in the people. Everything could now be achieved.

It was a low shebeen at the edge of a large tract of bog, a bleak and lonely place where only the curlew's cry broke the silence. Men's souls and minds were as dark and heavy as the peat about them. During the summer they cut the fuel with wooden slanes, carving the soft sods out of the black banks and throwing them to dry on the heather. At the edges of this great and sullen tract they tried to grow potatoes and pasture mangey cattle to sustain their existence.

They were the tenants at the edge of existence, burdened with taxation, threatened with expulsion from these thin acres at the whim of some middle man who had bought part of the land at the bankruptcy courts.

Johnny Appelby had been drinking at the shebeen all day. He had walked down the open road in the morning, knocked up Mrs Flood and ordered a tumbler of raw whisky. He had bet all his money on Appleby's Fancy, at fifteen to one, and since he returned to Ireland he had been drinking heavily and boasting of his achievements.

The men who drifted in that evening sat on rough stools in the cramped place, their clothes scented of turf. They had been working all day in the bog and looked at him with dull eyes.

'A bottle of poteen between the men,' Johnny Appelby told Mrs Flood.

'Are you sure you can pay for it?' she asked in a hard voice.

'Not only could I pay for it but I could pay for every bottle of drink in the house and the house itself if I so cared,' he said, patting his pocket. 'Good fortune has favoured me well during the last months. Appleby's Fancy romped home in England and he carried my last shilling on his back. He was a great horse but not as great as Pegasus. Now let me tell you the story of Pegasus.'

They feigned interest as with sweeping dramatic gestures he described the buying of the horse and the preparation for the race, the journey to England and the victory.

They listened to his story, drinking the poteen he bought for them. When it was very dark they left the shebeen together before he had a chance to finish one of his stories.

'Out you go now,' Mrs Flood said. 'I cannot wait up all night listening to stories about horses. You have a good distance to walk home but luckily there is a moon. Otherwise in the state you are in you could end up in a bog.'

'Could I not sleep here the night? I have ten miles of walk ahead of me. Surely you are not going to send me out into the blackness? I left you good custom,' he complained.

'This is not one of the town hotels. If you don't move I'll have to get the man of the house to throw you out,' she said roughly.

'I'll go, I'll go.' He took hold of the side of the table and got up. His back was stooped and he limped. Outside he looked about him. The moon was to the west and lit up the small road. He was

300

weary and staggered from one side of the road to the other.

Finally he reached the end of the bog road and moved between limestone walls where the land was lush and the hawthorn bushes scented with autumn fruit.

'Where am I now?' he asked at the crossroads. He sharpened his mind and staggered forward in the right direction.

They descended upon him from the shadows, someone bringing a cudgel down on the back of his head. The dried shell of bone was too brittle to stand up to the blow and he fell easily to the ground.

Warm blood was flowing down his neck on to his shirt as they went through his coat pocket and took the two sovereigns and several shillings which he possessed.

'Well, how much did you get on him?' Mrs Flood asked when they knocked on the door early in the morning.

'Two sovereigns and some shillings,' they told her and placed the gold and silver pieces on the counter.

'So he was boasting. He could not buy out the house after all. I'll take the sovereigns and set them against what you all owe me. If the police found you with gold they would put you in jail. You can have the shillings. Did he recognize you?' She peered suspiciously at each set of eyes.

'Sure, how could he? It was pitch-dark and the crack he got on the skull must have softened his brain,' one laughed.

'Did you murder him?' she asked anxiously.

'He was alive when we left. He had a soft skull like the shell of a duck egg,' another replied.

'Keep your knowledge to yourself. Go about your work and say nothing,' she told them. Mrs Flood was a large, heavy woman with an angry mind. They were deeply in debt to her and she dominated their lives.

He was bleeding and unconscious when he was discovered by one of the servants, who was on her way to Dillon Hall. She immediately summoned help and his light body was laid out on a hay cart.

When Elinor Dillon heard the news she directed that he be brought to the house, Tadhg Mor lifting the frail figure and carrying him to a guest room. He undressed and washed him and

301

laid him out on the bed. When Elinor came to see him he looked like a small child beneath the large blankets.

He never regained consciousness, though for two days he held on thinly to life. His face lost its hard lines and softened into gentleness.

As he lay dying, memories were stirred. Men talked on his uncanny knowledge of horses, aware once more that he had helped to save the fortunes of the estate. The work in the out-houses ceased as his life faded. The kitchens beneath the house were filled with people waiting for news of Johnny Appelby.

'It was murder surely,' they said. 'It points towards the black bog. The Flood woman had a hand in it.'

When Johnny Appelby died, his body was set out in a coffin in the hall. People came a great distance to pay their respects to the little jockey and horse trainer. Later he was carried to the old churchyard at the edge of the estate. Elinor Dillon following directly behind the coffin. As he was lowered into the grave she felt that some part of her life was buried with the small man, and she wept a little. People were surprised; it had been said that after the famine no tears remained in her body.

When the funeral was over she called some of the tenants to the house and talked to them. When they departed she was certain where the murderers lived. Next day she directed John Perdue the solicitor to purchase the bogland and three days later the tenants were evicted. She left Mrs Flood isolated in the wide bog where she survived for a year, the shebeen decaying about her. Grass grew on the thatch and in the yard outside the house and finally she left carrying a small suitcase of possessions.

While John Dillon and others of the Independent party were enjoying the banquets and honours conferred upon them, Daniel Parr was busy. He moved quietly through the country staying at the houses of landowners who shared his views. He was certain that if he could buy John Sadlier of Tipperary then others would follow. Checking through his dossier he noted that, despite the man's public image of wealth, he was in fact speculating in America with money from his own joint stock bank.

He approached Sadlier's house at dusk, having made an appointment two days earlier. It had given him sufficient time to gather accurate and damning evidence against him.

John Sadlier was just finishing his dinner when Daniel Parr entered his dining room. Every object seemed to be made of silver, the mirror frames, the cutlery, the plate, the tankards and door handles.

'I call this the silver room,' he said directly. 'I was always satisfied with silver. Firmer than gold you know, and it wears well. Gold is too soft a substance. You will have some wine, of course.' He ordered the servant girl to bring a bottle of port.

'Now what is the nature of your visit, Mr Parr,' his voice was plump and unworried. 'As you know we do not belong to the same political party and I do not think that we might have much in common.'

Daniel Parr disliked this businessman who was dismissive of his presence. He kept control of himself and watched the sensual way he poured out the port, his eyes brightening at its deep colour.

'But who does belong with the Independent party?' Daniel Parr asked directly. 'I know that there is dissension among the members. Some feel that they were forced into their present position. They are waiting for some courageous man to lead them out of an allegiance which weakens the power of the Crown and the government.'

'All parties have their differences. The Independent party is no different from any other,' he answered, drinking his port with relish and wondering where the conversation would lead. He had a business meeting in Clonmel later that evening with an American stock dealer.

'Then you are not aware that others have already accepted offices in the event of a new government being formed? Surely you do not think that the Earl of Derby is going to hold on to power and be wagged by the Irish Independent party. Already a new government is being formed which will render your party useless. Do you think that the landlords will adopt the Land Bill containing Sharman Crawford's measures? I can assure you that some of the Irish members have already accepted appointments in the next government.'

John Sadlier lost his casual interest in Daniel Parr and became cautious and cunning.

'Name those who have accepted these offices,' he said fiercely.

'My dear Mr Sadlier,' Daniel Parr said, disdain in his voice. 'You do not think that I would betray their trust. But I will call out fifteen names. Five of them have accepted appointments and financial backing as a result of their decisions.'

He listed fifteen names slowly, in order that he could think about it.

'Moore, Dillon and Lucas would certainly not accept office. They are men of principle,' he commented.

'No one is a man of principle when money and position are presented to them, I can assure you. And of course several of them are in financial difficulties. You may not know of these things but as the government representative it is my business to know them. Tonight you will meet Mr Wayne, the American stock dealer, and buy £25,000 of stock from him,' he added coldly.

Suddenly John Sadlier was startled into interest.

'How did you obtain that information? It is private. It does not concern you.'

'Perhaps it may not, but it would interest your customers if it were known that you were using their money in doubtful deals. Now let us get down to some serious talk. I did not come here to be trifled with by a businessman of doubtful integrity. Let me give you some of the information in the possession of the British Secret Service concerning you activities.' He opened a file and read out a list of secret dealings. John Sadlier did not utter a word.

'Now, Mr Sadlier, I will make you an offer. You vote with the next government when it is formed. For this allegiance you will be paid £20,000 and you will receive the position of Lord of the Treasury. Your file will remain a secret and your financial dealings will not be disclosed.'

John Sadlier took out a handkerchief and wiped his forehead. He felt ill and the port seemed to have lost its flavour. He looked at the ferret-eyed man sitting neatly in his chair.

'What must I do?' John Sadlier asked weakly.

'Sign this pledge,' Daniel Parr said.

John Sadlier rushed his signature across the page as if it were tainted.

'This is blackmail and treason,' he said when he had finished, trying to salve part of his conscience.

'Not at all. Not at all, Mr Sadlier. Do not let such words enter your vocabulary. You have done a noble and patriotic deed. You have saved the Empire and you have pleased your Queen. Sleep well tonight. Perhaps some day you will aspire to the position of "Sir". The Irish respect titles and positions more than money. Lord Tipperary is a grand-sounding title. Mull it about in your mind while you mull your port about in your mouth. Test the title upon yourself. I shall show myself out; obviously you have much to think about.'

As Daniel Parr rode towards Waterford, flames of pleasure warmed his mind. He had found the first weakness in the Irish party.

In December, from his seat in the House of Commons, John Dillon watched the Irish Independent party fail. He listened to the debate between Disraeli and Gladstone, a coldness about his heart. Daniel Parr sat on the far side of the house, a grimace on his angular face. The Tories were defeated on the division by nineteen votes and Lord Derby immediately resigned. The new government under Lord Aberdeen would hold for five years. It was only a few days later when the appointments were published that he realized how corrupted the Independent party had been.

'Keogh, Solicitor General. Sadlier, Lord of the Treasury. Monsell and O'Flaherty also enjoying honours. They have been bought out. Sinister forces have been working against us,' he told Lucas when they met at his house in London. His mind felt broken.

'Nothing can be achieved through legal or parliamentary channels. I believed once in reason, honesty and diplomacy. Now I have my doubts. Perhaps Mitchel and others were right. You achieve things only by force,' he said darkly, bunching the paper in his hand and throwing it on the floor.

'But you are a reasonable man, John. If you give up then all hope fails,' Lucas protested.

'I was a reasonable man. Now I must reflect on all that has happened.'

When it was announced that Daniel Parr would have the title 'Lord' conferred upon him, he realized how active he had been in bringing down the Independents. All his efforts had been in vain and once again he grew introverted and sullen.

305

# Chapter 29

From his desk at the *Herald* office, Kevin O'Donnell looked down on the bustling traffic at the corner of Broadway and Ann Street. He held a pencil in his teeth which he chewed nervously. A carriage marked 'Broadway and 23 Street' slowly made its way through the turmoil of the traffic. Women in bonnets and crinoline skirts walked independently along the sidewalks.

In two years he had established himself at the *Herald*, his first articles defining his beat on the New York waterfront. Through Liam Flaherty he could receive direct information on all that was happening in the dark places of the city. When he went into the Bowery or visited the Beer Gardens, he was protected by one of O'Flaherty's men. His latest article was on houses of assignation, dealing with the cheap hotels and bed houses. He had discovered a ring of prostitution which centred on the first-class hotels. Many bankers and lawyers kept their women there. He was doubtful if the editor and chief would let the article through.

At that moment the five editors were discussing it in the Council Room on the third storey.

'And I say that we will lose advertising patronage,' the editor told Richard Alexander, a frown on his forehead. 'Sure, you can let this young man dig up what he can find on the waterfront and in the low bordellos. But this is coming uptown. Some of the fancy hotels are listed here and I don't think our friends the bankers will like it one bit. They carry power in this city.'

'The *Herald* carries more. We live in a democracy and the press must be given its freedom. Every statement has been double-checked. It's a darned good story and, it will spread circulation,' the sub-editor argued. 'Let it run.'

'Then we have the religious groups to reckon with. We know all this goes on and they know it goes on but officially we are a puritanical society.'

'I'll stake my reputation on it,' the sub-editor interjected. 'I'll stand as guarantor for the story. If there is trouble then I will take the blame.'

'Very well. Let us have a head count.' The editor counted the hands. They were in favour of the article.

'Then we will run it, but look out for more trouble. The mayor of the city and the politicians won't like it. That young man is either going to become famous or infamous. Now let's get back to our desks.'

'Well?' Kevin asked anxiously, when his editor returned.

'You got me into a lot of trouble. I've staked my reputation on this article. Let's see what happens. In the mean time forget the scandals and do some honest work. Give me more political articles on the Irish. They are a political race and they are a gathering force in City Hall.' He was still nervous about the decision. 'I hear there is a lot of political talk and meetings. Something is in the air so go find out what it is. I'll remain here and sweat.'

Kevin left the building, making his way to the docks to ask Liam Flaherty if any more political rebels had arrived in New York.

The saloon bar was crowded with sailors but he had put on a rough coat and did not seem out of place in the bar.

'Liam's in his office at the back,' the barman told him winking, 'and does not wish to be disturbed. Some gentleman with him. Arrived in a French ship. You better wait until he is finished.'

He might have left the bar had not Liam Flaherty emerged and called to him.

'I think there is somebody here you might like to meet.' He took him by the sleeve and drew him into a snug.

'Meet John O'Mahony,' he said directly. Kevin looked at the stranger's taut and exhausted face. He knew this man had taken part in the abortive rebellion at Ballingary. John O'Mahony's piercing eyes tested his integrity. He could see that he did not approve of the saloon bar or the loose women who frequented it.

'Would you do me the honour of staying with me tonight?' Kevin asked him directly. 'I would like to discover what is happening in Ireland.'

'Certainly. I have nowhere to stay. You are a correspondent I believe and I am interested in newspapers. Every movement should have a newspaper. The *Nation* set Ireland aflame in its day and Mitchel had the *United Irishman*. We were friends. Told people how to build barricades so little wonder he was transported. But maybe not for long. Let us go to your lodgings. I need a wash.'

He shook hands stiffly with Liam Flaherty and marched on to the street.

'What type of man is this Flaherty? Can he be trusted? I was given his name in Paris,' he asked gruffly when they got into a cab.

'You can trust him with your life,' Kevin replied.

'I have,' he said. As the cab made its way through the teeming traffic his eyes were filled with wonder. He looked from side to side, eager to gather everything into his alert mind.

'You like this city?' he asked.

'Of course I do. I came here penniless and now I have secure work. I like what I am doing and I feel I know this city better than any place on earth. It is full of excitement and interest and I have established myself as a journalist. But tell me about France.' He was sure John O'Mahony could give him a good story.

'The Republic is dead. I was at the barricades with Stephens. We threw them up in the streets and fought behind them until we were crushed. I saw freedom and revolution die on rubble.' His voice was gruff, his expression stony.

'Why come to New York?' Kevin asked. 'You will not be able to throw up barricades here.'

'There is no reason to. I believe that our interests can be best furthered in America. There are many Irish here who can be drawn into the cause.'

'You believe that you can do this?'

'Yes. I must have a plan of the city and its history. I am never comfortable in a city unless I have memorized the street plans and know the alleyways and warrens. One must be able to disappear at a moment's notice.'

'This is the heart of the newspaper world of New York.' Kevin pointed out Printing House Square.

'How are the presses run?'

'A huge steam engine with 150 horsepower drives the presses. Shafting and belting carry the power in every direction from the engine.'

'I must see this great engine,' he said eagerly.

'Very well. I will bring you to the basement in Spruce Street and you shall see it in operation.'

They left the cab in Printing House Square. John O'Mahony

308

looked at the five-storey buildings carrying the names of the New York papers, his eyes filled with awe. To the left of the New York Times building stood the Tribune and beside that the Sun.

'Very impressive. Imagine the power these papers exercise. And you say all the presses are driven from a basement somewhere?'

'Yes. Follow me,' Kevin directed.

They entered the building in Spruce Street. Kevin was recognized by the security man who permitted them to pass down into the basement. As they walked down the stairs they could feel the whole building pulse with power. In the basement John O'Mahony looked at the massive engine which ran all the presses. Men moved about it, keeping a close eye on the wheels which carried the black belting. He led O'Mahony to the great furnace, where men who were stripped to the waist stoked fire with coal. The heat was intense and the noise dominant.

'What is the population of the city?' O'Mahony asked later as they waited for a cab.

'Over half a million.'

Their conversation was interrupted by the arrival of an empty cab.

The house Kevin lodged in was in a quiet street. He paid the cab and carried O'Mahony's bags to his room. He showed him a small bedroom where he could wash.

'Very good. Then I shall rest. I am much obliged to you. I have certainly fallen in with a friend. The place is neat and tidy and fresh. A man needs little to survive but he must have order.' He spoke with military formality.

Kevin left him and set off for the waterfront. When he returned that evening he found John O'Mahony sitting at his desk with a manuscript set out before him.

'It is Keating's *History of Ireland*,' he told him. 'Some day I hope to make a good translation into English. It will be my monument. He conceived the history book while hiding in the Glen of Aherlow in Tipperary. He travelled up and down Ireland in disguise consulting the old vellum manuscripts. A great past would have perished had he not undertaken this work. When I translate it, it calms my mind and gives me a noble vision of the past.' He closed the manuscript reverently and turned towards Kevin.

'Now tell me of your life,' he said with honest interest. 'Tell it to me in Gaelic for it is a sweet language and warms my heart.'

Kevin gave him an account of his life, even telling him what had happened in his youth when they had thrown Valentine Parr's body over a precipice. And then he told him of the Piper and his vast store of legends. He had forgotten the Piper but now as he spoke about him he remembered the past and his intense love of the Irish language history.

'Do you think the cause is dead, Kevin O'Donnell?' he asked when he had finished his story.

'I have given it little thought since I came to New York. Here one's perspective changes. I enjoy my life so why should I think of Ireland and its troubles? They look insignificant here. You could fit Ireland twice into many of the American states and yet she carries more grief and sorrow and bother than all of America. I do know that Irish clubs have formed in some districts and I take an indirect interest in them. But they are only places where exiles gather and talk of home. They have no political purpose.'

'No, the cause will never die. I carry it in my heart. So do Stephens and Michael Doheny and others. But we must band together and recruit men into clubs and I must meet your friends in the army. Here in America we have the training ground for soldiers. They must be formed into clubs and given a cause. That is why I came to America. Revolutions begin in small rooms. I have met the revolutionaries of the world in Paris when we sat in small cafés during cold evenings, our minds alight with plans. I have known great men starve for their convictions. We formed circles which were secret and difficult to penetrate. The uprising will come from America. It will take years to organize but I believe in my heart I will see the day when the Union is broken and Ireland will be a democracy.'

Kevin was sceptical of his ideas. He could not see him binding men into clubs and organizations.

'I must find work. Tomorrow could you give me a list of the smaller newspapers? I will visit their offices and seek employment. Like you I write.'

'Let me invite you to a meal at one of the city restaurants. They

310

say they are as good as the restaurants in Paris,' Kevin said.

'I only visited the cafés where the food was cheap and where there was a fire. Stephens and I lived in penury until I got a job teaching. But now that is all behind me and I look forward to life in this city. It will be my pleasure to accept your invitation.'

During the long meal O'Mahony began to relax. He drank some light beer which stimulated him. He was a natural story-teller and he entertained Kevin for several hours. As they walked home he sang, his memory seeming to have an endless store of Irish songs.

'I learned them at Kilbeheny in County Limerick as a young boy from the travelling poets and musicians,' he explained as they reached the lodgings. Before they went indoors he took a look down the gaslit street.

'I like this city, Kevin O'Donnell. Part of my destiny lies here. Good night, New York.'

O'Mahony stayed with him for a week, neat in his behaviour and tidy in his habits. He knew the economy of small spaces from living in Paris.

He acquired a large map of New York and pored over it like a strategist. When he committed it to memory he had Kevin test him. He was delighted that he could almost remember a whole page at one glance.

He purchased a book containing military history and statistics. His mind was always anxious for knowledge, and no time was ever wasted.

One day he found him committing to memory the rare flowers of America, running through the Latin lists as if he were reciting a poem.

'Of what earthly use is such information?' Kevin asked, laughing.

'It keeps my memory agile. Besides, everything is connected to everything else. And that reminds me; I think I have enough information concerning the American armies North and South to meet your friends if that could be arranged.'

'Of course it could be arranged. But surely you do not think that because you have studied some dry manual that you are an expert on American military history. And do not think that you can form them into some sort of revolutionary club. Perhaps two years ago that might have been possible but they are American soldiers now.'

'That is what you believe, but their memories have only to be stirred. We do not so easily forget the past. I know how revolutions are created.'

Four days after he had arrived he met his three friends at the Battery. They invited O'Mahony to a restaurant but he refused. He said he preferred to walk in the park during the day but Kevin knew he had little money and would have been embarrassed sitting at a table and have others buy his food.

His three friends during their time with the Irish regiment had been in action along the Mexican border. They had become professional soldiers and liked army life. John O'Mahony listened to them for an hour.

'How many Irish at your barracks?' he asked intently. They thought for a moment.

'Perhaps a thousand.'

'One thousand trained men. Imagine what one could do with a thousand properly trained soldiers. And what of their allegiance?'

'It is to themselves and their regiment,' Desmond Hogan answered.

'And what of their allegiance to Ireland?' he asked sharply.

'They remember Ireland and they talk of home and some believe that a day will come when they get the opportunity of returning and breaking the link with England. But there is no organization to rally them together.' As he spoke, his eye was turning to a pretty girl passing by with a parasol on her shoulder.

'Then you must list these men for me by their regiments. I will go to your barracks and give a lecture on military history. It will give me a chance to meet them.' He felt so secure in his belief that he did not entertain the thought that Desmond Hogan might refuse. Kevin's friends grew tired of walking the streets with O'Mahony and eventually they persuaded him to come with them to a small restaurant.

'At present I am a man without means but that shall not last for very long, I assure you. On your next visit to New York I shall treat you to a meal. By then I should have settled into some proper position.'

He came with them to the railway station and waved them goodbye. Kevin knew that he would keep in contact with them. He was a tenacious man with an overriding passion.

'I have obtained a position,' he told him one day when he returned from work.

'Where?'

'With the *Home Journal*. I shall write upon domestic issues. Already I have purchased several books on the matter. It has endless possibilities. My first article will deal with the Singer sewing machine. I have spent a day looking at one of these curious objects. I have actually tried to sew with it and it works. The *Home Journal* has its offices down by the quays so I can make several contacts there. I watch men coming and going and get to know the sea captains.'

'Do you ever rest?' Kevin asked.

'I'll rest the day the Union is broken and we live in a free country. It will come, for the seeds of revolution are in the air and they have a fine ground here. The next invading army will not come from France but from America and it will come in iron-clad ships.'

He was making his long speech as he packed his things neatly into the two travelling bags. He shook Kevin's hand firmly and left the house without giving a forwarding address.

Kevin watched him walk down the street, his gait distinctly military, and his head held high. The city lay before him.

He followed the destiny of this revolutionary, watching him move through New York with his lists, building up an army for the future.

He frequented the low haunts of the sailors from Irish ships and recruited them into the organization now called the Emmet Monument Association, its purpose to invade Ireland with an Irish American army.

Kevin was with John O'Mahony the night his translation of Keating was published. He took a copy from the column of books and put his signature on it.

313

'Some day you will come in with us. We need men who can write and you have followed the growth of the organization. Whole Irish regiments have taken a promise to sail for Ireland when the time comes. More will follow. Do you believe me?' he asked with shining eyes. 'Do you believe me now?'

'You are up against a well-organized empire. Do you think that you can fight the might of Britain?'

'It's worth a try,' he said simply. Kevin doubted the logic of the whole organization, yet he was drawn towards the men who formed the club. Gradually he cast aside the reasoned doubts and succumbed to a great wash of emotion. He began to speak Irish when he found the opportunity, to be part of the movement founded by John O'Mahony.

But there was something else stirring in America and Kevin was more aware of it than O'Mahony. The American Union would be tested. He had read the sentimental novel, *Uncle Tom's Cabin* and he noted the effect it had upon the northern mind. His interest was drawn towards the conflict, knowing that the spectre of civil war lay somewhere on the horizon. The American Union might not hold.

# *Chapter 30*

The children ran across the wide lawn towards their mother. Peter Dillon was nine now and his sister Catherine seven years of age. They were healthy, handsome children and she gave them the attention that had not been afforded her in her erratic childhood by the sea.

'You give them too much affection,' her husband told her. 'Let the servants take care of them as they do in other houses. They will come to depend on you too much and it will make them soft and emotional.'

She wanted to explain her feelings towards them but she knew that he would not understand her. She felt that she had no one to whom she could confide. Her brother was in America and only

Tadhg Mor, who always remained near her, knew her thoughts and fears. The Piper had drifted out of her life, though she had heard that he still travelled the countryside, led by a dwarf. The tragic image disturbed her.

'And I notice that they are picking up the barbarous Irish language. I heard both of them chattering with the blacksmith at the forge. They seem to be quite fluent in the peasant language.'

'It is not peasant,' she answered back angrily. 'It is a warm and tender tongue, far more expressive and deep than English which lacks any feeling. I insist that they speak Irish with the blacksmith. It is part of their heritage, as much as English and as much as French.'

The children ran towards her, their arms outstretched so that she could catch them and swing them about. She felt intensely that they were of her flesh and of her flesh alone.

'Tadhg Mor carried us all the way to the shore on his back,' Peter cried. 'And he made all kinds of strange faces. We asked him if he would row us to the island some day and he nodded that he would.'

'Hurry. The carriage will be soon here to take us to Galway,' she told him.

Each morning she went to the schoolroom set aside for them. They worked for three hours and then they were free. Catherine was both intelligent and strong; even at seven she could handle horses well. She had a natural understanding of animals. Peter had a strange softness and at an early age loved the sound of music. His eyes would brighten at the sound of a musical instrument and already he could play short pieces on the piano. He had all the gentle characteristics of the Piper, Elinor thought.

'Will Galardo win today?' Catherine asked her mother.

'Of course he will. I'll let you bet a gold coin on him, and you can watch him romp home.'

'Mother, will the leaden weights not drag at him?' Peter asked, anxious for the horse.

'No. He does not feel them on his back. He is strong and capable. I am certain that he is a winner.'

Indoors she called the maid and together they prepared them for the drive to Galway. Already a cart had gone ahead with their luggage. It was a pleasant June day and the sky carried no grey cloud.

At twelve o'clock they were ready and the carriage was brought to the front of the house. It was polished and shining and Tadhg Mor had put on his best frieze coat and cap. He had shaved himself severely and his neck was scarred. He had decided to place half his money on Galardo and was very excited by the race. He had watched him grow since he was a foal running in the Round Field and he knew that he was a winner. Elinor had bred another good horse and the Parr animal would stand no chance against him.

Elinor Dillon was proud of the stables. Joe Lavelle from Tipperary was her new trainer. He was a sober man and unlike Johnny Appelby in every way, but he understood horses and was as anxious as Elinor to breed winners. Galardo was the foal he had chosen to be trained specially to win. His legs had been hardened on the shore of the lake by continuous exercise. Joe Lavelle was painstaking in every detail and never left anything to chance.

The sale of the yearlings provided Elinor Dillon with money to extend the estate. She bought up two encumbered estates and annexed them to the Dillon Lands. Daniel Parr watched her grow prosperous.

'And this is the Member who most recently had called to the House of Parliament to give tenants fixity of tenure and to socialize the land. He should look at his wife's practices instead of listening to the sweetness of his own voice,' he told his agent who had informed him of the land purchase.

Parr's position had been advanced considerably in London. He had control over the Irish situation, and was able to buy men's allegiance with his devious methods. He had close contacts with the Secret Service and his network of spies in Ireland was now recognized and funded. The Nationalist party was destroyed and it would not recover from the shattering blow.

He had watched Sadlier fall into disrepute. His speculations in America had failed and he had been exposed. When the papers reported that Sadlier had committed suicide he felt no compassion.

'He was a jumped-up counter boy, a self-inflated financial frog who thought he had regal rights,' he told his friends.

And now Keogh, as a result, was showing signs of mental instability. He walked in his sleep at night crying out that he had betrayed Ireland and sometimes even in company his head shook and he had to put his hands to his face to stifle his memory.

Parr had been married for several years. His wife had produced three daughters and a still-born son. A doctor told him that she might not give him any further children, which meant that his title would pass to Peter Dillon, the only male heir out of the Parr line.

'The women of the estate can give me male bastards who will eat into my lands but you give me whimpering girls,' he told his wife. 'Do you realize there is a possibility that a Dillon may yet be Lord of Erris?'

'But I cannot control these matters,' she cried in fear.

'There is a weakness in your line somewhere,' he told her. 'It didn't come from the Parrs. In every generation we produced a male heir.'

Obsessively he walked the large room where the portraits of his ancestors hung, thinking about the position in which he now found himself. He could not let the title pass to the Dillons.

The city of Galway was always in a state of excitement during race week. The countryside was abandoned and the city streets were bursting with chaotic and misspent energy. There were sporadic faction fights in the narrow streets as old angers erupted. Men and women engaged in raw combats as a wild hate surged through them. In the shebeens men drank raw liquor in the dense half-light. They sang songs in Irish, their arms on each others' shoulders.

A small man made his way through the masses of people in Shop Street. He wore a green coat, shiny with age. His nose carried a perpetual drip which he wiped away with his sleeve. His boot soles, studded with nails, made a scraping sound on the stone sidewalk. He wore a black patch over a blind eye and looked more peculiar than sinister. His figure was slight and the coat was far too large for his meagre body. He was known in Galway as One Eyed Muldoon.

He travelled to all the race meetings, sleeping rough in back

317

sheds or ditches. His voice was high and castrated and carried a good distance. He carried with him a roll of ballad sheets tied into a coil by string. When he found a suitable spot at Shop Street, he put his hand in his pocket and took out his ballads. He drew phlegm out of his throat and spat it on to the dusty road, then scanned the sheet and began to sing.

> A tree has been planted in Ireland
> And watered with tears of the brave;
> By our great-grand sires it was nourished,
> Who scorned to be held like the slaves.

It drew a circle of attention to him. He had special effects which caught the eye of people and he used this to advantage. He beat out the metre with his heavy boot on the ground. He looked towards heaven with one eye and then dropped it towards the crowd at the end of each verse. He finished off his ballad with the words:

> Then gather beneath its broad branches
> All ye who dare strive to be free.
> And Heaven will surely protect those
> Who guard Ireland's liberty tree.

He got a good round of applause when he was finished and felt well satisfied.

'A penny a sheet. A penny a sheet. Sing the new ballad of Ireland. Sing the song of liberty,' he called out as he passed round the green, badly printed sheets.

When they disappeared and he was about to move towards the corner of Ayre Square, a policeman grasped him by the shoulders.

'This is sedition, Muldoon. You are fermenting discord with such metrical executions,' the policeman said grandly.

'I don't understand all them grand words. It's only a ballad and Muldoon has to make a copper or starve. Sure it is only rhyme made up by somebody and him in the horrors of drink.'

'It was composed by a felon. Come along with me to the barracks for you have some explanations to give to the sergeant.

318

The policeman shook him and the ballad sheets fell from his hand. They were scattered on the sidewalk and spread by the wind.

'Oh, look at my living being blown down the streets of Galway. You whore's melt but you'll have no luck for this, no luck at all,' he cried in anger.

'No lip from you, Muldoon, or you will be charged with insulting an officer of the Crown.'

'Sure if a man farts in Ireland it will be construed as insulting to the Queen,' he said seriously. By now a crowd had gathered behind the two figures, listening intently to the conversation.

'You'll be transported to Australia, Muldoon,' one cried.

'And well shot of this country I'd be,' he called back.

Finally they arrived at the police barracks, Muldoon becoming quiet with awe.

'Do you ever wash yourself, Muldoon?' the policeman asked. They were in a small room where the stench from Muldoon's body became entrapped.

'I'm as clean as a schoolmaster's hands. Nobody ever found fault with me before.'

'That's because nobody has been so close to you.' The policeman left the room with the offensive ballad, taking it to the sergeant, who examined its contents. He recognized the imagery and knew how it could stir the public mind.

'I'll ask him where he purchased it and then throw him out. There is a stench from his clothes that you would not get at a cesspool,' the policeman said.

'Very well. But I don't think that Muldoon would be any party to rebellion or even know the meaning of the poem.'

When he returned to the room the smell had become intense and there was a strong undertow of urine to it.

'You will save yourself a lot of bother, Muldoon, if you tell me where you bought these seditious scandal sheets. Otherwise you will be in jail for a year,' he said grimly.

'Sure, I'm a faithful subject of the Crown and has served the little queen well here and abroad. I have a scar of a sword on my backside which I would gladly show you as proof and evidence.'

'Never mind your backside. It does not relate to the issue in hand. Where did you get the ballads?'

319

'To tell the truth I got them from a man in Athlone. Devil an eye did I ever lay on him before. He gave me a fistful of them into my hand for nothing and I put the air to the ballad myself. I tried the Londonderry air but it did not work and the Coolin but they have not fire to them,' he chattered on.

'Will you stop, Muldoon? Could you recognize him if you were to see him again?'

'I could, I could,' Muldoon cried out. 'He had a scar across his face and spoke with a Dublin accent. I'd know that because I've a good musical ear.'

'Shut up, Muldoon.'

'I'm only trying to help.'

'Anything else about him?'

'He walked with a limp, just like this,' and he began to limp across the floor.

'Stop, Muldoon. No acting. I want a clear description.'

'And he had a stutter.'

'Anything else?'

'His front tooth was missing.'

'And anything else?'

Muldoon concentrated deeply. 'As far as I remember he had only one ear. Yes, he had only one ear. It was dark and I could not see too well.'

'That is all. You may go but don't sing that ballad again.'

'Indeed, no. I'll sing songs about love and young men and women getting drowned in cold lakes. That always stirs people's hearts. There is many a tear I brought to an eye with my rendering of "Young Sally".'

By now the stench was too overpowering. The policeman rushed to the door and down the corridor to the latrine where he vomited heavily. When he returned he looked white.

'Did you have a seizure?' Muldoon asked sympathetically.

'Out, Muldoon. Out. If you could barrel that stink of yours, you could destroy a regiment.' The policeman pushed him out the door.

'There is no need to be insulting,' Muldoon said, looking back. He drew in the free air of the city and hurried down to the twisted streets where he felt safe.

Daniel Parr sat behind his desk. There was a knock at the door. He limped over and opened it to the sea captain. He was well-dressed and his buttons were polished. He had a serious face and Daniel Parr was always impressed by his presence.

'You had a pleasant voyage I hope,' Parr said with formality.

'We ran into a storm nearing New York but otherwise it was an uneventful journey.'

'How did you find New York?' he asked. The sea captain put his hand in his pocket and took out a black leather-bound notebook which he handed to Parr.

'You will find all my information and impressions here,' he said. 'I have found change in the last year. There is a new spirit in the Irish immigrants. They talk of a rebellion in Ireland and slowly they are being formed into clubs. Before this they had been a shapeless mass. I have made out a list of the leaders, with a short biography on each. I have named the clubs and you will also find the names of some of the sea captains and the sailors who are drawn to the cause. You must keep a close eye on America. They have no formal plans but I expect O'Mahony and some others will draw these up. There is talk even of secret societies. They take oaths. But it is impossible to get exact information. You must have men living in America who will penetrate these organizations.'

Daniel Parr listened carefully, then took out a bag of sovereigns and gave them to the sea captain.

When he left the room Daniel Parr reflected for a moment, wondering what motivated this man. He held no allegiance to anyone. He was quietly married in Galway and had a pleasant family. He went to Church each Sunday and went about his business unobtrusively. Yet he was the most capable spy he employed and had been the cause of several men's death.

He thumbed through the pocket book. Kevin O'Donnell caught his eye and instantly he recalled the attempt on his life. He read eagerly through O'Donnell's biography. He had a good position in America. His voice was being listened to in the papers. That he was a friend of John O'Mahony meant that he was up to his eyes in rebellion. He became angry when he read of his success. He considered employing an assassin to kill him. But his

thoughts were interrupted when his servant knocked on the door.
'My Lord. Your carriage has arrived to take you to the races.'

John Dillon watched the entrance of Daniel Parr, his carriage
flanked by four soldiers drawing up behind the stand. They
saluted as he descended and he took his place in a special box on
the stand. Women curtseyed to him as he passed through their
ranks and men bowed stiffly. Like everybody else at the racecourse they were aware that he held the purse and the power.

John Dillon knew that this was the man who had destroyed
the Irish Independent party. He had become angry and frustrated
during the last two years. On several occasions in London he had
sat drinking in his rooms instead of attending the House of
Commons. Nothing could be achieved in open debate and he was
coming to believe like others that only a revolution would startle
them into any change.

His thoughts were broken by the roar of the crowd and he
immediately turned his eyes towards the course. He had almost
forgotten that his wife's horse was running against Parr's. It was a
flat race and the horses came to the turn bunched. The Parr horse
was in front by a head and he watched them settle into the long
straight run which ended in the stand. He wondered where his
wife's horse lay and then saw him on the outside, an ideal position. But the Parr horse was moving away from the rest, his head
and body moving in a convincing rhythm. He had power and drive
and he thought for a moment that the victory would be Parr's. He
looked towards the box where Parr was on his feet pounding on
the timber frame urging him home, his cold expression unusually
excited. He was roaring at the top of his voice. On the field, the
Parr horse was ahead of the race and seemed a convincing winner
until he saw the Dillon colour move forward and was instantly
reminded of Pegasus at the Grand National. It seemed that the
other horses had become slack. First he was beside the Parr horse
then yards to the finishing line his wife's horse increased speed
and won the race by a length. He looked across at Daniel Parr, his
fists clenched in anger. Their eyes met and John Dillon laughed.

That evening the Dillons held a victory celebration.

It was late when they left Galway and Elinor fell asleep on her

322

husband's shoulder. When they turned through the gates she awoke to look at the lights burning in the windows in welcome. Her mind was filled with contentment at the sight; the house and the land were a bond of security against time and history.

The Home Office was aware that Fenian feeling was growing in Ireland. It could be a danger to the general peace and might stir up old memories and hates. It was decided to dispatch Lord Dunraven to Dublin Castle to oversee a general operation against the growing menace. Quietly he slipped over to Ireland in the packet boat and installed himself at the Castle.

## *Chapter 31*

By 1860 it was evident to John Dillon that the desire for rebellion was in the air. He suspected that the men in the estate were forming secret clubs, and that guns were being smuggled into the country. Men had new confidence in themselves, no longer trusting the parliamentarians.

*The Times* called the talk of rebellion a cancer eating away at the hearts and minds of young men. It was everywhere; in the market place, in the army, among the minor civil servants and the peasantry. A generation had grown up since the famine, with the dark memory of what had happened branded on their minds. Mass graves were pointed out in lonely fields or beside the walls of the workhouses.

James Stephens had set up a wide network of Fenians all over the country. He had been on the barricades and had studied French insurrection.

'Never let it be the work of amateurs,' he argued with friends. 'A popular rising by the people with pikes and forks is a brave but ridiculous sight. They may exemplify bravery but they are soon cut down. The military forces are always too powerful. You must lay down wide foundations and you must strike when the enemy is weak. You must be so well organized that if one member of the group is caught and tortured he can only tell very little. The starfish's leg is cut off but it quickly recovers. That is how I plan to form a secret organization. It is everywhere and has no centre.'

O'Mahony slipped back to Ireland in 1856. Dressed as a beggar he walked three thousand miles through Ireland and became know as the Hawk. He met some of the parliamentarians and found them fatuous and without ideals. He discovered his strength among the lesser men. The movement he had planned in Paris began to take shape in Ireland and in America. He formulated a fearsome oath which bound them to the organization.

'I, in the presence of Almighty God, do solemnly swear allegiance to the Irish Republic now virtually established; and that I do my utmost, at every risk, while life lasts, to defend its independence and integrity; and finally, that I will yield implicit obedience in all things, not contrary to the laws of God, to the commands of my superior officer. So help me God. Amen.'

The British government was not yet aware of the organization's power. In England even warders in the prisons were bound by the oath. The common man, so long powerless, felt a new sense of importance. Perhaps the old dream which had lain dormant in their minds could come true.

The appointment of Lord Dunraven to Dublin Castle was most important to the British Secret Service. The Fenians were not aware that he was already planning their destruction.

Kevin O'Donnell was present when the two men met in New York. They differed in temperament but both were intense in the same belief. They met in O'Mahony's small house where Stephens smoked continually. O'Mahony stood firmly by the window, his hands behind his back and looked out at the small rose garden as he spoke.

'Money is scarce. I cannot raise the sums you request.'

'Then we will have to organize a patriotic parade and if necessary I will address them. Men are filled with spirit and the sense of revolution, but we must buy guns. This time every man must be properly armed. They must be bought in America and shipped to Ireland. More soldiers must be recruited into the organization.'

'America could be moving towards a civil war. If the South attempts to secede Lincoln will try and hold the Union. This he believes in above all else. If America engages in civil war young Irishmen will be caught up on both sides,' O'Mahony said anxiously.

'Good. Let them be tested by war. When this civil war is over we will have the fighting force we need. They will be hardened in battle and many of them will be leaders of men. And when the year for action comes they will be ready. I have already met some of the Irish regiments, brave men all. This civil war could be a blessing in disguise. You have seen how trained troops cut us down on the barricades. Well, it will never happen again.' Stephens's voice rose to an emotional pitch.

O'Mahony studied him.

'Do you believe that this will happen?' he asked.

'Of course I believe it. I know the temper of the times. Would you have believed eight years ago that we would have this vast organization ready to move against the enemy? Every day it increases, and if we do not take this rising tide then we may have to wait for ten more years before we move again.'

Kevin listened all evening as the two men spoke and argued, reflecting that in this small room in an insignificant suburb of New York a vast rebellion was being planned.

That night as he walked home he felt a great emotion move through him and began to believe in this new organization. He knew he must take the oath. It was fearful and terrible and would put him outside the safe boundary of the Catholic Church. Cardinal Cullen of Dublin had spoken out against it. Neglected by his clergy he would feel lonely and isolated and he agonized over his decision for a week. Then he met his friend Desmond Hogan again. He had risen through the ranks and was now a commissioned officer, his soft, boyish looks replaced by a lean, firm face. He still possessed his easy laughter and he slapped Kevin heavily on the back when they met.

'You think too much. I can see your forehead knitted with worry. Perhaps the archbishops are against it but I know many a poor priest here in New York whose heart beats as brightly as our own. You believe in the cause and you will not outrage your conscience. The whole regiment has taken the oath. If your conscience comes against you later you can break it. That's your way out.'

Later that week Kevin was sworn into the Fenians by Desmond Hogan.

Daniel Parr looked at the paper on his desk containing a list of ten men from the insignificant village of Cahir. He had other lists from other areas which all confirmed his fears. He could keep accounts on important and dangerous people but he could not accept that the Fenian menace was growing so rapidly. For seven centuries the peasant had been harnessed to the earth like a beast of burden. Firm and punitive laws had ground him into subservience, but now Parr knew that the situation was getting out of control. He could not visualize a rebellion. His own class would become extinct, something he would not contemplate. He was Irish and he owned Irish land. His children were Irish. He would not have their patrimony taken from them by revolutionaries. He must move quickly against sedition.

'There must be a core that I can penetrate,' he argued to himself. He brought the same argument to trusted friends.

'I have had peasants brought before me. I have tried bullying and threats. I have tried to buy their knowledge but they are grim and resentful. They despise us and all we stand for. They are united to one another and with other cells. I know from America that guns will soon be smuggled into the country ready for a rebellion. When it does come it will be widespread and well-planned. What does one do confronted with such a danger?' he asked.

His friend a judge pursed his thick lips and reflected.

'You have lists of sprats. They are of no account. Of course there is a well-organized centre. This James Stephens has travelled the width and breadth of Ireland recruiting men into the organization. It is rumoured that cells exist even among the constables and the soldiers. They are eating into the lower substance of authority. Never mind the outlying cells; look to the inner ones, the ones in which the poison is generated. You will be able to buy your way into them. When the time is ripe, arrest them in a clear sweep. Imprison them but don't hang them. A patriotic martyr is a dangerous symbol.'

The frown cleared from Parr's forehead as he considered the judge's opinion.

'Perhaps your advice is correct. There is no need for immediate fear. There has always been talk of revolutions in the taverns and in the mud cabins. But I must be vigilant.'

'And consider this fact. Have some of your money placed in England. Just in case. The day the great houses begin to burn marks the end of the ascendency,' the judge added casually.

This last remark unsettled Daniel Parr. He did not belong in England. His family had owned their estates for three hundred years. He was Anglo Irish but not British. He saw union with Britain as a guarantee that the Parr family would continue to thrive as they had through all the generations. On his way home to his estates he reflected on what the judge had advised him. He must never travel without an escort. For the first time in his life he felt insecure; the poison of Fenianism was getting to him.

When news of Lincoln's election reached South Carolina feeling ran high. The legislature declared that the United States of America was now dissolved. Other southern states joined the secession, feeling that it was time to do battle. The military force in the North was weak and Britain and France would swing in behind the South. When Lincoln blockaded the South the country was set for civil war. Desmond Hogan and the men serving under him waited for the time when they would be tested under fire.

A dangerous optimism gripped the North. Horace Greely, catching the war fever, printed 'Forward to Richmond' on the front of the *New York Herald*. The city became excited, convinced that a quick victory would bring the South into submission.

It was a warm summer's day and the trees were in full bloom. Desmond Hogan and his men gathered in a field close to a wood, stacking their rifles into pyramids, drawing off their haversacks to drink water from a stream close by. Their feet were blistered from the long march and they cast aside their shoes, feeling the relief of the cool air on the skin. Across the field a wagon had set up a food kitchen and soon they smelt beans and meat cooking.

327

'Eat well, lads, for it may be our last meal for two days,' Hogan advised them. 'We sleep for eight hours and in the morning we move against Beauregard.'

'Is that the name of a town or the name of an enemy?' one of the men called.

'He's a Confederate general. Have you not learned their names?'

'To tell the truth I don't know the names of our own or where I am. But march us in the right direction,' he laughed.

Since the beginning of the march the men had felt they would have an immediate and easy victory. Marching down the lanes of Virginia they sang revolutionary songs to keep their spirits high.

That night they gathered around small fires, talking in quiet voices. A soldier played on a harmonica, the plaintive and lonely sound adding to the bleak time of the night, when soldiers reflect before they go into battle. It would be their first taste of fire.

Hogan came upon one of his men sitting alone, drinking from a bottle of rum. He put the rim of the bottle in his mouth and drank deeply.

'You fool,' he told him. 'Don't your realize that you will need all your wits about you tomorrow? We are not going on a picnic.'

'Easy for you to talk. I was a poor immigrant and I joined the army for the silver dollar in order to have a full stomach. When I joined there was no talk of war. Now I have to face an enemy I don't know and don't hate. Worse still I'm told that there are Irishmen with the Confederacy. I have no wish to kill my own.'

'I could have you court-martialled for such talk,' he said angrily.

'Court-martial me if you want and march me before the generals. I don't wish to fight,' he answered sullenly.

'What is your name?'

'Cornelius Huggins of Beltra, Mayo.'

'I'm ashamed of you, Huggins.' With that he swept the bottle from his mouth and hurled it into the darkness.

When he saw him two days later, lying dead in a puddle of his own blood, he felt that he had been harsh. This more than any other sight on the battlefield moved him to tears.

They took up their positions in a confused countryside, the hedges and woods isolating the regiments. It was impossible to set up

328

communication lines as they waited for the enemy. Desmond Hogan rode up and down behind the double line of soldiers, their guns ready, eyes straining for the first sight of the enemy. A vast silence covered the woods and the open spaces, the men mute with fear. And then they saw their enemies with their slouched hats, their blanket rolls slung across their bodies, the Virginia rifle musket beside them. They marched forward and they heard the stamp of their heavy boots on the ground. Suddenly the cannons concealed behind Hogan's men in the woods spoke out. The flash of shrapnel broke about them and some Union soldiers were cut down, crying out in agony. Confusion began to spread.

'Hold the line,' Hogan roared. He signalled for the discharge of cannon, watching it cut into the ranks of the Confederates. Gaps were blown in the wall of men.

'Fire,' he cried out and there was a staggered volley of fire. The Confederates began to charge, screaming in high-pitched voices. He ordered the second row to fire, but, the enemy continued to advance before his men had time to rearm. He ordered them forward. Before he could give further orders both sides, inexperienced in war, charged in a raw, angry fashion. Men hacked at each other or used the butts of their guns. Soon the ground was littered with torn and bleeding men and his regiment might have been destroyed had not reinforcements come down the hill. The enemy withdrew, giving him a costly victory.

As he looked at the casualties he realized for the first time in his life that war was not a game. Men with whom he had spoken the previous night were dead. Others lay with their stomachs torn open, or their faces shredded, waiting to be carried off the field to the military hospital. He counted his men. Nineteen had been killed and more would die before nightfall. Sick with the carnage, he withdrew his men and reformed them into smaller lines.

He was not to know that Confederate reinforcements had arrived and were making up for the losses all along the front. The next encounter was from a distance and the Union soldiers held their position. But further up the long line a Northern regiment panicked and fled as Confederates poured through. The message was carried to Hogan and he ordered a withdrawal. As they left the field and entered a wood they ran into a confused mass of retreating Union troops. Panic spread across they countryside. Men threw down their muskets and sought safety in flight. The First Battle of the Bull Run had been fought and lost and it was clear to all that the Civil War would be long and protracted. There would be no easy victory for either side.

# Chapter 32

The ship under full sail moved across the even waves with speed. Behind her lay the wide tract of the Atlantic, querulous and strange. They had tacked south to catch the winds and run into a storm. It raged wildly for a single day, throwing the waters into a boiling cauldron. Several spars had snapped and the sails had been carried across the waters liked wounded birds. Then it had moved north to trouble other waters and within a short time the ship had been set in order and moved easily north-east towards Ireland.

Kevin O'Donnell had changed over the years. His experience in New York had made him a man of the world, shrewd in his judgement both of people and events.

'And you think that this rebellion will gather force?' Captain Irwin asked him as they sat in his cabin over dinner.

'Initially when I met John O'Mahony I thought that the whole thing was a dream. But I have seen enthusiastic young men drawn into the movement, many of them hardened by the Civil War. They know what fighting is about. However, it will take two years to stock enough guns for a general rising.' He smoked a pipe, a habit he had picked up from Stephens.

'Beware of the Home Office. I have enough knowledge of the sea and the affairs of men to know that already they are planting spies in your midst. Watch out for them,' the captain advised, pouring Jamaican rum into their glasses.

'Spies know the penalty they will have to pay. The principles have been well established. Of this I am definite. If the British intelligence service think that they will penetrate the organization with impunity then they have a surprise in store. We have taken the sacred oath. Our lives and our occupations are at stake.'

The captain looked at the young man who was so certain in his beliefs. They had met in Liam Flaherty's pub and Kevin had supervised the cases of revolvers being carried on board. He had purchased them secretly in New York City. They were deadly at close range and the British police and soldiers had no equipment to match them.

The ship slid quietly into the Galway harbour, Kevin recognizing many of the landmarks on the coast as they approached. He felt an indescribable delight at the sight of Ireland. He did not believe that his heart could be so stirred and understood now why this island had been often compared by the poets to a seductive woman. He no longer sought vengeance on Parr; his political ideals were greater than the downfall of a single man. He wished to see the country free from external rule. Ireland should be ruled by her own people, Protestant, Catholic, pagan and dissenter. They belonged to its earth, and were part of its substance.

He watched as the wooden crates were lifted from the hold of the ship and set on the granite wharf. A carter was on hand to receive them. He wore a red scarf about his throat and sat stolidly on the shaft of his cart while the guns were loaded.

'That is one certain and self-assured Fenian,' the captain said as he watched the carter directing his horse down through the confusion of the quays.

'I can assure you that these men have serious intentions. You cannot buy their allegiance with money,' Kevin told the captain.

When the operation was completed Kevin turned to him. 'I will bid goodbye to you but will join you again in three months time and return with you to New York.' He went to his small cabin and got his travelling bags. Within minutes he was lost in the maze of narrow streets.

He discovered Tom Kenny's pub. He looked quickly about before entering to see if he had been followed. Tom Kenny was a bulky, bearded man with a strong, confident face. He glowered at Kevin, suspicious of strangers.

'What can I do for you, sir? I see that you are a stranger to Galway?'

331

'I bring gifts from America,' Kevin told him, his eyes expressionless.

'Sure, sir, if you bring gifts we must treat you well. Come down to the privacy of the snug and we will give you a good Irish welcome.'

His manner had become bantering and he placed his arm on Kevin's shoulder and led him down to the end of the bar.

'Tell us of this great war that's going on. It is said that Irishmen fight on both sides and that it goes first one way and then another. And I believe you have buildings of six storeys in New York, the likes of which have never been seen before.' He spoke in a loud voice so that everyone could hear.

Immediately they were inside his manner changed and his expression darkened.

'Are you sure you have not been followed?' he asked anxiously.

'Certain.'

'Parr's agents are everywhere. One has been shot and others have taken fright but he offers high bribes to poor men.'

'No. The revolvers should be in the warehouse by now. Make certain they get to all the cells. Better to distribute them in the cities and the towns. If we do call a revolt it must be rapid and effective. Have your men prepared.'

'Half-prepared you might say. I cannot wait for the day. The air of freedom is about and men are anxious for a rising.'

'Hold them back. Temper their enthusiasm. It may take perhaps two years to arm them,' Kevin cautioned.

'And what of America?'

'We will bring back men tested in battle to organize them, have no fear. The organization is strong in America.'

'Do you think we stand a chance against the forces of the Crown?'

'We do if your organization is not penetrated by spies. I must leave now that I have made the connection with you but I will see you before I sail.'

He walked up through the limestone houses, listening to the steps and voices. There was a pungent smell of people living in a narrow, confined place and he knew that he was safe. He compared it to the vast expansive streets of New York, where vision seemed limitless. Passing a public house he heard the music of pipes and stopped to listen. He recognized the music of the Piper and his heart began to thump with emotion. He went down two limestone steps into the pub. It was early in the day and the place was almost empty. The sad music filled the rooms.

The place was cold, even in summer, and wet turf smoked in the hearth, giving off a rough smell and choking the throat. The Piper sat by himself on a hob, his frail body drawing warmth from the reluctant heat of the fire. Kevin noticed how old he had become. He approached the old man with awe; above all others he had inspired him and informed his heart. He stood before the Piper who looked up with eyes whitened by glaucoma.

'Who is the gentleman that stands before me?' he asked. 'Has he come to buy an old piper a drink?'

'He has come not only to buy him a drink but he invites him to the best hotel in Galway so he can eat like the lord he is.'

The Piper broke off his playing and stared in amazement. Then he put out his hand and drew Kevin to him.

'The dark boy, the dark boy. And where have you been all these long years?' he whispered, drawing him down to his side. 'I heard that you tried to kill Parr and that there was a wide search for you. It lasted a whole month and I feared for your life. Where did you hide?'

'In the woods with Bartley Gaynor. Even when the soldiers and the dogs combed the woods he hid me. Then I was brought to Galway and taken on board a ship.'

'And did America take you to its heart?'

'I have good employment and have some to Ireland to write some articles on the present state of the country.'

'And you are up to no devilment I hope?'

'Well there is a bit of devilment in it too. I am one of the boys now.'

'And so am I. I took the oath. I may have no eyes but I have ears and a piper is welcomed in many a place and because I am blind they assume that I cannot hear. I believe that guns were expected from America. Are you behind that?'

'I am, but keep your voice low. Let us leave the place and go to a hotel. You know me as John O'Donovan. I have grown a beard

333

but you must be careful. Parr still has a price on my head.'

The Piper packed his pipes and they left the bar, Kevin noticing that his stoop was permanent and that he dragged his feet behind him.

After the Piper had eaten they went to a lodging house and sat and talked about the past. He heard about his sister and her children.

'I rarely make my way to Dillon Hall these days. I prefer to remain in the towns. It's more comfortable there and many of my patrons have died. Who needs a Piper to play for them now when they are dancing to these waltzes and other queer-shaped dances? But I can tell you that the enmity between the Parrs and the Dillons still festers. Parr is now a lord. They say he destroyed the Independent party with his bribes and promises. John Dillon no longer sets his hopes in parliamentary reform but I have heard it whispered that his sympathies lie with our cause. If Parr were to find that out, then he would have his bloodhounds ready. But the country is wild with rumour. Some say the rebellion will be next year, others in six months. This time there will be no coming back, this time we will be a freed people.'

'I don't know. I cannot promise but the preparations are well under way. Men are training and when the Civil War is finished in America, soldiers will return to Ireland. We will not go into the field untrained and without experience. Our only fears will be from the spies. The castle will not rest until it penetrates the organization. But let informers beware; we will deal harshly with them.'

'It's grand to hear your voice. I wish I was young but I feel the weight of age on my back and in my hips. I don't travel as much as I did. I keep to Galway City and I play in the public houses. It's sad to think that I have such a low circuit but such is life. But now you must be about your business and I have to return to the public house. I will see you again. My heart goes with you in your travels.'

He brought the Piper back to the narrow streets and said goodbye. He made his way to the more fashionable part of the city, having arranged to contact James Stephens at the Central Hotel.

334

John Dillon watched his daughter take the fence. She held the reins confidently and had a natural control over the horse. Her blond hair flowed back on her shoulders. She waved to him and continued towards the next fence. The Dillon interest in horses had been passed on to her.

It was a warm dusty day with hay dust and the heavy scents from the woods and hedgerows in the air.

He waved to his daughter and followed one of the forest paths. In Catherine's presence he could banish political anguish but alone in the woods harsh reality began to trouble him again. Like many others he considered a change was necessary. He could no longer take an onlooker's stance. The House of Commons was a farce. His sympathies were like this new movement which seemed to be sweeping the country. He knew that several of his tenants had been sworn into the Fenians. Suddenly his thoughts were disturbed by a rustle in the undergrowth. The branches were pushed aside and the wild figure of Bartley Gaynor appeared, his eyes bulging and wide. In the bend of his arm he carried a small pup. He stroked it with his centre finger affectionately.

'Sorry for disturbing you, sir, and I hope I didn't frighten you but I have a gift for your young lady. I have watched her grow from the cover of the woods and I want her to have this pup. It is the best of the litter.'

'Will you not come and present it to her?' John Dillon said smiling at the puppy.

'And frighten her? She would think that I am a wild man. No, Sir John, I said I would interrupt you in your walk and give it to you. It is out of my bitch Hazel and it's the brightest of them all. I had to destroy the others save one. You have your law and the wood has its law.' He tickled the puppy's head and would not look directly at John Dillon.

'And are our laws any better than the laws under which you live?' he asked, testing him. It was a difficult question for the recluse.

'To tell the truth I know little about the English law. I am satisfied with my own and I hope you are with yours.'

'But the laws of the woods are harsh.'

'Maybe. Nature set them down and I live under them. They are fair in a hard way and we all abide by them. Anything else would be strange to me. But I must be going back to my hut. I don't trust the foxes. Good day to you.' He handed the puppy over.

John Dillon continued walking. During the last few years he had travelled to England as an Independent candidate, but had little power in the House of Commons. Periodically he made a speech on land tenure and on the Disestablishment of the Church of Ireland, arguing that the lands held by the Church should be sold off for the relief of poverty and for the encouragement of agriculture and fisheries. It made him unpopular among many of his Protestant neighbours. He further argued that the ballot should be secret. Refusal to vote for a landlord's candidate meant duress and evictions. On several occasions evicted men had made their way to Dillon Hall in order that he might bring their plight before the House of Commons. He had watched his words fall on deaf ears.

'We have no redress before the law, John Dillon,' a group of men had once told him in his office. 'We are honest men and we suffer injustice. Do you expect us to look on while the work of our hands is knocked down and turned into grazing land? There is little we ask. We are weary of the law and we will take it into our own hands.' He had looked at their worn faces. They had laboured honestly and long on land to improve it and had been beaten by the system.

His sympathies now lay with the Fenians but to take the oath meant that he would place both himself and his family in danger. He considered his position for a long time, finally deciding to associate with the Fenians. The first step was to place the ownership of the estate and lands in the name of his wife Elinor, so that it could not be touched if his allegiance was discovered. When he emerged from the woods much later he felt relieved that he had come to a decision.

James Stephens and Kevin O'Donnell met in Galway. Stephens arrived on a coach from Athlone sporting a loud tweed coat and a bowler. He carried a suitcase full of tobacco samples. When he opened it in his room the scent of the tobacco was thick and sweet.

'I draw in that scent every morning. It fills my lungs with pleasure and my imagination with scenes from Egypt and India,' he said.

'But most of it comes from the Southern States of America,' Kevin protested.

'Never mind, never mind. It reminds me of Egypt and India. Leave me to my fancy. And I may add I sell this tobacco all over the country. There is no better place to find men for the organization than in a tobacconist shop. If you can bring in the owner then you have a double bonus. Thoughtful men smoke pipes. But down to the present business. The guns have arrived and have been distributed.'

'Yes. It was a smooth operation. They have been delivered to the cells in Galway. Better have the towns well served with guns; you can never spark a revolution from the countryside.'

'Good. I believe you are to travel through Connaught. I can give you some contacts which will be useful. By the way, do you know John Dillon?'

'My sister is married to him. I have not met him personally. I had to flee to America. Why do you ask?'

'I have some personal business with him. I would like to know his background. I did meet your sister in Paris some years ago. I had to warn her against her brother-in-law. He is connected with the British Secret Service.'

Kevin sat on the single bed and gave a correspondent's view of John Dillon.

'You mentioned the name Parr frequently. I know his name and he is to be avoided. We know that he is head of the Secret Service in Connaught. I have considered the idea of having him assassinated, but he is as cute as a fox. He moves carefully and never to a pattern. But his day will come. He has his spies everywhere and that is why we have to move cautiously. Fortunately I have countered him. Five men came from Athlone with me and at this moment they have the hotel covered. They can smell out a spy a mile away.'

'What will they do if they discover one snooping about the hotel?'

'Take him to one side. Use moderate force on him to extract

337

information. And if that is not forthcoming we give him a final choice. The final choice is never refused.' He put a finger to his temple and pulled an invisible trigger. 'But now I must rest. I have an important journey to make after dark. I shall see you perhaps before you return to America.' He shook his hand firmly and said goodbye. When Kevin left the room James Stephens lay on the bed and thought seriously, his mind working in different directions. He prepared for his meeting with John Dillon and fell asleep. Outside his door a Fenian kept guard.

He left the hotel by the back entrance that night, wearing a large cloak and a wide-brimmed hat. His clothes were a dark colour and he looked like an anonymous shadow. He could not be recognized as the tobacco traveller who had entered the hotel that morning. Beside him rode his chief contact in Galway and both carried revolvers.

They spoke very little on the way, avoiding the towns in order to remain inconspicuous. The constabulary were on the alert and horsemen passing late through the towns would be entered in their logs.

When they reached the edge of the lake, a light wind was whispering in the sedges. Lights on the distant shore made interrupted lines on the spread of water. They passed over the bridge the horses' hooves ringing out hollowly on its limestone surface. At the gate they reined back the horses, moving slowly up the avenue. As had been arranged there was a single light burning in the house. Stephens dismounted and walked across the gravel to the front door. It was opened quietly and still wearing his heavy cloak and hat he followed the servant upstairs and was shown into the library. John Dillon rose from his chair and came to meet him.

When they were sitting in wide armchairs John Dillon said, 'I presume no one knows that this meeting is taking place.'

'No. I received your letter in Dublin and it has been destroyed. I thought at first that it might be some type of trap but when I considered your stand in Parliament and read your speeches I knew that there was no reason to doubt your integrity.'

'For the moment I do not doubt yours. I know of your

338

activities. You have set a flame that will not be extinguished.' He looked carefully at Stephens's cold eyes as he spoke.

'This flame has been well tended. This will not be a rebellion in a widow's cabbage plot as they like to remember the rising of '48 when hunger was stalking the land. This has its roots in France and America and force will be used if necessary. We no longer trust the members of the Irish party. They belong to another time and these times are urgent.' His voice was cold and certain. For two hours they explored their positions, each trading intimate details of their plans and ideals.

At three o'clock John Dillon took the Fenian oath, promising allegiance to James Stephens and those belonging to the inner circle. It was a decision he had not taken lightly and he knew that he was placing himself outside the law. When Stephens had left the house and passed into the wood, Dillon sat and reflected on his decision. There was a new excitement in his blood, a patriotic purpose. As the logs crumbled in the hearth and became a steady glow, he went out on to the balcony. The sky was lighting with a summer dawn. There was a fresh breeze from the lake and a stirring in the roof of the woods.

# Chapter 33

Daniel Parr finished breakfast with his wife and daughters. It was always a formal occasion. His children were growing up and he was thinking of their future. His eldest daughter Caroline possessed considerable presence and personality. She was his favourite and he granted her liberties which he did not grant the other two. She would inherit the estate on his death. In the last year they had been confined to the limits of the estate and a teacher had been brought from Galway to instruct them. When they did travel they were escorted by a troop of soldiers. He had heard through one of his sources that members of a secret society had planned to abduct them and demand the release of prisoners in Galway jail.

He spent some time in his office, checking over his papers. They contained information on the Fenian clubs in Galway.

'It continues to grow and set down poisonous roots everywhere. No sooner have we located one cell than it splits and forms two more. Who is behind it?' he asked himself, as he waited for his escort to arrive.

At ten o'clock his carriage was brought to the front door, flanked by eight horse-soldiers with loaded guns. He left his room and said goodbye to his family. He sat well back in the carriage, his bodyguard beside him with a pistol in his hand.

When they left the estate he became anxious. Popular feeling ran against him and his death would be welcomed in many homes. Even as he passed through the villages men turned their backs on him in defiance. Ten years previously they would have raised their caps.

The coach did not drive through the centre of Galway where it could be halted in the traffic and confusion. Somebody in the crowd could assassinate him and disappear into one of the narrow streets. When he arrived at the station policemen were waiting for him. They brushed people aside and permitted him to walk directly to the train. Alone in a private carriage and surrounded by armed men, he felt partially secure. Notices have been nailed to the trees in his avenue and with every warning notice came the feared coffin lid badly drawn with his name inscribed upon it. Even in the fortress of Dublin Castle he felt uncertain. It was said that some of the constables had taken the oath and that information was carried directly from the Castle to James Stephens.

Lord Dunraven looked at Daniel Parr's narrow face and sinister expression. He found it difficult to sit on a chair and when he talked or argued with himself he had to walk up and down the room. Lord Dunraven considered how much he should disclose to him. He possessed a mass of information on the Fenians, set out in huge folios in the library behind him.

'We must act now. Bring in the leaders and sentence them to penal servitude. Better still, hang them. Make an example of the ringleaders and all the outer cells will die. That is your answer.' Parr pounded his fist on the table.

340

'If we knew who the leaders were. Remember this movement is well-organized and although we can give you single members we have no idea who is at the centre. This man Stephens is and so is Luby and O'Mahony in New York. This is all known to us but we possess no documentation. Until we gain entrance to the main centre and have definite information then we cannot move against them. And so the matter must rest.' He spoke in the detached voice of an aristocrat. Daniel Parr felt that he despised him.

'No. It will not end there. I believe that the constabulary of Connaught is riddled with Fenians. We need a man who can weed out the vermin. You cannot act against these Fenians while they have informers in the barracks. They are warned of every movement in advance. Why, the Fenians have penetrated my estates and nailed warnings on my very trees.'

'Then you shall have the man. He has just arrived from England and his name is Sergeant Grinling. He is to be posted to Tuam. I think that you will have much in common.' Lord Dunraven was certain that both could be used by him to contain the Fenians in Connaught.

'And where can I meet him? I am most anxious to make the acquaintance of a constable who is above suspicion,' he said sarcastically.

'Are you implying that I am not doing my duty?' Lord Dunraven asked sharply.

'You can imply what you like. I wish to meet this man. Remember I have power in London. I have rendered good service to her Majesty the Queen. You are well aware of my position.'

'I know, my Lord,' Dunraven said, using the title disparagingly.

'I will go and meet this man.' He snapped Sergeant Grinling's address out of Lord Dunraven's hand and left the office.

He found him in his private quarters. Parr was impressed by his physical presence. He was a tall, well-built man, clean-shaven and smelling of soap and scent. Everything about his uniform and boots spoke of order and cleanliness. He sat behind a large desk which carried a column of files.

'Have a chair, my Lord,' he said courteously. 'I believe we see eye to eye on certain issues. I have read your files in London and committed most of the Fenian names to memory. I am checking

341

the more recent ones now. If sharp action is not taken soon then the very presence of Britain on this island could be in jeopardy.'

'I have given Lord Dunraven the same warning but it has not penetrated his mind that unless he takes immediate action we could have a rebellion on our hands,' Parr said excitedly.

'No, the rebellion is some way off. I have studied the various reports. They have no military leaders. At present it is a large but ineffective organization. However, I fear the American Irish. They collect money for arms and when the American Civil War is finished they will have trained soldiers better than any troops we have in Ireland. In the mean time I will weed out all Fenians from the constabulary. I have only to find one weak link, apply some pressure and then move against all the others. We must bring them into our net. What will really set them back is to expose some Fenian of note whom people respect, and destroy him. I have checked in all the documents but I have found no one of importance. The Fenians remain small farmers, shop assistants, school-teachers, and a few solicitors. Look, I have the numbers here. The big fish has not yet entered the net,' he passed across a folder which Daniel Parr eagerly examined.

'Sergeant Grinling, it will be my pleasure to work with you. I have found a just and dedicated man at last. Let us seek them out and destroy them.' He declared this with missionary zeal and handed back the folder. 'I shall see you in Galway. Good evening, sir.' He left the room filled with satisfaction.

In the mean time Lord Dunraven had ordered his coach to be brought to the cobbled courtyard. He quickly washed and shaved, changed into evening dress and set out to meet Elinor Dillon. The coach sped towards Rathfarnham, his thoughts only of the beautiful woman he was about to meet.

He had come to Ireland a year previously to take charge of intelligence operations at Dublin Castle. Lord Dunraven was sharp and intelligent enough to destroy the Fenian movement and had worked with the Secret Service since he first entered the Home Office. His urban manner gave little indication of his ruthless mind.

His transfer to Ireland had given him an opportunity to renew his relationship with Elinor Dillon. They had met officially at the

Viceregal Lodge in Phoenix Park and after that secretly at his house at Rathfarnham. It was a blind passion which consumed both of them. Again and again Elinor Dillon had made a strong resolve that she would not meet him, knowing how dangerous the liaison was. A breath of scandal and Parr would use it against both her and her husband. But as the train moved through the midlands she knew she must be with him again. Her passionate nature, restrained for so long, was like a wild storm within her. When the passion subsided and she had time to reflect she hated her weakness and her infidelity.

Lord Dunraven took delight in her physical presence and in her conversation. She had a mysterious quality that he could not fathom, holding some secret that he could not penetrate. He knew that she had been born by the sea and that her mother had been French. She spoke of the giant who protected her but gave hardly any information about herself beyond that. She loved him with her body and only part of her mind. Sometimes she seemed to slip into a mysterious past that was lonely and full of solitude. His heart was filled with delight as the carriage entered the avenue which led to his country house. The lights were burning in the bow windows and she was standing there looking into the darkness. When he entered the room she threw her arms about him and they held each other firmly for some time.

'I have thought of you all day. I summoned the carriage immediately to the Castle courtyard when I was finishing some tedious business. That dreadful man Parr insisted on having a meeting with me.'

Immediately her mind became sharp.

'Surely you could have dismissed him and sent him on his way?' she said, in order to discover information.

'He is our most important agent in Connaught. He has access to more secret information than anyone else in that province. He is obsessed with this Fenian threat, and fears that they intend to assassinate him.' He laughed and drew her away from the window.

'Is there a Fenian threat? I read about it in the newspapers but there is no evidence of any outrage. Should we all fear for our lives?'

'Not for the moment. I think that we have everything under control.'

'Are you certain?' she continued.

343

'Let us not consider the subject. I have been dealing with it all day. I wish only to be with you and hear about all that you have done since our last meeting.'

Lights were burning everywhere, giving an enchantment to the small intimate rooms with their mirrors and paintings. Dinner was set out on a side table and the main table carried silver plate and decanters of red and white wine. He took the covers from the plates, carved the meat finely and set it before her.

'And how is the book advancing?' he asked when they were settled.

'I spent the whole morning with the printer. We have finally corrected all the proofs and it should be published in the spring. I made a promise to Robert Dillon that I would see it through the press. He dictated the final pages to me so I have a keen interest in it. We had to shed some of the chapters in order to publish it as one volume. I know the old man would weep if he knew but I wish to have him remembered.'

'You are quite an authority on Marie Antoinette and the French Revolution,' he said, raising his glass and sipping some wine.

'On all revolution. And that is why I am interested in the Fenians. They interest me for I believe that their ideals have been inspired by the French Revolution.'

'Perhaps. But so has every revolutionary group in Europe. However they have no royal family to bring down in Ireland,' he reminded her.

'There is a ruling class in Ireland, possessing all the wealth and land. I believe that the similarities with France are greater than you think.'

'They have no leaders. The Revolution was carried forward by intense and intelligent men. As yet the Fenians have no outstanding men in their ranks. But enough of such conversation. Surely you did not spend all day with the printers?'

'I treated myself to a new ballgown.'

'Red?'

'No, blue. I have grown tired of red. It is too violent a colour and has gone out of fashion. And I bought several bonnets, but you have no interest in my bonnets.' She smiled, kissing him on the cheek.

'I am interested in everything about you. I wish I could take you to the Curragh Races in your new bonnet?'

'And create a scandal. No, we must be satisfied with our time here. I cannot be seen with you.'

'You could divorce your husband and come and live with me on my English estates? I will not be always tied to Ireland,' he said seriously.

'You do not understand my position and I do not think you understand Ireland. You promised not to raise the question. We have an agreement,' she said looking seriously at him.

'Very well, I will not bring it up again.'

'I do not know if I can discover a good excuse for coming to Dublin when the book is printed. I cannot think of a good reason for leaving Dillon Hall.'

'Some reason will present itself. It always does. Have some more wine and let us think only of the moment.'

Their conversation drifted to more pleasant things. Next morning they intended to ride across the Wicklow mountains. They would set out early and reach a small lodge beside Lough Dan nightfall. With wine and conversation the evening passed into night. They drew the curtains and sat before the autumn fire. From conversation they moved evenly into the pleasures of love, the fire throwing light on the movement of their bodies on the woollen fleeces. It was late when they drew away from each other, satiated and alone. Her mind returned to her estate and her carnal reason. She thought also of the unimportant men who were arming the Fenian movement. She knew that many of the tenants on the estate had taken the oath. They were brave, honest men who loved the land in an intense manner which the man lying beside her could not understand. She knew that her lover had lists of these men, cyphers in his folios. He could move against them if he so wished and destroy their small existence. She thought of her brother shooting and maiming Daniel Parr. Her body drained of pleasure, her mind was able to settle on these matters. She was passionately in love with this man beside her and passion was minding her mind. She reflected on his position in Ireland as government agent. His purpose was to destroy those whom she loved. She did not belong with him or his breed; he was closer in mind to Daniel Parr than he was to her. Her allegiance lay with her husband who had worked so hard in Parliament and was little rewarded for his efforts. She had come from the sea edge and from ordinary people, the people who were looking for common and decent rights.

That night the storm began to move across Ireland from the west. All day it had battered the coast and islands, tearing boats from their moorings and breaking them like matchsticks on reefs. It bore down on the woods, uprooting great trees which could not bend under the fury. Small thatched cottages on exposed places were unroofed and even the solid mansions had their slates lifted and carried away.

For Maud Dillon there was excitement in the confusion and disorder. From the upper room of her two-storeyed house she watched the branches of the trees bend and sway wildly under the primal force. A wild plan formed in her mind. She had been rejected by her lovers and her family and she possessed an estate of only a hundred acres on the edge of bogland. Her hair was grey, her body unwashed and her life in confusion.

She went to the kitchen where an old woman was cowering in the corner.

'I want a sharp carving knife,' she said, her voice filled with energy.

'Not to do yourself harm mam, I hope?' the old woman asked.

'No, but to do others a deal of harm which they have earned during many years.' She pulled out the drawers and threw their contents on to the table, spreading them flatly. She picked out a large sharp knife and tested its edge.

'This will serve my purpose well,' she told the woman pointing the blade at her. 'I will return after midnight and no one must know that I have left the house. Do you hear, mad woman?'

'I do, my lady, but it is a perilous thing you do going out on night like this when the elements are in rage. I heard a tree smash to the ground.'

'This is the weather I like. I have never been afraid of a high fence or a storm. Have the fires roaring when I return.' She pulled open the door and crossed the yard to the stables. She found th

346

horses nervous, their eyes bulging with fear. She saddled a heavy horse and urged him from the stable. The wind was to her back as she rode out of the yard. All about her the storm raged, tossing her hair and her cloak wildly. The confusion brought satisfaction to her mind.

It was dark when she reached the entrance to Dillon Hall. She knew that nobody would be about and that her access to the stables would be easy. She urged the horse forward beneath the chaffing branches. She rode directly into the yard, knowing exactly where Pegasus was stabled. She dismounted and opened the door. The crying of the horse was not heard, when she savagely cut his hamstrings and then in a final explosion of violence prised out his eyes with the knife. His warm blood poured over her hands and was absorbed by her sleeves.

'I have had my revenge,' she cried as she rushed from the stables, mounted her terrified horse and rode out of the yard. As she came to the end of the avenue she saw the waves of the lake boil in fury. She would swim the horse across the lake. He refused but she drove him forward with the point of the knife. The horse was frightened by the noise and confusion and gave a wild start, throwing her from the saddle. She held on to the reins as he turned for the shore, but her wet clothes began to draw her down. She struggled for some time then sank beneath the waves.

Later that night Tadhg Mor went to the yard to check the stable doors. He discovered Pegasus crying out in agony. He rushed across the yard and woke the servants. They opened the kitchen door and he charged up the stairs to John Dillon's room and brought him to the stables. When he saw the animal in agony he ran back to the house for his gun. He put the barrel to the eyeless horse and drew the trigger.

Next day when the storm had spent its fury the body of Maud Dillon was found on the shore, her long grey hair tangled and filled with coarse sand.

Elinor Dillon and Lord Dunraven did not make their journey to the Dublin mountains. The storm raged about the house and they remained in the comfortable bed, burning the passion from each other's bodies.

347

# Chapter 34

Tadhg Mor went each morning to the quarry which lay on the edge of the estate. Here in the arena cut from the side of the hill he gathered stones and put them in a cart. The stone mason watched his activity, never daring to interrupt him. Having chosen from the best of boulders he moved out of the quarry without a gesture, his expression plain and stolid. Holding the reins he led the horse through the wood to the Round Field where Pegasus lay buried. At the beginning he heaped the stones about the grave in singular mounds. Nobody questioned his purpose, not even Elinor Dillon, and he told no one of his intent.

When the yard bell sounded for work he fell into the same routine. Once when a stable boy asked him for the use of the cart he was struck to the ground. That single gesture affirmed that Tadhg Mor wished to be left alone. In the vaulted kitchen beneath the house, the women wondered what was happening. They felt that he was clearly mad. Even when he came for his supper he took the plate from the table and ate his food in the corner of the yard. He ate mechanically, his eyes looking towards the middle distance.

'He is struck like the lunatics,' Mrs Coyle remarked. 'He is acting as queer as any inmate of the asylum in Galway. If he took a fit in that mood he could destroy us all so, whatever you do, don't cross him. Leave him to what ever odd plan he has.'

'Well, if he continues, the whole of the Round Field will be covered with heaps of stones and there will be no training of the horses there. The master should be told about it,' one of the stable boys told her.

'The master has his own plans and worries. His mind is intent on other things these days, and he seems to have lost interest in the estate. His only certain interest is in the Collins woman. He has been seen at her cottage again. She's a saucy one who never did a day's work in her life but flaunting herself in front of men. You would think, to see her in the church on Sunday, that she was some type of lady rather than a kept woman.' Mrs Coyle gossiped to the other women as they stood around the deal table preparing the dinner.

'He's not up to it any more they say,' one of the young women observed.

'Where did you hear such filthy talk?' Mrs Coyle asked.

'Things have a way of getting out,' the young woman persisted.

'He's a fine healthy man,' Mrs Coyle continued, anxious to know more, 'and there is no base for such talk.'

'The Collins woman has a friend in Ballinrobe who makes dresses for her. She was overheard talking to her in the backroom.'

'Sure, what would he be going to the Collins woman for and a fine woman like Lady Elinor in his bed?' Mrs Coyle wanted to know.

'Fine for what, I ask you?' the young woman said. It was too much for Mrs Kelly, an old woman who had kept her patience during the conversation. She rushed round the table and caught the servant by the ear and dragged her screaming to the door. 'Out of the house. I heard the last bit of scandal from you.' Then she turned to the rest of the servants. 'You should be all ashamed of yourselves. I have been here all my life and I have never heard such talk. The Dillons have kept you in food and shelter when others starved and it little befits you to talk in such a manner. Back to your work. And another thing, I don't want to hear any more talk about the men drilling at night time. If that goes beyond this kitchen we could have the guards down on us. These are strange and strained times. Now there is a dinner to prepare.' She glared at them angrily.

The conversation in the kitchen and on the estate often turned towards the Fenians. Their husbands had been drawn into the movement and they drilled secretly in remote corners with wooden guns. They formed into small battalions and discovered a new energy among themselves. Some of them had privately asked John Dillon for advice on the matter, feeling that it would be betrayal of confidence if they had not let him into their plans.

'Keep your councils to yourselves. Nothing will be achieved through parliamentary reform and always keep an eye out for the spy among you. I wish to know nothing else of the matter.' He told them.

The men drank in a small public house in Ballinrobe. It was at the far end of the town and out of sight of the military barracks. Here they met other Fenians from Mayo and north Galway and pooled their information. They knew how many soldiers were in the cavalry barracks and how many policemen lived in the town. When a stranger entered the public house they talked of the price of cattle and the weather. And they always kept an eye out for an informer among them. Every cause had been destroyed by somebody who sold information to the enemy.

The station-master joined the organization in Ballinrobe, keeping a close eye on all new arrivals to the town. Every stranger was a suspected spy.

They set about organizing themselves and reading the Fenian literature. For two years they had drilled with wooden weapons until a stranger brought them a crate of rifles and ammunition and some military manuals. He was obviously disguised, spoke very little and departed into the night.

The manuals had been printed in America. They were clear and sharp and easy to understand, not only explaining the use of arms but setting out the principles of warfare. They read them slowly and in groups.

There was no particular hour when the movement became firm and established but by the year 1864 Daniel Parr knew that he was surrounded by enemies. The Fenians lurked in every street of every town. They were in the barracks and in the civil service and no single arrest would be effective. They had not broken the law but he knew that in the event of a general rising his class would be swept away. No military force could contain them. And now soldiers were returning from the battlefields of the American Civil War. When he travelled through the province of Connaught he wore an uncomfortable sheet of moulded steel on his chest. He had heard the rumour that he was marked for assassination, although Sergeant Grinling had assured him that there was no basis for his fear.

'And are you party to everything that goes on?' he asked him when they met at Dublin Castle. They sat with Lord Dunraven in his office and considered the Fenian presence in Connaught. On the table lay files and lists of Fenians and their sympathizers.

'Of course I'm certain. I have had some of my men set up ambushes along the routes you take. A good marksman could have picked you off on numerous occasions.' Parr looked at Sergeant Grinling in surprise. He had not expected anything so direct.

'You mean that I am not well protected by my own soldiers?' he shot back.

'It is impossible to protect you. You will always leave a weakness and that is when they could move against you,' he replied, drawing straight lines on the sheets of paper before him.

'Give me an instance when I leave myself exposed,' he insisted angrily. 'Give me one occasion.'

'When you visit your tallywoman on Saturday evenings. That is your most vulnerable point. There is always a weak point in every scheme.' He did not look at Parr as he spoke.

'Point taken,' Parr agreed hastily and went on to consider another point.

'I need some reassurance that we are going to make a move against them. What can you give me? I live in a state of siege and so do my family.'

Lord Dunraven considered what he was going to say for some time. Parr was beginning to lose his nerve. His face twitched and he paced the floor more frequently when he was talking. The Fenian menace was taking its toll on him.

'I have to consider the country in general. We know that guns are being smuggled into the country. We know that the trail leads from Birmingham and Manchester to the ports. We let these through in order to give the rebels a false sense of security. However I do have information for you. We have penetrated the inner circle in Dublin and recently we have added a new name to our lists. He may be the prize we have been looking for. Here is his name.'

Lord Dunraven wrote it down on a sheet of paper and passed it across the table. When Parr looked at it he gasped in amazement and forgot his fear. His mind was suddenly filled with new intent. Sergeant Grinling looked at the name, nodded his head and said impassively, 'This is where we can break the movement if we can get a damning conviction.'

351

'Then it must be arranged, Sergeant Grinling. But it will be arranged from this office. I have placed private information in your hands. Keep your lips and confidence sealed. We will meet here in two months' time. In the mean time I will deal with the matter in my own way.'

Daniel Parr could not believe his good fortune. He no longer felt afraid of the assassin's bullet and felt that nothing could touch him now. He would have his vengeance against John Dillon and he might even bring down the woman with him and the whole estate.

When they left the office Lord Dunraven walked to the window and looked down at the Castle yard with its polished cobblestones. On the opposite side of the quadrangle lay the centre of his operations. In these rooms five civil servants sifted through the information sent in by every agent in Ireland as well as England. On the walls hung maps not only of countries but of cities accompanied by detailed information. It was through these offices that Lord Dunraven could slip secretly into the city. Through a series of old wine tunnels he could make his way to the corner of Dame Street.

He left the window and stood in the middle of the room, his brow furrowed with thought. Despite his controlled voice and manner he was well aware of the gathering menace. He feared the reports from America. Already many soldiers had returned from the Civil War and were training men in the hills.

He checked his silver watch. Bells rang for six o'clock all over the city. At this moment the central cell was meeting in Roache' Hotel at Stephen's Green and John Dillon was expected. Lord Dunraven walked across the quadrangle and entered the office where one of the best men was waiting for him, dressed in tweed to look like a bookie. Lord Dunraven studied him for a moment.

'Perfect for the occasion. You know precisely what you are expected to do. Everything should be prepared at the hotel. Make sure you pick the right fancy woman. She will be waiting for you at Stephen's Green. Report back immediately after the meeting.'

The man went into a cellar beneath the building which led to nearby pharmacy shop. He walked through the shop into Dame Street and briskly along the pavement towards Trinity College. He made his way up through Grafton Street and on to Stephen's Green with its seven acres of park land. He met the prostitute by the railings and arm in arm they crossed the road and entered Roache's Hotel. He noted that there were two spies in the foyer room. He winked at the waiter indicating that he needed a room for an hour or two. Upstairs he took a key from his pocket and entered a room. They locked the door and took a picture from the wall. A small hole had been bored in the partition. He took a small horn from his pocket and, placing it on the hole, listened carefully. He remained in this position for two hours, writing rapidly in a notebook which the woman held for him.

The conversation in the other room turned to the smuggling of arms into the country.

'We cannot increase the flow from England,' Stephens told them. 'If we do, we will attract attention to ourselves. Already some of our shipments have been seized in England. Some of our men are under observation and we have had to reorganize the circles. But we should now turn our attention towards France and bring them in through Galway and Limerick ports which are not as well guarded as other ports. The west is the exposed flank. We can store them in the warehouses and then distribute them throughout the province.'

'Have we made contacts in France?' a member asked.

'Not only contacts but I believe that we have friendly ship captains who will carry them straight from the capital itself. They have to be bribed but the money has been transferred to a bank in Paris. I cannot be more explicit at this moment. Obviously a thousand guns will add greatly to our stocks. When the guns have been deposited in the warehouses in Galway you will be informed. That concludes our meeting. We may bring forward the day of the rebellion if the arms come through. And now leave the room in twos and threes. You know the various ways on to the street. Good night. The day draws near.'

After ten minutes there was silence. Then a door opened and a chair was drawn aside and somebody took a seat. The spy continued to write down the conversation.

'Are you prepared to go to France and settle the deal John?' Stephens asked. 'I have ordered money paid into a Paris bank.'

'I have some business to attend to in the city. I can use it as a cover and no one will suspect me. We will use one of my brother's ships and I will sail with it. I don't think that I will attract attention to myself. I intend to bring my daughter with me; our roots were originally in France.'

'You place yourself in great danger,' Stephens told him.

'I know of the danger and I have placed my property in my wife's name. Perhaps she is suspicious of my activities as a result. But I believe that this is the only way that we now can settle our problems. When we have broken the link with the Crown then the question of land and property can be solved. I no longer believe in the English Parliament. I have attempted to bring our case before the House but it failed. This is now the only course open to us.'

'Prison is a lonely place, you know. If you are caught then there is little we can do for you. Justice will be rough.'

'I have considered all these matters. I hope that the day will come when the arms can be used. I hope it is not a wasted effort.' He spoke passionately, ignoring Stephens's warning.

'The day will come. We will sweep the militia into the sea. I have not laboured this long and suffered so much to see my attempts frustrated. We have gone so far that we cannot turn back. My best wishes go with you. I shall not see you again until you return from France. We will meet in Dublin when the guns have been distributed. I have given you a list of all our contacts in Paris so it should be a smooth operation.' The two men said goodbye and after a while the spy heard the sound of doors closing. He replaced the picture and remained in the room with the woman for half an hour. Arm in arm they left the hotel, walked past Stephen's Green and turned into Grafton Street. As they went along the pavement they heard a young man singing a Fenian song. He parted with the woman at Trinity College and returned to the Castle through the pharmacy. He went immediately to Lord Dunraven's office and handed him the notes. He scanned them rapidly.

'This is the information we have been waiting for,' he told him. 'I wish you to go to London by packet boat this very night. We must move rapidly now.'

*　*　*

While her husband was in Dublin, Elinor Dillon waited anxiously each morning at the window of the study. She looked towards the long road which bent along the edge of the lake. She had told the stable boy to wave his hand as he approached. On two mornings he had come from Tuam empty-handed but today, the third morning, he carried the parcel. She rushed down the stairs and was waiting for him at the front door. When he placed the heavy packet in her hands she looked at it for a moment before tearing off the paper which covered the books. The spine carried the title Marie Antoinette and beneath it the name of Robert Dillon in gold lettering. Finally the work had been seen through the press and the author was guaranteed some small immortality. She opened the biography and flicked through the pages with her thumb. The print, which she had chosen, was strong and firm, and the quality of the pages rich. The chapters were set out in heavy Roman numerals. She bent it backwards to test the stitching. Having tested the quality of the binding she began to read random sections. It was difficult to believe that it had once been a large cumbersome manuscript. She was so familiar with the text that she recognized each line. The book was a living thing, a monument to a man's life. There was no one to whom she could show it and her pleasure was private. In the library she placed it on the desk where Robert Dillon had laboured so long to bring the work to completion. She began to cry, her strong shoulders shaking. She put her hand to her face and blocked out the light, wishing that the old man were present to see his life work set between covers. She sat in his chair for a long time, feeling empty and dry.

Her thoughts were interrupted by a knock at the door.

'May I enter, mother?' her daughter asked.

'The door is open. Come directly in.'

'You are crying, mother. I have never seen you cry before. Have you received some terrible news?'

'I do not cry when I receive bad news any more. No, I cry because I am happy. Your grandfather's book has been published today and I have placed the first copy on his desk. He should be here to join in our triumph. He spent his whole life writing the life of Marie Antoinette and I do not believe that he ever knew what was going on around him. His mind was always in France.' She handed the book to her daughter.

355

'You should feel proud of him. However, we must get on with living. Have you packed all your bags? You have to make a long sea voyage. I hope that you remember both your manners and your French. I have the most pleasant memories of Paris and I will return again some day when the business of running Dillon Hall is in order. I will give you a copy to bring to your uncle. It is the best gift you can bring him.'

'It will indeed surprise him. You have described the estates in such a detailed way that I feel that I can already find my way through them. I know exactly where the stables are and where the lake is situated. I have been thinking about it for the last week,' she said excitedly.

'You will enjoy every moment of it, particularly the rides through the parkland. I wish I were going with you.'

'But you could come. Nothing is preventing you.'

'There is always some business or other to attend to,' she said evasively.

She looked at the young woman who had grown so quickly in the last few years. It was difficult to believe that she was only sixteen years of age. She was already an accomplished horse-woman and spoke French fluently.

Catherine Dillon was excited at the prospect of travelling to France in her uncle's ship. The arrangements had been made by her father and the letter from Dublin confirmed everything. On his return they would leave in the first ship sailing to France. Elinor went with her to her room and watched her put out her dresses for packing. She was not as tall as her mother, but lighter of body and moved with a delicate elegance. They talked for about an hour and then Elinor left the room. Her horse was saddled and waiting for her to ride through the estate.

As she approached the Round Field she heard the ringing sound of limestone rocks thrown into place. Once a week Tadhg Mor drew stones to the centre of the field from the quarry. Now his pyramid was almost finished, rising up from the centre of the field in tiers. It was firmly built and would stand for a long time.

'You never tire of your task?' she asked Tadhg Mor.

'No, my lady. It gives me peace and Pegasus deserved such a monument. When we are dead and this estate derelict people will

356

emember that a wonderful horse once coursed about this field
nd they will ask about it and perhaps may ask about us. I will have
ft something to mark my presence in this world.'

'You are sad, Tadhg Mor.'

'No, my lady. I am not sad, but I wonder what may happen to us
l. I feel the world changing. I met the Piper in Galway and he
ld me so. He tells me that these Fenians are everywhere and that
me day the great houses will burn.'

'Do you believe him?' she asked.

'Yes. He is wise and thoughtful. Being blind he is given over to
uch thought and his ears are sharp. I believe what he says, that
mething terrible must happen. The country is arming and
eople's minds are full of memories. They will bring down the
reat houses.'

'And do you wish that the great houses should be brought
own?' she asked, looking carefully at his face.

'My lady, I love this house and the life about it. I'd slaughter the
enians if they came near it. We have worked for this house, you
nd I, and no one will touch it. Your children and their children
ill be here when the other houses are gone. They grow every day
nd I watch them eagerly. It seems only yesterday that I carried
em on my shoulders. I grow old, my lady. I have my small house,
y food and I follow the seasons with joy. I wish to grow old in
eace and I see no reason to change. The new masters the Fenians
romise might be the new tyrants.'

'I do not believe that it will come to pass. But tell me how the
iper is. He does not call to the house any more.'

'He is completely blind and looks older than his years. He
emains in Galway and rarely ventures out from the city. When
e does he is led about by a hunchback. They depend upon each
ther. But he can still play a fine air.'

'When you see him tell him that I invite him to the house. If he
kes, we will place a cottage at his disposal. I would like to see him
gain,' she said sadly. 'Why does he not come and visit me? I'm
ure he would like to talk with my son and daughter. He did play
r them once and wrote a special tune for each. Sometimes they
sk for him and wonder what has happened to him.'

'It's difficult trying to communicate to him through the dwarf.

357

He is ashamed of his appearance and wants you to remember him as he was when he came to visit us by the sea. He had his pride and that is all that is left to him now.'

'I am sorry that such changes have taken place.'

'We all grow old, my lady. That is why I build this monument.' Having said that he returned to his work. She turned her horse and left the field.

The carriage brought the Dillon family to Galway. They had received news the previous evening that the ship *Sophie* would sail for France in the morning. Although the accommodation was slightly cramped it would be a new experience both for John Dillon and his daughter. Elinor Dillon stood with her son on the quay and watched the ship move slowly out of the dock on a light sail. When it was clear of the pier it began to unfurl its sails. They fell magically from the yardarms and slowly bulged under the wind. Elinor and her son mounted the carriage and drove home. The departure of John Dillon and Catherine was noted by a man in grey fisherman's clothes. He left the quayside, hurried through the city, changed his clothes in a small boarding house and emerged later with a travelling bag. At the station he took the train to Dublin. When he arrived at the Castle that evening Lord Dunraven set his plan into action.

# *Chapter 35*

John Dillon stood on the deck of the *Sophie* and watched the heavy sails catch the wind. The coast of Ireland lay to the east, a blurred line on the horizon. To the west lay the continent of America, still embroiled in civil war. At the edge of his mind a fear lay brooding, like a black dog ready to spring. He drew in the bracing air to clear his mind of such doubtful thoughts and felt bright and sharp again. The sea had always brought him a deep peace.

Catherine crossed the gangway to talk with him and he

watched her with pride. She walked briskly, her blond hair taken by the wind and thrown wildly about her face. She stood beside him, put her arm in his and laid her head on his shoulder. They stood in silence, looking at the grey waves.

After several minutes she spoke. 'I had been watching you before I mounted the stairs. The expression on your face was very sad. What were you dreaming about?'

'What do you imagine I was dreaming about? Make a guess.'

'I could say that you were remembering some events in your life but that would be incorrect. I think that you are troubled by the present state of Ireland. Do not think that I have not noted your movements during the last two years. I have heard strangers coming to the house at night time and leaving before dawn; shadowy figures without substance. I believe that you are caught up in some secret organization, perhaps with the Fenians. You leave the house and set out on business and I never know where you have been. Can you not share your thoughts with me? I am a young woman now.' She spoke seriously, looking to see her father's reaction.

'Perhaps I have failed to notice or perhaps a man feels old when he admits that his daughter is a young woman. You have grown up and taken on responsibilities. Your mother was very young when she took over her hotel in Tuam. I must take you into my confidence more often.'

'Then why not take me into your confidence now? I am not blind to what is going on about me. I feel you carry too many private troubles,' Catherine said firmly.

'It would not be wise for me to let you know what is going on. In the event of failure or trouble I do not wish to have you drawn into my life. It is enough to say that I feel very strongly about the Fenians and their beliefs. The information I carry with me is dangerous.'

'But why did you not stand against Daniel Parr at the last election? You would have been a Member of Parliament. You could have changed the course of events.'

'Because the House of Parliament is not moved by logic. It only faces its obligations when it is pushed towards a crisis. They will only listen to the reason of force and not the force of reason. I spent nights preparing speeches to deliver at the House of Commons, but the members were not moved by my passion. They toddled off to their clubs. I have chosen a different path.'

'And a dangerous one. You are playing into the hands of the Parrs. He will move against you,' she argued.

'Do not tell me that the hates have been carried into the third generation. I thought that you were remote from these things.'

'And so I am. I am growing into a different world. I bear no grudges against Daniel Parr's children. I have my own life to lead and I intend to follow it but I do not wish you to be harmed. I think that you are reckless,' she said accusingly.

'I have always been reckless. It is one of my many faults. You have watched me all your life and you know what manner of person I am. No logic will change my ways.'

'I will always be at your side,' she said simply.

'I do not know if I deserve such affection and such help.'

'You do.' The light faded and it became cold. They left the deck and returned to their small cabin but some barrier between them had fallen. He had come to accept that his daughter was now a young woman bearing the responsibilities of life.

They never again returned to the subject of Fenianism. She knew that his voyage to Paris was more than a family visit.

They were two days out to sea when John Dillon made his first approach to the Captain Jacques Le Clos. He was a squat man with large and powerful hands, scarred with rope burns. He wore a cap with a greasy leather peak and his brown teeth bit heavily on a pipe stem which never left his mouth. He spoke broken English and his eyes moved constantly over each rope, sail and knot looking for weakness.

'Even in my sleep I know if something is wrong. At night I know by the sound of the rigging if all is not well. The sound of the wind and the sea tell me when the storms are coming.'

The conversation had no general direction until John Dillon asked him, 'Did you ever wish to own you own ship?'

'Many times, but I was not born with money. Had I money I would return to St Malo, purchase a small vessel and trade along the coast. It is more interesting. I would travel from harbour to harbour, picking up custom.'

'Then I could put some gold in your purse if you are willing to listen to my proposal.'

'Let me hear your proposal. I will listen but perhaps I may not accept,' he said cautiously.

John Dillon explained how he wished to have several cases shipped from Paris to Galway with no questions asked concerning their contents.

'You place me in a dangerous position. What if we are intercepted on the high seas or at Galway? I value my freedom and have no wish to rot in a British jail.' His voice was hard and avaricious.

'You have placed yourself in a dangerous position before. I know that you have smuggled criminals out of France for a price. You trade where the money is good.'

'I would need at least £300 for such an undertaking,' he replied. They haggled over the price for a day, finally arranging that he would carry four or perhaps five cases on board for £100. John Dillon would give him £20 when they reached Paris and the rest would be handed over when the cases were delivered at a warehouse in Galway.

The journey passed quietly. An easy wind took them down the channel and soon they passed Pointe de Barfleur. They passed Le Havre on their right and entered the mouth of the winding Seine. Jacques Le Clos had judged the tides well; they were on the turn and could carry him towards Rouen.

Having anchored for the night at a small port, they set sail early next morning. Catherine Dillon watched the landscape from the deck of the ship. The morning sun filled the horizon with silver and she watched it pass across the sky, noticing how it changed the landscape. Villages were thrown into high relief, the edges of buildings sharpened and the earth seemed to respond to the heat. The fields were vast and edged with tall poplar trees, men and women like heavy-sculpted figures worked through the drills and the crops, sometimes straightening up and waving to them.

He came and stood with her.

'It is very strange,' he said, 'and something for which I could never find a reason, but the Dillon women have always been drawn to the earth. They have cared for the Hall for two generations and I suspect that you in your turn will follow your mother's steps.'

361

'It is in my blood. If the land fails it is because we fail.'

'Then I think you will be impressed by my brother's château and estate.'

His face was bright when he spoke of his brother and how he had come to own the estates. He also described Edward Dillon's wife and told her that he had heard that the marriage was not only childless but that they now lived in different wings of the house.

While they were pleasantly engaged upon their voyage Lord Dunraven made his way to London. He sat in a panelled room just beside the New Parliament buildings, admiring at the Clock and Victoria towers which had been recently finished. He was proud of the great building which had arisen from the ashes of the fire of 1834. His father had brought him to see the smouldering ruins and he had watched the honey-coloured building rise stone by stone. It marked the beginning of a new era. A capable queen sat on the throne, huge wealth was flowing into the city from the colonies. London was linked by a vast network of railways to each corner of the country. Gaslights filled the city, their warm glow making the nights less dangerous. He was part of this new prosperity and he would not have it poisoned by the cancerous Fenian cells. Soon it would be time to move against them but it must be a sudden and subtle move. He had invited two ministers to his rooms. His butler announced that they had arrived and showed them into the room.

'Well, Lord Dunraven, I presume that you did not bring us here to talk over simple trifles. Your arrival from Ireland must herald important happenings. The cabinet is disturbed by rumours of a Fenian uprising,' one of the ministers commented.

'Yes. I wish to put some proposals to you. I know it would be in our interest to sweep through Ireland and England and destroy the Fenians but they are now so numerous and so widespread that the present soldiers garrisoned in Ireland would not be capable of the task. And of course we have no capacity for them in our jails. Our approach must be much more sophisticated.'

Both men were listening closely to his suggestions.

'I have spent a considerable amount of time charting their organizations and movements. I know where some of their cells

362

have stored guns and ammunition. Most of them come from the farming classes and from the lower rungs of society and civil service. The lawyers and professionals, seeing that their best interests are served by their allegiance to the Crown are firmly with us, as is the judiciary. So we must move against the most eminent man in their ranks. His name is John Dillon and he was once a Member of Parliament. At this moment he is on his way to Paris to buy guns and ammunition for the movement. He is the man we must pursue. So I have come here to set the plan before you. I will need large sums of money to buy men's allegiance and I wish to have control of the army in Ireland if necessary. Once we have him in our net we will move immediately against the central cells. The organization will then fall apart.'

'But we would be investing you with most unusual powers. The Viceroy in Dublin would have to be informed about this matter,' the Defence Minister told him sharply.

'Tell him what you have to tell him but, for goodness sake, do not confuse him. He is a most pleasant man. He throws balls at the Castle and the Viceregal Lodge and he invites the Irish to these sumptuous occasions. He dines well for his country and rides well in the hunts but he cannot make rapid decisions. He is not aware of the danger in which the country now lies. Do you know that I prevented an assassination attempt upon his life and he is not aware of it. He could have taken fright and returned to England.'

'You exaggerate, I am sure,' the minister for finance added, pouring himself a second glass of brandy.

'I do not exaggerate. I measure each statement I make. A move will soon have to be made and I wish to know where I stand. Authority for these powers must be arranged before I leave London.'

'The Prime Minister will have to be informed,' the Finance Minister told him.

'The Prime Minister should be here with us now. If there is a Fenian rebellion the government will fall. It will have to rush through measures in the House which will be unacceptable in Ireland. You will alienate the whole nation.' Lord Dunraven was regarded by many as a popinjay who flitted about elegantly from one social event to the next, but the two ministers felt they were talking to a future leader of the party.

'The Prime Minister will be immediately informed of this meeting.'

'Of course he should. You surely do not wish to have to go to the country during a rebellion. This Fenian matter, if it is handled properly, can be quietly destroyed. Let some madcap general loose in Ireland and you will have an uprising on your hands. know the temper of the times.'

He could see the anxiety on the two ministers' faces, as they weighed up his proposals.

'Yes. We believe that your assessment of the situation is correc and it is well balanced. We will let the Prime Minister know of thi meeting. You will have direct access to his office.'

Lord Dunraven listed his specific requests and they agreed to each one.

Sitting alone, Dunraven knew that he had placed himself in a position of considerable power. He would use his link with the Prime Minister's office to his advantage. He had now virtua control of the military forces in Ireland if he wished to use them. I would be highly beneficial to his political career if he suppressed the Fenian movement.

At two o'clock, there was a knock on his door and Harold Bazin entered, dressed formally in black. His skin was dry and sallow and Dunraven often wondered what racial mixtures lay within him. He had a file on him but the earlier years were blank At Oxford he had developed a carefully correct accent but there was something continental about his gestures and tone. He was based in Paris where he dealt with the underworld, knowing the city's docks, alleyways and brothels better than he knew the main thoroughfares of London. Even on the warmest days he wore hi heavy black clothes but he never sweated, as if his blood and body were cold. He always travelled with a young man from the Secret Service which led Lord Dunraven to believe that he was a homo sexual. Bazin listened intently while Dunraven explained his plan nodding his head with approval.

'I want every movement John Dillon makes followed. You have access to parts of the city where others cannot go. Make no effor to intercept the guns; that can be done much later. Find the gunsmith and the dealers and offer them large sums if they wil

364

sign statements against him, and promise that no reprisals will be taken against them. Have them witnessed by the best lawyers in Paris and sent directly to my address in London.'

'Would it not be in our interests to have his brother Edward implicated in the plot?' Bazin asked.

'No, he is one of our agents, carrying court rumour to London. He does not have to know what is going on.'

'Perhaps, but he is Irish and we have given him large concessions. He has become a rich man on his wine and shipping business. He may have served us well but have we not served him well in return?' Bazin spoke in a passionless voice; his eyes were cold and sinister. He was a creature of the night, always carrying a neat revolver which he had used on several occasions to assassinate men because they threatened his organization.

'There is no way in which you could implicate him,' Dunraven said, not committing himself to any position.

'There are always ways, Lord Dunraven. Nothing is impossible in these matters. Leave it in my hands. You wish to alienate the people from the Fenian movement? Well, this may help you.'

'Very well, see what you can do. All the money which you need is available to you. I will not question how it is spent. I think our business is finished and I bid you good day.' Harold Bazin bowed from the waist and left the room. Dunraven felt the dark presence of evil about him as if Bazin's breath carried a contagious plague.

As the *Sophie* approached Paris, John Dillon came on deck to see the city as the ship passed slowly up the river. He had followed its transformation by Louis Napoleon and Hausmann through the French journals which were delivered each month at Dillon Hall and already he could see vast changes. Once a huge tangled slum had existed between the Louvre and the courtyard of the Tuilleries Palace, where cholera had festered behind delapidated façades. The slum had been levelled to the ground and now the full beauty of the Louvre was exposed to view. Further upriver the water-pumping station on Pont Notre Dame, set on thick wooden piles and carrying a tower, had been dismantled so that the lines of the bridge were visible. The ruined buildings on the Ile de la Cité between the Palais de Justice and Notre Dame had been levelled to give a view of the Cathedral. Hausmann was ripping out the old, rotten, medieval gut and replacing it with proper streets and sanitation.

He had only a quick view of the city and he would have to take much longer to explore the changes. At the quay a coach was waiting for them to take them to his brother's château. They passed up the quays and then through the Champs Elysées. At the Bois de Boulogne he noticed that the formal roads had been altered, paths and avenues leading in many directions now and two small lakes developed. On the slopes above the lakes people picnicked in small family groups. They left the park and made their way through the village of Sèvres. Soon they swung through the gates of his brother's estate.

'It is far more beautiful than I imagined,' Catherine said.

'Wait until you see the stables and the horses. And of course the forests and parklands. You will be happy here.'

'And what of you?' she asked turning to him sadly.

'Oh, I will be happy in my own way. You take care of yourself and enjoy all the delights of the place.'

His brother came down the steps to greet them. They threw their arms around each other and then took stock of the changes brought about by the intervening years. Then he turned to his niece and kissed her hand and cheeks.

Later the two brothers sat and talked while Catherine noted the difference in their characters. Her uncle had a fine, detached manner while her father had a stronger, more direct presence. She felt that he did not belong with such refined luxury and that he was not easy here. Most of their lives had been spent apart and Edward had become a Frenchman. There was a certain tragic quality about her father's face, as if he had never been totally happy in his life, she thought. Her mother often explained to her that her father should have possessed the French property, yet, seeing the brothers together, she wondered how he would have managed it.

Catherine was fatigued and excused herself, a servant showing her to her room, where she lay on the bed and fell asleep.

Jacques Le Clos had a stolid peasant mind. As he made his way up the Seine he considered many things. He was weary of the great tracts of sea, weary of a lifetime spent working for others. He had begun his career as a cabin boy under a rough captain. He had been a sailor on board a ship which carried French criminals to penal colonies. Some had died in the fetid hulks, their bodies giving out an early stench of decay. Under the hard sun others went crazy and had arrived at the equatorial colony demented. It had been a world of sweat and urine and human excreta and men turning to unnatural perversions. He had been forced to whip one of his companions who had murdered a prostitute in a New Orleans brothel until his back was torn and raw. He had watched naked Nubian women sold at secret slave markets, their ebony bodies and perfect limbs haunting him all his life. Later they were carried on board their ship from Zanzibar to the Middle East and delivered to wealthy Arabs.

He was stirred with early memories. He would be like Georges Le Tour from his fishing village – Le Tour owned a large boat – and he would sail down the western coast of France, the landfall and a safe harbour always in sight. Perhaps he might marry a peasant woman, sensual and not too bright. He had carried this vision across the seas and in rough cities.

He knew he was in possession of information which could bring him a substantial sum of money. Added to what he had already set aside he could perhaps buy his own ship and ply the Atlantic coast. He knew that information of this nature could be sold in Paris like any other commodity. He had made considerable sums before from British agents with his knowledge of foreign ports.

He remained on the ship where everything had been secured, only leaving when the Seine was charged with maroon evening light. He made his way along the left bank of the river, past Ile de la Cité and turned into rue de Sartine. It was a narrow street filled with the stench of human filth, tall houses with bulging walls which never let in direct light. The cobbled stones were hard and dry and the channel which ran down the centre was choked with filth. There were plans to demolish the area and drive a new boulevard through it. He did not like this place but he had been lodging here for years and could rent a cheap room above a tavern. Un Merle had a door with flaking green paint, the windows dusty and grilled. He pushed it open and went down three steps into the semi-darkness. The thick smell of candle wax was everywhere, the acrid air stinging his eyes for a moment, drawing tears. The owner placed a rough bottle of wine before him and Le Clos counted out the exact price between thumb and finger, testing each piece, reluctant to let it go. Everywhere there was the sound of muffled and unclear voices, heads bent over tables in conspiratorial groups. He drank the wine slowly, letting it cut into his throat. He began to think of having his own ship. He would not always be a hired captain.

He watched his contact making his way down the room. He wore an old military coat and a torn cockade and was known in the quarter as the Soldier.

'May I have some of your wine, sir?' he asked when he sat down. Le Clos looked at him sullenly.

'Buy your own wine. I have earned mine with the sweat of my brow.'

'Very well. I see old veterans are no longer honoured in this land of liberty, fraternity and equality.' His voice was high-pitched, deliberately loud.

'Bugger your liberty, fraternity and equality. We are as unequal now as we ever have been. We have new masters and a new emperor. At least before the bloody revolution we had a king. Now we have an emperor who just pulls down Paris.' Le Clos felt tired and irritable after his voyage.

'Not even a quick mouthful?'

'Very well, a mouthful,' Le Clos conceded. The Soldier took a swig of the bottle, wiping his lips with the back of his hands.

'Very well. Have you some merchandise for me?' he asked.

'This time I wish to meet the real buyer. I have good cloth to sell.'

'Can I not purchase it?'

'Bring me to your employer.'

'He is out of the country.'

'When will he return?'

'Perhaps in two days' time.'

'I will meet him then. Mention the name Dillon; it will interes him. I have nothing more to say.'

368

The Soldier did not leave immediately. Halfway down the room he stood to attention and sung the Marseille for which he was given a glass of wine. Then he made his way out to the street. Le Clos nursed his bottle until it was time to sleep.

Two nights later the Soldier entered the tavern, eager to talk to Le Clos.

'The merchant is at a house in rue Saint Victor and is willing to do business with you.'

'What number is the house?'

'Seven.'

'I go alone,' Le Clos said sharply, 'when I've finished my wine.'

He would let Harold Bazin wait. He had no liking for the man and knew his reputation.

Later he made his way to rue Trouvée and from there to the wider rue Saint Victor. Bazin was waiting for him in a sparse room, his person precise and neat in his customary black garments.

'Could you not have done business with the Soldier?' he asked.

'I would do business with him normally but I think that this present matter is important,' Le Clos answered.

'What makes you think so?'

'You contacted me immediately after my return to Paris.'

'I presume John Dillon has made you a substantial offer. We now his purpose in the city.'

'Yes. He made me an offer.'

'How much?'

'Two hundred pounds,' Le Clos said slyly. 'Can you better it?'

'Liar. Do you think I am a fool? Give me the real figure and I will eble it.' Harold Bazin spoke sharply. 'And do not trifle with me.'

'One hundred and twenty.'

'I shall give you £400. I am being generous to you.'

'May I have the money now.'

'You are greedy. Tell me what happened on board the ship,' azin demanded.

'I'll talk for money. Twenty English pounds and its equal in ench money. I am poorly paid by my employer.'

'Later, later.' Bazin was getting annoyed with the stolid sea cap-in and his pecuniary mind.

'Now or I'll not talk.'

'For £5 and its equivalent in French money,' Bazin bargained.

'That will do.'

Le Clos told him all that had passed on board the ship and Bazin listened intently. A subtle plan had already formed in his mind.

'You wish to have your own ship, you once told me. Is that not correct?' he asked.

'That is correct.'

'If you follow my instructions and do exactly as I say, you will have the price of your own ship. Are you willing to follow my instructions?'

'I will do as you direct.'

'Then £200 will be given to you before you leave the house. You will receive the rest when the guns are aboard the ship.'

'Very well.'

Bazin took a large envelope from his pocket and passed it across the table to Le Clos. With a peasant's gesture he tore open the envelope and counted the money, transferring it into a money pouch he carried round his neck.

'Our business is finished for the moment but I will contact you again if further business arises. There may be further money for favours rendered,' Bazin suggested.

'I am always willing to do business with such a generous man as yourself,' Le Clos said as he left the room.

'Do you believe that he was offered £120 by John Dillon?' Bazin's companion who had been listening in the next room asked.

'Of course not. The man is a peasant and a liar but he is central to our scheme. He will have his money but he will never own his ship. He will be got rid of when the time is right.'

Le Clos' heart was beating with delight when he reached his lodgings. He would soon have his ship, but he must be careful. Harold Bazin was a ruthless killer and he must make his own contingency plans.

370

# Chapter 36

Two days after her arrival at the château, Edward Dillon took Catherine to see the stables and the paddock where the horses were exercised each morning. He wished her to choose a suitable mount in order that they could ride through the park. The evening of their arrival she had expressed a great interest in the horses, and Edward talked to her for some time.

Catherine watched the horses frolicking about the paddock. She picked a brown chestnut three year old, with sharp eyes and sensitive nostrils. Her uncle stood beside her, watching her eyes as they assessed each animal.

'I'll have him saddled for you,' he said, calling a groom to take the horse back to the stable.

'Why did you choose such a horse?' he asked her.

'Because he has enthusiasm. He is bright-eyed and loves to run. He is the type of horse I would feel most comfortable with,' Catherine said without hesitation.

'And how does the strain compare with Dillon Hall?'

'Ours are more suited to heavy ground and colder conditions. In general they are sturdier but that could become a defect. We need a new strain perhaps. My mother is the expert at our stables, but sometimes I disagree with her.'

He was impressed by her certainty, finding many things to admire in this young woman. When the horse was brought she put her foot in the stirrups and mounted the saddle with a quick athletic movement. She took the reins and gave the spirited animal a slight tug to the bit, establishing a relationship with the animal immediately. She spoke to the horse and patted its neck to give it confidence.

When she was ready they made their way along an alleyway filled with the scent of roses, emerging on to the wide parkland. They reached the middle of the vista then wheeled their horses about and began to ride gently forward, the ground soft beneath the hooves. Soon they gathered speed and rode at a faster pace, kicking up a spray of torn earth behind them. Edward Dillon let Catherine go ahead, content to watch the free manner in which she rode, with none of the stylized postures of French women. The wind was in her hair, tossing it about, and there was a look of delight on her face as she looked around to see if he were catching up on her.

The parkland stretched for two miles and then swung about in a curve towards an artificial lake. After riding over three miles of parkland they dismounted.

'I have never ridden on such fine turf,' she said. 'It could have been created for horses. It has no rough tufts or hard patches.'

'It is indeed fine turf. The kings of France and their ladies rode here and Louis XIV had a hunting lodge built at the centre of the forest where he could rest after a day's hunting or even stay overnight. You will see it in the afternoon. At the further end of the lake is an alleyway which takes us to more parkland, and beyond that are my wheatfields. But tell me about yourself and your ambitions.'

'To find happiness close to the earth and husband it well. Own my own house and my own horses and win the Grand National. I'm afraid that little else interests me. Of course, I would like to see father enter politics again; he was a marvellous parliamentarian. Now he does not have the same interests.'

'You are like all the Dillon women, never ones for convention. Your grandmother and your mother followed their own laws.'

'I follow my own destiny. I am not a hot-house plant,' she told him with conviction.

'And are you political like your father? Do you spend time dwelling on the history of your country and its domination by England?' He watched her face carefully as she answered.

'I like to follow what is happening. You cannot live at Dillon Hall without being caught up in politics and I cannot be close to my mother without taking an interest in the estates. But tell me how many acres of forest lie about us?'

'Three hundred and fifty. Two acres are cut each year and planted. The oaks planted this year will be felled in two hundred years' time.'

Their conversation became taken up with the estate. Her eye was not only taken by the beauty of the park but also by the wealth they produced and could sustain. When they reached the wide

372

wheatlands, ripe under the warm sun, she gathered the grain from the wheat ears and drew in the scent as if she wished to know its quality and worth.

'Do you have your own mill, Uncle Edward?'

'Yes, at the end of the wheatfields. We grind our wheat into flour and it is sold on the Paris market. You are looking at the best wheatlands in France, stretching from here to Chartres.' Everywhere she could see the heavy-eared wheat swaying under a light wind.

'I would like to see the mill before I return. Is it powered by wind or water?'

'Water. We have harnessed the lake. The fall of water powers the mill. But since you are curious about these things let me bring you to the mill.'

They mounted their horses and followed the lake into a gut where the mill stood.

'I am impressed by the way you use the power of the water,' she said after they had visited the mill. It was late in the day when they finally returned home through the forest. Everywhere shafts of light fell in patterns on to the forest floor. And there was a clearing in the woods with a fine stone lodge like a small palace. It had six rooms and when they went in she discovered food laid out for them on a table.

'I hope you are hungry for I have had all this prepared for you. I thought that you might enjoy supper in the King's Lodge.'

'I am very hungry and I would love to drink some wine. My mother has often spoken to me of your vineyard and we have your wine with our meals at Dillon Hall.'

'Let me indulge your tastes.' He asked a servant to carve the meat and set it before her. Then he took a bottle of wine and half filled her glass.

'It is light and sparkling, the best which our vineyards have produced in the last twenty years. It is seductive and elegant.' He smiled at his own description.

'Well, I know I won't be seduced and I feel elegant here,' Catherine said laughing.

The wine was like satin on her tongue.

'You keep the best wine in France.'

'I will have two barrels of your choice shipped to Ireland.' Edward was enjoying the occasion more than he could ever have imagined. Time seemed irrelevant surrounded with so much beauty. Outside, first twilight and then night came to the forest.

They left the hunting lodge much later. She felt drowsy when she mounted the horse and followed her uncle in the darkness.

'I have had a wonderful day and a wonderful evening,' she told her uncle. 'I would gladly have slept at the lodge but I know my father would have worried. I have never felt more close to the presence of the forest.' She told him in a tired voice.

'If you wish you could stay there for a few days. One of the servants will keep you company.'

'I would choose to be by myself and perhaps a dog. I never sleep at home without a dog in my room. I feel protected.'

'It will be arranged.' He kissed her gently on the cheeks.

She did not meet her father that night but went to her room washed and slipped into bed. Her dreams were filled with luxuri ant images.

Her uncle sat in his room and considered many things. He was impressed with his niece Catherine Dillon. She was an intelligen and warm person whose life was uncluttered with trivial matters Soon he would have to make a will and as he considered his life and the future of the estate he saw this woman as the only person to whom he could entrust it. He would like to think that when he was dead it would continue to prosper. His life had not been happy. His wife lived a single life in her own rooms and they rarely met. Sometimes she moved to her apartment in Rome and he might not see her at all during the winter. He had a mistress in Paris whom he visited twice a week, a middle-class woman, dis creet and comforting, who knew his sensual desires and satisfie them. But he was without intimate friends. Now he had to decide who would inherit his estates and fortune. As he grew older his mind turned towards these things and to the Dillon line. He thought that he had banished that thought from his mind foreve but in middle-age old echoes returned to him. In his niece he had found someone who would give great care to all the things he loved.

* * *

374

That night he made a new will, drawing up a detailed account of how he wished his property to be managed after his death. When he was satisfied with the contents, he made a copy. Next day the two documents were witnessed by his lawyers and signed by him. One was lodged with his lawyers, the other sent for safe-keeping to his bank. When the documents were sealed he felt that he was mortal and alone.

John Dillon had risen early and taken the coach to Paris. At rue de Vaugiraud he dismissed the coachman and arranged that he would meet him the same place at five o'clock that evening. He then made his way north through rue Pot de Fer turning into the narrow rue Mezière. He remembered the address of the arms agent and knocked at the door of a tall building. He found Le Blanc dressed in a silk dressing-gown, sitting on a chair, rubbing the back of a luxurious cat. The room smelt of perfume and stale air as if it were sealed off from the city. Paintings of pubescent girls with luminous flesh hung on the walls. He was neatly dressed and his manner of life gave no indication that he dealt in guns. They talked for two hours and John Dillon told him of his requirements. Later they had lunch at an expensive cafe at rue de Varenne. When they returned to his house a gun had been delivered for John Dillon to examine. He was satisfied with its quality, which was as good if not better as any gun bought in Birmingham. He told Le Blanc that he would have to test it to see how it performed. Two days later he was driven to a forest to the south of Paris where he fired the gun several times. It was accurate to three hundred yards.

'It is a worthy gun,' he remarked, looking at its lines. He had handed many guns when he hunted in Ireland and knew that the gun he held in his hand was better than those issued by the British Army.

'I sell you one of the best guns in the world,' the agent said. 'It will have no markings of course and nobody will trace it to its place of origin. As my dealings with you are illegal and these guns are hard to obtain, they are expensive. You of course understand that, Mr Dillon,' he said before quoting a price.

'Very expensive and I will need some documents to give my people,' John Dillon told him. 'They are anxious to know how the money was spent.'

'I shall give you a document but it must not fall into the wrong

375

hands. My government does not wish me to sell weapons abroad. Perhaps they might fall into the hands of our enemies and be used against France. One never knows where a gun may end up. Perhaps in Germany or Russia. I have to be careful in these matters.'

'I have no intention of that ever happening. Both of us are men of the world and it is not in our interest to disclose any part of our business so you need have no worry concerning such matters.' Dillon took a bundle of notes from his money belt and handed it to Le Blanc.

'It will take a week to assemble 120 guns. You may examine them in their crates before they are closed. I presume that you have arranged to transport them from France.'

'That has been arranged.'

'Then I hope that you have an enjoyable time in Paris until we meet again.' He stood up, bowed in a gracious manner and closed the door behind him. John Dillon tried to assess his character as he walked down the street towards rue du Four. He believed that he was a man who lived in a constricted world of pleasure, unconcerned with what he sold as long as he turned a profit. He perhaps took pleasure in the fact that the rifles were of excellent quality but never considered that they caused death.

He returned late that evening, sitting with his brother and discussing the great changes which had taken place in Paris. They found a common bond of interest here and they did not attempt to talk of politics.

In the mean time Le Clos was moving down the Seine toward Le Havre with a cargo of flour. It was a safe voyage and sitting on the deck, smoking his pipe he had time to think about what had happened. He carried money with him which he had withdrawn from a bank in Paris. As he watched the flat lands he made slow plans in his mind. He had been offered more money by Dillon and Bazin, than he had ever hoped to save in his life. He was not interested in their politics or their purposes. Dillon he could deal with, Bazin was a different matter. He was drawing him into web of intrigue and he felt that danger lay about him. He had known men who had been killed by Bazin and he would have to move with great care. He had one advantage over this man; Bazin had underestimated his intelligence and cunning. In a slow hand he set down his meetings with both men. When he reached Le Havre he lodged his money with a small bank. Then he went to a lawyer and explained to him that he had made out a certain document which should be delivered to the newspapers if he failed to return to his office after six months. He paid his fees and left, feeling satisfied that he had taken some steps to protect himself. That night he sat in his cabin and drank a good bottle of wine.

Every move that John Dillon had made had been followed by Harold Bazin. He sat in his room, a map of Paris spread out on a table and followed each activity. He even knew that he had stopped off to have lunch at Bois de Vincennes. Now his men were following Le Blanc. They knew the factory in which the guns were made and they knew the warehouse in which they were stored. One night he had examined the quality of the rifles which John Dillon had purchased and saw that they were superior to those used by the police and the army. The warehouse was close to the quays and the cases could be easily transferred to the ship. His plan was coming neatly together and John Dillon was falling into his trap. When he sailed for Ireland on the *Sophie* he would be a marked man.

Le Clos returned from Le Havre. One evening he was contacted at his lodgings and taken to a large house, standing in its own grounds, in the city suburbs. As he entered the gates he felt some panic but controlled himself; Bazin was not as yet ready to move against him. He was shown into a well-lit room where three men sat at a table. Bazin entered and took his place, his hair immaculate, his face well-shaven.

Le Clos felt ill-at-ease in this comfortable room and surprised that the information which he had sold had stirred such great interest. Obviously John Dillon was a man of some importance. The guns would be seized in Galway and the man taken prisoner. This meeting suggested however that Bazin's plans were more subtle than he had originally believed.

'Please be seated, Monsieur Le Clos,' Bazin directed. 'As you see I have invited two lawyers to be present and a secretary. You may feel free to speak in their presence. They are men of integrity and are employed to make our business legal.'

'Our deal was private. I gave you information and I did not wish it known. You betray me,' Le Clos said harshly, coarse anger stirring in his heart.

'Our former deal is known only to both of us. The present deal needs to be witnessed,' Bazin persisted, rubbing his thin fingers slowly together.

'I do not make such deals. I wish to leave immediately. I did not expect such company. I wish to return to my lodging.' He rose to leave but a hard hand pushed him down into the seat. Le Clos felt threatened.

'Now, Monsieur Le Clos, let us discuss the proposition I wish to make. We are men of the world. You wish to possess a ship of your own. I wish to reprehend a criminal, perhaps two criminals.'

'And what will this be worth to me?' he said stonily.

'It will be worth the following sum of money.' He ordered the secretary to place a large amount of money in neat bundles before Le Clos.

'How much?' he asked.

'Enough to buy a small ship.'

Le Clos touched the money, his greed stimulated. He considered the neatly stacked pile of money, wondering if it might be counterfeit. But the notes had been already used so he was certain that they were real. He took a bundle from beneath the pile and tested each note, trying to contain his excitement.

'And how Monsieur Le Clos, let me tell you how you must earn this money. When you have done your business you can take two-thirds of it. The rest will be given to you when you return to Paris and the mission is a success. I know you can write so I wish you to copy out a document stating that John Dillon bribed you to carry guns abroad the *Sophie*. The second must be written twice. It will be sent to Edward Dillon when you have left port. The documents will bear different dates. Do you understand?'

'Yes. Where are the documents?'

'In the next room. The secretary will show you to a desk. Everything is carefully set out. When we are satisfied with your penmanship and you have signed a legal document stating that you sent the letter to Edward Dillon, the business will be concluded and you will be free to leave with the money.'

'Will my master suffer as a result of these documents?' he asked.

'Not necessarily. It is a precaution I have to take. Things have to be seen to be legal.'

As Le Clos left the room he felt black of heart and for a moment almost hesitated. Then banishing his scruples, he followed the secretary into an adjacent room and laboriously wrote the documents. He left the house late that night, his money in a leather satchel, knowing he had betrayed John Dillon. Only when he counted out the money behind closed doors did his qualms vanish. At last he was a rich man and would achieve his dream. Next morning he took most of the money aboard the ship and hid it in his cabin, placing a small sum with his bank.

John Dillon made an inspection of the guns two days before the Sophie sailed. He was satisfied and directed the man with Le Blanc to secure the lids. That night the cases were carried on two handcarts to the ship. Le Clos was waiting by the quayside, holding a lantern to direct them on board the ship. The cases were placed at the edge of the hold beside casks of wine and other casks piled on top to conceal their presence. Little conversation passed between them, John Dillon finding the captain moody and sullen. When the hold was secure and their business finished they slipped into the darkness of Paris, each going their separate way.

John Dillon looked at the single lights in the darkness of the Bois de Boulogne and considered his position. He was now committed to revolution.

Next day he went riding with his daughter. On several occasions he had invited her to visit Paris but she expressed no interest in the city. The château, its stables and lands had drawn all her attention. Each morning she had visited the horses, watching them exercised on the long tract of land close to the château. Each day she rode to a different part of the estate and walked it carefully. She has passed through the wheatfields and seen men cutting the rich harvest.

'I have had few occasions to talk with you. The city has occupied all my time. I wish that you had come with me and noted the changes which have taken place. It is now a splendid place, improved beyond all measure,' he told her as they rode together.

'I had an interest at the beginning but I have fallen under the spell of the château and its lands. Each day I discover something new about the place. I have no wish to see Paris.'

'Have you lost your taste for life?' he asked.

'No. My taste lies here.'

'Would you remain here?' he asked, looking keenly at her.

'Yes, if my uncle would have me. I will leave with great reluctance. I detest the thought of returning to Ireland. The winters are too cold and the days wet and miserable. I would thrive under the warm skies of France.'

They rode in silence.

'What do you return to, Father?'

'I do not know.'

'I hope it is not danger.' Her father did not reply but he spurred his horse forward. She knew that something was troubling his mind.

Two days later they left the château. Her uncle had spent the previous evening pleading with her to stay for six months and take charge of his stables and the farm. It would have been an easy decision to stay.

'I wish to be with my father.'

'Why?' he asked. 'Surely he can attend to his own business? I feel your destiny lies in France. You speak the language and you take delight in what it has to offer. I have to show you the vineyards in the south-west. That is another part of France which you would come to cherish.'

His voice had a pleading quality. Her uncle was lonely and needed her presence.

'It would be easy for me to stay with you but I am haunted by some strange fear. I cannot account for it but it is always at the back of my mind. I will spend the winter thinking about it. Then will give you my answer. I will never forget our day in the forest and our evening at the hunting lodge. It will always haunt my memory.'

All these thoughts were in her mind as she kissed her uncle goodbye and entered the carriage. She looked at the château caught in the morning sun, the light giving brilliance to the silver stone. The rose gardens were heavy with perfume and the stable

380

boys were leading the horses out for their morning canter. She began to weep as they drove down the avenue and did not look behind her.

The ship slipped anchor and moved down the Seine. John Dillon did not know at that time that he would never visit Paris again.

## Chapter 37

Daniel Parr rarely went to race meetings any more and when he did he was well protected by soldiers. His life had been threatened and he was convinced that he would be assassinated. Sergeant Grinling assured him that he had been given every protection but he was still not satisfied. The danger was brought home to him as he passed through the village of Oughterard on his way to Galway. It was a pleasant place with a good salmon river and a narrow bridge which divided the two sections of the village. His driver barely noticed the man looking over the parapet of the bridge. As he slowed down, the man pulled a revolver from his belt and rushed at the door of the carriage. He had time to discharge a shot at Parr before a soldier cut him down. It grazed Parr's head and knocked him unconscious. He was rushed to Galway but the wound was superficial.

He felt threatened at every turn, never sleeping in the same room for more than three nights. If he heard a sound at night, he would leap out of his bed and call for the guard at the door.

Despite his fears, his mind was filled with energy. His old enemy, John Dillon, was falling into the trap set for him. He had received a message from Dublin where Lord Dunraven set out in detail what had occurred in France, the exact date of departure for the Sophie, the expected time of arrival and the cargo. He even knew the location of the warehouse in Galway.

He felt that the old war between both houses was finally coming to a close and he would satisfy his need for revenge. He would destroy John Dillon and the pride of the house. Elinor Dillon would know the bitter taste of humiliation.

Desmond Hogan said goodbye to John O'Mahony and Kevin O'Donnell on the quays of New York in spring 1863. He was a gaunt figure with no loose flesh. He carried a bullet scar over his left eye. The bloody years of the Civil War, the slaughter, the long marches and days of hunger, the sweet stench of decaying corpses under a hot sun had made him cynical. He often thought that the next battle would end his life but it was never so. Men had been torn to pieces beside him, horses maimed as he rode into battle. Yet always he led a charmed life.

After the battle of Antietam he had walked across the west side of Haggerton Hike, the earth littered with dead. They were torn by bayonets, their intestines pouring out of their stomachs. The guts of a man like those of animals, man himself an animal on the battlefield. On either side lay Irishmen, drawn to a cause on a foreign soil. In a single day's battle more than 25,000 men had lost their lives. He raged at the hopeless loss of life, at McClellan's errors of judgement. Had McClellan launched a full-scale assault the Southern line would have been broken, but he chose to fight piece-meal and gave Lee the advantage. Lee later retired, claiming victory. The earth was wet with blood, the field irregular with carnage.

That night after the battle, he sat alone under a tree. About him campfires threw the bodies of weary soldiers into relief. They were tired after the battle, each man mute, absorbed by his own thoughts. Some drank whisky to kill the images of slaughter. Even at night the burials continued by lantern light; the dead carried in canvas stretchers and laid in long graves, not unlike the mass graves he had seen dug beside the workhouses during the famine. Somewhere in the distance two shots rang out and later he heard that two scavengers had been killed. They followed the armies like pests, slinking into the distance during the engagements, then emerging at night time to rob the bodies of dead soldiers.

It was well past midnight when he reached a final decision. He remembered the past; it came to him in clear pictures. He had paid his debt to America. He felt that it was time to return to Ireland, to settle old scores.

382

He returned to his quarters and spoke to some of his trusted men, who like himself had taken the Fenian oath. He told them of his decision. They gave him what small money they had, together with some which had been collected from the pockets of dead comrades. They had been with him throughout the war.

He took his horse and left the camp under the cover of darkness, reaching New York five days later. He contacted John O'Mahony and told him of his desire to return to Ireland.

'In six months' time, perhaps in a year, we will be ready. You will meet Stephens in Galway. We need leaders, men who are tested in the field of battle and have fought under fire. Guns have been smuggled into the country in preparation.'

He had returned to Ireland and spent nine months training men at hidden locations in the country. He sat in small cabins and spoke with men who were willing to die if necessary for the cause. They were waiting for the word from Dublin, knowing that every police barracks in the country could be destroyed on a single night. The rising would have to be all over the country in order to stretch the forces of the Crown; if it were not it would fail.

Desmond Hogan carried a revolver and Springfield rifle. He demonstrated their uses and let each man handle both weapons. He believed that the contours of a gun in a man's hand gave him a taste of power.

His name was already known to Sergeant Grinling but he moved so swiftly and cautiously that he was never traced. Grinling considered him the most dangerous Fenian in Connaught.

The sergeant was anxious that John Dillon should be captured in the warehouse with the guns which were now on the *Sophie*. It would deal an immediate blow to the Fenian centre at Dublin, catch them off their guard and perhaps throw the various cells about the country into panic. All that was necessary to prevent a general uprising was the slaughter of some rebels caught attacking a barracks and the heart would go out of the rest of the rebels. If necessary they could cut the Fenians at Galway to pieces. He visited Parr on his estate and they stood over a map of the quays. They had to arrange the disposition for their men. They had been especially trained for their mission at Athlone. None of them had taken the Fenian oath and each man's salary had been doubled during the days of training. In addition they were promised large sums of money if they accomplished their mission. At this moment they were spread out in various hostels in Galway. They had visited the quays and knew the precise positions they had to take up.

'Tell me again the exact nature of their training?' Parr asked anxiously.

'These are men who are both intelligent and loyal. They know exactly what is expected from them. If the opportunity is presented to them they will engage every Fenian in the vicinity of the warehouse once Dillon is captured. Nobody is aware that these men have been trained, not even the Fenians.'

'Yes. They must cut down the Fenians. That will be the element of surprise. They will not be prepared for the reception they are going to receive. This will mark the end of general rebellion. They will scurry back to their rabbit holes and never emerge again. Are these good marksmen?'

Sergeant Grinling explained how they had been brought from Dublin and billeted in Athlone. Each man could handle a gun accurately and many had already seen active service.

'Each one knows his position and if there are changes of plan he knows how to act independently. They have rehearsed the whole operation several times.'

'This is our single chance to deal a deadly blow to Fenianism. But we must catch Dillon with the guns. We will have documents to prove that he purchased them in France but he must be caught in the warehouse. And remember the *Sophie* must be permitted to sail from Galway. We do not for the moment wish to implicate the captain.'

'Is there any particular reason for this?' Grinling asked. 'It would tie up everything neatly if he was arrested.'

'I have received orders from Dublin so they must have their reasons. I believe the captain has already signed documents which can be used against Dillon in court. It would not be my way of doing things. As soon as the ship is sighted off Galway we will put our plans into operation. We must not fail. My life has been threatened and if they succeed then we will be engaged in a conflict which will cost both money and lives. Let us drink to the success of our plans.' He poured out two glasses of tawny whisky and toasted the plan. Sergeant Grinling who rarely drank, sipped the liquid.

If Lord Dunraven thought that the polished manners and foppish ways he assumed in the social circles of Dublin covered his more sinister activities, he was greatly mistaken. Every movement he made was followed. Two policemen at the Castle were Fenians and they carried information to Dermot Redmond who dealt with Secret Service matters. He kept a small tobacco shop opposite the main gate of the Castle and appeared to lead an innocuous life. He relayed his information to the central cell and to Stephens, when he was in Dublin. He had a special file on Connaught and was taking a keen interest in Parr's and Grinling's visit to the castle. Even the dispatches to Parr were counted. He knew that something important was about to happen in the west of Ireland and when Stephens visited his office and examined the file his eye caught the name of Elinor Dillon.

'Could you explain this matter to me in more detail?' he asked, his face expressionless.

'It is merely an unimportant note. Apparently this woman is having an affair with Dunraven. They meet at his house in Rathfarnham and I believe that she has visited him at his rooms in the Castle. I did not think it merited much importance.'

'I'm afraid it does. We have never been able to gain access to the files. Perhaps with some persuasion she may be prompted to help us. I must visit Dillon Hall and meet her. Make arrangements with the local Fenians to throw protection about the place while I am there and contact Desmond Hogan. I wish to set up a meeting with him. He had doubted our ability to bring guns into the country and is straining for a rising. I must reassure him of our best intentions. It is matter of much urgency that I get there as soon as possible.'

He left the building by the back entrance, his mind much troubled. He had to reassure Hogan and he had to meet Elinor Dillon. It was a distasteful task.

When he boarded the train in Dublin two days later he was securely protected by two bodyguards who sat in the compartment on either side. He looked out at the wide spread of country, the rain coming in from the west out of a dark sky. It lashed against the window, pouring down in diagonal tracks. His mind became bleak and introspective. The long train journey, the thick damp weather, the perpetual rain across the window gave him time to think.

The train halted at each small station discharging small groups of passengers on to rainswept platforms. It was late when he got to Tuam where a covered carriage was waiting. Desmond Hogan was inside and drew him into the carriage. Stephens knew the man as a serious soldier.

'Will this cursed rain ever end?' Desmond Hogan asked as he looked at the dismal appearance of the town.

'Not now and not ever,' Stephens said. 'I have walked the byways of Mayo and Galway in the perpetual rains until my very bones were wet. If anything is guaranteed to sap a man's determination it is rain.'

'And if the year of the rising is not brought forward it will be sapped without any rain. I have asked for directions from the central council and all I receive are vague answers. And we need arm.' Hogan said in a hard voice.

'They are coming. They are on the sea and soon you will have them in your possession.'

'I hope you are not making false promises. I wish to see the guns as soon as they arrive, and I want the right to distribute them.'

'You will have your guns within the next week.'

He told him when the guns would arrive.

'They will be stored at the Dillon warehouse. They have a depot at the quays.'

Hogan was satisfied with the information and relaxed a little.

They arrived at the Dillon estate late in the evening. Stephens could do his business and return to Tuam before morning. He could sleep during the day and return to Dublin. The cloak of darkness was their best protection.

Elinor was expecting the visitor. He simply stated in his note that he was a old friend from Paris and she wondered who it might be. She had received a letter franked at Tuam post office which stated briefly that a member of the Central Fenian cell would visit her. The letter was unsigned and the name of the visitor was not given. It was after midnight when the bell in the hall sounded. Tadhg Mor knocked on the drawing-room door and showed in James Stephens. He looked at the dignified woman and remembered recalling their meeting at the Irish College in Paris.

'My name is James Stephens,' he began awkwardly. He felt uncertain in this woman's presence.

'So you are the visitor from Paris. We met before briefly concerning private matters at the Irish College. You are the elusive Mr Shook of the English newspapers. You have set up your organization in every corner of the country as you planned. Will you have some wine after your journey? I believe that you have something to discuss with me. Please sit down.'

'I prefer to stand,' he said, trying to gain control of the situation.

She asked Tadhg Mor to bring them some wine.

'Before you begin, Mr Stephens, I suspect that my husband is a Fenian,' she began directly. 'Why he became a Fenian I can guess. I presume that his visit to France is on their behalf. Was it the nature of your business to tell me this or is there something of which I am not aware?'

'These are dangerous and testing times in which we live. Soon we may be engaged in a struggle against the British army. I believe that you know Lord Dunraven. Your relations with him are of no importance to me but they might be to your husband.'

She reflected for a moment. She should have been angry with the impertinence of this man and dismissed him from the house. Then she realized that probably others in Dublin knew of her affair. She did not know how this affair could affect her husband but obviously if the Fenian leader had come to her house concerning the matter it must have political undertones.

'I am friendly with Lord Dunraven,' she began coldly. 'I do not see how this friendship could in any respect affect my husband.'

'Perhaps not. You are correct in your suspicions of your husband being a Fenian. We fear his name is on the files at Dublin Castle. If this is so his mission to France could be in danger.'

'What mission?' she asked, worry entering her mind for the first time.

387

James Stephens reflected seriously and decided to confide in Elinor Dillon.

'He is going to bring in several crates of guns through Galway port. If this were known at Dublin Castle and your husband captured, the consequences both for himself and the movement would be very serious. There is no way we can get our hands on these files, as we have never succeeded in gaining access to Lord Dunraven's office.' Now she saw the purpose of his visit.

'You wish me to obtain the information?' she said directly.

'That is why I came here but perhaps you may not believe in our cause. I do not know.'

'You suggest that Lord Dunraven could at this moment be plotting the destruction of my husband? You are bound to know more than you are telling me.'

'That could be the case. They are preparing to spring a trap at the Castle. The only mission of importance we have in hand is bringing in guns from France.'

'What do you wish me to do, Mr Stephens? I am interested in the welfare of my husband and that of this house. My relationship with Lord Dunraven is of little consequence when I consider wider issues. Of course he is well informed about the Fenians. He detests the word Fenianism and has little regard for you. He belongs to the English aristocracy and thinks that you will be crushed like vermin. Do not think that I am hostile to your cause. But I have to keep my counsel to myself. This house must be retained by the Dillon family therefore we must not let those in high places know where our allegiance lies. We have stood by the people during bad times when there was no movement to voice their angers. I do not wish to see the common people damned by harsh laws. I myself am one of them. I have been at my husband's side and know the corruption in high places. I have seen a fine political movement destroyed. The present state of things must be preserved against all change; vested interests dictate policies Mr Stephens.'

He felt encouraged by her admission. There was something in her strong beauty which moved him to awe.

'Very few owners of the great houses think in your terms.'

'Only the files could tell us if Lord Dunraven has this information

It would also give us the names of the spies in our organization. You are only one who can obtain access to them. Could you arrange to meet him in his office at the Castle? He arrives each morning at ten o'clock. He changes his route each day but we are well-informed of this. We can arrange to have his coach delayed for one hour.' His mind was racing with plans.

She fell silent for some time. She had been unfaithful to her husband, now perhaps he was in danger from her lover. She must discover the truth.

'Are you certain that you can delay him? she asked.

'It can be arranged.'

'This is a dangerous undertaking,' she reflected.

'I know. But there is nothing else we can do. Remember time is running out.'

'Very well, I will obtain access to the files.'

'I am in your debt.' They made final arrangements and he left at two o'clock, Tadhg Mor showing him to his coach. She remained for an hour in the room, reflecting on what had just happened. She felt that her affair with Lord Dunraven was drawing to a close. If all that James Stephens suggested was true then her lover was a most dangerous man. Her passion had blinded her to the true situation in Ireland. Next morning she set off for Dublin. Immediately on her arrival she dispatched a note of Lord Dunraven, suggesting that they should meet at his office at ten the next morning and received a positive note in reply.

That night she stayed at the Shelbourne Hotel, her mind fraught with worry. She went over the layout of Lord Dunraven's office, planning all her movements once she was inside it. She sat at the window of her suite and looked down at the mass of trees lit dimly by gaslight. Somewhere in the city the Fenian organization had been alerted of her presence and would obstruct Lord Dunraven on his way from Rathfarnham to the Castle.

At half past nine, she walked down the steps of the hotel, dressed in a long blue dress and a green cloak, her hair arranged in small ringlets. She wore expensive scent and her finest jewellery. When she reached the Castle gate she showed the constable the note she received from Lord Dunraven and he let her through.

She controlled a twitch of nervousness on her chin and walked to the entrance of the building where Lord Dunraven had his office.

'I am expected,' she said to the guard outside the door, handing him the note.

He showed her in. 'Lord Dunraven will be along presently. He arrives punctually at ten. It is just past ten now but I expect that he will be here in the next few minutes.'

And then she was alone in the room. For a moment she was frozen by fear and dared not move. Then she forced herself forward, her hands sweating. She looked about her and reached for the folio marked 'County Galway'. It was bound by a red ribbon which she undid. She opened it, trembling. What she read startled her: knowledge of all her husband's movements were noted. They were leading him into a deadly trap. She read letters from Parr and Sergeant Grinling containing comprehensive knowledge of all the Fenian activities in Galway. She discovered a file on her own brother and read it quickly. She began to pant with fear and checked her watch. It was a quarter to eleven. Quickly she memorized the names of the informers set out in a long list then closed the file and returned it to its place as coach wheels crackled on the courtyard. A soldier rushed to the door and Lord Dunraven descended as the clock in the tower sounded eleven strokes. She admired the precision of Stephens's plans.

'You are late,' she said angrily when he entered the room. 'Burke's peerage makes very boring reading.' She snapped the heavy book shut on her knees.

'It was most unfortunate,' he said, 'a horse took fright in Harcourt Street and crashed directly into my coach breaking a wheel. Accept my apologies.' She stood up and controlled her feelings. This man was planning to trap her husband but he acted as if he knew nothing and she wondered what type of mind could divide love and loyalty in this way. She had an excuse to walk directly out of the office and should have done so but he put his arms about her and kissed her. He smelt her scent, felt the opulent flesh beneath the clothes and his desire for her grew strong. She hated the treasonable sensuality of her body. She remained in his office while he attended to some business, watching him put his signature on official forms, unable to judge from his expression what they contained. As the clock bell rang one they left the office and went to Rathfarnham. As they travelled through the city she tried to recall all the names she had seen on the lists. Time and again she went over them, knowing that they were of vital importance to Stephens. She wondered why she was in the coach and felt that this was the last time she would be with Dunraven. When they reached his house and were secluded by the walls she forgot her responsibilities. Her passionate love for this man blinded her reason.

When she left his house next morning, she looked back at him standing in the doorway and knew that the affair was over. Serious political matters were now engaging her mind and she intended to be in Galway to warn her husband of the danger. She could not know that a strong, southerly wind was carrying the ship to Ireland, and it would arrive two days ahead of time.

## Chapter 38

When John Dillon went on deck it was to take exercise and clear his head of the stuffy air in the cabin. He felt constrained by the small space, the low ceiling with its heavy beams, the windows which looked on to an uneventful sea. There were no books to read and his mind was inactive.

He began to drink whisky two days out to sea, sitting dourly on his bunk, a heavy glass in his hand. He said nothing but looked blankly at the wall. His mind was filled with forebodings and he wished that the guns were delivered and that he was back on the estate. He dreamed of spending a day at the hunt, recalling his youth in the saddle, the wild enthusiasm for the chase.

He could never again live these times or regain his vigour of mind. When he recalled the demented time at the Brass Castle in the company of filthy whores and their pimps, his body seemed still defiled.

He had not drunk whisky for two years. Now there was a fire in his stomach and only whisky could fuel it. He had locked himself in his cabin and refused to talk to Catherine. One morning she found the door unlocked and went inside. His face was unshaven, his shirt front open and a half bottle of whisky lay beside his bunk.

He opened his eyes and looked at her.

'Why did you not tell me?' she said. 'I would have come and talked to you. Look at you: you are unshaven and unwashed and I'm sure the sailors are talking about you.' The tears ran down her cheeks.

'I should not have touched the poison. I thought that a single glass would be sufficient, but no. The hot thirst began to rage in me.'

She wet a towel and began to wash his face. Then she took his soap brush, lathered his face and shaved him until his skin looked polished and clean.

'I know your humours. This dark cloud will pass over and soon we will be back at Dillon Hall. We shall spend a day riding together.'

'I have thought a lot of Dillon Hall. We will take the pathway by the lake and go up through the forest to the mountain. We will look down on the earth as the Greek gods do and laugh at the small activities of man.' He smiled and quoted a Greek passage which she did not understand.

'It is from Theocritus,' he said. 'Let me translate it for you. "Sweet to me it seems is the whispering sound of the pine tree goatherd, that murmurs by the wells of water; and sweet are your piping." It is something from an abandoned memory.'

He looked at himself in a small mirror. His face was still blotched and his hands shook, but the cloud within his mind was passing away. The sun began to shine on the sea again, turning grey water to a fresh, vigorous blue.

On the deck they could see the hills of Ireland and affection warmed his heart. Why were men willing to engage in wild enterprise to free her? Why had men suffered torture and exile for her?

'What are you thinking about?' his daughter asked.

'I am thinking of Ireland as a country where men live in a democracy forging their destiny. There never should have been a Union; was one of the great mistakes. But now it is coming to an end.'

'Do you believe that all this will happen or is only a dream?'

'Once it was a dream, but no longer. Forces are gathering which are certain to change everything. I know it in my heart. I have never felt so certain in my life.'

On the horizon, the shallow hills of Clare were visible and the Aran Islands rose up out of the sea. They were interrupted by Le Clos.

'I believe that we have some business to attend to,' he said dourly. 'Could you come to my cabin? Under these fair conditions we will reach Galway in the next three hours.'

John Dillon left his daughter on deck and followed the captain. She had an intuition that the captain was a dangerous man and wondered what business they had. She wished that they had disembarked and were on their way to Dillon Hall.

He sat at the base of a tower set on a high hill overlooking Galway city and harbour. He cut shavings from a dark lump of tobacco into the palm of his hand. When he had cut enough he put it into a leather pouch and pulled the mouth closed with a leather thong. Then he rubbed the shavings with his palms until they were teased into tangled shreds and drew them into his pipe.

He had been stationed at the tower for two days but had sufficient provisions for a week. At night another soldier came to relieve him and he slept on a rough mattress on the second storey. Suddenly in the distance his eye caught the suggestion of a ship's sail. He pushed the pipe into his pocket and mounted the tower. He took the telescope and trained it on the sails, certain it was the *Sophie*. He discharged the gun beside him, then another and so he continued until all the guns had been fired. He looked towards the east where a flag had been raised on a mast. His message had been received. His business at the tower was finished. He pushed the telescope together, placing it in a leather cylinder, gathered up the guns and put them in a strong bag. He went down the circular staircase, lit his pipe and watched the *Sophie* make her way towards the harbour.

This was the signal that Daniel Parr and Sergeant Grinling were waiting for. They had set up their headquarters close to the quays at a vantage point where they could observe every movement. They dispatched two men into the old quarter of the city. The trained gunmen, dressed as dockers and sailors, began to move into position as had been planned. No one noted their appearance, even the ship close to the warehouse which had been docked three days earlier did not attract attention. Twenty men were now in position.

'This is the day when the menace of the Fenian tide will be turned,' Parr said in a venomous voice. 'For too long we have watched them spread their tentacles across the country until the very order on which the country rests is under threat. I have waited patiently for this day and we cannot afford to make one single mistake. If Dillon is caught in the warehouse with the guns panic can be spread through the papers and we will be able to introduce every punitive law necessary. We will make an example of him.'

They entered the warehouse and climbed up the wooden stairs having practised the movement days beforehand. Positioned between the bags of grain and far above the floor they lay in readiness. They had a clear view of the open space on the floor close by the door. Each man placed two loaded revolvers on the rough surface of the bags. Light poured in the door and fell slantways on the dry and dusty floor. They were startled for moment when a pigeon eating grain flapped its wings in awkward panic. It crashed against the roof several times, then found the door and flew out. The palms of their hands were sweating and they rubbed them dry on the sacks. There was silence again and they breathed the rich scent of wheat. Time passed slowly as they watched and waited.

Desmond Hogan, dressed as a sailor, walked up the quays. His hands were deep in his pocket, each hand holding a revolver From beneath his peaked cap he scrutinized the movements of the quays. Heavy carts pulled by lumbering Clydsdale horses drew the cargoes to the warehouses. The guns would be delivered to his best fighting men within two days. If Stephens refused to set a date for the rebellion then he would take it upon himself to order his men into the field. He felt the old excitement mount within him He believed in the cause, he had old scores to settle and the tim was ripe. Already there were sufficient civil war veterans in the country to carry out a successful rebellion. He left the quays and walked towards where his soldiers had drawn up their horses and carts, eight men in all. When the arms were delivered to the warehouse they would move down along the quays at intervals of an hour, collect a specific number and move off. Each had been given a destination.

'Nothing can go wrong. I have checked the quays. You will not be noticed and besides you are covered. I have set armed men on guard and they will move down beside you on the sidewalk. The ship may not arrive for two more days. I have no way of knowing.' The men reminded him of other soldiers he had marshalled before going into battle. Their hands were restless, their bodies like tight springs.

John Dillon now picked out individual marks on the landscape. He had been familiar with the city of Galway since childhood and he felt exhilarated to see her. It was like returning to a favourite mistress. He watched intently as the ship sailed past the harbour wall and then moved slowly towards the quays. The dockers drew the ship up towards the quay wall, securing the ropes to the huge bollards. The voyage was over. John Dillon noted that one of the servants was waiting patiently with their carriage.

'You must return immediately to Dillon House,' he told Catherine. 'I notice that Seamus is waiting for us. If I know him he must have been here for the last week. I have business to attend to and once it is finished I will ride home. I need the bracing air. Perhaps tomorrow we will have our ride across the mountains and watch the countryside in its autumn mood.'

'Better be a week early than a day late,' Seamus said when he came on board to collect the luggage. 'It's great to see you all back. The mistress of the house is in Dublin to buy clothes and will be back tomorrow. It's a bleak place without you. The mare Regina had a fine foal while you were away. My eyes tell me that he's a winner nearly ready to take the fences and him five days old. And old Nell Jones, the washerwoman, died at long last. She never knew her own age but she must have been a hundred for she recalled men coming home from the Battle of Clontarf. We waked her for a week.'

He prattled on while he went about the business of securing the large chests to the back of the coach.

'I'll soon be with you,' John Dillon told his daughter as he closed the door. Seamus gave the horse a neat flip of his whip and the carriage rolled across the rough surface of the quays and disappeared.

Looking around the deck of the ship, he noted that Le Clos seemed anxious. He was calling to the carters in broken English to hurry, as if the cargo carried a plague. John Dillon watched the casks of wine roll slowly down the gangway where they were caught by four men and lifted upwards on to the carts. Then they were taken to the warehouse.

From their positions high up in the warehouse, the soldiers watched the carters curse and swear as they heaved down the casks of wine. They noted how one of the carters remained behind and bled the casks with a fine auger, letting the red liquid pour into a bucket. Then he plugged it and passed on to the next barrel. It was neat, professional work and when he was finished he disappeared with the bucket.

They followed his actions with interest; it helped the time to pass. At half past four the cases carrying the rifles arrived. They were placed on the floor and the carter left. The soldiers checked their pistols. Their mouths became dry and in their minds they went over the general plan.

John Dillon entered the warehouse to examine the boxes. He stood in the shaft of evening light by the door and looked up the quays. Soon they heard the rattle of iron wheels on the pavement and a small cart entered the warehouse. The soldiers watched eagerly as the cases were prised open. They could see the guns neatly laid out on straw. One of the men took out a gun and handled it expertly.

'Perfect for the job. They are better than the British rifles and they handle easily. We are now equal if not superior to the field.'

There was a knock on the door and a second cart entered. The net was ready to close on them.

'Surrender,' a voice called out from the darkness above them. 'You are covered.'

Two of the men panicked, drawing their revolvers and shooting into the darkness. The fire was returned and bullets cut up dust from the stone floor. They rushed to the door, where withering gunfire caught them from the ship opposite the warehouse. The men fell, their bodies torn by bullet wounds.

Hogan walked behind the third cart. The sound of muffled gunfire from within the warehouse had an instant effect on him. He saw his men rush into a hail of gunfire.

'We have been trapped. Run for cover,' he told his men. 'I will draw their fire.'

He moved to the front of the cart and fired accurately at the soldiers on the ship. Two of them fell forwards on to the quays. The rest took cover and he stood alone for two long minutes. Nobody emerged from the warehouse. Then a single bullet from behind cut into his clothing, searing his flesh. He knelt on one knee and picked off the soldier who was fumbling with his gun. There was no more he could achieve so he ran to an alleyway and disappeared. His mind was angry that he had missed all the signs of a trap. He had not been alert.

John Dillon watched as the four men with revolvers trained on him descended the wooden steps. A man lay bleeding to death at his feet, the others torn by lead groaned in agony. They lay on the pavement, blood pouring from their bodies. This was the first encounter he had ever had with immediate and bloody death and he was accountable for it.

The soldiers stood about him, their eyes intent upon their prey. 'Can you not help the wounded men?' he asked. 'Did you have to shoot them so savagely.'

'They are the casualties of war. It is not a game, sir. You are under arrest for gun running and treason,' one of the soldiers said.

While the sentence was being uttered Sergeant Grinling entered the warehouse.

'Why do you stand idly by?' he called to the soldiers. 'This man is a common and dangerous criminal. Secure him with chains. There is a prison cell waiting for him.'

John Dillon felt alone and deserted. He thought of the promises he had made to his daughter which could never be fulfilled.

'March him through the city to Nuns Island. Let him smell the sea and look at the blue sky for he will not see them again. Let the common people watch the felon Dillon dragged through the streets,' Grinling ordered.

His feet and hands were manacled and he was marched across the blood of the dead men. He felt soiled and indecent, and his mind was dumb with shock. Crowds had gathered to watch the spectacle of his humiliation. The sky was very blue with small fluffy clouds. He dragged his constricted steps across the Corrib bridge and on towards Nuns Island. He looked at the grim building, the gates of the prison thrown open in anticipation of his arrival. He passed through and they clanged behind him.

The city was alive with rumours. Some said that the Fenian rising was general all over the country. Others believed that it was only local and had been suppressed. It was said that Fenians everywhere were being rounded up and brought to prison, that the Fenian menace was at an end.

Desmond Hogan finally reached the cellar. An old woman came down from the woollen shop above, tore open his jacket and examined the long bullet scar.

'You will be safe here,' she said, 'and you will be mended in few days. Better stay under cover for the city is crawling with soldiers like maggots in meat.'

'And the prisoner?'

'You mean that fine nobleman, John Dillon? Parr has his hand upon him now and I hate to think what's in store for him. But you be easy and slow. There will be no call to leave this place for the next week. I'll carry you all the news.'

She closed the door and mounted the rickety steps to the ground floor. Hogan felt that their cause was now hopeless and vowed revenge on those who had set the trap. He would deal with each one separately when the time for reprisals came.

When Elinor Dillon arrived at Galway station she knew that she was too late. Everywhere they were talking of the rebellion. The trap had been sprung.

# Chapter 39

The prison lay within encircling walls like a sad island. Minute, barred windows let in the short light.

Dillon was dragged forward by the soldiers, falling twice on the stone slabs. They butted him with rifles as he struggled up, encumbered by the heavy chains. His mind reeled with chaotic images.

No one spoke to him as he passed down through a dark hall. Men peered at him from the darkness through small oval holes in their doors, cursing him as he passed by.

The air was thick with the smell of unwashed bodies and excrement and he felt for a moment that he would retch. Oil lamps burned on the walls offering the only light. He was led down the long corridor to an iron door. It was unlocked and creaked open. Only the lamp carried by a warder threw moving light on to the stone roof and wet steps. They were moving down beneath floor level. He felt he was being interred in a stone tomb and the world of large cut rock was pressing in on him. There was a final door at the bottom of the steps. He was pushed inside a narrow room, barely high enough for him to stand. The roof was arched as it was in the kitchen cellars at Dillon Hall.

'I protest,' he began when he saw the room. The soldiers did not answer, one slapping him across the face and drawing blood. In silence they stripped him and he felt the humiliation of their fingers as they probed his body. Finally they chained his hands behind his back and secured them to his chained legs. The soldiers and the warder with the light withdrew. The door was slammed and locked and he was left in utter darkness and silence.

And then he felt cold, his bare feet drawing it out of the stone floor, his body out of the air. Later his teeth began to chatter, despite his attempts to grit them together. He dragged himself to the door and tried to look through the small window but it was covered from the outside. He walked towards the wall in small, shuffling steps, his naked body pressing against the wet stone. Time began to play tricks on him. He could not imagine that it was day outside, that the sun was now setting towards the west. Time was banished, space drawn into its limits. Involuntarily he wet his legs with warm urine, the sensation of heat giving him comfort for a moment. He recalled his last moments with Catherine and hoped she was safely back at home.

She reached Dillon Hall at two o'clock. She noted the small changes which had taken place on the land as she passed through the estate. Her presents were carried into the drawing room and spread out on the table. Some of them were for the servants but she decided not to give them until her father arrived. She left the house and visited the stables to look at the new foal, a tall, gangling creature still finding his feet. She put her arms about his neck and hugged him. She went to each stable, checking the horses to see if they were well bedded and fed. Later she returned to the drawing room and waited for her father. At eight o'clock she saw the coach sweeping along the avenue at great speed and knew that something was terribly wrong. Her mother rushed into the main hall.

'It's your father,' she cried. 'He is in Galway prison. I could not gain entrance. There was a gun battle at the warehouse and several men were killed.'

'But I was with my father six hours ago. How could it have happened so suddenly? I cannot believe it.'

'It happened suddenly because it was planned in advance. The men did not stand a chance. They walked into a trap.'

'And father, was he wounded?'

'No. They were careful about that. They want him as their prisoner.'

'And what will they do to him?'

'I do not know. I cannot imagine him confined in a small cell; it will surely break his mind.'

'We had planned to ride across the mountain tomorrow. I knew something would happen. I should have warned him. I knew that he was on Fenian business when we were in Paris but instead of being with him I spent my time in the forests and in the fields. I will never forgive myself.'

Elinor Dillon held her daughter in her arms while she cried. Her heart was dry. She stared at the wall with its silk paper, its gilded mirrors. At that moment she hated herself. Had she reached Galway a day earlier she could have warned him of the danger. Now she did not know where to turn. Even Tadhg Mor would not have condoned her action if he had known what had taken place. Waves of remorse passed through her mind. She had betrayed her husband and her children for her sexuality. She felt that at that moment she did not deserve to be mistress of Dillon Hall.

'We must see him, mother, and bring him some comfort. He needs us.'

'He needs us and we cannot be there. I am sure every obstacle possible will be placed in our paths. We can only wait and see what tomorrow will bring.'

She remained with her daughter for many hours. It was well past midnight when she finally went to bed. Her sleep was haunted by images of her infidelities.

During the first four days in prison John Dillon's memory was heightened by the darkness. The great and the insignificant events of his life passed before him. So real were his recollections that sometimes he almost forgot that he was in the cell.

He heard the thunder of hooves approaching, and taking panic clung to the hand of his mother. She brought him to a wide field and he watched the magnificent animals pass before his eyes. He remembered feeding the horses from a wooden bucket with Johnny Appelby, their wet, rough tongues leaving light slime on his hands. The carriage was drawing away from the house and the family were on their way to the races at Galway. It was a summer's day and men were moving in the meadows, set out in a staggered line, the scythes moving in unison. He was drinking in some low shebeen and singing with the labourers, having just returned from a political gathering in Tuam. Then he was racing across rough land, the fox in panic before him. His wife was sweeping down the stairs in a light dress, which brushed against the steps. He visited the Brass Castle where images were never certain. He was in a dank cave eating from a tin plate, calling for rough poteen. And he saw the wide sea of faces beneath him as he spoke from a political platform.

Every moment he expected the iron door to creak open, to be

401

placed in a comfortable cell and given food and clothing. Then he could prepare for a fair trial. But nothing broke the tedium or the silence.

The news of what had occurred in Galway quickly reached Dillon Hall, and spread rapidly into the villages. People were stunned when they heard that John Dillon was a Fenian and was now imprisoned in Galway Jail. As the day passed further news arrived. They heard of the battle at the warehouse and how men had been shot down without a chance as they tried to escape. The Fenians of the area met in the woods and discussed what they should do. Some suggested that they attack the prison but they were poorly armed and inexperienced. Many suggested that Parr should be assassinated. But when they had considered all the possibilities it was obvious that nothing could be accomplished. It was rumoured that Fenians were being rounded up all across the country and they feared for their own safety.

John Dillon did not know how long he stood in the solitary cell, his arms aching behind his back. It could have been an hour, it could have been a day. Weariness set in and he fell on his knees and rolled over on his side. The cold in his body was intense yet he began to sleep. He was aware of water in the cell and awoke with a start. Somebody was pouring water beneath the door and the level was rising about him. He would drown. He pulled desperately at his chains and they chafed his wrists, tearing into the flesh.

'Let me free,' he called. 'Animals are not treated in this fashion.' His voice filled the cell and thundered in his head. He drew himself into a corner and fell asleep in a squat position.

The governor of the prison protested to Daniel Parr at the brutal treatment of John Dillon.

'He is not a criminal, he is a Fenian and a felon,' Parr insisted. 'He has plotted the overthrow of our established order. If you fail to carry out my orders then I will get someone who will carry them out. And do not clean out his cell; let him lie in his own filth until the stench suffocates him. We must break him. He must confess to his crimes and put his signature to a statement. Do you hear? He must be brought so low that he is willing to confess to anything I wish.'

As he talked, more and more insane ideas poured into his mind. Finally he was tired.

'And he may have no contact with his wife or with others. What happens to him is secret and must not be discussed outside these walls. Good night.'

His coach was waiting for him in the prison yard. He drew his cloak about him and entered. The horse soldiers drew up beside him and the gates were thrown open. The city was buzzing with rumours of the Fenian rebellion. He had given the news to the papers and they were eager for details of how guns had been secured in France and brought to Ireland by John Dillon. It was obvious, he told the journalists, that the whole family was involved in the Fenian rebellion.

After dinner with his family he retired to his office, throwing himself into the armchair and looking at the fire. He felt the heat in his body. The timbers had been set by his ancestors and now he enjoyed the rewards. The house and the lands were more secure now than they ever had been. His family would flow on until the very end of time.

In the mean time Le Clos was on his way to France. He had called into Limerick Port and taken on a cargo of stinking hides. He was anxious to be on his way, calling at the men angrily to hurry with their task. Finally the hold was filled and he slipped out into the Atlantic and the security of wide seas. It would be an uneventful voyage and the stench of cattle hides was not offensive to him.

One evening out from port he locked himself in his cabin and gave orders that he should not be disturbed. His mind turned slowly and with care. He set out his bank books and his loose money on the table and counted it with pleasure.

The figure was large and satisfying. He could buy his small ship. He put aside his accounts and his money and took out a bottle of good wine from Vouvray. He dashed it into a glass and had a large mouthful. It was mature and rich, suitable to a man of substance.

A good sum of money lay in a bank at Paris. With it he could not only fit out his ship but buy trading cargo. He could sail from port to port, captain of his own ship. The voice of avarice was loud in his ears, advising him to go to Paris. He began to think with shrewd peasant logic.

He knew too many secrets, had been drawn too deeply into a

403

plot. He was a small fish and would be easily consumed by th
secret shark. It would be madness to remain in Paris. His li
would already have a price upon it and there were assassins in th
alleyways who would kill for a whim. No, he would not remain i
Paris, neither would he go to Bordeaux. It was too accessible t
British spies and he was known in the ports. His mind turned t
the warm Mediterranean. He was growing old and the cold wi
ters plagued his bones. He remembered small ports where the su
was hot and the days slow. Rich and gaudy flowers grew i
gardens and fruit ripened in autumn. Fires were rarely lit i
winter.

'I will go to the south and trade in the Mediterranean. There
am not known.' It was a decision he would not revoke, certai
that his councils were wise.

Two days later Le Clos arrived at Le Havre. He abandoned th
ship, and caught a train to Paris. He went directly to a bank an
withdrew his money. He took a cab to the station, purchased
ticket and travelled south.

Lord Dunraven received the news of John Dillon's capture
day later. He was at a viceregal dinner party in Phoenix Park whe
the news was brought to him by letter. A young lady from Londo
dressed in silk chatted away beside him as he broke the seal an
took out the single page. He read the contents with satisfactio
His schemes had been successful and he could relax. The mo
public and important Fenian had been captured. The plan ha
gone smoothly. It had been worth setting the trap and he believe
that there would be no uprising. The slaughter of the men at th
warehouse would be a reminder to all rebels that the governmen
was serious in its intent. It remained to round up the inner circl
in Dublin. The dinner was an occasion of gaiety and light conve
sation. The viceregal lodge was famous for its fine food. It was sai
that the Queen did not dine as well at Buckingham Palace. A fou
piece orchestra, set in a wide alcove and discreetly cut off by larg
fronds, played a slow waltz.

'I hope you are not called away on some urgent business, Lor
Dunraven,' a gentleman across the table asked.

'Not at all. It is a matter of no serious importance. Even if
were I do not think it would draw me away from the exceller

table and delightful company.' He took his glass and toasted the young beauty from England.

'Have you been to see Lady West's folly?' he was asked.

'Each time I see Lady West I see folly enough,' he said lightly. 'I have heard about it. It is a small, gothic palace with Irish round towers. A disastrous marriage of two styles and a monument to the foolishness of the lady.'

The guests began to laugh. Having caught the attention of the table he told a witty story of Lady West and the interment of her second husband.

Three days after John Dillon had been captured, Sergeant Grinling took control of Galway prison. The Habeas Corpus Act had been suspended by Parliament on receiving news that a Fenian rising was imminent in Ireland. John Dillon was at the total mercy of his enemies. Sergeant Grinling lost his temper as he stood before the governor and warder who stolidly refused to obey their orders.

'You will lose your positions and your pensions for this insubordination,' he said viciously. They were afraid of this callous man. 'What will you say to your wives and children when there is no bread in the house and the rents fall due?'

'That, sir, is something we shall have to face. We cannot tolerate the injustice done to John Dillon. It is a breach of the penal code,' the governor said.

'Breach of the code,' he called. 'What code does this felon follow but the code of a secret organization bent on disrupting the order of the state. You are dismissed. Take your belongings and leave the prison.'

Twice during the next week he was approached by lawyers on behalf of Elinor Dillon demanding to see the prisoner. He slammed the door in their faces.

In his dark cell the humiliation of John Dillon was complete. After three days his mind began to break. He was prevented from sleeping during this time by a warder banging his door each hour.

'Talk to me, please. Let me hear a human voice. Speak to me and let me know that I am not buried in this bleak hell. I am not an animal. I am not an animal.' Tears streamed down his face. He felt that he was an animal. He could never get away from his own filth floating on the water about his feet. He shuffled about in the darkness, moving from wall to wall, knocking his head against the dank stone and crying out in anguish.

His body was constantly cold. He tried to recall pleasant moments in his life, fresh spring mornings when the dew was on the grass and he had taken his black mare down across the lawn to the lake.

His stomach went into spasms of hunger. In an effort to relieve the hunger he knelt on the floor and drank the foul and soiled water.

Then the rat came, introduced into the air vent above his head. He heard it scrape on the lead lining and give a small screech. For a moment the sound was welcome. The animal dropped into the water, lashing about struggling for survival. He kicked at it in the darkness and screamed when it touched his body. When he lay down to try and catch some precious sleep, it climbed on to his body and began to gnaw at him. In his imagination it became monstrous, growing and growing until it filled the cell. He screamed for help but no voice answered.

They left John Dillon alone in his cell for ten days. He was given no food during that time and the only water he drank was fetid and soiled with his own waste. He never slept and flesh fell from his limbs, making the manacles loose about his ankles.

John Dillon heard footsteps outside the cell and a light flickered. The door was thrown open and the sun seemed to scorch his eyes. He turned away from its burning presence and cried out in idiotic laughter. He began to cry, his whole body shuddering with sobs.

Even Sergeant Grinling was appalled by what he saw. The man who had once stood in Parliament and whose powerful voice had sounded beneath the great roof was a whimpering animal. His body was filthy with his own excrement, his shoulders skeletally thin and his buttocks sunken.

'Turn him towards the light,' he directed, his voice a little uncertain.

Sergeant Grinling was startled by what he saw. John Dillon had become an old and white-haired man. His eyes stared ahead and could not focus on a single object. He began to sing simple nursery rhymes.

'Undo the chains,' he ordered. The warder took off the chains, his wrists and ankles running torn wounds. He continued to hold his hands in their chained position.

'Bring him to the infirmary. Have the doctor patch him up. It will not serve our cause for him to be seen like this. He cannot stand in a courtroom in his present condition.'

The events which occurred within the prison trickled out, at first vague rumours. Men howled at Sergeant Grinling as he passed through the city and women cursed him. But he held his poise and was unruffled.

John Dillon saw the golden disc of the moon outside his window of the infirmary. It looked wondrous and soft, pouring its shafts of light on to his bed. Once there was a moon upon a lake, a lake before a great house. It made a pathway on the waters. A spring moon on the late dew, and the autumn moon on leaves, scrolled and copper-coloured on mysterious pathways, which led to the great house. The winter moon on the hard frost.

He rose from his bed and walked to the window, wanting to reach out to the moon. But there was something in the way. He smashed the window and looked at the clear moon. His hands were red and he gasped in wonder at the live fountains pouring from his wrists. It was a ritual sacrifice to the moon. He held his hands up towards it and watched the blood flow. He was free, rising to the moon. He felt a lightness of spirit and smiled at the gentle shield of silver.

Next morning they found him dead beside the window, blood thick and dry on his wrists and on his nightshirt. There was a smile on his face. When news reached the other prisoners they broke their silence, banging their tins and buckets against the doors and crying out at the warders.

News of his death reached Dillon Hall late that day. The people flocked to the lawn of the house and waited for Lady Elinor to appear.

Eventually she came on to the balcony with her daughter, both weeping. She looked down at the upturned faces.

'I have just received the news of my husband's death. I have not been permitted to see him and I have no clear idea of what has happened. I can only wait for further confirmation. Perhaps it is a rumour. I will travel immediately to Galway.' She went indoors and when they emerged later both she and her daughter were dressed in black. Tadhg Mor was with them, mounting the front seat of the carriage. The people ran down the avenue after them.

As she went through the countryside she remembered how many times she had taken this road with her husband. They had passed along it in victory and defeat. The city of Galway was going about its business as usual and it was only when they crossed to Nuns Island and she saw the grim prison she fully accepted the fact of his death. They dismounted in the yard and were brought to the small prison mortuary. In the whitewashed room, her husband lay on a plain stone slab. She did not recognize him. He had aged beyond belief. His wrists had been torn by chains and severed by glass. She wept that he had suffered so much and she wept at her own infidelities.

They remained in the mortuary for an hour. She left the prison and ordered a coffin. It was brought to the prison and later that evening she brought the body through Galway in a hearse. By now news of what had happened in the prison had been passed through the city and people stood in silence on the pathways as the cortège passed through.

The body was brought to Dillon Hall and set in a triple-shelled coffin. All night she sat in a chair and kept vigil over the body, reflecting on his sad past and on her own life.

Next day hundreds of people came to pay their respects, filing past the coffin, praying for a moment, and passing out on to the lawn. The bell tolled every hour through the wood.

After Requiem Mass in the family chapel men from the estate carried the coffin on their shoulders. It was an autumn day, leaves falling in the woods and a sight ripple on the lake.

Beside Elinor walked her son Peter, tall and dark-haired. He had a retiring and distinguished bearing. He had been educated at a private school in England and for three years he had studied at Cambridge. His interests were of a literary and legal nature and it

408

was expected that he would establish a reputation for himself at the law courts of London. Her daughter Catherine also walked beside her mother. She held back her tears, not wishing to demonstrate her feelings in public. Her mind, like that of her mother, was firm and certain and she could be trusted to deal with all the business of the estates in Ireland and in France. The fortunes of Dillon Hall could now pass on to a new generation.

# Epilogue

Daniel Parr sat before the table through the night, knowing that John Dillon was interred in the vault beside the lake. His plan had failed and the dead man was now a patriot, his name revered for ever more. He had not destroyed the Fenian movement; he had given it purpose. The death of John Dillon should have been gradual and insignificant.

The bottle of brandy he had placed before him was empty. He listened to the clock sounding the hour. It was five o'clock and in two hours it would be light. The Fenians would have left the estate, disappearing into the shadows, and he would have survived another night. The shutters were still closed, and his servants were asleep.

He would wait until the clock sounded seven hours before undoing the shutters.

Desmond Hogan's mind worked with cold precision like the clock in Parr's mansion. He had escaped from the wood after he had shot Grinling. It had been an easy task. Having reached the wood he mounted his horse and met his men on the edge of the Parr estate. Their orders were precise. Parr had left his house unguarded, having expected trouble during the funeral and posting his soldiers in Galway. This was the time to move against him.

He climbed the Scots fir and settled on a large branch, an American rifle resting on his arm. If he failed in his first shot then he had a second rifle set aside for another attempt. He wrapped his cloak about him and waited for the dawn.

In the great room the grandfather clock sounded seven. Daniel Parr waited for the final stroke of seven, then drew aside the iron shutters letting in the weak autumn light. He opened the french windows and went out on to the damp gravel. As he breathed in the clear morning air, a shot rang out. Parr held his head and

410

staggered back into the house leaving Hogan uncertain whether he had killed him or not. He climbed down from the tree and disappeared.

In Paris Bazin calculated that his evidence had reached Galway but waited for a week before setting off in his carriage to Edward Dillon's château. He would confront him with the forged evidence, which was witnessed and signed. Edward Dillon would never carry diplomatic dispatches to England again and his reputation would be destroyed.

He reached the château early in the morning. There was a light fog in the stretch of parkland behind the house and heavy cattle browsed in the open space.

He was ushered into the dining room where Edward Dillon was having a light breakfast. Bazin noted how fastidiously he ate his bread.

'Ah, Monsieur Bazin, to what do I owe such an early visit?' he asked nonchalantly, wiping the crumbs from his upper lip with a table napkin.

'To this,' he said and took a parcel of documents from his pocket. 'I have evidence that you are a Fenian. You plotted with your brother to have guns smuggled into Ireland. These documents are signed by Captain Le Clos. Read them. Your friends in England will not be pleased at your duplicity. At this moment your brother is standing trial in Ireland and the evidence brought against him will be also brought against you. I have it all secretly located. Not even your Lord Dunraven knows where the evidence lies.'

'And your dubious friends? I am sure that they are aware of its existence,' Edward Dillon said.

'Of its existence but not its location. It is all here in transcript if you care to read it.'

'Dear Monsieur Bazin, I'm afraid that you have not been in contact with London or read the English papers. You have been so involved in your own plots that you do not realize that you are exposed as a foreign agent. Your sharp practices are already known to the British public and at this moment you are not a very desirable person in any country. The Fenian leaders have revealed the plot against my brother. Your correspondence to Dublin has

411

been intercepted by them and published in the *Freeman's Journal*, and *The Times* has republished it.'

'What do you mean?' he asked incredulously.

'I mean this. Read.' He handed him an English newspaper. As he read the news item his face turned ashen. The Paris plot, the forging of the evidence, both Dunraven's and his own name mentioned. The plot had not succeeded; John Dillon had died before his time.

His throat was dry as he looked at Edward Dillon.

'I acted on orders,' he pleaded.

'You have destroyed my brother and now you set out to destroy me.'

'I acted on orders, I tell you.'

Edward Dillon sounded a bell twice. Two men emerged from behind the curtains carrying revolvers.

'Meet the Fenians you have plotted against.'

'No,' he cried and tried to rise from his seat.

'Tell us what you know,' one of the man demanded.

Bazin knew he was cornered. He spoke for two hours and gave them accurate information. Later they buried him in the woods.

Lord Dunraven looked at the woman who rode beside him. She was considered one of the great beauties of her generation and in addition she possessed a great fortune. Their marriage would unite two old families. He was still a young man and his political future was in the ascendant.

As they rode through his estates he could scarcely believe that two months earlier he had been in charge of the Secret Service in Ireland. He had almost forgotten that John Dillon had died or that his wife Elinor had shared his bed. His plan to destroy the Fenian may not have succeeded and many of his agents had been exposed but he knew that the Fenian movement would fail.

He looked up at the sky. Above the woods he saw birds migrating from the north. Winter was drawing in upon the landscape.

THE END

# TRINITY

## by Leon Uris

Ever since the publication of BATTLE CRY more than thirty years ago, Leon Uris has continued to write bestselling novels. Each displays all of the author's skill, for he is a writer at his best when the subject seems almost too big to handle. One of the most popular storytellers of the twentieth century, more than 5,500,000 copies of his novels have been sold in Corgi alone.

In TRINITY, he writes passionately about the tragedy of Ireland – from the famine of the 1840's to the Easter Rising of 1916, a powerful and stirring novel about the loves and hates, the defeats and triumphs of three families – a terrible and beautiful drama spanning more than half a century.

552 10565 1

**PAST CARING**
*by* Robert Goddard

'THE BEST FIRST NOVEL I HAVE READ FOR A LONG TIME. REFRESHINGLY ORIGINAL AND A GOOD EXAMPLE OF WHAT IS CALLED COMPULSIVE READING'
*Victoria Holt*

Why should distinguished Edwardian Cabinet minister Edwin Strafford resign at the height of his parliamentary career? Why does the woman he loves so suddenly and coldly reject him? Why, seventy years later, should people go to such lengths – even as far as murder – to prevent the truth from being revealed?

Martin Radford, history graduate, disaffected and unemployed, leaps at the chance to go to the island of Madeira, and begin the hunt for a solution to the intriguing secret of Edwin Strafford's fall from grace. However, his seeming good fortune turns to night mares as his investigation triggers a bizarre and violent train of events which remorselessly entangles him and those who believed they had escaped the spectre of crimes long past but never paid for . . .

'COMPELLING. MOVES AT THE PACE OF THE BEST OF TODAY'S THRILLERS'
*Western Morning News*

'HORNET'S NEST OF JEALOUSY, BLACKMAIL AND VIOLENCE. ENGROSSING'
*Daily Mail*

'A COMPLEX TRAIL OF BLACKMAIL AND MURDER RECOMMENDED'
*Daily Express*

0 552 13144 X

# IN PALE BATTALIONS
*by* Robert Goddard

'SHADES OF DAPHNE DU MAURIER'
*Today*

Six months after her husband's sudden death, Leonora Galloway sets off on a holiday in Paris with her daughter Penelope. At last the time has come when secrets can be shared and explanations begin . . .

Their journey starts with an unscheduled stop at the imposing Thiepval Memorial to the dead of the Battle of the Somme near Amiens. Amongst those commemorated is Leonora's father. *The date of his death is recorded as 30th April, 1916. But Leonora wasn't born until March, 1917.*

Penelope at once supposes a simple wartime illegitimacy as the clue to her mother's unhappy childhood and the family's sundered connections with her aristocratic heritage about which she has always known so little.

But nothing could have prepared her, or the reader, for the extraordinary story that is about to unfold in the pages of IN PALE BATTALIONS.

'AS THE LAYERS OF MYSTERY AND DECEIT ARE EXPOSED AND REMOVED, ONE APPRECIATES NOT ONLY THE CLEVERNESS OF THE PLOT, BUT ALSO THE LAUDABLE CLARITY AND RELEVANCE WITH WHICH IT IS CONVEYED'
*London Portrait*

'IF YOU THINK YOU'VE GOT IT ALL FIGURED OUT BY THE END OF THE BOOK, TRY AGAIN! GREAT FUN'
*Book People, Switzerland*

552 13281 0

# A SELECTED LIST OF TITLES
## AVAILABLE FROM CORGI BOOKS